AUTHOR
Profile

SCOTT JONES has written hundreds of articles and columns for many newspapers/magazines in the USA and Thailand, and has authored five books:

—***Flesh and Blood and DNA: in her right mind and the wrong body***... a speculative sci-fi/adventure novel exploring dangerous genetic engineering

—***Turnabout: The world wasn't ready for Edna***... the finale to ***Flesh and Blood and DNA***.

—***Life in the Laugh Lane: facts, fiction, and photos from America to Asia***... laugh out loud, real-life travel tales.

—***Can you spare me a smile?: a copious compendium of comedic commentary***... A fine line separates fact from fiction. This sequel to *Life in the Laugh Lane* lurches back and forth across that line.

—***Five Lives One Dream: Five souls intertwined though they've never met***... a meta-fiction novel of action, love, and adventure which spans the spectrum from severely humorous to deadly serious.

Scott has performed his unique style of original music, comedy, and stand-up photography in Asia, Canada, and all fifty states in America. He edits and designs other authors' books while living with his wife and two huskies, Sirius and Aurora, the Exalted Rulers of Their General Vicinity.

He was born in Fargo, North Dakota, but he takes pills for it.

PREPRESS
Impressions

"Intriguing. It unfolds fast 'n' furious!"—*Washington*

"It's great! The story is absorbing and mind-boggling. A first-rate book."—*Florida*

"Loved it! A fantastic piece of work."—*Myanmar*

"The characters are rich and fascinating. Now that I've finished the book, I am sad, as I won't be spending time in that world anymore."—*Mexico*

"A beautiful work! You've written an incredible gift to this planet, a very healing book about the brevity and beauty of this time we each have."—*Minnesota*

"I love the movement and the idea. The writing is amazing and wonderful. Besides, it's a really fun read."—*Oregon*

"The words are alive. A splendid journey in a seminal book. An inspiration for me."—*Thailand*

Five Lives

one dream

FIVE SOULS INTERTWINED THOUGH THEY'VE NEVER MET

KING COBRA PRESS.COM

A SCOTT JONES NOVEL

COPYRIGHTS
and Credits

Published by Scott Jones and King Cobra Press in 2026

1 3 5 7 9 10 8 6 4 2
(The numbers above are on title pages in most books to alert us that writers, editors and publishers can count, but not necessarily in the right order.)
This is a work of fiction. Names, characters, places, and incidents are either the product of the author's imagination or are used fictitiously. Any resemblance to actual persons, living or dead, business establishments, events, or locales is entirely coincidental. When I read about what happens in Washington, DC, I'm convinced DC must be fictional, too.
ISBN 978-1-7342862-6-7

COVER AND TEXT DESIGN
Jacqueline Jones Design, San Francisco, CA
Scott Jones, Earth, Milky Way
COVER PHOTOGRAPH
Eukalyptus in Germany

For information or purchase of this novel and other books by Scott Jones, please visit www.kingcobrapress.com or amazon.com.

DEDICATED
to My Soulmate

You once said,
"Write something
from your heart."
So I did.
I wouldn't
and couldn't
have done it
without you.
You always
inspire me…
all ways.
Thank you
from the soul
of the heart
that wrote this.

THANKS
to All of You

My deepest gratitude to all my official and unofficial editors for their splendid analyzing, revising, excising, and literary massage:

Jonni Anderson for crossing all my eyes, dotting all my tees, and brain/heart storming along the way.

Victoria Lyons for being the first person to read this entire novel.

Michael "Bald Eagle-eye" Tangen for catching a bevy of things that crept by the official editors.

Stuart Land for saying, "You should write a novel." I laughed. It took me two years before I believed him and actually started.

Rebecca Weldon—with all three (or more) of the brains that must be living in her head, each speaking a different language—for guidance, great ideas, and companionship along the way. How many times did I ask her: "But why do you even know that?"

Jim King for answering all my flying questions and several others I didn't think to ask.

Polly Szantor for dialogue wrangling in the British-Indian Zone. Although I've spoken American for years, I'm still learning English.

All the regular and irregular editors at our Writers Without Borders meetings in Chiang Mai, who honestly told it like it is, even though it wasn't like it was for the person sitting next to them.

Lee Thomas for originally creating Writers Without Borders and having the eternal patience to put up with all the unruly and ruly writers who have wandered in and out of the group.

Composer Mitch Leigh and lyricist Joe Darien for writing the phenomenal song: "The Impossible Dream." And for Luther Vandross, who sang it and brought it alive like no one else. Bless all their departed souls on their journeys beyond time and matter.

Jackie Jones for working her magic with the book design.

Darlene and Ken Jones for having me in the first place.

And in a completely different dimension—my shoulders, lower back, cramping legs and hands all thank Chancellor the Husky for demanding I get the hell out of my chair and take us for a walk at least twice a day.

TABLE of Contents

FIVE WORLDS

RED ADMIRAL

In and out of New Delhi
Forty-two days ago

HAD SHE KNOWN THIS WAS THE LAST TIME SHE'D SEE HER MOTHER ALIVE, Red Admiral might have worn different clothing. She'd dressed up for the meeting, adding a white lace blouse to her daily denims. Well-heeled and strait-laced Chandra had dressed down in a gold chiffon sari.

"Really, Danielle, must you wear blue jeans?" Chandra didn't care much for her daughter, nor her long auburn locks, nor the nickname Red, spawned by her strawberry-blond British father.

"Did you come to meet me or my clothes?" At the post-teen age of forty-seven, Red mistakenly thought she could select her own wardrobe.

"Well," Chandra huffed, "I certainly should have chosen a less luxurious spot for breakfast."

"Like Bangladesh so your friends wouldn't accidentally see us together?"

Chandra ignored her daughter's jibe. "I saw one of your father's so-called friends, Baldev Gupta, at the Butterfly Conservatory Benefit last night. He should've been in the cage with the bugs."

Red stiffened. She owed Baldev two million rupees after a recent poker fiasco.

"The Public Prosecutor's office has been investigating him for years," Chandra droned on, "but he always manages to crawl through some loophole in the law."

"And why are you telling me?" Red asked flatly.

"He started talking to me about Admiral Aviation, but I walked away. If you meet him, I suggest you do the same. Perhaps if your father hadn't associated with creatures like Baldev, he might not have disappeared."

"Any new clues about his case from your ex-minions at the Prosecutor's office?"

"No. You know good judgment wasn't your devious father Danny's strong suit. His big head was screwed on crooked at birth, and his little head screwed anything with two legs."

Red's eyes rolled back as her head rolled to the side. "How often do you have to tell me this? The last time I saw you, I heard those exact words."

The rest of their meeting was forgettable. Red chewed and Chandra spewed unwanted wisdom. At the earliest civil opportunity, Red escaped.

"Thanks for the meal and all the advice, Mother dear." She pointed up. "I must fly."

An hour later Red Admiral was in the air, in her world. She loved to put Danny Boy's old crop duster through its paces. In the open cockpit, the wind whipped her hair back and forth behind the leather helmet and goggles. Red's devilish smile matched the teeth painted on the nose of the yellow and black Tiger Moth biplane.

She soared under power lines, dropped to six feet above the field, and released a cloud of chemicals that drifted like a shroud over the cotton. The prop slashed through a flock of butterflies, spitting a bluish haze of body parts into the breeze. Red rose above the fence at the end, sailed down to the river, banking with the curves of the valley, anticipating her favorite maneuver. The arched stone bridge ahead looked too low and narrow to allow a plane's passage. She sailed underneath with five feet of clearance for each wingtip, her wheels nearly touching the water, and then pulled the stick back hard.

"Mmmm…" she moaned with glee, the g-force flattening her slim body against the seat.

As Red powered straight up preparing to loop backward, a searing pain stabbed through her brain to the back of one eyeball like a dagger driven into the top of her skull. Tears streamed down one cheek and her vision flickered between single and double.

I've got to land! Now!

Unable to see through the deluge in her left eye, with her right she spotted a road bisecting two fields. Spasms in her neck muscles tightened into a noose, but she wrestled the duster around and dived toward the ground. Red hit the rutted road, bounced hard, then ricocheted off to the side, scraping bushes with her tires. Reining the plane back over the road, she cut the throttle, hopping and skidding to a standstill.

She shut down the engine, elbowed the door open, and stumbled out onto the wing. Flinging off her helmet, she collapsed in a heap, her hands a vice on her temples.

On the other side of Delhi, a cement truck driver lost control and smashed through a bridge railing. The truck, Chandra's Volvo, and two other cars plummeted into the holy Yamuna River below—the "River of Death," one of the most toxic waterways on Earth.

As daughter and mother had begun their day, they ended it together in the same building: Red in the hospital emergency room and Chandra in the morgue.

ANGEL PHOENIX

Near La Paz, Bolivia
Twenty-nine days ago

Clad in a grubby poncho and ragged, baggy pants, Angel Phoenix limped along with a cane in one hand, pushing an ice cream cart over the cobblestones with the other. Adobe homes and hovels built next to and on top of one another lined both sides of the skinny street.

Earlier that week at dusk, he'd dropped from a plane from 20,000 feet, soared nine miles wearing a Ninja Birdman wingsuit before opening his chute to ease into a soybean field near La Paz. His mission: to locate, extract, and return seven-year-old Greta, the kidnapped daughter of a Dutch oil company president. Angel had sailed in unnoticed, except for a few farmers who argued among themselves whether they'd seen an Andean condor or a black-and-white flying mattress.

For the third day in a row, the familiar ice cream theme tinkling from a plastic speaker announced his arrival. Angel switched it off and paused in front of a burly thug standing under the roof over the doorway of a windowless hut.

"Hot day. Cold ice cream," he hawked in Spanish, smiling beneath his wide-brimmed straw hat.

The thug understood, but replied in English. "Too fuckin' hot." He walked to the cart and leaned over to view the selection as Angel raised the lid.

When the thug stuck his hand into the freezer, Angel slammed down the lid, pinning his arm. A second later, Angel chopped the man's throat to sever his cry as a karate kick buckled his knees. As the thug slumped to the ground, he plunged a tranquilizer dart into the back of the man's neck and then dragged him to the side of the hut's doorway.

Angel snatched a popsicle from the cart and stuck it in his pocket. After days of surveillance, he knew the code. He rapped on the door three times… two times… once… then leaped to the other side of the street while gripping his "cane"—a three-foot bamboo hanbō with a metal chain concealed inside and secured to one end. As the door cracked open, Angel took two steps and launched his body horizontally through the air, his boots leading the attack. The impact catapulted the man behind the door backward over a chair, then headfirst into the fractured wall. As Angel's momentum carried him into the room, he kicked off the door to the right, landing on his side. He flipped upright while flicking his wrist to release the chain. Before the third thug could rise from his stool toward the gun in front of him, Angel swung the hanbō, wrapping its chain around his neck, and yanked the choking man over the table. Another dart put him away as Angel's boot crushed his face into the tile floor.

"Greta, darlin'," Angel crooned to the trembling, blindfolded girl tethered to a rickety chair, "are you okay?"

She nodded.

Angel spoke softly as he removed the blindfold. "Your Mommy and Daddy'll be glad to see you."

Greta's saucer eyes blinked, frantically scanning the room while he untied her. Whether relieved or terrified, he couldn't tell.

"I'll bet you like ice cream, don't you?" An orange popsicle appeared from his pocket. He removed the wrapper to reveal a whole stick and half a melting popsicle. "Oops. I busted it."

Greta took it hesitantly. "Who are you?"

"You can call me Uncle Angel. I'm here to save you."

"They were mean to me," she stammered, her voice slipping into a sob.

"I'll bet they were." He rubbed a few soothing circles on her back. "How's that popsicle?"

She looked him in the eyes during her sample lick. "It's good. I like orange."

"I didn't break this, though." He took out a tiny stuffed bear from his other pocket. "He's soft and cuddly. Give him a hug while I take care of the bad guys."

After Angel tied them together, emptied their guns, and smashed their cellphones, he kneeled next to Greta. "How 'bout a piggy back ride?"

"Okay."

He lifted her onto his shoulders. "Let's go home." As he walked outside using the hanbō cane, a butterfly landed on her leg. "Look at our big blue buddy! It's good luck when one lands on you."

Angel turned on the tinkly jingle as he strolled behind the cart. Kids emerged from doorways and got free frozen goodies. The word "free" seemed to spread telepathically.

He leaned over and challenged two newcomers in Spanish. "You can both have free cones, but first you must become men." Angel peeled off his thick gray eyebrows and stuck them on one boy's face, then ripped off his mustache and beard and pasted them on the other boy. They pointed at each other and giggled. He set all the boxes of ice cream on the ground and the gaggle of kids dove into them.

Angel took Greta off his shoulders and snuggled her into the cart. "We're gonna play hide 'n' seek now. You hide in here. It's cool."

TIGER BROOKS

Mooswa Park, Canada
Fourteen days ago

"DITCH THE NET AND DIG THE DITCH, YOU TWO!" The ranger slowed on the dirt road, shouting out the window of his truck. "I'm gonna chop that thing into kindling if I see it again."

Tiger ran a hand over his wet face and through the curly locks stuck to his forehead. Shrugging his shoulders and eyebrows, he turned to his workmate.

Logan frowned back at him. "What's with you and bugs, anyway?"

Working at the state park during summer vacation kept Tiger outside and in the woods, but he didn't like being harassed about his passion for insect collecting. He mainly kept to himself.

"They're amazing," Tiger said, folding the net into his pack filled with specimen boxes. "And can do stuff we can't. They can fly. An ant can lift fifty times its own weight. We're sweatin' after a few shovels of dirt."

"So what?" Logan pitched a hefty rock out of the ditch. "I could do that with a hang glider and a dozer."

"They're vital to our survival." Tiger spoke like he was reading a book, though he might as well have been talking to his shovel. "If insects disappeared, all life on Earth would end in a few decades. If mankind disappeared, all other species would flourish."

"Yeah? Well, if you disappeared, the ranger wouldn't be yellin' in my direction."

Later on at home, after scrubbing the ditch off his skin, Tiger surveyed the take of the day in his attic laboratory—all duplicates of those he'd already captured. Tired of the local species, he knew where to find the exotic ones he'd dreamed of owning. He descended the steep stairs from the attic, sat at his desk, and surfed the web. He'd saved enough money to order three: rhino beetle, Atlas moth, and blue morpho butterfly. He heard footsteps outside the door and his father's voice—"Tiger!"—and switched windows on his computer to golf.com website.

MORPHO

Amazon Rainforest, Brazil
Nineteen days ago

THE HORNED SCREAMER'S CALL CUT THROUGH the spider monkey chatter and cicada buzz in the treetops.

"Yoik-yok! Yoik-yok!"

A natural steam bath, the jungle dripped on itself through mist permeated with the enticing aroma of tropical flowers and fruit.

Perched on a pea plant in dense undergrowth, Morpho devoured a leaf until his stubby legs held only the naked vein at its center. An eating and excreting being, he'd shed his motley hide five times as he grew. Morpho himself was a potential meal for lizards or flycatchers, but the white and red venomous bristles protruding from his yellow and brown rumpled skin kept them at bay.

Nothing about his fat caterpillar form gave a clue to the elegant blue morpho butterfly in his future. No iridescence or smooth scales. No shimmering sapphire. No blue at all.

His body had bloated until his skin seemed as if it might rip open. It was time to change. Morpho inched down the stalk and over soggy moss, then crawled up a wide trunk in search of a sheltering branch to sleep.

MONA ARCADE

A strip mall in Mission, Texas
Yesterday

"All these drugs aren't for me, you know."

Mona set three bottles on the counter, one for her and two for a couple of elderly friends—laxatives for her, diet pills for Sasha, and sedatives for Yves. As the cashier rang up the sale, Mona considered switching their medicines. *Sasha should relax more and Yves could lose a few pounds.*

Mona hobbled through the parking lot with a walking stick, her sandals sticking to the asphalt. On a torrid dry day in Mission, Texas, the long-armed saguaro cacti prayed for visits from stray dogs.

"Ma'am! You forgot your drugs!" The cashier smirked as he ran up—this had happened before. "Do you want these pills, or is your cash another kind donation?"

Crimson crept across Mona's face. "Good heavens! Thank you. Do you sell memory pills?"

"I don't think so. I could use 'em, too."

"I'd probably forget to take them."

"You're Angela Mariposa, aren't you?" the cashier asked, reaching into his satchel. "The famous painter?"

"Me? No." Always trying to keep a low profile, Mona had never gotten used to this. "Famous in my own mind, maybe. Or infamous."

"I bought a pack of your butterfly postcards. Would you please autograph one for me?"

"If you like. Might increase its value by a whole penny."

Once she'd signed her fan's card, Mona used the paper pharmacy sack to grasp the hot chrome handle of her Ford Ranchero. After dropping off the diet pills at Sasha's condo, Mona headed home. She reached across the seat to grab her bottle of laxatives, but her fingers couldn't locate the bag. She looked over. No bag. Must have left it at Sasha's.

She stopped at the curb and searched her purse for her cellphone. No phone. It was charging at home. *Criminently! What good am I?*

Mona knew of a shopping mall with a pay phone, drove a mile up the road, and parked next to the booth, a tall rectangular oven. She looked up Sasha's number, punched it in, and set her address book under the phone.

"Sasha Goldberg here, the world's oldest living realtor. What can I do for you right now?"

"It's Mona, the world's most forgetful artist."

"You left your sack."

"That's what I thought. I'll be back in ten minutes."

As she pressed the buzzer at Sasha's condo, the door cracked open four inches and a hand poked out holding the paper sack. Mona could see half of a wrinkled grin through the gap.

"Thank you, Sasha." She sang the words like they were a cuckoo clock chime. "Please don't tell anyone."

"Good luck, sweetheart," Sasha said with that knowing look of hers. "Do you need a map to your house?"

Mona pulled the door closed and plodded through the sweltering heat to the Ranchero—red-orange, thirty-five years old, no air-con. When she got home—wet—she poured a dose of medicine—Merlot—into a mug full of cubes, then sat on the davenport and opened her purse to get Yves' phone number. No address book. It was baking in the phone booth.

"Lord help me," she confided to her raised mug. "Takes a serious commitment to forgetting to forget something while calling about something I've forgotten."

MORPHO

Rebirth

An internal alarm signaled silently. His world was dark and still; the sun outside brilliant. Arising from a death sleep, Morpho stirred in a womb he'd created by himself, for himself. The emerald-green pod—shaped like a short, pregnant banana suspended from a branch far above the forest floor—repelled predators with an ultrasonic sound when touched.

Reborn in a strange new form, Morpho twitched. He squirmed. He secreted enzymes to dissolve his organic cage. Testing his redesigned appendages, he clawed the wall until it parted. A shaft of daylight drew him out of his womb into dense air, so sultry and humid it almost seemed solid.

Clinging to his split chrysalis pod, he pumped liquid life into wet crumpled wings on his back. They thickened, widened, and lengthened until five times as long as his body and twelve times as wide. He soon dwarfed the womb from which he'd emerged.

Once a slave to gravity, the sluggish caterpillar with eighteen fat limbs was no more. After his wings had dried in the sunlight, the transformation into a blue morpho butterfly was complete. With his two front brush-foot legs tucked under his thorax, his svelte black body balanced on four slender rear walking legs between powerful wings shimmering as if illuminated by a sapphire light within.

Instinct overriding fear, Morpho shed the cocoon, and his wings caught the wind. Climbing effortlessly above the canopy of trees, he gazed down on the world he once knew but had barely seen, finally free to fly and explore.

He sailed over, around, and through the sea of foliage. The bright blue of the topside of Morpho's wings and the dull brown underneath flashed with each flap, creating the illusion he was disappearing and reappearing, transporting invisibly from place to place to confuse birds.

Speckled seed pods dangling like grapes captured his attention, and he darted through the leaves to inspect the foreign shapes. Then, attracted by scarlet trumpet blooms overhead, Morpho soared up and relaxed to surf the breeze.

Charcoal-colored clouds towered above, but the green ocean below dropped away to burnt earth. The rainforest floor was covered with tree corpses, smoking pyres, and square yellow Caterpillar bulldozers and tree harvesters lumbering along trails of packed soil. As the temperature rose and the updraft lifted him higher, the activity in this new world below compelled Morpho to fight his way down.

Assaulted by oily fumes and smoke, he faltered, nose-dived toward a Caterpillar, and landed on its smooth, vibrating skin. Hard and hot, it burned his feet. The cacophonous clatter sent tremors through him. Flapping frantically, Morpho retreated to the safety of the jungle.

TIGER

Real Dreams

Dawn slipped through the window blinds and drew amber lines on the bedroom wall that crawled down across Tiger Brooks' head as it twitched on the pillow. He wrinkled his nose, sniffing a funny smell that wasn't unfamiliar, just not quite right. Still on the edge of a dream, Tiger cracked open his eyelids through the sleep crust and squinted across to the table. Without his glasses, he saw only a blur.

Damn… must've left the killing jar open.

Tiger's fingers searched for his specs on the nightstand, where Tony the Tiger silently shouted from a half-empty box of Kellogg's Frosted Flakes, "They're GR-R-REAT!" Nearby two yellow and black striped tiger swallowtail butterflies lay side by side, resting in peace under glass. He stretched a leg from under the warm blankets until his toes touched the cold linoleum floor and recoiled. When both feet found their slippers, Tiger stumbled across the room to check the jar.

It's tight. So is the acetate bottle. What's that smell?

Still groggy, he slumped onto the chair. His forehead settled into his arms on a table cluttered with specimen jars and envelopes, tweezers, a magnifying glass, and a pinning block with insects suspended in the air on long thin pins. The odor slipped away and scenes from his dream flooded in. The corners of his lips rose into a smile, and Tiger rocked his head from side to side. His eyes fluttered open as he remembered it was Friday.

Today is introduction day at school!

He leaped up, stuck one arm in a Detroit Tigers baseball jersey, and draped it over his lanky frame. He bounced downstairs into the kitchen and slid across the tile, colliding with the breakfast table.

"Mom! I was flying! It was so awesome!"

"Whoa! Careful!" Doris Brooks whirled around in a rainbow apron, waving a spatula, her blond hair bundled in a purple towel. "When? Now? You just flew into the room!"

"I broke out of my cocoon and flew over the rainforest," Tiger stated matter-of-factly, his brown-black uncombed hair attempting to escape from his head.

"Hey, Hon, are you okay?" she asked, putting her arm around his shoulders and touching his forehead to check his temperature. "Are you awake?"

"I was flying right before I woke up. I really was! I mean, it was dream, but it was real. I could even smell it."

"Well, dreams can seem real, eh?" Mom said, handing him a plate of flapjacks. "Sounds like you had a whopper. Can you stop soaring long enough to eat?"

"Sure, I'm starving." Tiger sat down and dug in.

Walter Brooks had paused outside the doorway to listen, but now plodded in, following his paunch that stretched out every wrinkle of his white polo shirt. He plopped into his chair, which squeaked and pleaded for mercy. "Son, I think you've been sniffing too much of that paint thinner in your room."

"It's not paint thinner," Tiger grumbled. "It's ethyl acetate. I even smelled it in my dream. The dream was real."

"I have a real dream, too." Walter Brooks furrowed his brow along lines written during a decade of concerted frowning. "I dream you'll trade in your butterfly net for a golf club, or a worthwhile tool of some trade and become successful like your namesake Tiger Woods… instead of a bug doctor."

"Walter…" Mom hissed, sticking eye daggers into his skull. She set a plate of pancakes in front of him, letting it drop from an inch above the table for impact. "It's a beautiful morning, Walter, but you may have to go to your room. Let him be… what he wants to be."

"Yes, dear," Dad mumbled, then attacked his stack of flapjacks, filling the puffy face peeking through a circle of salt-and-pepper hair, bushy sideburns, mustache, and beard—all a little heavy on the salt.

Seated at one end of the table with Mom and Dad on each side, Tiger looked as if the creator had crossbred him from a fifty-fifty mixture of his parents' genes. Some of his parts were exact replicas of theirs, some exotic hybrids. On Tiger's face, his dad's curly locks trailed alongside his mom's high cheekbones. Dad's round nose rested between Mom's sapphire-blue eyes. Dad's black and Mom's white skin colors had melded in their son to become a cocoa complexion that appeared to glow.

"It's not 'bug doctor,' Dad. It's entomologist, a scientist. I like the name Tiger fine, and I love woods, especially walking in them—with a net, not a golf club."

Walter poured another glob of maple syrup onto his plate and shook his head in disappointment. "Well, you might consider helping me in the family construction business."

"I dunno, Dad. I saw what you did to our woods out back. You and your Caterpillars bulldozed the fir trees and built houses out of them. Now the only green thing standing is a pole with a sign that says Pine Boulevard."

"Look here, son, if I didn't work," Dad griped, pointing around the room with a forkful of pancake, "we wouldn't have this food on the table, or the table, or this kitchen, or this house. Now eat those jacks, boy! You're skinny as a damn pole."

Doris transformed into Queen Brooks the First with a towel for a crown. She spoke each word precisely, jabbing the air with her knife dripping syrup into her orange juice. "Walter-Percival-Brooks-the Second!"

"Sorry, sweetheart." Dad spoke to his empty fork, knowing the wrath that might be unleashed after his full name was taken in vain. Doris could inject venom into "Walter" alone, add arsenic with "Walter Percival Brooks," but when she included "the Second," it was time to flap the white flag.

"Seems to me like you're in the deconstruction biz, Dad. You know..." Tiger paused and raised a finger to his lips. "I think I dreamed about people like you last night."

Walter had zoned out, becoming one with a mouthful of pancake.

"Thanks for the cakes, Mom. Gotta go." Tiger grabbed his backpack, butterfly net and jacket, then pushed open the screen door.

"Hey, Tiger!" Mom shouted. "You might want to wear pants instead of your pajamas, eh?"

"Good call." Walking back through the kitchen, he said, "Dad, do me a favor—please stay out of the rainforests," then ran upstairs to change.

"What'd he mean by that?" Dad asked between bites.

"I don't know. You tell me," Doris hissed. "What are you doing messing around in his dreams?"

MORPHO

Survival

Lured by iridescent flashes in the bushes, Morpho flew toward them while other primal alarms signaled inside. *Drink. Mate.*

Suddenly Morpho was surrounded by scores of himself. After tapping wings with some males and territorial skirmishes with others, he joined the crowd on the rainforest floor. Antennae smelling, leg sensors tasting, they sucked fermented nectar of rotting fruit through flexible snouts until the waterlogged air began to sweat rain. Intoxicated by their fermented beverage, the diners flapped erratically, seeking shelter under umbrella leaves.

In this steamy sanctuary, delicate bodies united. Morpho mounted his newfound mate, his twin with nearly identical markings. Motionless for a moment, he appeared to be standing on a mirror. They turned as if slipping away from each other, then raised their wings and folded them together like curtains covering their coupled bodies.

Lost in the serene union, the butterflies paid no heed to the hooting and hollering of birds and monkeys, or to the low buzzing, or to the vibration of the ground coming neither from bees nor thunder.

In slow motion, a sky-scraping tree leaned, hesitated, and then its core split apart. Cracks and groans stabbed the air as its crown of foliage, fruit, and branches toppled lesser trees like sticks. Charged with fear, Morpho wrenched away from his partner and lurched up into the falling sky, but found no passageway through the chaos as trees, vines, bushes, and leaves pounded him to the forest floor.

TIGER
Introduction Day

Tiger's English teacher, Kirby Smothers, had given the class their first homework assignment two days earlier.

"On Friday, each of you will introduce yourself to the class, using whatever words, pictures, props, or backup singers you choose. Think of it as Show and Tell about you. No longer than five-minutes or you'll get the hook. Be creative. You'll be graded by your classmates, not by me."

Tiger fidgeted in the chair, anticipating his carefully crafted speech as Kirby told the class too much about himself. He was an odd fat fellow but fun to watch. Kirby diagrammed his life on the board with gusto as dangling chins flapped on his extra-wide tie, sold exclusively in the men's department of Goodwill Industries.

Tiger shook his head and wondered. *With a head as big as Kirby's, why are his eyes, nose, and mouth all crammed together in the middle of his face like they're magnetized or something?*

The first student introduced himself semi-creatively; the second half-wittedly. On Tiger's third day as a sophomore, many faces were new to him, but he knew his turn had to be soon because his last name began with a B. The third girl droned on forever while Tiger tapped rhythms on the desktop with his fingers. Though confident of the intro to his introduction, Tiger wanted to get it over with before he forgot the rest.

"Thank you, Miss Borman! Our next contestant is Mr. Tiger Brooks," Kirby announced in his game show host voice. "Come on down and tell us who you are!"

Tiger ambled up to the podium, set things from his backpack on the inner shelves, and one essential item hidden on its slanted top. He took a deep breath. "Hi, my name's Tiger, as in 'Woods.' And Brooks, as in 'babbling.' At first I didn't know what to say about myself, but I sat down to think about it and had lots of ideas. I grabbed the nearest paper and wrote 'em down."

Holding onto the first sheet, he flicked a roll of toilet paper over his clipboard and the podium. It bounced onto the floor and unfurled down the middle aisle between the desks. The room erupted in giggles.

I got 'em! Tiger carried on as if reading from the roll. "I was born during the Chinese Year of the Tiger, like most of you. We're supposed to be powerful, courageous, and brave, but also friendly, kind, and caring. Tigers are natural leaders and love to be the center of attention, but I'll be quick. I know each of you is dying to get up here, too."

He held up photos of Tiger Woods, a pack of Cincinnati Bengals cheerleaders lounging in bikinis, then two hardcover scrapbooks.

"I like to collect stuff. Tigers, of course. And stamps and coins from other countries. I hope to travel around the world, and they help me imagine I'm already there. I love to collect insects. No one knows for sure, but there might be thirty million different kinds of insects on the planet—ten quintillion bugs alive every day. Ten quintillion is a one followed by nineteen zeros. That's 300 pounds of bugs for every pound of human!

"After I catch 'em and put 'em in a killing jar, I pin 'em to this mounting board with little paper strips to hold 'em so they look lifelike. Then I display 'em in these glass and wood cases I build in my dad's workshop. I caught these beauties here in Manitoba. A male and female tiger swallowtail. They're almost the same, but she's got this band of blue at the bottom of her wings. I think the world's most beautiful butterflies aren't in this part of the world, and I want to study them where they live. So maybe I'll be an entomologist. That's an insect scientist. I don't know for sure, cuz I love to sing and play the piano, too. Maybe I can do both. I'll be an entomusician and write songs that bug people." He flipped the rest of the toilet paper over the podium. "Well, that's more than enough about me. Thanks for listening. Oh, yeah. I have a friend collection too, and I hope you'll all be in it. But don't worry, I'd never mount you or put you in a case!"

Most of the class cheered or clapped, but not Dick Hedlund, a sour boy in the back. His immobile mug perched above a neck wider than his head, while his hands cracked walnut-sized knuckles. His vacuum gaze said he'd pressed dumbbells 10,000 times, but never flexed his brain. Dick hated school and its students, especially the ones who liked it. English was the worst. It might as well have been a foreign language to Dick. He excelled in gym, but spelled it "jim." His only goal in life was to get the hell out of there. Soon he'd have to give a stupid introduction, and all he could think of was a threat: "My name's Dick. You wanna make somethin' out of it?"

Tiger tried to jam all his props back into his pack as Kirby proclaimed, "Good job and best wishes with your billion bugs! Okay, let's see who's the next lucky guest on our list? Miss Gemini Cavalier… come on down!"

Tiger spun around, bumped into Gemini, and spilled everything from his pack onto the floor. He may have been good with his hands, but the rest of his body seemed to be constructed of elbows and knees—and he was never quite sure where they were.

Gemini leaned down to help him, gave him a thumbs up, and whispered, "You were great!"

For Tiger, it was one of those unforgettable moments when time vanished. His elbows and knees melted as he gazed into her sparkling black eyes, like dark passageways that concealed bonfires around the next bend. Her dark chestnut hair was as curly as his, though Tiger's went up, and Gemini's cascaded down her back to her waist. Outside, lightning struck and thunder rumbled. Inside, Tiger wasn't thinking, only feeling. *Is this me… or Morpho on the mirror in the dream?*

"Sanks, but I'm thorry. I mean…" Tiger stammered as he grappled with his mess. "I'm sorry, thanks, you're great… I mean… to say I was great. Thanks for your help, but don't help. Good luck. I'm sorry."

"Forget it," she said. "See ya later."

Somehow Tiger's elbows and knees hauled him back to his seat as Gemini perched on the edge of Kirby's desk, then paused and surveyed the class, her lips lounging in a calm smile.

"Hi. You can call me Gem. I'm new in town, and now I have one goal in life—to survive winter in Canada. I've seen snow, but like, only in pictures. I was born in Africa and got used to forty degrees above, not below. I might have to wear everything I own, all at the same time."

Other kids laughed, but Tiger's tongue was tied and dry, his eyes mesmerized. *"You can call me Gem." I will call you, Gem.*

Gem beamed at her classmates, talking with her hands as much as her voice. "Papa's from Quebec and Mama's from Italy. They were missionary teachers and built a school in a village in the Congo rainforest. A couple years later, Mama got bigger… not because of the food. That wasn't in Plan A. Papa started working on Plan B… B for baby. The villagers made a stick crib, a wooden stroller, and some clothes. Since the baby'd probably be born in April, during the zodiac sign Aries, they'd name it Aries if he was a boy, or Arielle if she was a girl.

"Well, Arielle came out just fine, but Mama wasn't feeling very good. The village doctor rushed in, took a look at her, and hollered, 'Sahib! There's another one in there!' Papa hollered back, 'But I only have one crib!'

"So they named me after the zodiac sign Gemini, which means 'the twin.' It was April 1st. Papa still calls us his two April Fools, the best mistakes he ever made. They tell Air and me the story every year on our birthday. We're identical twins. Sometimes we even dress the same, so be careful what you say to her about me, because she might be me!"

Tiger was bound in her spell. *She doesn't dress like anyone from around here. Is that a poncho? Are those pants she's wearing or a skirt?*

Gem rested one hand on Kirby's desk and tapped the side with her foot, relaxed, as if she were talking to a few friends in her living room.

"After a few years of learning more from the villagers than my parents could ever teach, they got tired of trying to turn those perfect black people into white Christians. We moved to Arizona, where Mama taught in a Navajo reservation school and Papa worked on his master's degree. It was even hotter than Africa. We'd complain about the heat, but Mama'd say, 'It's not so bad. It's a dry heat.' Papa'd say, 'Sure it is. So is fire.'"

"Anyway, now we're here..." She stretched out both her arms, palms up, and looked out the window. "In Canada, ready for something new like snow and sleds. If I survive—and if I ever grow up—I want to be a photographer and filmmaker." She held up the feathered handbag draped over her shoulder. "This isn't a purse. It's a camera bag. Scene one, take one." Gem grabbed her Nikon, flicked off the lens cover, and focused on the class. "Do something awesome that'll get us a million clicks on YouTube, but won't get us arrested."

As the class went semi-bonkers, she walked back and forth grabbing close-ups, monkey antics, and hand gestures she'd have to edit out.

"Okay, cut!" Gem shouted and drew her finger across her neck. "I'll send you all your royalty checks. How much is zero dollars divided by thirty actors? See ya later. I might call you up to borrow some thermal underwear." Gem strutted to her seat while Kirby tried to calm his students.

Tiger had never experienced the sensations stampeding through him. He wanted to see the world, but felt the world had just come to see him.

She lived in a rainforest. I dreamed of a rainforest and thunder. It thundered when we met a few minutes ago. Mmm... those eyes... like deep caves.

For the rest of the hour, Tiger hovered in limbo between last night's dream and future dreams. The bell buzzed like a chainsaw. Kids encircled Gem's desk to watch themselves on her camera screen. Standing in the hall, Tiger took in the scene through the doorway and sighed.

Oh well, she's got everything. And I've got bugs.

ANGEL
Home Sweet Womb

THE STEREO SYSTEM AUTOMATICALLY CLICKED ON AT 9:09 A.M. and orchestral music wafted through the air. Luther Vandross' velvet voice enticed Angel back into the conscious world with the song "The Impossible Dream."

To dream the impossible dream
To fight the unbeatable foe
To bear with unbearable sorrow
To run where the brave dare not go

Angel lay on the bedspread facedown, fully clothed, still wearing sneakers, as if he'd collapsed forward, legs spread, arms out, and scattered the contents of his pockets on the nightstand—three passports, two cellphones, wallet, keys, foreign coins, a switchblade, and business cards with no contact info, only a name and six words.

Angel Phoenix
Odd Jobs
On-site Research
Special Deliveries

Angel stirred and turned his head. He hated alarms. This gentle routine reminded him to be aware of his dreams before they slipped into the void. His grandmother Dao—"star" in Laotian—had taught him dreams are "messages from your soul and the universe." The words of the song inspired him and captured his life mission, so he let it loop. He called it "The I'm Possible Dream."

To right the unrightable wrong
To love pure and chaste from afar
To try when your arms are too weary
To reach the unreachable star

His windowless bedroom was a high-tech tomb with arched ceilings lit by track lights. Above topographic and world maps, two metallic Bose speakers hung on the narrow slate walls at each end. A tall silver air-con tower hummed to an audience of rumpled shirts, shorts, socks, documents escaping from folders, black utility bags and packs strewn on the floor along the side wall.

Angel groped under the bed for his dream diary to jot down a few notes, then paused. *I've had flying dreams before, but never as a butterfly. And this seemed like two dreams. One in the jungle… and one with teenagers in… Where? Canada?*

He groaned and sat up as his bones echoed his groans. He scribbled down what he could remember, which included seeing one of those blue morpho butterflies sitting on Greta's leg in Bolivia. Sometime last evening, he'd gotten home and had hit the sack hard. After four flights in twenty-some hours and a thin slice of shuteye, his arms, legs, digestive system, and head were in different time zones. *Okay, skin first, stomach second, muscles third, brain tomorrow.*

His clothes created a black cotton trail out of the bedroom, through the living room, and into the bathroom as he stripped down to his Superman briefs. Inside the resounding tiled walls of the shower, Angel crooned along with the music, wrestling with Luther over the exact notes of the melody. Luther won.

This is my quest
To follow that star
No matter how hopeless
No matter how far

His subterranean catacomb was shaped like a turtle—an oblong shell for the main room with four separate legs serving as bedroom, bathroom, workout area, and equipment storage. Two tunnel exits with four-inch steel doors lead out of the head and tail. Every doorway and ceiling arched into a semicircle. No windows or skylights. The "roof" of his sanctuary was three feet underground.

With no appointments on the agenda, Angel dressed as comfortably as possible—soft Abercrombie T-shirt, blue hoodie, jeans with more holes than denim, no socks, and buckskin moccasins. Although pushing thirty-three, he could have passed for nineteen… and often had. He'd inherited his short height, smooth tawny skin, brown eyes, and dark hair from his Laotian father. With his mother's California Caucasian DNA in the mix, people might mistake him for Native American, Latino, Asian, Arabic, Jewish, Italian, or just another random face in the crowd… and they often did, exactly as he had planned.

To fight for the right
Without question or pause
To be willing to march into hell
For a heavenly cause

Leaning on the kitchen counter in the main room, Angel took the bread out of the toaster, browned to the exact shade perfect toast should be, opened the jar of Skippy Peanut Butter, the only kind of PB worth entering the mouth, and meticulously spread it to the edges with special attention devoted to covering every corner. A solid foundation was imperative before starting the same process with Heidi's Organic Raspberry Jam, the only kind of jam worthy of a PB partnership. His bedroom and sock drawer might be disheveled, but in other areas—missions, motorcycles, or bread spreading—strict adherence to discipline, systematic methods, and precise preparation were critical.

The type of bread didn't really matter, since it fell under the technical term PBDV: Peanut Butter Delivery Vehicle, a category including apple slices, crackers, a knife or spoon, and if no one was watching, an index finger.

MORPHO
Fate

Except for the perpetual buzz and rumble in the distance, silence surrounded him. Morpho tried to move, but his wings were soggy and stuck together, pinned to the rainforest floor by debris. Through a gap in his trap he saw sky above, though no amount of struggling brought it closer.

Time tortured Morpho as daylight departed. Twigs snapped. Leaves crunched. A human face blocked out the sky, then the eye of a young brown-skinned boy replaced the face. A babble of clicks and hisses pierced the stillness.

"Aqui está um belo azul!"

Fleshy fingers on a hand the size of Morpho plucked away sticks and leaves, grabbed his torso, and lifted him out of his prison.

The foreign noise grew louder, closer.

"Papa vai ser feliz."

Straining for freedom, Morpho flapped and fluttered, but the fingers tightened into a pinch. The hand slipped into an envelope held by another boy, to preserve the precious wings. The second boy dropped the envelope into a plastic jar held by a third, who tightened down the lid and dropped the jar into his rucksack.

Morpho was back in the blackness that began his day, but now, twitching and squirming did nothing. A sharp chemical odor dulled his senses, slowed his convulsing, and sealed his doom.

TIGER

Surprise Attack

Block by block, Tiger floated toward home, barely aware of where he was, but his inner entomologist remained conscious of small creatures flitting through the air. Movement—light blue flapping a few yards inside the park—suddenly refocused his attention.

Hmm. Silver-spotted Skippers. I've got one, but its wings are torn.

Like a knight drawing a sword from a scabbard strapped to his back, Tiger slipped the net from his pack and crept toward the bushes. He knew Skippers lived up to their name and flew fast and erratically. Tiger missed on his first swing, then raced after them across the wide expanse of grass. As he leaped up and caught one in midair, something hard and heavy slammed into his right side. Tiger flew six feet to the left. He hit the dirt flat on his back, smacking his head on the ground. Stunned, he tried to suck the wind back into his lungs, but three beefy bodies piled on top of him.

"Hey, Tiger, ya little pussy," a voice jeered.

"Who… Who are you?"

"Yer worse nightmare."

"Lemme go!" Tiger struggled, but with two kids sitting on his shoulders and one straddling his stomach with two hands on his throat, escape wasn't an option. "Let me go!"

Dick Hedlund slapped him across the face. "Quit yer squirmin', Brookshit."

"Ow! I don't even know you! What'd I ever do to you?"

"Yer trespassin' on our field."

"Your field?" Tiger shot back. "It's a public park!"

"Shut up, Bugboy! How's it feel? Pinned down like your precious butterflies?"

Tiger's dream flashed back and he shuddered. *I'm paralyzed on the rainforest floor.*

"Pretty fancy net ya got here." With one foot on the handle, Dick snapped it in half with his free hand. "Aw, it busted."

"Eeeiiiaaaiiieee!"

For five chilling seconds, an unearthly scream cut through the neighborhood. Its shrill alien tones rose and fell and strangled each other.

Dick jerked his head around. His neck hairs stood erect and then went limp. He spied two girls standing like statues, scowling at him. Dick blinked his eyes as if seeing double. They looked alike, dressed in the same clothes with the same colors, but in different places. One of them aimed her camera directly at him.

"Get the fuck off Tiger!" the screamer commanded.

The words stabbed him like sharp blades, but the "fuck" gave them an extra twist. Dick swore under his breath, wondering where the damn weird twins had come from. They weren't there a minute ago. "Who's gonna make me?" he shouted.

The other twin screamed—"Eeiiaaaiiiaaaeee!"—a little louder, lower and longer.

Dogs perked up their ears and started to howl. Cats slunk under chairs. A few frightened leaves fell from tree branches. Dick's eyes widened and scanned past the girls to people coming out onto porches across the park.

The three captors relaxed their grips, and Tiger lifted his head. *Gem! That must be her sister Arielle.*

"Dick Hedlund, if you don't get off him in ten seconds," Gem ordered, "I'll email my movie of your little mugging here to the police, the TV station, and a hundred of my friends. One more click and it's on Twitter."

"His name is Dick?" Air asked, screwing up her face.

"Yeah, he's in one of my classes," Gem said.

"Fits."

"We were just helping him up," Dick grunted. "He got in the way of our football game and fell down."

"OMG! What language is he speaking?"

"Bullshitese," Air said, hardening her glare at Dick.

"Hey, Dick," Gem snarled. "What's your father's name?"

"What's it to you, anyway?"

"I thought he'd like to meet ours." Gem punched a key and put her cellphone up to her ear.

"Let him up," Dick growled to his friends.

Air stretched out her hand to Tiger. He rose slowly, brushing leaves from his hair and dirt off his clothes. *The dream again. A hand picked me up.*

"Papa…?" Gem asked. "Got a minute…? Since you're the principal of our school, I thought maybe you'd met Dick Hedlund, one of my classmates…

No? He's here with a couple of his buddies… Just a sec. Lemme get their names. Hey! Dick's sidekicks!" she demanded, pressing the phone against her chest. "What're your names?"

They glanced at each other with pursed lips, both sides sagging into timid frowns.

Air drilled them with narrowed eyes. "Wouldja like to hear us scream again… together?"

They both muttered quickly.

"Thomas."

"Harry."

"Papa!" Gem smirked into the phone. "It's Dick Hedlund and Thomas and Harry… No, I'm not joking. I'm here with Tom, Dick and Harry."

Air covered her eyes and shook her head.

"They've got a big problem and might wanna talk to someone about it. I thought maybe they could come and see you… Okay, thanks, Papa. I'll let 'em know… See you at dinner… Love you, too."

"Smile, Tom, Dick and Harry." Gem snapped their photo as Tiger waved his broken net like a victory flag and grinned, eyes and teeth braces twinkling. "Papa says you're all welcome to stop by his office anytime and talk."

"You're both crazy," Dick said, nervously watching several adults walk toward them across the field.

"Oh… he noticed," Gem cooed to Air. "How sweet."

"Maybe you'd better go now," Air suggested, invading Dick's space. "We'll tell those witnesses over there we were playing a game and you lost."

"Yeah, hide and seek!" Gem taunted. "It's your turn to hide and practice your English."

Dick and his sidekicks backed away, then retreated into the trees.

"Papa's studied bullshit for years," Air barked after them, "and he doesn't like it."

"You guys saved me… er, I mean, girls. Soldiers?" Still dazed, Tiger sighed, "Thank you."

Gem held his arm gently. "Are you okay?"

"Ya, a little shook up, that's all."

"Nice to see you again." Gem kneeled in the grass. "Let's pick up your stuff… again."

"His name should be Dick Hed, forget the 'lund.'" Air handed Tiger the remains of his net. "Your net's history."

"I dunno what their deal was. They just attacked me!"

"Brave warriors," Air grunted. "A surprise ambush, three against one.

On the reservation, they'd've been history."

"Dick's in our English class," Gem said to Air as she held up Tiger's pack and slipped it over his shoulders. "A real jerk… probably jealous cuz Tiger actually has working brain cells."

"Where'd you learn to scream like that?" Tiger asked. "In Africa? From horror movies?"

"In Arizona from our Navajo nanny. It's supposed to scare away wild animals, evil people, and dark spirits… and let the whole tribe know something's wrong."

"I think Dick almost broke his neck when his head spun around," Tiger said. "Your screams were like a thousand fingernails scraping on a blackboard."

"You could do it," Air assured him. "Just yell like hell and give it all you've got."

Tiger tried to get the bows of his mangled glasses to stay behind both his ears. "You live near here?"

Gem pointed down the street. "Fourth Street and Thirteenth Avenue. So easy to get around this flat town. Go straight, left or right. That's it."

"Well, I'm right on your way home. First Street and Tenth Avenue. How about a glass of cold root beer… in return for saving my life?"

"Thanks, I'd like to," Air said, "but I've got a violin lesson. Wish I'd brought it. I could have stabbed them with my bow. See you at school." As Air loped away, she shouted over her shoulder, "You owe me one!"

"Root beer sounds okay to me, Tiger. Am I in your friend collection now?" Gem asked.

"You're president and Air is VP of security."

"Do collections have presidents?"

"They do now."

ANGEL
Talk of the Town

A CELLPHONE RANG. ANGEL DIDN'T LIKE TO GET CALLS. That meant someone, somewhere, might know where he was. Or which cell tower zone he was in.

Shit. From whom and why now?

The only calls he really wanted were from a couple of women who didn't know Angel existed, and he hadn't figured out how to meet. When he finally located which cell phone was ringing, he looked at the number but didn't recognize it and let it go into voicemail as he let "The I'm Possible Dream" flow through him.

And I know if I'll only be true
To this glorious quest
That my heart will lie peaceful and calm
When I'm laid to my rest

After breakfast, he listened to the voicemail.

"Hello. I'm trying to reach Angel Phoenix. This is Jonathan Skipper, Deputy Administrator of the DEA. We have an urgent confidential issue to discuss with you. Please call me back ASAP at 202-555-7977. Thank you."

Deputy Administrator? Angel pictured a thin secretary with a tin badge and a squirt gun, searching his place daintily and confiscating his stash of ibuprofen. On the web he verified the number as the Drug Enforcement Administration Headquarters in DC. He decided to make this deputy wait a while in the outer office like the corporate fat cats do.

Angel didn't want to return the call. He'd been around the world in the past eighty days—three times. Tired of war, he longed for peace. He remembered the good ol' days when calls revved him up and he could tell people how great he was—when he considered himself a superhero and had a flight jacket with embroidered angel wings on the back sporting the name "Supero." Now he hardly dared tell anyone what he could do or what he had done.

Optimistically, he imagined they might want him to talk to kids about the dangers of drugs. He could tell them how he'd tried "Mr. Happy" in junior high school, but turned into Mr. Sappy until he realized he already was Mr. Happy without "Mr. Happy."

"Yeah, right," he sighed to his glass of milk. "Dream on, Angel."

The Deputy had said "urgent confidential issue." That meant Mr. Despicable and his Dreadful Minions in some shit hole. He guessed the DEA wanted him to save someone. That was his specialty. He hoped the job would be in a couple of weeks, but they never were. Angel downed his drink and then washed the dishes.

And the world will be better for this
That one man, scorned and covered with scars
Still strove with his last ounce of courage
To reach the unreachable star

As Angel tried to decide what he might say to this deputy guy, his dreams wafted back in. *Introduction day. The kid got 'em going with toilet paper.*

The more Angel thought about it, the more he remembered other scenes from the dream, as if they were still alive and playing inside him. That Tiger kid inspired him to have some fun with his intro phone call to the deputy, even though the funny bones at the DEA were likely under lock and key. *I'll just be me... well, one of me. Since I'm at home in the woods near whistle-stop Pokeberry Ridge, Georgia, I might could give 'em a right good taste o' the talk o' the town.* He punched in the deputy's number.

"Good morning. DEA. How can I help you?"

"Howdy, ma'am. I am returnin' a phone call from a Dep'dy Jonathan Skipper."

"May I tell him who's calling, please?"

"My name is Angel, darlin'."

"Angel Darlen?" she asked.

"No, ma'am. Jus' Angel."

"Jess Angel Darlen?"

"Darlin' as in sweetheart, ma'am," he enunciated in plain Yankee American. "Would you please be so kind as to notify Deputy Administrator Jonathan Skipper that Angel, as in Angel, will be on this telephone line for eleven more seconds?"

"Please hold."

"Bless yore sweet heart!" He only had to wait for nine.

"Is this Angel Phoenix?"

"Who all's askin'?"

"Jonathan Skipper. I called an hour ago."

"How'd y'all get this here number?"

"I'm holding your unique business card."

Angel clicked through the DEA web pages on his laptop as he replied. "Ain't no number on my bidnis card."

"The number was written on it by an FBI friend of yours."

Oh, the FBI: Fucking Bunch of Idiots. I'm surprised we're still friends after that last mission. "I got a heap of gubmint buddies. This friend of mine got a name?" *It must've been Bernie.*

Seriously perplexed, Jonathan held up the card as he studied the photo of Angel Phoenix in the thick file on his desk and wondered what the hell was happening. He was looking at Jackie Chan, but talking with Andy of Mayberry. "They'd rather not say, or I don't recall. Which answer would you prefer?"

What's with these people? Paranoia plus amnesia. It's like talking to me. "Done disremembered, mmm? Mister Skipper… 'preciate the call, but I reckon y'all got the wrong number."

"Mr. Phoenix, we don't know each other, but I've heard about you and your singular skills. We may have an odd job for you requiring on-site research and a special delivery."

Jonathan's photo smiled at Angel as he scanned the deputy's bio on the DEA Leadership web page. "When?"

"Now."

Angel got up from his sofa and started pacing around his round coffee/dining/operation planning table. "Cain't do it. Been mighty busy lately and I am plumb tuckered out. I'm fixin' to put up my dogs for a spell, and so far I've only had ten hours of vacation."

"Angel, I understand this is short notice—no, it's immediate notice—but will you please come to our office in DC and talk with us in person? It's a matter of life or death. Your trip here will be on us, all expenses paid, first class all the way."

"When?"

"Now."

"Dad gone, Jonathan, can't you use any other words 'sides now when yore talkin' about time?"

"Later."

He's quick. I kinda like this dude. "Whereabouts this odd job o' yourn?"

"Not in Cleveland," Jonathan said.

"Good. The Land of Cleve. The Mistake on a Lake." Angel leaned on the counter and scooped out a fingerfull of peanut butter. "That only leaves us the rest of the world. Is it in a farn country?"

"Asia."

Smart ass. "Right big country... Jonathan, how 'bout we play a game of Clue? You be Kernel Mustard and I am Perfessor Plum. D'it happen in the ballroom?"

"No, but you'll need to come here to the library, and then we could meet later in the dining room. Let's just say... on this odd job you won't have any trouble asking where the bathroom is."

Hmm. An English-speaking country? Singapore? Hong Kong? India? Oh god, not Pakistan. Or... just how much does he know about me? "Will I need to wear a tie?"

"Don't bother. You'll meet many beautiful ones."

It's in Thailand. "Y'all could sweet talk a kitty cat outtava tall tree. How long y'all think this odd job'll take, Jon?"

"It must be finished within the week."

"Lordy, lordy. I'll have to have an argument with myself and it might could get vi-o-lent. Angel may be willin', but frankly, Dep'dy, the Devil might not give a damn. I'll call back in a few."

"In a few what? Minutes? Hours? Days?"

"Hold yore potato, Jon. Sooner than later, sometime after now. Y'all are nervous as a long-tailed dog in a room full of rockin' chairs."

"I'm holding my breath," Jonathan said and hung up.

Angel flopped onto the sofa. He tilted back his head, shut his eyes, and gazed at the Devil in the mirror in his mind. For some people, a little white angel and a little red devil stood on each shoulder and yelled back and forth. But Angel looked the Devil straight in the eye and saw himself. He knew the reflection in a mirror is reversed, the words on his Atlanta Braves baseball cap backwards—right is left and left is right, though up and down are the same. You had to consider both sides and then decide for yourself which direction was heaven or hell.

This time Angel started the silent conversation. "I'll probably have to save someone."

"You've already saved enough souls. Save yourself and leave the rest to me."

"I should at least find out what they want. I'm already time-zoned out. Another day won't matter. I can visit my mother next door in Laos."

"Take a break, Angel. Heaven can wait."

"Maybe you're right. I'm gettin' sick and tired of my life. I don't trust anyone. I hardly have any friends. I live in a fuckin' cellar."

"That's not so bad. Try living in hell."

"No, thanks. I've been there and back."
"Haven't you been in hell enough lately?"
"I am what I am. I do what I do. It's my mission.'"
"Angel, what is devil spelled backwards?"
"Lived."
"Angel lived. See? We're stuck with each other."
"Whatever. I'm goin'. You comin'?"
"My way or yours?"
"I'm sure it'll be a little of both."

TIGER
The Secret Laboratory

GARLIC GRABBED THEM BY THE NOSE when Tiger and Gem walked into the kitchen. His mom chopped vegetables at the counter, keeping a steady beat with her ten-inch cleaver and belting out "Stairway to Heaven." She wasn't a singer, but the louder she sang, the more she thought she might be—especially while holding a knife.

"Hi, Mom."

"Oh!" Doris swung around clumsily and knocked a couple of carrots off the counter.

Gem stood behind Tiger, taking it all in, her dark eyes saying, like mother, like son.

"Hi, Tiger." Then Doris saw Gem. "Oh…! Hi…!"

"Mom, this is Gem Cavalier. Gem, my mom."

"It's nice to meet you, Mrs. Brooks."

"It's nice to meet you, too, Gem. What a marvelous name!"

"Thanks."

"I promised Gem a glass of root beer," Tiger said.

"Hmm. Sorry, but I think your dad finished the last one—soon after he finished the first five." Mom rummaged in the fridge. "How about some orange juice? Or water, or tea? Milk? I've got some apricot nectar!"

"I like apricot nectar," Gem replied.

Mom poured two mugs, stuck in straws, and set them on the table, almost spilling one.

Tiger's eyes widened as he shook his head behind them. *Jesus. Will I ever get out of that dream? Now we're going to suck fruit nectar like Morpho and his mates.*

"Since Tiger loves butterflies, I got these mugs on the internet. They're little paintings of monarchs done by an artist named Angela Mariposa."

"They're cute. So is her name," Gem said. "It means Angel Butterfly in Spanish."

"Would you like to join us for dinner?"

Standing behind Gem, Tiger cringed inside. *No, no. We're not meeting Walter Percival the Second yet.*

"Thanks for the offer, but my parents are expecting me."

"How 'bout if I give you a tour of my room?" Tiger suggested to Gem.

She nodded quickly.

"Okay… well, have fun!" Mom turned back to her vegetable hacking. "Tiger's got a bunch of fantastic collections up there. Remember, Gem, you're certainly welcome to stay and eat with us if you…"

Tiger and Gem were already halfway up the stairs.

Above the bedroom table where Gem and Tiger sat with their nectars, a white ceramic tiger head roared out of the wall, lips curled and fangs bared, next to a Tiger Airlines travel poster and a painting of a saber-toothed tiger battling a mastodon.

"Is your dad really the school principal?" Tiger asked.

"He's just Papa, but he is Papa the Principal. I don't make a big deal out of it. Everyone'll find out soon enough."

"Your papa sure came in handy on the phone today. I thought maybe you were bluffing."

"Nope. I could've sent the movie with a couple clicks."

"To the police and TV station?" Tiger asked.

"Well… eventually." She slurped on her straw. "This nectar is great!."

"Thick and cold. That sounds like my dad."

"I'd like to meet him. Your mom's a bundle of energy."

"Doris seems to be growing younger, getting into the 'new age' while Walter's getting into old age. I'm kind of amazed they're still together. She's a vegetarian; he's a meat and potatoes man. Golf shows excite him and put her to sleep. She works out. His only exercise is to eat faster."

"Sounds like you take after your mom," Gem said, glancing around his equipment-laden lair. "This looks more like a wizard's workshop than a bedroom."

"I experiment on myself in my sleep. I've got another brain in a jar under the bed." Tiger rose and opened the door to a small closet. "Come and look at this. We're only on the wizard's main floor."

"Okay, bro. Lead the way."

Inside the closet, two steps on the right went up to another door, which he opened to reveal another set of stairs.

As Tiger led her up to the dimly lit attic, a musty odor crept into Gem's nostrils. She could only make out hazy shapes until he flicked the switch. Racks of specimens and tables lined the walls below display cases teeming with insects, butterflies, moths, stamps, coins, and skeleton keys. In the middle of the room, a model train on tracks steamed through tiny towns, forests, and tunnels.

"The secret laboratory! Where's Igor, your hunchback assistant?" Gem asked. "Like, do you have a white lab coat for me to wear?"

"Igor only limps over at night in the spring and fall. He might be in tonight. This is my inner sanctum. No one else comes up cuz it's a furnace in the summer and a freezer in the winter."

"Very impressive. You've been busy up here."

"I guess I get it from my dad. He builds houses. Gets concrete things done." Tiger picked up the Great Northern locomotive from the track and gazed at it wistfully. "We had a good time making the train layout together, but that was a few years ago."

Gem pressed her nose against a glass case and peered at the skinny labels sticking out like miniature shelves on pins below the beetles. "You keep track of all that data for every insect? How can you write so small?"

"Small mind and too much time."

"In the Congo, Papa used to battle beetles, bugs, slugs, and rodents. He planted a garden with seeds from America: pole beans, sweet corn, monster tomatoes. He put nets over the plants, sprayed them with natural sprays, and dusted them with like, I don't know, dust, and built a bamboo fence around the whole thing to keep out the other million critters. One night, snorting and grunting woke us up. We lived in a wooden house on stilts next to the river and no one dared to get up except Papa. He went to the window as a herd of hippos tramped through the garden. They flattened everything! After that, he didn't mind the bugs so much. Like, when a beetle steps on a tomato, nothing happens. But a hippo? You get ketchup."

"Wow." Tiger had mentally left the room and was living in her words. "That would not happen in Canada. I'd love to have been there. Or to go there. I've never been in a jungle."

"I miss it. So many trees to climb, creatures to talk to… a great place to grow up."

"In class, you said you hadn't grown up yet."

Gem shrugged her shoulders. "I started, but I don't plan to finish. Right now I'm working on growing in."

ANGEL
Fun on the Phone

While Deputy Jonathan waited for an answer, he'd perused the DEA file on Angel in depth. This enigma was born in Laos, came to Los Angeles with his parents, and later moved to Phoenix.

Angel Phoenix joined the Marine Corps, earned a black belt in their Martial Arts Program, served in several Marine Air Ground Task Special Forces in Iraq and Afghanistan, then left the Marines to become a "freelance commando" with sketchy addresses in Montana, Brazil, Spain, and now somewhere in Georgia, maybe, while traveling most of the known, and unknown, world. Jonathan had an inkling this hillbilly was only one of many characters ambling around in Angel's brain.

After checking flights on the web, Angel called back. "You win, Dep'dy. I'm on my way, if you say so. Ain't but one nonstop, first-class, roun' trip Delta ticket to Warshinton left."

"You're a good man. Book it and bring the receipt. We'll reimburse you tomorrow. What time will you arrive?"

"3:53 p.m. at Ronnie Reagan Nashnal on Delta 1125 from Atlanta. Best check with the airline 'fore yore man leaves to git me, cuz I reckon y'all know what Delta stands for…"

"I do not know. Please enlighten me."

"Doesn't Ever Leave The Airport."

Jonathan laughed out loud. "That I will remember. Will you be spending the night with us?"

"If the job's really odd, I might be needin' some local edgy-kayshun… topo maps and everything like that." Angel sat cross-legged on the sofa, swiping out the last islands of peanut butter from the jar. "And vittles. Steak 'n' taters. And I can't live without my grits."

"We could put you up at the Hilton, or would you rather rest your dogs in a log cabin?"

"Ain't got no cabins at the Hilton?"

"Not in DC. I'll ring up the Kuntry Kitchin over yonder. They may have a bunkhouse out back next to the cornfield. You can grind your own grits."

Jonathan's catching on. "I reckon I could handle that."

"We'll be meeting with Administrator Victoria Lionel and some other people as well."

"Administrator Victoria?" Angel asked, clicking to her bio and photo on his laptop. "Zat like a sec-e-tary or somethin'? She take notes?"

"I'd say… no. Think of her as Director. Top Gun. The Big Cheese. The Administrator, with a capital A, is in charge of an administration."

"Okay then, Dep'dy Gun, Dep'dy Cheese. I need to hit the highway real pronto-like. I am halfway between the boondocks and the sticks. Two hours outta Atlanta."

"Angel?"

"Dep'dy?"

"Thank you," Jonathan said, sincerely grateful.

"You are welcome, sir!" Angel snapped, now a respectful Marine cadet at attention. He stood and saluted. "If you need any assistance seizing illegal moonshine in the Appalachian Mountains, I'm your man, sir!"

"Now I must be speaking with Angel Phoenix the Second." Jonathan fully understood this soldier was definitely a long-term resident of the twilight zone, perhaps exactly what they needed.

Angel paced around the room again—not with trepidation, with pleasure. "Chai, na khrap. Acha rao ja dühm bia sawng kuat kühn?" Angel said in Thai, knowing from Jonathan's bio he'd worked in Bangkok. *Yes, sir. Maybe we'll have a couple beers tonight?*

Jonathan shot back instantly. "Angel Phoenix tee Sahm. Dai, dai. Pom rahk bia Singha." *Angel Phoenix the Third. Sure, I love Singha beer.*

"¿Cómo se siente ahora, señor Skipper?" Angel asked in Spanish, assuming every DEA agent must have been to Mexico. *How do you feel now, Mr. Skipper?*

"¡Hola, Ángel el cuarto! Me siento mucho mejor, gracias." *Hello, Angel the Fourth! I'm feeling much better, thanks.* "So, señores Phoenixes. Should I send a bus to fetch all of you at the airport?"

"No, sir! A car will be sufficient. We all live comfortably in one body. We'll be wearing this."

"This what?"

"This!" Angel pointed at his clothes. "Doesn't the DEA have some electronic device that can see through phones?"

"Not yet, but I'll bet y'all're wearin' of them straight jackets." Kentucky Fried Jonathan quipped. "Think y'all can squeeze into one hotel room?"

"Yes, sir! With two double beds, if you please, sir! I can order a cot from room service if necessary."

"I could invite our staff psychiatrist to the meeting," offered Deputy Jonathan.

"No, sir! I think people who see psychiatrists should have their heads examined."

"Good luck, Angels one through four. See you in six."

"Sawatdee, khrap! ¡Adios! I'll see y'all before y'all see me," Angel rattled off in Schizophrenese and then punched out.

"Well, that was fun," Angel confessed to the cellphone in his hand. He grinned and stroked his chin.

Do I have to shave since I'm only meeting with the DEAD—the Drug Enforcement Administration Director?

RED
What a Bitch

The outpatient cancer ward in the outskirts of New Delhi had severe off-white walls—very off-white, as far off-white as Bombay is Off Broadway. Like much of India, even though the hospital was a relatively new building, it seemed impregnated with centuries of grime.

Entering through the open-air arches in the corridors, hungry mosquitos cruised into rooms in search of liquid meals. No one had researched whether they suffered from side effects of the chemotherapy drugs in their blood buffets—hair loss, diarrhea or constipation, depression, problems with concentration, judgment and reasoning, mood swings, and loss of memory—but the mosquitoes definitely did not lose their appetites.

Dressed in an Armani business jacket, perhaps fashionable a decade earlier, blue jeans, and a scarf covering what was left of her auburn hair, Red Admiral lay on her back, motionless on the rusting bed. A clear bag of chemicals dripped down the IV tube into her wrist as soft feminine snores gurgled out of her nose and mouth.

Two dark-skinned nurses wearing bright-white sterile uniforms stood in stark contrast to the dingy walls, similar to the millions of women outside dressed in saris floating like butterflies above the trash-lined streets. One nurse held a clipboard with Red's medical file, as the other tapped the bag and impatiently looked down at the unconscious patient. She spoke in Hindi with no attempt to lower her voice.

"What a bitch!"

"That's what everyone thinks," the other nurse agreed. "Asleep like this is the only way I can stand her."

"I've never even seen her smile. She only barks like a chained dog."

Making his rounds after an arduous night of surgery, Dr. Bankyopadhyay—Dr. B to his English patients—had stopped outside the door to listen to the voices coming from the room. Short, stout, and unassuming, Dr. B had the countenance of a fire hydrant. Once the nozzle opened, the intensity of his energy could wash away people's pain or tear them to pieces. He stormed in and commanded with a whisper, "Both of you, into the hallway at once!"

The nurses scurried out and took refuge against the wall, bowing their heads to deflect the doctor's wrath.

Leaning forward, Dr. B stabbed his stubby forefinger at them. "Who do you think you are, speaking about a patient like that?"

"Doctorji, she doesn't speak Hindi." The defiant nurse feebly defended them. "She wouldn't understand us even if she were awake."

Dr. B's choler swelled and his green scrubs seemed to deepen in color. "Did you perform lab tests to determine this absurd hypothesis? She has lived in India for thirty years. Even if she chooses not to speak Hindi, do you think she understands nothing? That she cannot feel the loathsome tone of your voices? Have you not learned in your waking hours that people hear and learn in their sleep?"

She backed down and bowed her head even lower. "I am sorry, Doctorji. It will not happen again."

The other nurse tried to be invisible.

"It certainly will not happen again! We are here to assist in patients' healing, not add to their suffering. If I witness this behavior one more time, or even hear of it, you will find yourselves mopping floors in the basement or at the morgue where your pathetic words will fall on dead ears. Karma will then deliver you to your dismal destinies, perhaps with the same affliction tormenting our patient here. Give me her file and go." He grabbed the clipboard from the nurse and pointed fiercely down the hallway. "Now!"

The nurses scampered away as Dr. B waddled back into the room to check on his patient. The file reminded him this was Red's fourth visit and that previous treatments had lasted about four hours. She'd slept each time, awakening dizzy and exhausted.

"Begging your pardon, Doctor Bankyopadhyay."

Startled by a voice speaking English, Dr. B turned awkwardly to confront a familiar face. "Azeez! I did not see you come in!"

"I am being here for three hours," Azeez announced proudly, pointing across the room, "eating and reading on my mat on the floor behind the other bed."

Dr. B bowed his head. "Then I offer you an apology for the disgusting behavior of our nurses toward your employer."

Azeez stood erect, almost rigid, in his tricolored uniform. A long-sleeved white shirt, always pressed, matching his beaming smile. A black leather belt and dress shoes, always polished, matching his thick combed hair. Milk chocolate-brown trousers, always creased perfectly, matching the hue of his face and hands. Dr. B had never seen him dressed differently and wondered if his clothes were surgically fastened to his body.

"I am sure you are right and they are wrong," Azeez said, his head bobbing from side to side, "but I think Miss Red is most happy being a bitch. I hear her saying it to many people. Let me see if I am remembering her exact words... she says them very loudly and they are sticking in my mind somewhere. Oh, yes! 'You are goddamn right I'm a bitch, and don't you forget it!'"

"That does sound like Miss Admiral." Dr. B chuckled, then switched back to his serious demeanor. "Nevertheless, the nurses' words were malicious."

He walked over to Red, felt her pulse, and noticed the REMs behind her closed, pulsing eyelids. "She must be having vivid dreams. Look how her eyes bounce back and forth under the lids."

"I am hoping they are sweet," Azeez said softly. "How much longer is her treatment lasting today?"

Dr. B watched the flow of the IV, checked his watch, and scribbled a few lines in her file. "About an hour, I think. Why don't you wait in the lobby? The divans are quite comfortable."

"Thank you, but I am wanting to be near when Miss Red awakens and needs me."

"As you wish. You are indeed a kind and devoted servant. I hope she appreciates you."

"For fifteen years Miss Red is taking care of me, and I am taking care of her. We need each other."

"I see, Dr. Azeez. I will return in one hour."

Dr. B walked out to visit his other patients. Newly christened "Dr. A" went back to his mat, meal and book.

Now that these annoying distractions in their dining area had ceased, the mosquitoes dropped lazily from the ceiling, settling on Red's skin to finish their meals in peace.

TIGER

Met A Morpho Sis

"Do you remember your dreams?" Tiger asked Gem after they'd trekked down the attic stairs into his bedroom.

"No, I have so many. One second they're there, then they're gone." She sat down, took a sip of her drink and mused, "I love to dream."

"Ever dream you can fly?"

"Oh, they're the best!" Gem jumped up and stretched out her arms like wings. "I raise my arms and the wind carries me away! I guess some people fall and get scared, but that's never happened to me. How 'bout you?"

"Last night I had a dream that's been haunting me all day. Not haunting, like scary, just there… under the surface. So real."

"What d'you dream? Tell me!"

Tiger fiddled with the tweezers on the table. "I broke out of a cocoon as a wrinkled butterfly, then my wings grew, and I soared through the rainforest… in Brazil. It felt great. I even smelled things in the dream. And stuff happened today that seemed to come out of the dream. Kinda the same but different."

"Tiger!" his mom shouted from downstairs. "I forgot to give you a package the postman brought today. It's on the coffee table."

"Thanks, Mom. I'll get it!"

Tiger came back into the bedroom, humming and grinning. "Perfect timing. One of my dreams has come true."

"What is it?" Gem asked.

"Since I couldn't go to the jungle, I had a little bit of it sent here." Tiger cut open the package, lifted out three bubble-wrapped items, and meticulously dissected one. "This must be Hercules, the world's largest beetle. From South America." Tiger talked two tones lower in his professor voice. "Insects are part of the animal kingdom, and Hercules the Beetle is the strongest animal in the world. He can lift 850 times his own weight. That would be like you lifting sixty-five tons. Nine elephants!"

"I'd be squashed," Gem said. "Human ketchup."

Tiger finally got its display box unwrapped and held up Hercules—a five-inch, black and brown, shiny round tank with a curved horn instead of a gun barrel. He rested it in Gem's hands.

The words leaped over her lips. "I had one almost like this in the Congo! I'd put a string leash on him and he'd fly around my head. I named him Pinocchio, maybe cuz I thought his horn was his nose! Papa said it was a rhinoceros beetle."

"Same family as Hercules here, but not as big. These have longer horns and can grow to be seven inches long. In Asia, they use rhino beetles in gambling fights. People put a male on each end of a rotating stick, and the one that falls off first loses. They don't hurt each other like in dog or cock-fights… or die."

"I wish this boy were alive," Gem sighed.

"Me, too. He looks… I don't know… sad."

"Mine would stay still like this on my arm for a while and then we'd play together. He trusted me."

"Their entire lifespan is…" Tiger stopped to think. "About two years, but butterflies and moths only live for a few months. And only for a couple of weeks with wings after they come out of the cocoon." *In the dream, I only lived for a few hours.* Tiger spoke in chunks as he unwrapped the next bubble ball. "Get ready… for the largest… and most beautiful… moth in the world… the Atlas moth!" With a flourish, he set the clear plastic case in her lap.

Gem oohed as if she were watching a fireworks display.

"Mostly from Southeast Asia, but also found in…?" Tiger looked her in the eye, tilted his head, and raised both eyebrows, waiting…

"… 7/11 Stores!" Gem blurted out, pointing her finger at Tiger.

"Wrong."

"The North Pole!" She jabbed her finger again.

"Fat chance."

"My camera!" Gem said, holding up her bag.

"Possible," Tiger conceded.

"Your dream!"

"You're getting warmer."

"Brazil, of course," she announced nonchalantly.

"Bingo!" Tiger shouted.

"They're found in Bingo?" Gem asked in her silly voice. "Where's Bingo? In which church?"

The Atlas moth was truly a magnificent creature: beige, orange and maroon, ten-inch, multi-patterned wings with silver-gold triangular eye-like markings; bushy yellow antennae; a round, red-white-black-striped abdomen with dots along its sides; furry burgundy legs.

"Here's a bizarre fact for you. When they become moths, they don't have mouths and don't eat. They live on fat deposits built up when they were caterpillars."

"That is bizarre," she said. "Your last diet before you die."

"You know, I'm sorry." Tiger looked down at his bare feet. "I've been going on and on and on, being Babbling Brooks again. You probably don't care about any of this. I get carried away… someone should carry me away."

"Tiger…" She sang his name like a two-syllable song. "This is great. It takes me back to the Congo, and I hardly remember that part of my life. Ten years ago and it almost seems like a dream. I don't think I've thought about, or like, even talked about my pet rhino since then."

"Well, okay." Tiger dragged his eyes up from the floor to her face. "I can pretend I'm an Atlas moth without a mouth. I don't want to bore you to death."

"Don't worry. You're not. Now, what's that last bubble ball in the box?"

Tiger knew what it held and was almost afraid to open it. He unwound the bubble wrap and let it fall on the table. Transfixed, he stared at the blue morpho butterfly, pressed into white cotton under the transparent lid of the case—the butterfly from his dream. The butterfly he was in the dream. The butterfly that he, as each of the three young brown boys in the dream, had captured, pinched tightly, slipped into an envelope, and dropped into a killing jar.

Tiger's gaze roamed from Morpho's stunning wings to his segmented three-part body and halted. The head and the thorax where its wings attached were real, but shriveled and brittle. The antennae were fake—stiff plastic twine glued to his head. His abdomen below, fat and healthy in the dream, was made of flat, black paper. Tiger's soul shivered.

Gem watched his eyes—vertical pools of tears, frozen in time, the same blue of the butterfly's wings. She didn't understand what was happening, but felt the tension and saw his heart pounding through his T-shirt.

"Tiger…" she whispered. "What's wrong?"

"Wow… I… I was *this* blue morpho butterfly… in my dream last night," he stammered. "My name was Morpho. I flew through the rainforest. I drank nectar with other butterflies. Huge trees fell. I was trapped under sticks and leaves. I thought the first boy might save me, but he killed me… I was the boy, too." Tiger's tears fell.

"Come and sit down. Tell me everything."

Tiger set Morpho in Gem's lap, lay down on the bed, and put his arm over his wet eyes. "I only remembered flying before, and a couple other scenes from the dream, but the whole ending just came back to me. It was a nightmare. A real nightmare. I smelled the chemical that killed me."

Gem rested her hand on his shoulder and listened attentively as Tiger related all he could recall.

"It's different when I relive that dream now. Last night I was Morpho. It's like I wasn't thinking, or like the thoughts were all in colors… smells and tastes… or only feelings. Now when I think about it as me, awake, I feel like I'm above the scene looking down on it. Morpho had never heard a chainsaw or seen huge Caterpillars and bulldozers, but I know what they are. I've watched my dad use them to clear land. The rainforest was torn up for miles. It's weird, but I even remember seeing the word 'Brasil' painted on the dozers in the dream, but it was spelled with an 's' instead of a 'z'."

"I think that's how it's spelled in Portuguese," Gem said. "That's what they speak in Brazil."

"Poor Morpho only lived for a few hours. Most butterflies spend about 100 days as an egg, caterpillar, and cocoon, and then maybe two weeks as a butterfly when they can fly, feed, and mate. He only got to fly for a few precious minutes. Sad."

"You never know when your number's up. Yours could have been called today if you'd hit your head on a rock."

"You're right. Death by Dick. Well, if these are my last moments, I need something to drink. Can I get you some more apricot nectar?"

"Sure," Gem said. "You want me to come with you?"

"No, I'll zip in and out before Mom can start rambling on again."

Tiger went downstairs, brought back the whole bottle, and filled their mugs. "Whew. I know we only met today, but talking to you is like talking to a sister I don't have."

"Sometimes I think it's easier talking to someone you don't know than someone you do." Gem looked down at Morpho in her lap. "You meet a stranger and share a few moments. Then you go your separate ways. No gossiping with friends. No secrets to keep."

"Mom was probably keen on you staying for dinner so she could have another girl around the house besides her. Her Plan A included a son and daughter, but for some reason she couldn't have anymore after me."

"You and I could have met in a dream," Gem mused. "Or in a past life. Mama thinks dreams come from other lives, even other people's lives in the past… or even the future."

"It seems like our mothers are on the same wavelength. My mom says we just keep going round and round on the wheel of life until we learn enough to get off. You do good and come back in your next life a little further along. You do bad, you come back as a can of Spam." He shook his head. "I don't know."

"I'm still trying to work out the difference between good and bad."

"Isn't good, good and bad, bad?" Tiger asked.

"Not so simple. What's good for one is bad for another, and vice-versa, back and forth, all over again."

"Well, sister, will you please let me know when you've figured it all out?"

"That might be never."

Tiger lifted Morpho from Gem's lap and set it aside. "I'm pretty sure I'm done with this insect collecting. It might've been good before, but it feels pretty bad right now."

"Thanks for sharing your new friends… and feelings."

"Thanks for listening. How 'bout some fresh air, eh? Maybe we'll catch the sunset in my secret tree fort."

"Okay, bro! Lead the way." Gem jumped up, ready for another adventure. "I've got a collection of sunsets. My camera likes to bring them home."

As they walked down the stairs, Tiger stopped and put his finger to his lips. "Shh. Let's sneak out the front door. If Mom knows what we're doing, she'll want to join us. Dad's the opposite. We were on a trip and staying at a hotel by a lake. Dad was watching golf on TV. Mom asked him to come with us and watch the sunset. He said, 'No. Seen one, seen 'em all.'"

"Wow. Two peas in two different pods."

"Yep. When Mom and I walked out, she said, 'I feel the same about his golf shows. Seen one, seen 'em all.'"

ANGEL
Home Sweet Hell

To catch the flight to DC from Atlanta, Angel had to hit the road in an hour. He hadn't unpacked yet, and now he didn't have to.

Where's my damn duffel bag? Must've left it in the car.

After opening the locked, bolted, and barred steel door in the turtle's head hallway, he walked through a forty-foot, track-lit tunnel to another steel door with a fifteen-inch wheel like those on a submarine hatchway. No fancy electronics to hack. Entry—or exit—necessitated either keys, combinations, and elbow grease, or laser cutters and explosives.

This second door opened into a cramped, moldy root cellar guarded by cockroaches, centipedes, and mice. He skipped across the red clay ground onto the wooden staircase. Angel wasn't a big fan of any small creature lurking in the dark unless it was him. He yanked on a rope pulley to raise the trapdoor from his underground "Safehouse," which was also the bedroom closet floor of his topside "Fakehouse."

Two years ago he'd purchased this mousy, four-room mini-house on a half-acre lot from a feisty old gal recently sentenced to a nursing home. She and her unreal estate agent son had envisioned a ritzy subdivision a couple of miles out of town, but so far the only other takers were a whisky-blind hermit in a dilapidated shack and several thousand trees. That suited Angel just fine.

He'd left the house pretty much as it was, except for new aluminum siding colored in its original, wouldn't-give-it-a-second-look avocado green from the sixties. He'd decorated the interior in a Nuevo Leftoverian style with garage sale survivors from his previous apartments, including a massive old computer reincarnated as a fish tank and the shit-brown leather chesterfield couch which had kept him hot in the summer and cold in the winter. With lights on timers, window shades closed, and its owner in perpetual absentia, this facade fit his local persona of "that eggscentric travelin' buildin' consultant who rides up to the gen'ral store on a motorbike and tries to affect a Suthun axsent."

Angel could count the visitors to the Fakehouse on one hand. Only four—the sheriff, William Willard the postman, whom he called "Bill" since that's about all Bill ever delivered, and two young Jehovah's Witnesses selling God, their God, door-to-door.

The day the witnessing women had rung his doorbell, he'd introduced himself as Angel and invited the girls in. Visibly pleased by his name, they prayed he'd be their first receptive soul after two days of persistent peddling. The girls of God wore exactly the same clothes—white blouses, blue skirts, and black shoes—except for the size. One witness was rotund with severe acne and unkempt hair; the other rail-thin with a do kept in place by epoxy hairspray. Not one strand would've wobbled in a wind tunnel.

Angel directed them to the chesterfield to assure they were suitably uncomfortable with their sticky thighs glued to the fake leather. He came back from the kitchen wearing battery-powered, plastic devil horns glowing ominously, and handed them two blood-red raspberry sodas. They started to fidget as he spoke.

"Tell you what... you Joseph's Witlesses have done inspired me over the years. My full name is Angel O. Wrath and I gotta a message for the world. I am puttin' together an army of folks like y'all to infiltrate humanity, mate with the infidels, and alter the course of history through DNA." Angel walked toward them as he delivered his fervent plea. "Since you two ladies got hands-on experience with this door-to-door duty, I thought y'all might want to live on the other side of the fence. My fence. Remember, evil spelled backwards is live, live, live!"

After a few eternal, soul-searching seconds of smiling concretely and communicating with each other via rapid eye movements from Angel to the door, the girls jerked into a standing position in unison. Miss Thin stammered something about a forgotten appointment and apologized profusely. Miss Rotund silently perspired. Then they bolted out the door, threw a "God bless you!" over their shoulders, and ran across the yard as fast as legs hampered by tight sweat-soaked skirts and low-heeled pumps could carry them.

"Which God?" Angel yelled as they fled. "God spelled backwards is dog!"

A stack of religious tracts flew out their car window onto the lawn as they drove away, perhaps exceeding the speed limit for the first time in their polite pious lives.

There goes Anna Recksik and Fanny B. Joglin. Angel kicked himself in the brain for removing the whoopee cushion under the seat of the couch.

During the Safehouse construction behind the house, Angel had erected a tall, rectangular chain-link fence covered by opaque tarps. He hired "outtatowners" to do a quick covert job, while he told the townies about his "state-of-the-art, environmentally sound, septic and water reservoir system." In the local mind, this lowered him from being a Yankee (a nawthner who's jus' visitin') to a damn Yankee (a nawthner who's fixin' to stay) down to a crazy damn Yankee—"All I can figger is that there boy is tetched in the head. Best give him a wide berth." That suited Angel just fine, too. The tarps came down to reveal the one heavy-duty shingle on his Safehouse roof: an asphalt tennis court, nicely sodded around the edges.

Angel wasn't worried about the locals. The only crimes committed in Pokeberry Ridge were tunes brutally murdered at the KKK—Karla's Karaoke Kafe, an occasional kid napping at Our Savior's Primitive Baptist Church, and stolen glances at bank teller and third-runner-up to Miss Georgia, Georgeann Taggart, by henpecked husbands standing in line with their pear-shaped wives. Angel considered the way local men treated women in general as disorderly conduct, but with the formidable odds of several million good ol' boys to one Angel, fighting that battle with all the good ol' boys in Georgia would be like demanding that the Chinese Army stop breathing.

But today, the moment Angel cracked open the Fakehouse front door and peered outside, he felt something sinister in the air—that sixth or seventh sense inherited from his grandmother, more than a feeling, more like a knowing. He called it his "gutuition" because it ran from the space between the thoughts in his brain to the pit of his stomach and back again. Parked on the street to the right were two empty flatbed trucks. A Cat track bulldozer and shovel Cat excavator sat in the weeds on the vacant lot next to his.

They weren't there last night.

Angel stepped out onto his tiny porch, sat on the railing, and surveyed the neighborhood.

And no one's around today. A man drives the flatbed and then gets out to drive the rig. Where are our workers? Pissin' in the woods? It's not lunchtime yet, and they're religious about twelve noon in these parts.

A black and yellow striped butterfly danced in the air, zigzagged across his lawn, and landed on the railing.

"Hey! Aren't you a beauty?" Angel scratched his head. "I know you. You came from my dream. You're a..." He closed his eyes and coaxed back the image. "A... Tiger... Tiger Swallowtail..."

The butterfly slowly fanned its wings up and down as if saying yes. And seemed to stare him in the eyes.

"You're a little messenger from beyond, aren't you? There were Caterpillars in my dreams, up to no good. Will a tree fall on me, little buddy? Are some kids gonna attack me like Tiger?"

The swallowtail fluttered off as Angel walked the ten feet out to his aging Honda Hybrid sitting in the circular drive and retrieved his bag from the trunk. His "Angel Radar" went on alert, but didn't pick up any more signals until he glanced over at the Cats again. He knew from experience that both were overkill for clearing one lot. And the Ridge folks didn't go much for basements. No need for a furnace downstairs with one burning in the sky.

That shovel Cat looks like the same size I rented to dig my Safehouse. And that's got to be a D9 dozer like we used in Afghanistan. I might have to give Sheriff Dillon a call.

As thunder rumbled in the distance, Angel locked the front door, secured the trap door, barred the steel door to the Safehouse, and went to search for clean clothes.

Sheriff Dillon was Corporal Donny Dillon when they'd met a decade before as Marines in the Middle East. They served together in the same special forces teams and became fast friends that would last a lifetime. After they both left the military, Donny went home to Pokeberry Ridge and slipped into the law enforcement biz, finally replacing the slightly corrupt and exceedingly corpulent Sheriff Wiley Wilkerson. Wiley had occupied two offices: an official building with a jail cell and an informal room with a deep-fry at Digger's Donuts. He wouldn't take bribes unless jelly-filled pastries were involved.

Three years ago Donny had phoned his Marine mate to check in and invite him for a visit. Angel was free, he came, he stayed. It felt good to have one friend who understood him from the inside out and accepted everything he couldn't reveal to anyone else.

The shrill beeping of his perimeter alarm snapped Angel out of his reverie. He raced out to "mission control"—an entire wall of his main room. One large high-res screen displayed his computer, and the other, satellite TV. Below these hung eight smaller screens fed by bullet cameras mounted on each corner of the Fakehouse roof and on the four fence poles around the tennis court.

His two front video cameras told the tale. The shovel Cat tracked across his lawn from the right. The dozer headed toward his car in the front. Behind the unmarked silver van parked on the left crouched an olive-skinned man in fatigues, pointing an Uzi submachine gun at the side door.

"Son of a bitch," Angel said to the screens. "They were just waitin' to make sure I was inside." He'd expected this to happen one day, but not today, kind of like everyone thinks about death. He'd seen these raids in the movies and heard grim stories from his cohorts. The back fence cameras showed no vehicles and no movement.

Only three workers? Odds are in my favor.

The dozer hoisted up the Honda in its blade and smashed it into the front door of the house as the shovel Cat tore apart the roof. Three screens went blank.

"Fuckin' hell. I liked that car." He shook his head from side to side. "Now I gotta fuck with the insurance agent, too. Okay, time to play!"

Angel ran into the storage room, strapped on an ankle knife, and grabbed his camo jacket pre-loaded with his ninja toys, tranquilizer darts, and a short-barrel Glock. He didn't like to use guns, but a man with an Uzi in broad daylight might need extra persuasion.

He unbarred the back door and sprinted through the short tunnel leading to his garage behind the tennis court. It sat a few feet off the next street at the back of his lot. He'd designed the garage to look like an electric company relay building protecting high-voltage equipment that no sane human would dare touch.

Angel spun open the steel hatch above the stairs, flicked on the light, and snatched a crowbar off his workbench. He activated the hydraulic lift and raised the steel automatic door two feet off the ground. Rain dripped off the roof onto the driveway. Angel already had a plan.

Shovel Cat first, dozer second, Van Man third. I've got a plane to catch.

He crawled through the gap, kept low, and cut over into the dense trees on the lot to the right. He sprinted up even with the house, or what was left of it. Concealed behind dense bushes, he inspected the devastation. One wall still stood, but the shovel Cat was about to take it down. The dozer tracked over his Honda, crushing it into the garbage pile that had once received junk mail and monthly bills. With the Uzi dangling at his side, Van Man stared into the wreckage, as if the job was about done.

Out of their line of sight, Angel scampered up behind the shovel Cat, hooked his crowbar on an air vent, and pulled himself onto the roof.

Sweet! The cab door's open. Must be expecting me.

The Cat veered toward the rear wall of the house, and the operator cab door now faced away from the other men. The driver never saw Angel, only the curved handle of a crowbar flying between his eyes, one second before his afternoon cat nap. Angel dumped him out the door, jumped into the seat, and took control.

Feels good. I missed this machine!

The hefty bucket arm hung to the left. Angel hit the accelerator, turned his shovel Cat to face the dozer, and swung the bucket around, smack into the dozer's cab, shattering every window.

That's called a roundhouse punch with a six-ton arm.

He lifted the shovel high and hammered it down like a sledge, collapsing the dozer's roof. The Cat and its driver now dozed peacefully.

Three blows, two men down, one to go.

At first Van Man might have thought his hired morons had a freak accident, but with a fifteen-ton steel behemoth bearing down on him, his second thoughts must have scared him shitless.

Angel smiled defiantly behind the bucket raised like a shield in front of his cab. *Here I come. Your Angel of Destruction, rising from the ashes like a phoenix.*

Van Man panicked, sprayed his entire clip at the advancing shovel Cat in five seconds, and almost fell over backwards. If he did consider slipping in another clip, this thought was vetoed by his legs hightailing it out of the hell they imagined in their immediate future. He stumbled to his van, vaulted in, and frantically turned the key. Angel's bucket slammed into the windshield and crunched the hood. Van Man screeched backwards, leaving his front bumper hanging off the teeth of the shovel, then sped down the street.

Angel shut off the Cat, took a deep breath, and stepped out of the cab. Songbirds chirped. A fragrant fall breeze pushed through the exhaust fumes. The drizzling rain lulled the forest back to sleep.

He checked on the drivers. Shovel Cat Man was out cold with a purple and red horn growing out of his forehead. Dozer Man was cut, bruised, and moaning.

Like pesky mosquitoes spoiling a nice day. I wonder if they make a spray to keep assholes away?

Angel stuck two tranquilizer darts in their necks before dragging their limp bodies under a scrawny shade tree and sitting them on either side. Using duct tape, he wrapped the legs of each man together like a cocoon from ankle to waist, then continued round both men and the tree, covering torsos, arms, necks and heads, bypassing noses and eyes. He pressed harder on their scalps, so they'd remember the invisible Angel once again as tufts of hair tore from their roots when Sheriff Donny unraveled the tape.

Angel stepped back to admire his work and have a few words with his captive audience. "You were sitting ducks before and now you're sitting ducts! Two taped worms mating with a tree? No, a two-headed mummy wishing its mommy were here."

He thought it was bullshit in movies when the bad guys—or the good guys—were left alone in a room with their hands tied behind their backs by cub scouts, then cut through the ropes with a nail clipper, or stood up and smashed the chair. No way these Siamese twins could chew through a roll of duct tape or leave with the tree. He went into the Safehouse from the garage and walked to the main room, replanning the trip to the airport on his motorcycle. Cracking open a cold root beer, he phoned Sheriff Donny.

"Angel, my man!" Donny greeted him cheerfully.

"I was attacked by a few Cats."

"Pardon…? Cats?"

"Big Cats."

"Lynx? Mountain lions? What were y'all doin' to them?"

"A shovel Cat and dozer and a foreign cat with an Uzi. My house is a pile of rubble, along with my Honda."

"Are you okay, Bud?" Donny asked.

"I'm fine. They didn't know what hit them. Two are outside sleepin', duct-taped to a tree. One flew the coop."

"What can I do?"

"You could put up your pretty yellow police line streamers around the whole lot after pickin' up the garbage stuck to my tree. Please peel their duct tape off real slow. I don't know who they are, but they aren't local. And I don't know what they wanted, except to bury me. I'll ring a pseudo friend at the FBI, but I doubt they'll give a shit. I'm just their handyman who helps clean up their dirty work. You might send out an APB for a silver Ford Econoline with a crunched hood and no windshield or front bumper."

"I will do it. I'm on my way."

"Donny, I'll be gone by the time you get here. I've gotta start riding ten minutes ago to catch a plane and I don't know when I'll be back."

"I'll race y'all. I can git there in a flash!"

"Whatever you want. Be careful. I don't know if anyone else is hangin' around here, and I do *not* want to hear you complainin' in the hospital. This shouldn't be a thorn in your ass. It's a matter for the Feds. I've probably got footage of the deed on my security cameras, but no time to check."

"You be careful, too, Angel. Good luck. I'll take care o' this end. Keep the revs up and the rubber down."

RED
One Dream or Three?

Her legs kicking on the bed, Red awakened from her chemotherapy session at the hospital with a scream.

"Aaaa! Aaaaaaa! Azeez, help me!"

Azeez' book flew off his lap as he leaped up, stepped into his Styrofoam container of chicken masala, and raced over to Red, bedside by the time she had finished saying his name. He put his hand on her shoulder and gently rocked her. "Miss Red! I am here, Miss Red! Please wake up."

She dragged open her lids, squinting at Azeez as though he were far away. "Bloody hell. Where… where am I?"

"We are in the hospital. You were dreaming. You are safe and being here now with Azeez."

"I was in a jungle in Laos. Men with guns were chasing me," she stammered. "They shot me. My stomach hurts. Get the doctor."

Azeez reached for the call button across the bed. "Yes, yes. I will press the red button here."

Red grabbed his arm as it passed over her head, gripped it tightly, and lowered her voice. "I do not want the bloodsucking nurses. They're worse than the mosquitoes. I said get the doctor, damn it!"

"Yes, Miss Red, yes. I am going immediately. Please stay lying down and relaxing." Azeez grinned and scurried out the door, glad she was back, alive and kicking.

Red was one of those people who scoffed and said, "I don't dream," but this didn't feel like a dream. She rolled onto her side, put the pillow over her head, and tentatively returned to the jungle. She rewound the dream to flying off a cliff in Thailand, to Washington DC, to a motorcycle speeding through twisting turns, to a house in Georgia crumbling under yellow machines. Thoughts swirled and emotions pinched her heart.

Thailand? DC? Georgia? I've never been to any of those places, but I was there… No, I wasn't there. It was a bloke named Angel… or was it Tiger?

The name Tiger triggered another flood—a treehouse, an attack in a park, a live moth pinned to a board in Canada, more flying, another jungle, one that came crashing down on her.

Teenagers in Canada, butterflies in Brazil? I've lost the plot here. It must be the drugs… Morpho. I was Morpho and I died.

She had to shut it off. Flipping the pillow away, she lurched upright in the bed and reached for the ground with one foot. The floor rippled with waves, and her brain sloshed back and forth inside her skull. She caught the bed railing just before her legs gave way.

Pull yourself together, woman. You can do this.

Red clutched the railing and shut her eyes while the dreams and dizziness drifted away. When Dr. B and Azeez entered the room, she was leaning against the wall in the corner and staring out the window.

"Miss Admiral, I am glad you are awake," Dr. B announced. "Dr. Azeez here tells me you had a nightmare."

Red turned lethargically, glazed pupils floating above a wry smile. The fluorescent ceiling lights glistened off Dr. B's shiny bald head and Azeez' slick black shoes. "What in god's or the devil's name did you slip into my chemical cocktail today? LSD? Ecstasy? You could rake in the rupees selling it at dance clubs downtown."

"I added nothing new. To be effective, these drugs must build up in your system. We discussed the possibility of hallucinations and impaired mental abilities."

"I don't know if it was one dream… or two? Or three?" Red rubbed her eyes with clenched fists. "They're still brewing in here, like when you put down a good book but know the characters are still scuttling about on the pages and you might miss something."

Dr. B took Red's hand and led her to a straight-backed chair. "Come sit and tell me how you are feeling."

Azeez rested against the wall in a full squat, poised to spring into action, his eyes stuck on one sentence of his book while his ears followed every word in the room.

Red eased herself into the chair. Statuesque and svelte, she was about as tall sitting as the doctor standing in front of her. "I'm knackered and my body aches inside and out. Did your gang of nurses run me over with that bulldozer I saw parked out front?"

"I doubt it," Dr. B said, opening the file in his lap. "If they did, it should be noted here in your record. I am sorry, but pain is an unfortunate symptom of your ailment and the cure. May I get you some Tylenol?"

"B, actually I'd kill for a cuppa."

"I thought our hospital brew is not your cup of tea. I believe you once mentioned you would rather have a urine sample from a passing cow. That could be arranged. We are very efficient at collecting fluids."

"Have you sampled this so-called tea yourself?"

"Honestly," he sighed. "I avoid all the food here. You are fortunate you can leave to eat."

Besides Azeez, Dr. B was the only person Red truly trusted. He'd been her family physician as long as she could remember and used to call her "Little Miss Red" when she only came up to his waist.

Gazing through the thick square lenses that made Dr. B's eyes look as if they hovered at the end of two tunnels stretching three inches into his brain, Red twirled a few strands of the auburn hair dangling beneath her scarf. They fell off into her hand. She sighed and held them up. "I think you've administered your maniacal drugs so I'll end up looking like you."

"I confess," he sighed with a smile. "I was addicted to them for twenty years. I used to be taller than you and had a full head of hair. I had to stop taking them before I completely disappeared. Red, my dear, I have a suggestion," he said, removing the stethoscope from his neck. "I have finished my shift, and we can both leave. The lounge at the Eros Hotel serves a sumptuous high tea. We could have a chat about your dreams over a proper cup of tea and scones. It's not far."

"That sounds lovely. I'll fit in perfectly. Eros spelled backwards is 'sore.'"

"Do you feel up to it? I could call for a wheelchair."

Red sprang up from her seat. "I walked in and I'll walk out. Your nurses might dump me in the lift shaft. Azeez! Let's get cracking. The warden has released me from prison."

Before she'd finished speaking, Azeez had rolled up his book and food containers in his bamboo mat and was walking briskly toward the door. "I will bring the car to the main entrance."

"Wait." A spark of mischief glinted in Red's pupils. She pressed her hand on Dr. B's shoulder. "I changed my mind. Would you be so kind as to order the wheelchair? Azeez will escort me to the car. How long before you'll be ready to leave?"

"Seven minutes in the dressing room and seven more to the parking lot. I will be under the front canopy in fourteen minutes. My tongue is already tasting the tea."

As Dr. B left the room, Red turned to Azeez before heading to the washroom. "I'll be ready in five minutes. If the wheelchair hasn't arrived by then, find one."

"Yes, Miss Red."

Azeez shook his head—not a side-to-side, back-and-forth shake, but side to side from the top, as if he were shaking water out of his ears. In India, that meant yes.

Most places in the world, the standard side-to-side shake meant no, and the up-and-down shake meant yes. It had taken Red years to get used to the Indian side-to-side, water removal technique that would mean "I don't know" or "whatever" back in England.

When she'd ask, "Do you have anything besides curry?" and the stone-faced waiter wobbled his head, he wasn't a mentally challenged boy hired a few minutes ago, wordlessly saying, "I have no idea." When she asked taxi drivers to take her to the airport, they didn't mean, "Whatever. Maybe. Who knows? What's an airport?" They were silently saying "yes." Red tried to avoid the habit like Dengue fever, but found herself doing it, too.

When the doctor spoke, nurses jumped. The wheelchair arrived as Red waltzed back from the washroom like a reawakened force of nature. "Sit down in the wheelchair," she commanded, now taller than Azeez in her high heel boots.

"Begging your pardon, Miss Red?"

"I said I'd walk out of here. You will ride. Sit."

"Yes, yes, yes." Azeez lowered himself into the seat awkwardly, his head wobbling back and forth and up and down. The very idea of this scheme flummoxed him, but those feelings were business as usual with Miss Red. "I have never before been sitting in a wheelchair."

"Pray this will be your first and last time."

She spun him out the door into the dingy marble corridor. A few mosquitoes took up the chase. All movement at the reception desk came to a halt as they passed by. Azeez gave the nurses a thumbs up and a wide grin matching their wide eyes. Red remained stone-faced and mentally gave them a different finger. Dr. B was nowhere in sight when they reached the front curb under the canopy.

"Smashing," Red said. "I'll fetch the car. You sit. Stay."

Azeez' head now bobbled randomly like a plastic dog with a spring for a neck. "But Miss Red, I have come to be driving. You should not be driving when the drugs are driving you."

She pointed at him as if he were an unruly puppy. "Sit! Stay! If you get up from that chair, you're fired."

"Yes, yes," he said, raising his hands subserviently. "I am sitting and I am staying most definitely. Please be careful."

For the next few minutes, Azeez took a short course in Wheelchair Invalid 101. People walking toward him averted their eyes and changed course to avoid him, as if his legs might fall off or they might catch a deadly disease. He definitely did not feel valid.

Dr. B pulled up and rolled down the window of his silver Toyota Corolla. He didn't need expensive and fancy, just a seat and wheels. "Azeez! What are you doing? Where is Miss Admiral?"

"She is getting the car! Every day I am serving Miss Red. Every day I am cooking and cleaning and minding the store. Some days I am driving. Today I think I am acting in one of Miss Red's plays. I am sitting and staying here or she will be firing me."

Dr. B nodded knowingly as Red appeared in his rearview mirror. Like most folks, he could never predict what she might do or say next, just like her father, Danny.

She slithered out of her fifteen-year-old red Mercedes SL500 convertible, spick-and-span and immaculate—thanks to Azeez—then sauntered up to the wheelchair and rolled it toward the car, all the while smiling at Dr. B's stern face. She opened the door for Azeez and helped him into the backseat, then slipped into the driver's seat and pulled alongside the doctor's car.

Dr. B removed his sunglasses and stuck his head out the window. "What game are we playing here, Little Miss Red? Doctor's orders say you should not be driving under the influence of these drugs."

"B, please don't fret about me. Your drugs are on holiday. And you know there are no rules for driving in India. Only one simple guideline: survival. See you at the Eros. I'll save you a scone or two. Namaste!"

She sped off down the drive and squealed into the teeming traffic, barely missing the cow that could have given her a cuppa.

MONA
First Flight

Old man winter crept in gently, but relentlessly forcing fall to sleep. Cold drizzles became sleet rain then sheets of snow, blanketing every kaleidoscope leaf. Clumps of frozen fluff cascaded through the forest as if a billion crowds of flakes had joined hands and leaped off the clouds.

Inside the log cabin, homemade cinnamon-raisin bread and the wood cookstove flavored the toasty air. Mona stood on her tiptoes and rested her chin on the sill, her nose pressed against the windowpane. She watched Papa outside, bundled in his red plaid wool jacket, shoveling a footpath to Chester, their 1946 charcoal Chevy pickup purring by the garage.

"Hey, pumpkin!" Lily Arcade plucked a parka off the peg on the wall and walked up behind her daughter. "If you're finished eating, it's time to go to church then."

In the frost on the windowpane, Mona scratched her name with a backward 'n'. "Why?"

"Because God is waiting for us." Lily tucked Mona's arms into the furlined parka and gave her a hug as she zipped it up.

Mona looked up into her mother's eyes. "Papa says God is everywhere. Why do we have to go there?"

"So we can pray and sing together. Right foot." Lily knelt down and slipped one beaver-skin bootie on one petite foot.

"It's boring," Mona complained. "Why does the man in the dress talk so much?"

"It's not a dress. The pastor wear a robe. He's teaching us. Left foot."

"Last Sunday, the man next to me snored."

"Criminently! Aren't you Miss Grouchy this morning? Tell me one thing you like about church."

Mona pulled on her rubber galoshes and stepped outside. "When we leave to come home."

"Mittens." Lily held out the deerskin choppers that Mona's father had fashioned for her—thumbs in the two thin pockets, fingers in the two fat ones. Mona grabbed them and shuffled toward her papa. German Shepherd Shadow intercepted Mona halfway and tried to lick the cheeks off her face.

Papa Marco Arcade set his shovel in the truck bed, opened the door, and shouted, "Chester's all warm and waitin' for you, Mona Lisa." Mona jumped in, stood on the seat, and played with the knobs on the dash. Marco waited by the door as Lily gingerly stepped along the path, peering through the netting that hung from her feathered pillbox hat. "Careful, honey! It's a slippery one under the snow."

He helped Lily into the truck, then got behind the wheel and eased Chester into gear. A foot of snow covered the ground; the dirt driveway was merely a narrow white space between the trees. He couldn't take his eyes off the road he couldn't see.

"Lily, my dear, that was a mighty fine milkweed and mushroom omelet you made from your grocery shopping in the woods."

"Yah, I had to dig under the snow there and through the needles to get those pinie shrooms. Did you really like it?"

"Yah, you betcha." Marco took his hand off the gearshift lever and rested it on Lily's knee. "When have I ever said one false word to you?"

Lily smirked and put his hand back on the lever. "Not since we got in the truck."

"Mona? Remember when your mama made a whole meal out of grass clippings, the edible parts of a wheelbarrow, and leaves gathered from my jacket?"

"The leaves were from Shadow's coat," Lily corrected.

Mona wasn't sure what to believe. "I don't remember."

"Good, because your mother almost had to bury us out back. I had to make us new tummies out of goat skins in case she ever fed us that again, ya know. Instead of salt and pepper, she used sand and pebbles."

Lily smacked him on the shoulder with her beaver muff. "Your papa's makin' up stories again."

Near the top of the steep incline, the rear wheels spun, and Chester slipped to the side of the drive.

"Uffda, shoulda put on the chains," Marco moaned. "Mona, come out and help me get this boy movin' again." They shuffled through the snow-drifts to the truck bed, and Marco lifted her onto his shoulder. "You can make me some angels to help lift us outta here, but first I need your advice. Looky here. I got two tools. A shovel and a chainsaw. I'll give ya a shiny penny if ya can guess which one I'm gonna use."

"Silly papa. The shovel."

"Yah, well, we'll see about that." He dropped Mona in the deep snowbank, fired up the chainsaw, and felled a dead oak tree near the drive.

Mona lay flat on her back, waving her arms and legs in the snow in front of Chester so she could show off her snow angel to Mama.

Fifteen minutes later, Marco had cut the trunk into two-foot lengths and the branches into kindling. A truck with an empty bed skittered along like a leaf on ice. A full truck bed gave Chester the traction of a tank.

"Let's go, Mona! Here's your penny. The shovel woulda worked, but I wouldna had firewood to bring to the church."

As they drove past an open field, a black V of mallards sailed by in the slate sky, forging its way through the dense clouds of flakes. Marco poked Mona in the ribs and pointed through the windshield. "Look at those ducks, flyin' south, prayin' for sun and open water. Which one of you knows why one side of the V is always longer than the other?"

"Something about being easier to fly," Lily asked, "or the draft of their wings?"

"Mona? How 'bout you?"

"More ducks are on the long side."

"Well, I'll be. Aren't you the little crackerjack? That's two pennies in your pocket."

"Why can't we go south for the winter?" Standing on the front seat, Mona had fired her question three inches from Papa's ear, her fiery red-brown eyes flashing beneath jet-black eyebrows. "I wanna fly south to Mexico."

Marco and Lily's crystal blue eyes under Scandinavian blonde brows exchanged a silent glance that would be the seed of a private talk in the bedroom. Mona had been known to try to fly, and had the forehead scars to prove it.

"Gosh take it all, Mona. Flyin's pretty darn expensive." Marco raised his fox-fur cap and nodded to the side. "And your mama and papa have jobs here so we can live and eat and you can go to school."

"Chester can take us," Mona blurted out and rattled on. "You're a lumberjack. You can cut trees along the way. Mama's a nurse. She can help people anywhere. We can plant a garden in Chester's bed. Mama can go grocery shopping in the woods. You and Mama can teach me."

"You sure got it all figured out, don'cha? Well, keep plannin', Mona Lisa. Maybe someday," Marco sighed, "maybe someday."

Only a couple of miles away as the mallard flies, the one-room Little White Church in the Vale was little, white on the outside, white on the inside, filled with white Lutherans, and sat in a shallow vale, not deep enough to be a real valley.

Marco stopped in front of the walkway and came around to open the truck door. "You two head on in. I might come inside if I finish splittin' the wood."

"I wanna go with you, Papa," Mona pouted.

"You gotta keep your mama company. Sing like birds in there while I listen to the birds out here."

Marco pulled around back where the firewood was stored and stepped out of his truck as Pastor Amundson walked through the door on his way to the outhouse.

"Marco! It's good to see you." The pastor gave him a flaccid, three-fingered handshake and laid on the guilt. "Isn't it about time you joined us in the sanctuary?"

"Yah, but… I brought you a shi… a shipload of firewood here. I'm gonna split and stack it. If I put logs in your offertory plate, they won't be able to pass it down the row."

"Well, my son, thank you for keeping us warm. May Lily pass on my sermon, and may God be with you."

Marco tipped his head and spoke quietly to himself. "He is, every moment, every day, everywhere."

To the left of the pulpit, Clara Amundson's plump fingers caressed the keys religiously while her snow boots pumped the old harmonium organ pedals. Twenty-some manicured ladies sat reverently as their husbands prepared for their morning naps.

In her lap, Mona held a hymnal as her table, picked the yellow pencil from its round hole in the polished brown pew, and drew a V of mallards on the back of an offertory envelope. As the music faded, candle-carrying altar boys marched down the aisle, leading the pastor in his purple and white robes.

"Looks like a dress to me," Mona whispered to her mama as he passed.

"Shhh."

When she ran out of envelopes, Mona shifted her attention to the pastor's monotone chatter above the low drone of men's snores ending in snorts when elbowed by their wives. He was talking about flying. Her ears honed in on the bible verse he read—"But they who wait for the Lord shall renew their strength; they shall mount up with wings like eagles."

I don't think I have to wait for the Lord. Mona believed what her papa said about God living in her heart and surrounding her in every tree, creature, and stone. She remembered flying before, somewhere, in her dreams, perhaps before she could remember, before she was born.

"The woman was given the two wings of the great eagle so she might fly from the serpent into the wilderness, to the place where she is to be nourished for a time..."

Mona didn't know what a serpent was, but she imagined a wilderness in the south with dry mountains and expansive valleys covered in dense forests flowing from one to the other. She could smell the sage and mesquite, though she had no idea what they were either. She drifted off into this inner world until she had to stand and kneel and sing and sit and stand and kneel, and finally, Clara's feet on the organ pedals feverishly pumped everyone outside.

Marco and Chester were waiting right where they'd dropped them off. As Lily opened the door, Mona flew in and slid across the leather seat, dropping a flock of ducks on envelopes in her papa's lap. "Why is the man in the dress called a pasture, Papa? Does he live with cows like ours?"

"That's pas-tor, sweetheart, not pasture," he corrected as he flipped through the envelopes. "He's a man of the cloth, but don't ask me what that means. Ya sure, these are swell pictures you drew here."

"He said women with wings like eagles fly into the wilderness. I wanna do that."

With a déjà vu glance at Marco, Lily put her arm around Mona. "I think the pastor was talking about angels."

"You said I am an angel! Papa said I am an angel! He was talking about me! I know I can fly. I did it before!"

"You are *our* little angel," Lily assured her. "Many people fly in their dreams, pumpkin. Many people want to fly when they're awake. You've tried and it doesn't work."

Mona crossed her arms and legs and grunted. "I didn't dream it. It was real."

Those were her last words until they coasted down the hill to the cabin and an overjoyed Shadow the Shepherd. The snow had been busy and filled the tire tracks in the driveway.

"Come in and warm up while I fix lunch," Lily said, extending her hand to help Mona. "And I'll bet Papa's going to shovel some more."

Mona ignored her, jumped out, and scampered away, yelling over her shoulder. "I gotta make more angels."

She knocked off a few for emotional support, though Shadow dug out their hearts and destroyed their wings. Mona then lay in one spot in the snow, beating her arms and legs wildly. No longer making an angel, she was trying to lift off the ground. Disappointed though not discouraged, she spied the neat stack of firewood behind the woodshed, a makeshift shack with a flat roof sloping down from the front to the back.

I can't get off the ground. I need to start in the air.

She climbed the staircase of logs until she reached an overhanging maple branch and pulled herself up onto the roof. Her Shadow followed, but couldn't handle the last step, and ran to the front of the shed. Mona plodded through the foot of snow on the roof, lost in her vision of a warm wilderness.

Shadow didn't like it. She stared up at Mona, her high-pitched whines and whimpers masked by the scrape of Marco's shovel near the garage.

Standing at the apex of the roof, her toes straddling the edge, Mona was surrounded by white—the sky, the trees, the ground. God was everywhere like Papa said. She closed her eyes, spread out her arms, and waited for a puff of wind, for the perfect moment to realize her dreams—no fear, only resolve.

Standing on his hind legs and clawing at the woodshed door, Shadow burst into a cacophony of unearthly barking.

Lily threw open the door and rushed from the cabin as Marco turned, his gaze racing from Shadow up to Mona. In unison, Mama and Papa both screamed her name, creating her perfect moment.

Mona leaned forward and flew… straight down.

Marco was already moving when he screamed. The moment Mona dropped, he launched himself toward ground zero, arms outstretched in front of him, his heart propelling his feet.

This snippet of time froze, forever a snapshot in each person's soul, but witnessed from three different perspectives—one in ecstasy, two in terror.

Marco landed on his elbows, his rock-hard lumberjack arms bent into a cradle, and slid across the ice. Mona's chest hit his mittened hands and flipped onto her back in the snow… still and silent.

Marco rose on his knees, lifted her limp body into his lap, and pleaded. "Come back to me, my little butterfly, come back!"

Lily was petrified panic, hands folded in prayer, eyes beseeching the heavens.

Shadow tried to lick Mona back to life.

Eternal seconds passed. Haltingly, her eyelids fluttered open. With a faint Mona Lisa smile, she looked up at Marco and whispered. "I flew, Papa."

In her cozy open-air studio perched on a bluff above the Rio Grande River, Mona finished the final strokes of the painting in her easel.

On the canvas in front of her, from the vantage point of the maple tree behind the woodshed from her childhood, a monarch butterfly with a grid of black veins on its red-orange wings sailed off the roof over a snow-covered yard. Lily stood in the cabin door on the right; Marco shoveled on the left; Shadow howled in the middle.

Picking a thin brush, she dabbed it in black paint and wrote in the lower right corner, "First Flight, Wisconsin, 1947." And then signed it, "Angela Mariposa."

The scars of those distant days were buried under the creases in her forehead, but the joys still coursed through her bones. She gazed over the top of the oil painting through her picture window overlooking the Rio Grande, but only saw Papa Marco in her mind, with tears freezing on his cheeks.

I'll fill a canvas with his face… with a butterfly reflection in each eye.

Knowing she might not remember the inspiration, Mona sketched it in pencil on the thick drawing paper in her notebook. Donning her tattered straw hat, she picked up her piñon pine walking stick and drifted down the milkweed-lined path to the house with Marco, her German Shepherd, at her side.

I haven't made it to Mexico yet, but it's on my bucket list.

TIGER
Lunatics in a Tree

Gem followed Tiger through the backyard and behind the garage to a towering box elder tree with thick branches spreading out like elevated walkways. Aged two-by-four steps bolted to the trunk led up to a treehouse with a hobbit-sized door, white French windows, and orange aluminum siding. Gem started climbing immediately.

"From a secret laboratory to a secret fort! This treehouse looks like our home back in the jungle. You ever get hippos tramping through here?"

"Only my friend Otto," Tiger said. "Short fat guy. Never dared to climb up the steps. Wait a sec. You need the key."

Gem reached down and took the old three-inch iron skeleton key from Tiger's hand. "OMG! We had one like this, but it was carved out of wood!"

"Just trying to make you feel at home, I guess."

"It's very orange and not very secret. It's like a 'Here I am!' fort."

"It's my favorite color. Orange ya glad you're here?"

"Cute. Yes, I'm feeling fort-u-nut."

"You're cute, too. I thought of changing it, but how can you change your favorite color? It's not easy using it in a song. Can you think of even one rhyme for orange?"

Gem went through the entire alphabet as she climbed step by step. "No."

"Me either, so I looked it up, but only found door hinge. That's why they're orange. Orange door hinge. It's a short song. I'm still working on the music."

Gem unlocked the door, and they ducked into the treehouse. Faded insect, wildflower, and tree identification posters hung on unfinished boards. Linoleum left over from his dad's house projects covered the floor. A dusty stack of magazines, a few packs of ancient firecrackers, and two stools were its only inhabitants.

"Sorry it's so dirty." Tiger pushed open the windows. "I don't remember the last time I was up here."

"Did you build this yourself?"

"Nah. Dad built it. I handed him tools. Maybe eight years ago." They looked over the neighborhood as he gave her a pointing tour. "Chip lives there. Mike next door. Over there by the river is a softball field during the eleven days of summer and an ice-skating rink for the rest of the year."

"Liar. I've been here for three months and it was summer the whole time."

"Sure, but this is a freak year. Winter could hit later tonight. Last year we had to wear so many layers of clothing that if you fell down, you just had to stay there until somebody rolled you home."

"I may not make it," Gem shivered.

"See that garden down there? That's old Grumpy Groby's. We used to steal his tomatoes and raspberries at night."

Gem wagged her finger at him. "You're bad."

"We were. Our little boys' club was definitely bad. Chip, Mike, Otto and I. We'd phone in pizza orders and send three of them to Mr. Groby's house. One time he shot Otto in the butt with rock salt. Easy to do. Otto's butt was a big target. After that, we had to get him back. We got a bunch of dog shit in a paper bag, put it on Groby's front steps one night, set the bag on fire, and rang his doorbell. He came out and stomped out the fire, swearing, shaking his fist, shit all over his shoes. That's the closest I've ever come to dying. Not a bad way to go. Bustin' your gut laughing."

Gem wandered from the window and stopped in front of his posters of insects, moths, and butterflies. "Do you know what your dreams mean?"

"No. I've had a bunch of strange ones, like I'm naked at school in the hallway. Or I can't find the room for the final exam cuz I never went to class."

"You have Wi-Fi? I want to look up butterfly dreams."

"Haven't tried it out here. The network is our last name. Brooks. Dad set it up with a real tricky password. 1-2-3-4-5. Want me to write that down for you?"

"Thanks, I got it." Gem surfed on her iPhone as he looked out the window. "You ready, Tiger? Listen to this. It's about Morpho!" She joined him and read from her phone. "'Dreaming of a butterfly relates to rebirth and metamorphosis. Your subconscious is telling you to be mindful of changes taking place. They are natural for your growth. One thing may have to die so another may live. You should appreciate the shifts as they come, rather than fighting them.'"

"I'm sure not a fighter, probably not a collector either."

"Well, it kinda sounds like what's happening to you."

"I've felt it coming for a while," Tiger said, still gazing out the window. "A couple years ago, Dad bought me a BB gun. I'd shoot cans and targets, but one day I shot at a rabbit. I never thought I'd hit it in a million years, but it fell over and started screaming and kicking like it was trying to run away. Then it just spun around on its side in the grass. I felt horrible, but couldn't do anything to help it. After what seemed like forever, it stopped, and I went over and picked it up. It was still warm. Soft, furry and young… and dead. I cried then, too, alone in the backyard. From then on, I thought about that bunny whenever I killed the insects."

Gem sighed and nodded. "That must have been rough. I can't imagine killing any animals. That's why I like to shoot with my camera. I can print their pictures, give them away as many times as I want, and still keep them for myself."

Tiger sat on the floor, put his arms around his legs, and rested his chin on his knees. "Another thing hit me hard at Dad's church one Sunday. He's Catholic; Mom's whatever. I looked up at Christ nailed to the cross and thought, 'Jesus, that's what I do to my butterflies. I spread out their wings and pin 'em to a board.'"

"Like maybe you need a new road, bro. So what do you want to be when you grow up?"

"I've been thinkin' I should be a musician. When I talk about bugs, people make fun of me. When I play the piano and people sing along, we all have fun."

"It sounds like the music inside you wants to live. The bugs and bunnies are outside of you… dying."

"Could be," Tiger agreed.

Gem looked at the sun slipping down through the yellow and red fall leaves. "I seem to dream a lot around the time of the full moon. I think it's in a couple of days."

"Then I'll try to stay awake for a couple of weeks," Tiger said, recalling his nightmare.

"I've heard the full moon brings your subconscious mind to the surface, kind of like how the moon affects the tides. Seventy percent of the Earth is covered by ocean, and seventy percent of your body is water. Full moons bring out the lunatics, too. You know… moon, lunar, looney. Cities add more policemen because there's more crime. People do weird things."

"Part of my dream may have come from my mind," Tiger mused, "but the rest felt like it came from another dimension… or another being."

A red-orange butterfly flitted through the window, treaded air for a few seconds, and then settled on Gem's shoulder. Her eyes lit up as she let out a whisper of glee. "It's a monarch, isn't it, like on the coffee mugs?"

"Yup. She likes you. Not me. I must've killed her cousins."

"How do you know it's a she?"

"Males are larger and have black pheromone pouches on their underwings to attract females. It's good luck when they land on you."

"Well, I am lucky to be here."

"I'm surprised she's still around," Tiger said. "They're the only butterflies that migrate south for the winter, all the way to Mexico. Most of them are gone by now."

Like campers under the spell of a fire, they were silent for a few moments, listening to the crackling of their own thoughts and wondering about the universe. Then the monarch rose up, danced round their heads, and disappeared out the window.

"Thanks for stopping by!" Gem called.

"Mexico or bust! Hasta la vista, baby!" Tiger echoed.

As they gazed out the window where the monarch wasn't anymore, Gem asked, "So, Tiger… like when… when do I get to hear your music?"

"Maybe next time. I started writing a song for you, but I don't have much yet."

"Come on." She poked him in the ribs. "What do you have so far?"

Oh, what the hell. Why not? Tiger sung softly. "She's a gem… from Bethlehem."

"But I'm not from Bethlehem."

Tiger rhymed again. "You saved me, did you not? Or have you already forgot?"

"I didn't save you. I just helped you. I'm not God or anything."

Tiger put his hand on his heart. "God is here, Miss Cavalier."

"How do you rhyme like that all the time?"

"Now you're doing it, too! It's rhyme time! I dunno. It just happens. My brain slips into rhyming mode, but not many words rhyme with Gem. Them? Phlegm? BM?" Tiger heard his mother yelling from the house. "Mom's calling. Dinner must be ready. We'll have to catch the sunset another time."

"When's the next one?" Gem asked, wearing the sweetest smile he'd ever seen.

"We have them every day here. You're welcome any time."

"Like, which one do you think will be the prettiest?"

"We're going to visit relatives tomorrow night," Tiger replied, almost trembling. "Well… how about Sunday? I guess sunset and Sunday sound good together." He'd never asked anyone out on a date before, but it seemed like he'd just been asked out on one, and this must be how it's done.

"Sunday it is," Gem said as she crawled across the floor and dangled her legs out the door. "We'll have a treehouse picnic. Since you're providing the sun, I'll bring the sandwiches."

"Do I have to invite my mom? She'll be jealous."

Gem looked around the room. "I only see two chairs."

"Okay then, only you and me and whatever happens to fly through the window."

Tiger followed Gem down the steps, although he felt as if he could leap from the tree onto the back porch. They ran across the yard into the kitchen.

"There you are!" Mom said, stirring lots of green into a red sauce and spilling some of both over the side of the pan. "Where were you two?"

"Tour of the treehouse," Tiger said.

"You never gave me a tour," she pouted.

"Sorry, Mom. Mothers weren't allowed back then."

"I didn't think you still went up there."

"I don't. Today's a special day." Tiger wanted to poke Gem in the ribs, or at least catch her eye and smile at her, but he couldn't quite make himself do either one.

"Dinner's in a half-hour, whether your dad's here or not. Are you staying, Gem? I'm making my special vegetarian spaghetti that Tiger loves."

"Thanks again for asking. It looks and smells great, but I've got to get home."

"Mind if I borrow your car for a few minutes, Mom? Gem only lives a few blocks away."

"Of course you can! You have to take the old girl out once in a while so she feels needed. I hope you'll come over soon for dinner, Gem. We didn't get to chat much."

"I'd like that. It's up to Tiger."

"She'll be back." Tiger grunted in his gruff Terminator voice. "Even if I have to pay her."

As they left the kitchen, Gem said under her breath, "I can walk, Tiger. It's not that far."

"Sorry, not with lunatic Dick on the loose. Besides, Mom's car is the car for today. You'll see."

They walked outside to the garage, and Tiger lifted the door to reveal a 1967 pink Volkswagen Bug sporting peace signs and daisies on every body part except the windows.

"It's the only bug Mom can handle. She got it from her mom, Grandma Celeste. She's gone, but still with us."

Gem stroked the hood of the car. "Holy guacamole! Vintage Volkswagens, secret laboratories, clandestine closets, Brazilian bugs. I knew Canada would be cold, but like, I didn't think it could be this cool!"

ANGEL
A Surprise Defence

Swinging his crowbar like a cane, Angel whistled softly as he dragged his duffel bag to the garage. He flipped his cellphone in the air and smacked it into the back wall with his iron cane, scoring a home phone run. He fused the pieces into a blob of obsolete art with a blowtorch.

He took a new phone out of his duffel bag and used the crowbar to pry open its display pack—the impregnable industrial-strength kind consumers are incapable of cracking without sharp plastic slicing their fingers to the bone. Angel went through cell phones like toilet paper. They were cheap and useless once the wrong people had shit on you.

It's probably a coincidence the DEA called minutes before I was attacked, but these days you just never know.

He didn't believe in accidents and had experienced too much synchronicity to believe in coincidence. Things happen for a reason. Cause and effect. Signs were everywhere. if he was aware. But so far, he wasn't sure what to be synchronized with.

The top case on his motorcycle was reserved for specialized tools and weapons nicknamed "mind changers," so he packed a few clothes in his backpack and the sport bike's side panniers.

It better be casual day at the DEA, cuz they're gettin' jeans, T-shirt, and a baseball cap.

Angel donned full protective gear and snugged on his custom-made, home-modified Reevu helmet. It shipped with rear optics that allowed riders to see behind them, as if looking at a rearview mirror inside the helmet above the eye opening. He'd added two tiny cameras on each side of the shell and nearly had a 360-degree view, without rotating his head, like insects and crabs. With their compound eyes, flies know where the hand is coming from before the swatter knows where it's going.

He rode out the back street to the only road into his neighborhood in the valley, or as they called it in The Ridge, "back in the holler." At the T-junction, left went into town and right headed down the mountains to

Atlanta. Angel relaxed into the rhythm of the winding switchback road that he adored. Not for long.

Something buzzed by his left shoulder, and it wasn't a fly or honey-charged bumblebee. With his rearview optics, he saw Van Man barreling behind, Uzi resting on the dash, firing through his non-existent windshield. Angel slammed the bike down a gear, cranked the throttle, and pulled ahead. No way in hell or the Appalachians could a van keep up the pace of a seasoned biker on the tight curves, but he didn't want to meet any lucky stray bullets along the way.

"Mother of God. Some people never learn." Angel's hot words and breath steamed up the inside of his helmet's visor. *He must've been parked off-road near the T. He'll soon be hopin' he's got workers' comp. Let's play a game of jacks!*

Angel had a surprise for him, but needed to choose the right section of road. He remembered the barely traveled drive to a new development up ahead and prepared to lure his hunter into the trap. He lengthened the gap between his bike and the van by another 100 yards. When the road straightened, he throttled down to make sure Van Man saw him turn right, and then sailed around several bends.

Angel slowed to ten mph and pressed a button that released a cluster of tetsu-bishi out of a funnel from his pannier onto the pavement. These four-spiked metal jacks, or calthrops, were knife-sharp and shaped so one barb always pointed up. In their traditional ninja form, they were brutal on bare feet and rough on tires, but with Angel's augmentation of pressure-sensitive plastic explosives in each center, they'd be surefire mind-changers for Van Man. Angel sped ahead, pleased at his toys' even distribution across the pavement.

Van Man must have taken some in each tire because Angel couldn't quite count all the blasts. On four rims and ragged rubber, the van slithered across the road before pitching down the steep gorge, smashing through saplings and bushes, and splashing into the river thirty yards below.

Angel turned around and rode back to the van's exit point. Peering over the edge with his monocular, he saw a crumpled body half-in and half-out of the water. He flipped open his cell and phoned to ask if Donny would collect his roadside litter. The call clicked into voicemail.

"Sher'ff, I'm right sorry to bother y'all again. It must be a Pokeberry jam-packed day in The Ridge with all yore parkin' tickets and body pickups. I confess to bein' a litterbug. Would you be so kind as to fetch one man and his van out of a river? Bless that poor boy! He failed in his killin' spree two times in one hour. If that cat ever had nine lives, they're 'bout used up."

Angel left exact directions to the scene of the accident and his hapless assassin, then gathered his leftover jacks so he didn't blow up any locals.

RED

Harried and Hairless

Racing through late afternoon New Delhi traffic to the holy grail of high tea, Red and Dr. B attained incredible speeds of three to four kilometers per hour. His Corolla surged ahead a half-car length when an elephant blocked Red's lane. A one-legged beggar hopping from auto to truck to oxcart zipped past both of them. During their half-hour sprint, the population of India increased by 956 people, and British Petroleum took in another $25 million.

Red and Azeez arrived at the door first, just in time to open it for the doctor. Tucked among massive white pillars, under glittering chandeliers, and surrounded by fresh bouquets of exotic blooms, the Lobby Lounge in Shangri-la's Eros Hotel presented a relaxed atmosphere—upholstered sage chairs, creamy leather couches, and dim table lamp lighting. The dress code sign stated, "Smart casual."

Red positioned herself between her two escorts and held both of their arms, chatting with Dr. B as they walked in. "Jolly good you're here. You look like the GM of a posh resort in your khakis. Azeez could pass for a smart accountant, but I'm dressed casually stupid."

"You look fine. I am just happy you are alive after this last escapade. You ought to rein yourself in a bit. These drugs can affect you in ways you may not even notice."

"Yes, Doctor," Red said, punching each word, and then turned to Azeez. "I'm sorry. Dr. B and I need to have a private chinwag over tea for two. You can order anything your stomach desires… at a table for one."

"Yes, I am understanding."

"And no lip-reading."

"Yes, Miss Red." Azeez perched on a couch in the corner as a waitress brought the menus and waltzed away.

"He's too smart for his own good," Red said.

"Perhaps," Dr. B agreed, "but I think he is a most splendidly devoted servant. He does indeed care about you."

"Not many do," Red sighed, staring up and through the chandelier.

Knowing how true that statement was, Dr. B let it drop and picked up the menu. "Shall we share an order of scones and a plate of cucumber sandwiches?"

"As you wish. I may nibble a bit, but the butterflies in my stomach might play ping-pong with any nosh. Tea would be marvelous, but I refuse to do the prissy stiff pinky finger like those battle axes over there." She gestured to a table of four makeup-lacquered British ladies with high hive hair that could house colonies of bees.

Once they'd placed their order, B became the official Dr. B again, leaned over, and put his hand on Red's wrist. "I would like to know what you felt and saw during today's treatment."

Red looked down, folding and unfolding her cloth napkin. "They were far beyond any dreams I've ever experienced. Wild and vivid… So many places, so many lives. Three dreams wrapped up into one."

"Please tell me everything you remember. And don't worry. It's confidential." To Dr. B, the details of her dreams could reveal as many clues to her condition as an EKG or a blood test.

Bit by bit, Red eased into the virtual lap of this pseudo-father, and her naïve heart slipped out. Tea was served and sipped; scones delivered and devoured. For a half hour Dr. B listened intently, coaxing out the complete story of her dreams about Morpho, Tiger, and Angel while massaging her with the appropriate "hmm" and "I see" and "remarkable" as he chewed on his scones and her words.

"I don't remember anything else, but they seem unfinished, like a series on the telly… to be continued. Utterly real. Talking about them, I can almost smell the jungle." She raised her shoulders and shivered. "And feel the terror of being trapped."

"That is certainly quite a saga, and I am certainly *not* an expert on dream interpretation. Some say they are only whimsical fabrications of the brain. Others say they are messages from your soul or parallel lives in other dimensions. A psychiatrist might say every character in the dream is you playing a different role."

"The main characters might have had different names, but I felt like each one was me. No roles, no playing."

"Morpho was a butterfly," Dr. B recalled, "Tiger collected butterflies, and Angel seemed to get messages from them. They all had names of butterflies, as you do. A red admiral butterfly is even the logo of your company now, yes?"

"Spot on. I changed the name and logo after my father disappeared. You remember what it was before?"

"How could anyone forget?" Dr. B chuckled. "Danny Neville Admiral: DNA Crop-dusting. His sacred, sacrilegious slogan: 'Let us spray.' I miss that irreverent Brit."

"I only miss him every day. I wish I knew he was absolutely dead, so I wouldn't imagine he's still alive somewhere." Red crumpled her napkin and threw it on the table. "He'd never have left without a word. He was taken."

"I am sure he was. He had the gift of making friends easily. And the curse of making enemies easily."

They both took a sip of tea, mentally toasting Danny.

Dr. B leaned back in his chair. "I have heard that butterfly dreams mean you may be experiencing metamorphosis in life, like all insects. After its egg stage, every insect has three more: first as a worm or caterpillar, then through a transformation stage in a cocoon, and finally emerging as an adult, most with wings, but all with three body parts, six legs, and antennae."

"Well, aren't you a fount of useless knowledge?" From the same mold as her father, the soft tissue of Red was one molecule away from sandpaper. "Do you moonlight as a insect vet after hours?"

"Like young Tiger, as a child I was captivated by insects and considered being an entomologist. In fact…" Dr. B paused. "Since this is a confidential conversation, can I trust you to respect a secret?"

"Oh, absolutely. I love secrets."

"If you tell anyone, I may confidentially alter next week's dose of medicine to render you comatose."

"Cross my heart and hope to die, if you promise you'll save me."

"Perhaps you already know, but coincidentally my first name, Shaardul, means 'tiger' in Hindi."

"That's the secret? I can't call you Dr. Tiger?"

"We shall stick with Dr. B. The secret is…" A puckish smile crept over his face. "My mother named me Tiger in Sanskrit: Vyaghṛa."

"Blimey. Viagra, as in Viagra? You must be joking?"

"Unfortunately… no."

"How did you survive the playground in school?"

"One reason. Viagra was not introduced until the late '90s, decades after grade school. I changed my first name in 2000 after the millionth person said to me, 'Perfect name for a surgeon who can stay up all night.'"

"Well, your secret is safe with me, but please don't kill me if I accidentally call you Dr. V."

"Red." His voice lowered and eyes narrowed.

"Steady on, B. Take a pill. With the effects of your meds, I might not even remember today."

"Good." Dr. B took off his glasses. "But there is something I want you to think about and remember."

"What." Red crossed her arms uncomfortably. She knew specs removal meant lecture hour.

"I believe all diseases have causes. I do the best I can to deal with them on this third-dimensional, material level. You have handled, sprayed, or sold noxious chemicals your entire life. Even if your cancer is cured, chances are your current lifestyle will cause a relapse."

"Yes, Doctor, I remember. You've mentioned this before. I know you want me to sell the business."

"That is *your* choice for *your* life. This is what I want you to think about. Do you like butterflies?"

"Doesn't everyone?"

"How many have you killed?"

"I haven't a clue." Taken aback, she sat up straight. "None intentionally. They don't eat the plants."

"How many have you killed before they were cabbage butterflies, when they were cabbage worms? How many other insects have you killed?"

"How many zeros in a zillion?" Red raised her palms in front of her chest to defend herself. "I've no idea. Bugs are bloody pests. They destroy crops that feed people."

Dr. B pressed on further. "How many people have you harmed when your toxins spread over the countryside, when your pesticides were ingested with the food? How many cases of cancer have you caused?"

"Now you sound rather like my mother, you know." Her elbow on the table, she cradled her forehead with one hand, covering her eyes. "I suppose the wrath of karma is next on the agenda."

"You are in India, Red. Everyone lives, dies, and is reborn with karma. Everyone everywhere in the world."

"Right, then. I'll become a monk and never swat a malaria mosquito or step on a biting army ant… in my next life." She reached for her purse, stood and looked for the waitress, a washroom, any exit. "No, no, I see. I will be the mosquito. Perhaps I'll live at your hospital and drink Bloody Marys from your patients' veins like the rest of them."

"Please sit down, Red. I can see your mother's Indian fire burning in your eyes." Dr. B took her arm and eased her back down into her chair.

"My point is, and I apologize for my bluntness, you may be paying for your choices in life. I care about you. I always have and always will, but there is a limited amount to what I can do for you. I believe in science… and in signs. I think these dreams are signs you should seriously consider and perhaps consult someone who works in the spiritual realm, who might help you cure your disease with methods not taught in medical school."

"A witch doctor? Do you have any on staff?"

Ignoring her questions, he continued. "Some people have a gift of seeing and feeling beyond what you and I are capable of. They might be able to guide you to heal yourself."

"A new-age swami-rami? A bloomin' psychotic?"

"I was referring to a psychic," Dr. B said flatly. "Someone who could show you techniques to heighten your awareness or deeds that could reverse the karmic wheel."

"Oo… voo-doo. There is a right irritating chicken at home I'd like to sacrifice. I've been meditating on that deed for quite some time now."

"I can see I am talking to a red brick wall." Dr. B picked up the check. "Please think about it. Over the years, I have witnessed impressive results. Maybe Azeez knows of someone."

This last turn of the conversation pushed Red over the edge of exhaustion. "Cheers for your advice, B. I'll look into it, but right now, I am knackered times ten. Normally I don't last this long after my visits to your chemical torture chamber. I'll return once I've relieved myself of a few of your drugs."

While Red hit the washroom, Dr. B paid the bill and spoke with Azeez about spiritual advisors.

As the three of them walked outside to the parking lot, Red again grabbed both of their arms, this time for support. "My bed is beckoning me, Dr. V… I mean B. Thanks so much for ignoring your other patients. Next time tea is on me, with sacred scones and freshly immolated chicken sandwiches. Cheerio. Azeez, car!"

Dr. B grimaced. "You are very welcome. Until next week then." He walked with Azeez to the parking lot and said as they parted, "Please take good care of her."

"I am always taking most excellent care, Doctorji." He bowed his head slightly. "As much as she is letting me."

After helping Red into the Mercedes, Azeez headed into the setting sun and the frantic traffic. Moments later, a harsh voice came from the backseat.

"Dr. B will never sign the papers for the physical evaluation to renew my pilot's license. It's due in one month. Find a doctor who will."

"But Miss Red, you should not be flying in your condition. I am worrying about you every day."

"Just… find… another… doctor. Rupees talk."

"Yes, yes, Miss Red." A few blocks away from the hotel, while locked in a morass of vehicles stopped for a light, Azeez began, "Dr. B asked me to help find a spiritual advisor for you, and two of my cousins are most definitely successful at advising…"

He rambled on in his own world as Red grumbled in the backseat. "Confidential, my ass."

Two minutes later, during a testimonial of his relative's ethereal abilities, Azeez heard gurgling snores behind him, smiled, and drove in silence.

At home, an illuminated sign stretched across the top of the gate opening in the electric fence. The words "Red Admiral Aerial Application, Chemical and Fertilizer, Ltd." sat to the right of the red admiral butterfly logo: black wings with white blotches on its upper wingtips, red-orange bird-like shapes across the middle, and another red-orange strip with four black dots along the base of each underwing.

Azeez pulled up to a remodeled hangar next to the airstrip and helped Red out of the back seat. She thanked him numbly and stumbled through the door to her quarters. After shedding her jacket, blouse and pants on the way to the bathroom, Red splashed water on her face and glanced at the mirror as she fumbled for the soap. She didn't like the pale woman staring back at her. Red pulled the scarf off her head, and an unhealthy share of her leftover tresses came with it. She flung it into the corner.

"Fuck this."

She snatched the disposable razor out of the shower stall. Feverishly she shaved off her remaining greasy locks, backed up a step, and glared at the odd creature in the mirror. Two rivulets of blood from razor cuts ran down the sides of its face and dripped onto its shoulders.

"Brilliant. A cross between diehard Bruce Willis and a bald Indian guru—Bruce Gandhi. I'll have to buy a loincloth and a spinning wheel. I've already got the guns."

MONA
The Unbirthday Present

Every Friday afternoon (if they remembered it was Friday) Mona met her friend Sasha (if they both remembered when and where) at a different location (if they could remember where last week's rendezvous had been in order to choose a new one).

Over the years, they'd realized that Mona was space-challenged and Sasha was time-challenged. When they decided to meet on a specific street corner, Mona normally showed up on time, but a mile away, and Sasha on the correct corner, but an hour late. At seventy-three, Mona wasn't sure where she had done what, and at eighty-five, Sasha didn't even want to think about time. The task of finding each other became hopeless until they both bought cellphones, though they often forgot to carry them.

Mona rang Sasha. "I think it's Friday. Are we going to meet up?"

"It is? I thought yesterday was Friday. Good. Now it's a four-day weekend."

"Today's my birthday and I'd like to treat myself to a new pair of shoes."

"Your birthday? I thought you just had one."

Mona checked her desk calendar to make sure she had the correct day. "Not since last year."

"Well, happy birthday, darling! How old are you?"

"Seventy-three and counting."

"You spring chicken. Stop counting," Sasha grumbled. "Where exactly should we meet? I'm free at two."

"First I'd like to have a drink at L.O.V.E., you know, Loretta's Organic Veggie Emporium. We ate there once, down the block from a shoe store."

"How could I forget? I smuggled a burger in my purse. Loretta caught me and confiscated it. She probably ate it in the back room."

"I doubt it," Mona disagreed, remembering the squeamish frown on Loretta's face. "I think even her dogs are vegetarians."

"Your new shoes are on me, well, I mean, they'll be on you, but on me. Whatever. A happy birthday present."

"You don't have to do that, but I'll take it. See you at two!"

Mona had first met Sasha Goldberg twenty years before while searching for a small city with a warm, dry climate. Mission, Texas—population 40,000 natives and snowbirds—captured her attention because of its proximity to the National Butterfly Center. Though at that time Mona was officially a semi-starving artist, her butterfly paintings had garnered some recognition, giving her the means to dream of a serene country home. Sasha's ads leaped out from the others stuck on Mission's bus stop benches.

"Take a load off your mind and your feet. Relax and call Sasha Goldberg, the world's oldest living realtor."

Sasha's husband, Eli, had died abruptly after they'd arrived in Mission from New Jersey, ready to lounge around in retirement bliss. Sasha was not one to sit alone and mope. Eli had been a successful real estate agent, and it didn't seem too difficult, so she studied, got her license, and set up shop.

Besides the attraction of her singular slogan, Mona learned this mysterious Sasha drew intricate pen and ink pictures of each house she listed, and the new buyer could keep the original. On her maiden property tour near the Bentsen-Rio Grande Valley State Park, Sasha showed Mona a strange, one-story rambler that did indeed ramble on in two opposite directions, as if it were trying to escape from the towering desert fan palm tree growing through its center and sprouting out of its roof. Some thought the tree looked like a monster alien having a bad hair day. Artistic Mona imagined it was a lovely natural parasol.

Local legend said the house had been designed by the architect Frank Lloyd Wrong. It sat on an unkempt lot filled with wildflowers, chirping crickets, and more butterflies than Mona had ever seen in one area. For months no one had wanted to buy it, so the price plummeted. Mission accomplished: the whole place was the bee's knees. Mona evolved from Sasha's new client into her best friend.

At 2:37 p.m. Mona walked through the front door of L.O.V.E., which felt like traveling through a time warp to 1969. She waved to Sasha, already settled in a booth, apologizing as she approached. "I'm so sorry. I forgot where it was and drove around in circles. Have you been waiting long?"

Sasha looked at her Rolex. "A whole two minutes. I was only thirty-five minutes late, which is twenty-five minutes early for me."

"Did you order yet?"

"I didn't dare until you arrived. Loretta glared at me when I came in. I think she wants to frisk me."

Mona gave her the silent, wide-eyed, shut-up look, then stood to greet

Loretta as she walked up behind Sasha.

"Hi, Loretta! How are you this fine day?"

"Just dandy. I haven't seen y'all for ages."

They hugged.

Looking like a large, round loaf of whole wheat bread in a dress leftover from the musical *Hair*, Loretta set two menus on the table. "How's it goin', Mona?" she asked, completely ignoring Sasha.

"Too busy, but good busy. How's busyness here?"

"Can't complain. Lemme know when y'all are ready to order."

"Thanks, give us a minute. We're only having drinks."

Sasha perused her menu. "I assume you'll be having a sawdust shake, the one you had to eat with a knife and fork. I'd like tea, but I can only find a list of ridiculous names here: Jammin' Lemon Ginger, Candy Cane Lane, and Morning Thunder, which sounds like me in the bathroom at eight a.m. Doesn't she have tea, as in tea? As in Twinings?"

"She only serves Celestial Seasonings herbal teas."

"I see. Brewed by God herself, no doubt. Choose one for me."

"Do you like ginger ale?"

"Yes."

"How about lemonade?"

"Yes."

"Jammin' Lemon Ginger it is. I'm having her Bodacious Blood Builder: beet, carrot, and parsley juice. It's divine."

"Like my tea, I suppose," Sasha sighed. "Shall we pray while we sip?"

Other than their like-minded artistic bent and shared status as foreigners—anyone not born in Texas—they made an unlikely pair. Japanese Sasha had converted to Judaism for Eli, and that culture fit her so well God even forgot he hadn't chosen her himself. After sampling a plethora of religious rituals, Mona had settled into the universal church of the New Age in her old age.

Sasha's abbreviated white hair hugged her head so hard it had almost turned blue. Mona's lengthy black locks with a dramatic gray swath in the middle threatened to reach down and root into the earth if she sat still too long. Sasha wore an immaculately tailored dress and gold jewelry because it was gold and half of her last name. Mona had on a rainbow of cottons and exotic fibers, a red hawk feather she'd found and woven into her hair, and shoes made of organically grown hemp. No leather. No animal products. Sasha was a staunch carnivore. Mona was a strict vegetarian, although after an intense period subsisting solely on fruits and nuts, she had broadened her diet to include dairy and eggs, but still wouldn't eat anything that had a face.

Beneath her gruff exterior, Sasha had a massive heart. A natural-born marketer, she'd helped Mona, a natural-born artist, enliven her marketing DNA, generally DOA in natural-born artists—Dead On Arrival. Her butterfly paintings now graced calendars, greeting cards, coffee cups, and clothing, making her financially secure. Mona was both the child Sasha never had and the artist she'd dreamed of becoming.

Mona liked the fact that no matter how old she got, Sasha would always be older. As one who'd barely made it into the world, and never thought she'd last in it very long, her friend was a model of longevity and enthusiasm.

After hashing over recent events in Mission and chuckling through Sasha's endless horror stories about her clients, Mona went silent for a spell and then got serious. "I'm worried about my memory. It's getting worse."

"Forget about it," Sasha told her. "It's easier that way."

"Today isn't my birthday. It's tomorrow. I had the date right, but I hadn't flipped over the calendar. I've been living last month all over again."

"So what can we do about it? We tried once, remember? We enrolled in the 'Improve Your Memory in Eight Hours' seminar and forgot to attend."

"I don't know what to do, Sasha. I keep misplacing things. I must've been here fifty times, but today I pictured this place on the other side of town. That's pathetic."

"Welcome to your seventies. These things are business as usual. Wait until you hit your eighties. My mother had it together until she was 100, but lost it at 101. She'd tell people, 'Last year I was 100. Now I'm 200.' Then she died. Don't worry, girl. You've got a long way to go." She downed her last drop of tea. "Now let's get you your present."

"Okay," Mona said, exhaling a deep breath as she stood. "Did you like your tea?"

"It was tasty, but needed ice cubes and another vegetable. Fermented grain. Vodka."

As they left Loretta's and the '60s behind, Mona opened her sun umbrella and they shuffled down the street in its shade. Mission was fry-an-egg-on-the-sidewalk hot.

"The sporting goods store's a couple of doors down."

Shocked Sasha asked, "You want *sport* shoes? Are you losing your mind as well as your memory?"

"I need more support for these flat ol' feet on my walks," Mona held the door for Sasha as they entered Sports Universe. "A friend had a charming pair and told me she bought them here."

The spacious store had a department for every major physical activity that required sweating—team sports, tennis, hiking, climbing, or riding a stationary bicycle in the garage and then driving the car to work instead of riding a real bike. Sasha and Mona scanned the vast assortment of multi-colored, multi-soled, multi-use footwear covering the wall under the Shoe World banner.

"Sakes alive!" Sasha exclaimed. "I grew up with one pair of Keds sneakers. Rubber, canvas, and laces."

"Here's the style my friend wears," Mona said, picking up a New Balance cross-trainer off the shelf that seemed to have the different colored parts of nine other shoes stuck together in haphazard geometric patterns.

"A pragmatic selection, my dear," Sasha pointed out, mainly to herself. "Those will clash with any color outfit you wear."

Mona was too lost in the explosion of hues and textures. Two more pairs caught her eye. "These are cute! I'll try these on as well."

An acne-laden, towering salesman, his skinny torso perched on spindly legs, looked vacantly down at them. The name "Ignacio" was stitched over the pocket of his purple Sports Universe jersey. "May I help you ladies?"

"Yes, Ignacio, you can. I like these three styles," Mona said. "I'm pretty sure I'm size five… or six."

Sasha raised a random sneaker an arm's length over her head, an inch below Ignacio's nose. "Do these come in high heels?"

Ignacio appeared momentarily paralyzed and didn't know what to say. He searched through his tiny mental file on retail experience, flipped through his entire vocabulary, and came up with, "No."

After returning with several boxes, size five and six, Ignacio somehow squatted on the floor behind the slanted footstool, his knees level with his ears, and shoehorned a pair onto Mona's feet.

Sasha leaned over to him. "Do you have any specialized footwear for my morning exercise? I touch my toes 100 times… trying to tie my shoes."

He wasn't sure it was a joke, especially coming from the oldest person he'd ever seen, one who only said weird things. Luckily, the other woman started talking, so he didn't have to answer.

"Do you like this pair, Sasha? You're buying them."

"If you like them, so do I."

Mona tried the other two pairs, but her feet definitely preferred the ones her friend wore. As she formulated her shoe acceptance sentence, she bent down to tie her laces, and her Bodacious Blood Builder bubbled into a

Bodacious Organic Gas Builder. A rowdy puff of rectal turbulence escaped from her nether region, starting as the buzz of a seven-pound wasp and finishing like the gurgle of a half-submerged child blowing bubbles in a bathtub. Its odor followed, certainly noxious, almost venomous, possibly able to loosen nose hairs from the nostrils.

Instantly flushed and overheated, Mona jerked up and stammered, grammar and etiquette flung aside. "Thank you I'll take these I'm wearing them Sasha I'll see you outside." She bustled out the door as fast as her new New Balance cross-trainers could carry her.

Sasha, Ignacio, and the lingering vapors sat quietly for a moment. Wordlessly she paid the bill; Ignacio wordlessly accepted her cash. Head held a bit higher than usual, Sasha strutted out the door, trying to suppress her anger and a belly laugh at the same time. Mona was propped against the display window of the next store.

"By Jove, I thought I was going to faint, Sasha. I'm sorry. I just couldn't take it."

Sasha burst out laughing, leaning on Mona for support. "Did you see young Ignacio's face? I thought his pimples might pop as he tried not to crack up. Let's get out of here."

"Sure… now… I'm sorry." Mona looked around for her umbrella. It wasn't there. "Oh my god, I forgot my umbrella in the store! It doesn't matter. They can have it. I will never go in there again. Ever."

"We'll shrivel up like vampires under this sun without it. You stay here; I'll get it."

"No, no! Forget about it." She took hold of Sasha's arm. "That's what we do. We forget things."

"Mona, calm down. Ignacio's in the shoe department in the back. I'll ask at the front counter, and they'll get it. It's not a problem."

Mona took a deep breath, straightened her back, and stated, "No… I'll go. I can do this. I'll be right back."

She marched semi-confidently into the store and up to the front counter. No one was there. She looked around the room, and when she turned back, Ignacio strode through the curtained storeroom door behind the counter.

Before her brain could craft a coherent thought, she blurted out, "I forgot my fart."

This time she really couldn't take it. Her face paled as every blood cell in her body fled down into her new shoes. She tilted slightly, eyelids fluttering, and collapsed onto the floor.

Ignacio tore around the counter and froze, towering over her. She was very old a few minutes ago and now he assumed she must be dead. The only emergency covered during his recent Sport's Universe training course involved a fire extinguisher, but she wasn't on fire. Within seconds, other salespeople and customers had surrounded them.

Sasha peered through the window and saw a crowd of people hunched over a body. "This again," she thought. "Her disappearing trick."

It had happened when they were at the zoo and an orangutan suddenly lurched toward the bars at Mona. The management gave them both complimentary passes for life. It had happened when they were pulled over for speeding and the officer asked Mona to step out of the car. She fell out of the car. He turned into a kitten and didn't give her a ticket.

Adrenaline-charged Sasha barged through the door. "Ignacio! Call 911, for God's sake!" After successfully removing Ignacio from the scene, she wedged herself through the petrified gaggle of customers and counter help. "Stand back! Give her some air! My brother's a doctor." Sasha hunkered down close to Mona, squeezed a eucalyptus inhaler under her nose, and whispered into her ear. "Wake up, girl… Wake up now, before I have to give you mouth-to-mouth and smear my lipstick."

Mona groaned and sat up.

"Now stand up," Sasha commanded. "It's time to leave. Let's break in those new shoes of yours." She noticed the umbrella resting against the counter and snatched it, used it as a cane, and herded Mona outside. They piled into a taxi parked by the curb. "Tell me the location of your Ranchero and what happened in there."

Fortunately, Mona remembered where it was and gave Sasha the details as they rode, giggling like a couple of schoolgirls in the back seat.

When they reached the Ranchero, around the corner and one block over, Sasha stayed inside the taxi as Mona stepped out and insisted, "I'm feeling fine now. I can give you a ride home if you want."

"Thanks," Sasha said, "but I'll take the taxi. There may be another toxic air freshener bottled up inside you."

"All right, my guardian angel. Thanks for the drinks and my unbirthday present. You know, if I got a quarter every time Ignacio is going to tell this story, I'd be one rich lady."

Sasha wagged a finger out the window, vowing as she spoke, determined to have the last word. "Know this. I swear I'll never let you forget this day, no matter how hard you try!"

TIGER

It Was So Cold...

Grinning contentedly during the ride to her house in Grandma Celeste's VW, Gem glanced over at Tiger in the driver's seat. "I love this Bug! I've only seen them in pictures or movies... like snow. I hope I love snow this much."

"Snow's okay, but the cold sucks." Tiger wrinkled his face. "Someday I'll take you downtown at dawn when it's forty below so we can watch the firemen chop the dogs off the fire hydrants."

"Ha!" She paused, then frowned. "You're kidding, aren't you?"

"Well, maybe Chihuahuas. Canadians have a million jokes about winter. It was so cold..."

"How cold was it?" Gem chirped.

"Hitchhikers were holding up pictures of their thumbs."

"Can you drive me to California?" Gem pleaded, leaning over with hands folded in prayer.

"I like this one. It was so cold we had to chop up the piano for firewood. We only got two chords. Get it?"

"Got it," she said. "You 'wooden' think I'd know about wood, would you?"

"You're good. Here's a real fact you have to know, though. Your skin can freeze to metal if it's cold enough. For some strange reason, when it's 100 below, every kid in Canada has to put their lips on a swing set or handrail or something metal. I did it on the door handle of this car. Both my lips stuck tight."

"No!" Gem gasped.

"I wanted to throw back my head and scream, but I'd have ripped my lips off. What would I have yelled, anyway? Mom! Help! Bring your hair dryer out here to the driveway!"

"Like, maybe you could drive me back to Africa."

"Maybe next time, eh? Here we are at Fourth and Thirteenth. Which one's your house?"

"Straight ahead, the yellow and white house on the right."

Tiger pulled the Bug over in front of the walkway to her front door. "You got time for one more cold story?"

"Is it over an hour long?"

"One minute." Tiger held up his right hand. "Scout's honor."

"Hmm. Lemme look..." She rolled up her sleeve and checked her bare wrist. "Okay, I got a minute."

"First some cold facts," Tiger began. "Do you know that people here plug in their cars during the winter?"

"What? Plug 'em in where?"

"At home or when you're out. At some supermarkets, they even have outlets in the parking lots."

Gem looked down and shook her head. "I gotta have a talk with my parents. There may be time to get out while we're still alive."

"Cars have engine heaters to keep the oil warm so they'll start when it's arctic cold. After I got my license, I asked to use the car. Dad said, 'Okay, but be careful and don't forget to unplug it from the garage.' When I put on my parka, Mom said, 'Make sure you unplug the car.' I walked out to the garage, chanting, 'Unplug the car. Unplug the car.' I went into the garage, pulled out the plug, got in the car, and backed out. But I forgot to open the garage door."

"No!" Gem's mouth froze in her final "o."

"Yes! Hey, they just told me to unplug the car! They didn't say anything about opening the door."

"Bet they were pissed."

"Doris laughed. Walter didn't."

"Sounds like it's a good thing he's in the construction business."

"They're getting used to it. My full name is Tiger K. Brooks. 'K' stands for Klutz. You might want to stay away from me."

Gem raised one eyebrow and tilted her head. "That cold story was longer than a minute, you know."

"Sorry, I owe you thirty seconds." Tiger hung his head.

"You'll just have to listen to my hot stories later."

"It's a deal. Maybe they'll warm up the winter."

"Thanks for the ride, Tiger, and for sharing your dreams with me."

"It's the least I can do for someone who saved my life. My number could have been up!" Tiger paused, then started stuttering before his next words stumbled out. "And... um... speaking of numbers, would you give me yours?"

"Sure… 3."

"I just punch '3' and you'll answer? Or is it 333-3333?"

"You'll have to guess the others," she said coyly.

"2, 4, 6, 8, 11, 149, 955 and—"

"Wrong!" Gem interrupted. "Okay, fine. I'll trade you. What's your number?"

"7."

She took a pen and notepad out of her handbag, wrote down his phone number, then hers, tore the paper in half, and gave one piece to Tiger. "Don't give this to Dick."

"Dick who?"

Gem got out of the car, then stuck her head back through the open window. "See you later, Tiger."

"Call me Alligator."

"After a while…" She smiled, turned, and sauntered toward the house.

"Bye-bye!" Tiger called to her back.

"Butterfly!" Without looking behind, Gem raised both hands and flapped her fingers like wings.

Tiger watched her walk up the steps. *Pinch me. I think I'm still dreaming.* He waited until she went inside, then slowly pulled away, feeling as if his wheels were not even touching the road.

ANGEL
Invisible No More

Compared to his life-threatening workout at home, now a pile of rubble, Angel's two-hour ride to Atlanta was easy as pie and a piece o' cake walk in the park. No one tried to kill him, intentionally anyway, and he'd tuned down his Angel Radar to standby. Riding on two wheels in a sea of eighteen-wheelers presented moment-by-moment trials, but he loved feeling the walls of wind whip his bike and body back and forth as he wound his way through the semi-trailer hurricanes. It was like flying.

Most truckers gave motorcycles respect, the right of way, and the room to move, since they likely rode themselves. Four-wheeled vehicles posed the most ticklish challenges. If auto-maniac drivers even accidentally, maybe, once in a while, happened to see Angel, they preferred he wasn't there in the first place—nor anywhere for that matter. And definitely did not want him to date their daughters. They cut in front of him. The cut into him. They tailgated him. When he passed them, they got pissed and passed him back recklessly, millimeters from his side mirror.

During his first motorcycle safety course, Angel's instructor had said, "Getting angry will only eat you up, so lighten up. Road rage or old age is your choice: 'May he rest in pieces,' or 'He who laughs, lasts.'"

Those words had worked their way into his whole life. That teacher chiseled another commandment into his soul. "Thou shalt ride as if thou art invisible." Angel often replaced the word *ride* with *live*. And he did not like the fact that where he lived was now visible.

He'd hoped to stop at his second home, a self-storage unit near the Atlanta airport, but his watch said no way, thanks but no thanks to Van Man and the Morons. He left his bike at the "Park 'er And Lock 'er" lot and caught a shuttle bus. He stuffed his body armor and helmet into an airport locker before suffering through security just in time to board.

Angel seldom flew first class. He didn't need it because of his "efficient, compact stature." The extra cash wasn't worth the extra legroom, nor the extra ass room. Besides, he felt more comfortable with the lower-class folk on the other side of the curtain.

He loved to leave the ground behind, though he'd rather use his own wings, hang glider, or chute. As the plane took off and other passengers buried themselves in magazines, Angel closed his eyes and let the g-force turn him into a happy little kid again. But on this flight, the little kid inside was troubled. Angel had grown up with Marvel and DC superheroes in comic books and movies. Their honorable desire to help humanity was printed in gold foil on his list of core values.

His mother, Deborah Worthington, had worked with USAID in the Refugee Relief Department and was sent to Laos, where she met his father, Tay Sengtavisouk, a farmer and freedom fighter who'd lost most of his family during the Vietnam War. Named Christopher at birth, Angel spent his first few years in a tiny village near Luang Prabang.

At the age of six, he and his parents moved to the USA to his mother's hometown—Los Angeles, fifty-five suburbs in search of a city—with Tay's mother Dao, a shaman in their Laotian village. Deborah worked with a non-profit legal aid clinic. Tay started a Lao-Thai fusion restaurant.

The smog and the speedy lifestyle took their toll, so they relocated to Arizona. His father loved Phoenix and his new Thai-Tex-Mex restaurant became successful beyond anything he could have imagined in his homeland, but his mother yearned for the simple life in Asia. Eventually, they split up. Tay, Angel and Dao stayed in America; Deborah returned to Laos. Though his parents still loved each other, they discovered they loved each others' countries more.

Over the years, Angel learned that helping people wasn't as easy as the words rolled off the tongue. Help the "good" guys in "bad" lands, and the bad guys brought hell home to his doorstep.

Today had been his own personal 9/11… a turning point, or at least a curving point. His secure world in Pokeberry Ridge came tumbling down. He felt it might be time to replace his bumper sticker that read, "If you're not living on the edge, you're taking up too much room," with "Life is Short. Make it Wide." Then he remembered he didn't have that bumper sticker anymore. Or a bumper. It might be time to replace Pokeberry Ridge, too.

Life was narrow in The Ridge, as the locals called it. For three years he'd whittled down his oblique personality enough to fit into their nice square holes. He had a few friends, but only Sheriff Donny was like family. If Angel ever had a family of his own, he imagined making it with a casual, easygoing woman. The Ridge girls seemed heaven-bent on being straight-laced uptight ladies.

Bit by bit, Donny's biker buddies had accepted him, even though he didn't have a rhythmic rhyming name like most of the natives. Sheriff Donny Dillon. Dr. Darryl Darlington. Larry Little, loafer. Contractor Claude Conners and his wife Claudine, who both appeared to be attached to the moniker Claude 'n' Claudine more than the marriage. They called him "Angel Derangedalittle" and it stuck for a spell. His first name added a taste of exotic authenticity to the gang's national image in their local brains—Hell's Angel's Compatriots.

As the miles and months multiplied, he evolved into "The Alien." Angel didn't mind, since in his mind, he'd considered himself one for decades. When people asked him where he lived, he might say, "Earth, but I'm just visiting." No matter where he was, he felt like he had one foot in "where" and the rest of his body in "no matter."

Every time he rode his motorcycle, Angel wore his "robot costume" as the boys called it: full-face helmet, gloves, boots, and body armor from shoulders to ankles. The rest of the gang, mostly vets from one war or another, wore skull cap helmets, ragged Levis, and sleeveless black leather vests with patches and pins proclaiming:

"If it's too loud, you're too old."

"Three can keep a secret if two are dead."

"ABCDEFU"

His buddies were big and white with red necks.

Dr. Darryl had a Buddha body with a Bud-heavy belly. Like the rest of the boys, Darryl drank Bud Light with thirty percent fewer calories, so he could eat thirty percent more food. His stethoscope didn't dangle from his neck. It rested on his chest.

Massive Contractor Claude made his immobile living by dining behind his desk, telling everyone else how and where to build what. When he sat in a normal chair, you could barely see the chair.

Larry Little was scrawny tall, a six-foot-six stick. When he stood next to Claude, they looked like the number 10. Larry lived up, or down, to his name. He did little or nothing.

Sheriff Donny was big at birth, might have hurt his mama on the way out—a black body like a building, constructed from large bones and larger muscles. Nothing joggled when Donny jogged.

Without the biker buddy bond, they'd never have said more than "hey" to each other. They all devoutly rode low and wide Harley Davidsons—fat Fat Boy Specials, V-rod Muscle machines, or humongous Electra Glide Ultras with stereo systems, floorboards, picture windshields, and Barcalounger thrones for their "bitch on the back."

The Alien was small and chose to ride a thin, high-clearance Kawasaki KLR Dual Sport adventure bike so he could "boldly go where no Harley has gone before."

Angel thought of the time he'd taken his life into his own mouth after a buddy ride in a county Harley rally.

Built from knotty boards milled from the original chestnut logs of the 100-year-old Hitchin' Post Tavern, The Post bar had a grisly history odor. Local boys and babes had sucked in and squirted out a billion beers, a good share of them that morning once the graveyard shift from the paper mill slunk in after work. Steel-toed boots crunched goober shells underfoot. Butt smoke stained the air and tobacco chaw ate away the floor. Besides salty-fried, thirst-provoking snacks, the only meals served at The Post were raw eggs cracked into cold brews.

Claude, Larry, Darryl, Sheriff Donny, and Angel shot the shit around a rough oak table, customer-carved with broken hearts and bike epithets. Twelve Bud Lights and two root beers faced off on the tabletop.

"Y'all, listen up," Angel said, raising the bar of friendly provocation. "Who knows the diff'rence between a Harley and a Hoover?"

"What's ahoovah?" Larry asked, screwing up his face.

"A Hoover vacuum cleaner," Angel clarified.

The gang looked at itself around the table. It didn't know the difference.

"With a Harley," Angel told them, "the dirt bag is on the outside."

Time silently slammed on its brakes. The din in The Post diminished by four-fifths.

"I thy-ank we all best step outside," Darryl threatened, rising half-cocked from his chair, "and find out what you and yore little scooter's made of."

Angel smirked, accepting the challenge. "On the road or off?"

"Ona pavement, where real men ride," taunted swaying Darryl.

"I will take all y'all on after a few more beers," Angel bragged, pointing four spread fingers on his right hand at his four friends.

"Tain't fair. You been drinkin' root bee-ah."

In The Ridge, "beer" had always been a two-syllable word.

Angel declared, boldly going where no Yankee should have gone, "And after a few more bee-ahs, y'all won't even remember that I whupped yore asses,"

"Despite the look on my face, you are still talkin'!" Darryl warned. He chucked a peanut toward his mouth and missed. "Y'all got some big balls for a small fry."

"I say we take a rain check for when the Buds ain't pourin' down so hard," Larry suggested, then turned to Angel, and shouted in his ear, "Heylien!" In this itty-bitty Brotherhood of The Ridge, 'Hey, Alien' had become one word. "What's that 'KLR' on yore Kamikaze scooter stand for, anywho?"

"Kills Low Riders." Angel grinned mischievously as he sliced a middle finger across the front of his neck.

"Whoa!" the gang chanted in unison, tilting back on its four chairs.

"The Alien is cruisin' for a bruisin', he is." Claude hunched over the table to get right in Angel's face. "I might could fetch y'all a little ladder to he'p yore little legs git up on that tall Jap KLR o' yourn."

The gang gloated and clicked its beer mugs together.

"The older my bike gets," Angel admitted, "the more KLR stands for Keep Loctite Ready."

"Tell you what," Sheriff Donny sighed, "I got the same problem. I hafta drag a damn magnet behind my V-rod to pick up loose screws."

"Those loose screws drop from yore rod or yore head?" asked Claude.

The whole gang toasted except Donny.

This went on for another hour until they were all too juiced to ride, including the Sheriff. They careened out of The Post like bumper cars at the county fair, straddled their two-tired Harley wheelchairs, and gazed at the street.

"I do not 'member this bar bein' on a four-lane road," Darryl drawled, trying to maneuver the sticky words out of his mouth while keeping several marbles in.

"I am seein' at least *eight* lanes." Larry squinted in the general direction of his eight or ten pals and their bikes. "Hey, Darryls, did you and yore twins ride over here today on two, or three, Fat Boys?"

A lubricated controversy ensued over whether Donny, Darryl, Larry, and The Alien could all squeeze into the Barcalounger throne on the back of Claude's Ultra Glide at the same time, without using a bottle of olive or fifty-weight motor "awl."

Claude solved the mystery with five words. "Y'all try it, yore daid."

Once the Sheriff had extracted the cellphone from his tight jeans pocket with half the gang's assistance, he attempted to summon his deputy. He located the correct keys on his phone in the correct order on his third try.

"Dep'dy Stokes! I am orderin' you to apprehend four drunken skunks in the parkin' lot outside The Post, and transport them home forthwith! Be forewarned they are four-armed and dangerous as Aunt Bea at a Harley rally. And one of 'em might be disguised as me."

Angel helped spoon-feed the gang into the deputy's pickup, bought a six-pack of root beer, and rode home on his Kawasaki.

The news of this incident circulated through the entire population of Pokeberry Ridge faster than one email from the kitchen to the den.

RED
Bugged

RED SAT WITH BOTH HANDS COVERING HER FACE, elbows resting on stacks of bills and receipts. *I absolutely detest this.*

After weeks of procrastination, she'd dragged herself mentally kicking and screaming to her father's formidable desk to do the books for Red Admiral Aerial Application, Chemical and Fertilizer, Ltd. At this point, they weren't really books, only scraps of paper gathering dust and termites in cardboard boxes.

She lifted her head and gazed longingly out the two picture windows stretching the length of two walls that joined in the corner of the triangular-shaped room. The late afternoon sky was calm and clear, but she wasn't flying through it. A month had passed since she'd soared in her precious metal birds. Flying was her only genuine joy in life and the sole reason she kept the business going.

She missed the bygone days when she was merely a pilot and occasional mechanic, when father Danny shuffled the papers and took care of the bullshit. His canary-yellow-and-black DH.82 Tiger Moth biplane sat outside the window in the hangar, the toothy devil grin painted on its nose that seemed to shout, "Get out here and let's get crackin'!"

The Tiger Moth had been developed in 1932 for the Royal Air Force as a two-seated pilot trainer by British aviation pioneer, Geoffrey de Havilland, but Handyman Danny built a chemical tank in the rear seat compartment and modified the lower wing into a spraying system, transforming the Tiger Moth into a crop duster.

Geoffrey, also an avid lepidopterist, had originally modeled the Tiger after his DH.60 Moth designed "like a moth" since most moths fold their wings back along their bodies while resting. Pilots could tow it with a car or hide it from their wives in a neighbor's garage.

The Tiger Moth might still be seen at an air show, its single prop pounding the breeze with stunt cowboys gyrating off its twenty-nine-foot fixed wings. It spun, stalled, recovered, and performed aerobatics with precision, though in gusty weather the Tiger's lightweight caused many green pilots to plant themselves into the ground. "These old birds offer a purer form of flying," Red would say. "You fly by feel. You become the plane and the plane becomes you."

But whether she was finessing the Tiger Moth or either of her newer dusters, it lit her up to fly upside down, dive to within feet of the ground, to turn on an intangible dime while plotting her next powder swath over the crops.

She called it crop dusting, but was trying to remember to say 'aerial application' after she'd heard that flight attendants now use the term 'crop dusting' to describe the art of stealthily passing gas while walking down the aisle of passenger aircraft.

Recently her income had dwindled as expenses doubled. She'd auctioned one of her newer planes, but once she'd paid off its actual owner—the bank—the proceeds barely covered the price of its spark plugs. She'd sold her house to create her triangular condo in the hangar where the plane had been parked. From floor to ceiling, she'd built a partition from one side of the open hangar slanting diagonally to the middle of the back wall and divided the space into a bedroom, kitchen, bath, and the living room/office where she currently sat, wishing her workplace was in the clouds. *I hate being grounded. And now I've had to hire another pilot, draining my reserves even further!*

Groggy from her weekly chemo, Red sensed a nap attack circling, but lacking the energy to move to the white leather couch under the window, she rested her head in her arms on the desk and faded away.

When she awoke, the sun had set. The fluorescent beams from security lights cast a pale glow into the room. A dark foreign figure sat in the armchair directly in front of her desk, its eyes buried in deep sockets, staring at her. Red jerked up, one hand flicking on the table lamp, the other shooting toward the desk phone.

"Who the fuck are you?"

"Bug," he told her calmly. "We've met."

"Bug? How the fuck did you get in here? Azeez always calls when anyone arrives."

"It matters not, Miss Red Admiral," he said, still staring intensely. "I go where I want, when I want. That's what bugs do. They get into the system."

His manner wasn't threatening—his whole being was. His face and body were thin, like daggers. Black, stringy hair bound into a ponytail. One continuous black eyebrow stretched over both eyes. Black beret, gloss-black leather jacket, black jeans, and black sneakers. A living shadow.

At first Red thought he looked Indian, but his speech sounded international. Other species prowled inside him, treacherous ones. Red certainly didn't want to rile any of them, but her temper was a feral creature she'd never learned to control. Red mirrored his stare.

"What the fuck do you want?"

"I'm here to bug you as a service to a mutual friend."

"Who might that be?" Red asked curtly.

"Baldev Ishwar Gupta."

The mere mention of that name made her skin try to creep under itself. Red now recalled where she'd "met" this Bug, if it's possible to meet a black biting fly on the wall—at an underground poker game hosted by Baldev. This Bug wasn't the kind of person anyone wanted to meet, only the kind you wanted to get away from.

Bug snapped open a switchblade to clean his fingernails. "Do you know what the name Baldev Iswar Gupta means?"

"No," Red said, her courage eroding, "pray tell."

"Supreme ruler or protector… he who takes away."

"I suppose you're a grim reminder that my little debt is nearly due."

"Two million rupees is not a little debt, but there is indeed little time left." He rose and tapped her calendar on the wall. "One little week. You should've given Baldevji half that amount already, but in his benevolence, he granted you a great-hearted extension…" Bug turned fluidly and locked onto her eyes. "One… little extension."

"I am sorry for my delay, but I've had medical issues that kept me from—"

He interrupted her with a sigh and a flip of his hand as he sat again. "Yes, we know all about you, Miss Red Admiral, but you're not very red anymore, are you… Bruce Gandhi?"

How could he know that? I was alone in the washroom! I only said it to the mirror!

"We know when you are awake and when you are asleep and everything in between. But your problems are not our problems, unless you do not pay your debt, then *you* become our problem. Your deadline has already been extended. You wouldn't want your next deadline to be a permanent one, would you, Miss-ing Red Admiral?"

"Are you threatening me, Mr. Bug?" And then, in a moment she hoped to live to regret, her mouth ran amuck. "Bugs can be squashed."

"Oh, my dear Miss-fit Red Admiral," he chuckled and slapped his knee. Before she'd managed one blink, he flipped his switchblade into the chest of the carved wooden Samarai warrior standing on the shelf behind her. "My apologies to you and your lifeless guardian, but my knife has slipped from my fingers again. An epileptic fit, perhaps."

Red, and her mouth, were momentarily palsied. She felt like the Sphinx moth in her dream, pinned alive through its thorax onto Tiger's mounting board.

Bug's tone changed into a hissing buzz. "Baldev Gupta is an honorable man, but I do not share that trait. This bug is not benevolent and has learned to be violent, like the bee in your bonnet that stings to survive. You have one week, Miss-behaving Red Admiral. Let us hope it will not be your final seven days." He stood abruptly, retrieved his blade from the warrior, and seemed to move toward the door without using his legs. "Don't bother to show me out. You have no idea how I got in."

At the doorway, he picked up Red's cat by the tail and flung it across the room. "I hate cats."

And he was gone.

MONA
Painting the Past

CRITICS' OPINIONS ABOUT HER ARTWORK SPANNED THE GAMUT from spite—"The Angela Mariposa butterfly paintings spewing from the brush of Mona Arcade are monotonous pop drivel"—to awe—"Similar to Jack London, who presents his deep meditations on a creature and its place in nature from the canine perspective in *Call of the Wild*, Angela Mariposa transports us into the inner realm of butterflies. London writes like a dog thinks, and Mariposa paints like a butterfly feels. Her creatures are so lifelike you imagine they might fly right off the canvas."

Mona's singular paintings ranged from James Audubon realism with a modern flair to a cartoon series lambasting humans' inhumane treatment of her adopted babies.

• Two tiger swallowtails viewing a collection of tiny men in suits and ties mounted on long stick pins under glass with the caption, "I had to travel all the way to New York City to net these Stockus brokerinias."

• A sleek red admiral butterfly flying a biplane spraying dark clouds over a village fair.

• A thickset, silver-spotted skipper driving a truck with miniature people smashed on its grill.

• Colossal yellow-necked Caterpillars tearing apart skyscrapers as the population flees in all directions with the caption, "Damn the natives! We'll put 'em on a reservation!"

Her fallen arches buoyed up by new walking shoes, Mona strolled out to the studio to work on her latest suite of compositions called *One Life*. She was painting her autobiography with a monarch butterfly playing a leading role in each piece. Though her memory seemed to be slipping away, she marveled at how the distant past could become a detailed oil painting, yet the present often meandered by in vague sketches. During these project sessions, she entered a dream-like state. Entranced by the scenes and experiences of days gone by, Mona paid little attention to the painstaking process of painting. Mundane worries and anxieties vanished, unless they came from the moments relived. Now gave way to then.

Mona set a fresh canvas on the easel and picked up her pencil, but couldn't quite put her finger on the idea for the painting she'd had last month. After checking her notebook, she filled the canvas with a rough form of her papa's face. Like that day she jumped off the woodshed, tears ran down Marco's cheeks and froze there. Within a few moments, the brush strokes and the oils and colors and the recollections melded today into time immemorial.

Lily was a loving mother and confidante, but Papa Marco was Mona's best friend. Since his early teens, he'd been everyone's best friend, a boy scout straight out of a Norman Rockwell painting on the cover of Boys' Life magazine. Almost fifty, Papa was still a grown-up scout and still "trustworthy, loyal, helpful, friendly, courteous, kind, obedient, cheerful, thrifty, brave, clean, and reverent."

He'd nearly tarnished his spick-and-span reputation by marrying Lily in the late 1930s, a time in northern Wisconsin when a coupling between a Swede and a Norwegian was frowned upon as an interracial marriage. Lily was Norwegian and Marco was Finnish—with unmentioned strains of Russian, French, and Chippewa Indian. But thank god, they were both Lutherans and the local furor subsided. He had four words to describe his matrimonial choice, his demeanor, and his life in general: "Nice Finnish guys last."

Mama mainly lived inside the cabin and at the hospital where she worked, but Mona and Marco loved to live outside in the woods. He taught Mona how to stretch beaver hides, sharpen knives, forage for food, cook over a campfire, and make a shelter out of leaves and branches. She learned to be self-sufficient and to survive with a pack on her back.

Sometimes he'd disappear into the woods for a week, tending his trapline. Mona would miss him something fierce and worry, especially on those crystal-clear sunny days when she'd peer out frosty glass at the big round thermometer on the deck, frozen tight at fifty-three below zero.

She cherished the times he'd saved her from death by boredom at school. Art and biology were the only subjects that kept her in her body instead of mentally drifting out the window.

Appearing at the one-room schoolhouse at noon on a Thursday, Marco greeted the teacher warmly but adamantly. "Good day to you, Mrs. Swenson. I hope I'm not botherin' ya, but I need my Mona's help for a few days. I'll make sure she does her homework. You have a nice weekend now. C'mon, Mona."

"Zip-a-dee-doo-dah," Mona said under her breath, reaching down to pick up her rawhide rucksack from under the desk.

Outside, Marco opened the truck door for Mona. "There's stuff in the world you can't learn in that square box of a school. I already packed everything for both of us. Ready to hit the trails?"

"Everything?" Mona joked. "Did you bring my makeup? I think green would go with the leaves. Or maybe brown. Can we forage for lipstick in the forest?"

"Brown for sure." Marco grinned as he gunned Chester on the main road. "Plenty o' mud where we're goin'." In the truck bed, old Shadow and new Chipper surfed the breeze with their tongues flapping.

"Where are we going, Papa? Crystal Lake? Bent Oak Ridge?"

"We're goin' to harvest the trapline next to the Namekegon River. We got work to do, but we'll make it play as best we can. That okay with you?"

"Did you bring my pencils and my drawing book?"

"Son of a gun! Am I your Papa, or am I just some stranger that picked you up while you were hitchin'?"

"My favorite Papa in the whole world. You work and I'll draw you working. Is that all right with you?"

"Ya sure, you know it is, Mona Lisa. I gotta have proof I was workin' to show your mama when we get home."

A half-hour later, they reached the trailhead and unloaded their gear. Since every day above zero in Wisconsin was mosquito season, Marco rubbed bacon grease on their skin to keep the hungry suckers at bay. "Uff dah! These critters can drink a man dry. Officially the state bird of Wisconsin."

He said that every time, and Mona loved it every time.

They hiked for an hour to the campsite, dropped their packs, and spent the rest of the afternoon traipsing from one trap to the next. It tore up Mona to even catch a glimpse of the dead foxes and dried blood, but now trapping was Papa's sole job. The life of a lumberjack had worn Marco down, though that was okay with him. He preferred to be in the woods alone.

As the sun settled behind the trees, Marco pitched the tent while Mona gathered branches, sticks, twigs, and built a fire. They cooked dinner in one aluminum pot—rice on the bottom, a layer of cattail stems, wild chives, and dandelion greens over it all, and after ten boiling minutes, four eggs cracked in four depressions on top. Thimble berries and s'mores for dessert.

Once the metal bowls and spoons were washed, Marco tucked the remaining food into their packs and hung them high on a rope stretched between two silver birch trees, out of the reach of bears. Mona rolled in a couple of logs for sitting next to the fire and heated up water for their traditional hot chocolate bedtime chat.

Marco added a shot of peppermint schnapps to his cup and eased down onto his log with Chipper in his lap. Old Shadow slept at Mona's feet, bushed after one day in the woods. Shadow was on her last legs, but Marco didn't have the heart to leave her behind. He'd gotten Chipper, a one-year-old cocker spaniel, because "Folks say these are good for huntin' birds, but I think he'll be more for pettin'."

Most nights he'd take out a deck of cards and they'd play a game of cribbage while he told Mona tall tales of his lumberjack days, but that evening, Papa just wanted to talk.

"So Mona dear, how come you like the woods so much? You're a girl, a big girl, twelve years old, almost a teenager. What about dolls and dresses and fancy shoes? Are you dreamin' of dancin' with boys?"

"Papa." Mona looked down, her cheeks a shade redder than the golden firelight on the rest of her face. "I love being in the woods with you, or alone, like you. I love the pine smell, the wildflowers, the cute little beetles, the flocks of butterflies. The woods feel like a home without walls."

"You used to say you wanted to fly all the way to Mexico. You 'member that, Mona?"

"Oh, yeah." Her eyes perked up and flames sparkled in her pupils.

Marco pointed south with his tin cup of hot chocolate schnapps. "So you still wanna go to Mexico?"

"Like you said back then, Papa. 'Someday, maybe someday.' And maybe someday is getting closer. Mrs. Swenson set up a pen-pal program at school, and we could pick from a list of names and addresses from all over the world. Guess where I chose?"

"Um, lemme think... Minnesota."

"Silly Papa. You're not even close, but it does start with an M."

"Okay... Minneapolis, Minnesota."

"No. Merida, Mexico. Her name's Zarita Flores. She's twelve like me."

"Well, that sounds just peachy. You'll have to learn Spanish, and knowing you like I do, I'm sure ya will, amigo. Hola. Gracias. Hasta mañana. Friend, hello, thank you, see you tomorrow. Those are the only words I know."

"Where'd you learn Spanish, Papa?"

"Guess I picked it up from migrant workers over at the hospital."

"Hoo, hoo." An owl hooted in a tree near the campsite, like a warning of something sinister lurking in the darkness.

SUDDENLY ANOTHER MEMORY TRIED TO HAMMER ITS WAY into Mona's subconscious—a sketch in her notebook she wasn't ready to revisit. She shuddered and almost dropped her brush.

No time for that now.

She put the final touches on her painting and leaned back to take it all in. Mona looked at the two butterflies reflected in her papa's eyes. One was a red monarch and the other… She furrowed her brow and moved in closer.

A blue morpho! Where did that come from?

TIGER

Shoplifting Stooges

To the sweet sounds of Air's violin in the next room, Gem reviewed the mugging movie she'd shot in the park. She doubted she'd ever show anyone, but archived it on her hard drive in case Dick got out of line again.

Her papa knocked on the door. "Gem, are you up?"

"Sure, Papa. Come on in." Gem closed the windows on her computer screen as he sat down on the bed and folded his hands in his lap.

"Gem, dear. Do you want to tell me any more about Tom, Dick, and Harry?"

"Nah," she answered casually. "It was nothing, really."

"Nothing, eh? They were featured on the ten o'clock local news."

"What?!" Gem whipped around to face him. "What'd they do?"

"You go first. What did they do?"

"Oh, they were just being total jerks. Dick's a first-class bully. He and his butthead buddies attacked a friend of mine for no reason."

"Where?"

Gem told him the whole story, and he listened attentively until the end. "You are a gem with a heart of gold and nerves of steel. When you met Dick earlier, he may have been the Village Idiot, but now the web is turning him into the World Idiot. You and Air have got to watch the news report. I recorded it for you."

Gem fetched Air, and they both plunked down on the living room couch as Papa queued up the report on the TV.

The Channel Five logo danced across the screen to their up-tempo theme song. Anchorman Dennis Hedlund smiled blandly and began.

"Three Shoplifting Stooges! This late-breaking story has put our city on the map. No, on the globe! It's spreading on the internet like wildfire. Tonight we have a special eyewitness report for you from our head cameraman, Garth Winslow, who was at the scene of this crime that went south. Garth, what happened at the Foodfare Store today? You were there a couple of hours ago."

The camera panned out to include Garth, a normal guy dressed in a khaki vest with several functional square pockets, unlike suave Dennis in his shiny blue news suit and red power bow tie.

"While shopping for groceries on my way home, I noticed three young lads acting real weird, so I started filming them with my little digital camera." Garth's footage filled the TV screen. "See, they don't have a cart. They squint and look around, snatch things off shelves, and slip them into their pants. Watch this now. They dump entire boxes of candy in their backpacks."

"Sugar addicts looking for a fix. Do we know their names, Garth?" Dennis asked.

"Tom, Dick and Harry. We're not revealing their last names yet."

"Are those their real first names?"

"Yeah."

Dennis wilted. "Good lord, help us."

"That's them," confirmed Air to her papa.

"Losers," Gem added.

Garth continued his commentary. "Security must have been watching through that camera up there on the ceiling, because now a guard marches down the aisle toward them like a stormtrooper. They spot him, turn to split, trip and fall down, knocking over an elderly lady named Mora Archer. They leave her lying on the floor and run around the corner. The guard stops to see if she's injured.

"He'd called the police and a squad car with lights flashing pulls up in the front. Here, two officers question the manager and some customers. No one saw the shoplifters leave. At least ten people are snapping photos and taking movies with their phones."

"Publicity wannabes looking for instant stardom," Dennis grunted off-screen.

"I guess so," Garth said. "The manager and police head for the warehouse storage area, assuming the kids must be hemmed in there because the back doors and loading dock can only be opened with special keys. A girl comes up and says she heard a crash and shouting.

"Here's the best part. The officers cautiously approach the plastic curtains hanging in the warehouse door. Suddenly Dick, followed by a swarm of angry hornets, charges through the plastic, flailing his arms and slapping himself in the face and neck—and skitters right into the arms of the police! A shopper grabs a can of Raid from his cart, flips it to an officer, and runs away. Dick must have bumped into a nest while trying to hide. I don't know how many people got stung."

The crime scene faded, leaving the station's logo on the screen. Dennis had buried his head in his hands. Garth stared at him for a moment, and then spoke to the camera.

"The officers wouldn't let me film while they searched for the other two in the warehouse. Harry had ducked into the walk-in cold storage room, but couldn't open the door from the inside. He was half-frozen, but that's business as usual in Canada."

Dennis snorted and stared at his desk. "Meathead."

"Okay..." Garth said tentatively, puzzled by Dennis' terse comments. "Tom tried to climb on top of some major shelves, but they tumbled over on top of *him*. They found him trapped under jumbo cases of paper towels, diapers, and toilet rolls."

Dennis snorted again. "Was he on a roll? No, under them. Idiot."

"Right..." Garth said. "The good news? We should have more kids like this, ones who commit crimes and then capture themselves. Here's a clip of the 'suspects' as they're escorted into custody. Harry's blue-white from frostbite. Tom's bruised red and purple from cascading cases. Dick's face is covered with welts. He looks like a goalie for a dart team. I imagine their families are frantic at home, planning to relocate to another province."

"Or planet," Dennis fumed, frantically tapping his pen. "'That stupid ass."

Garth hesitated... then asked under his breath, "I thought we can't say 'ass' on TV?"

"We can't."

"But we both just did."

"Ha! Today we're going for World Wide Web Ratings! If those punks thought their reputations were bad before, this *rectum* for good! Ha, ha, ha. This *rectum*. Hee, hee."

Dennis laughed way too hard when he shouldn't be laughing at all. Crazy Jack Nicholson with a hatchet from the horror movie *The Shining* flashed through Garth's mind. "Denny, are you okay?"

"I'm *pooped!* Hee, hee, hee. What do you viewers think of this *crappy* situation as a *hole*?"

"Den, get a grip."

"I think these *asses* should be *wiped* out! Ha, ha, ha!" Dennis was so far gone over the edge it looked like a distant horizon in his rearview mirror.

"Let's take a break..." Garth pleaded to anyone. "Now!"

There wasn't much left to lose, but Dennis lost it. "But... But... *Butt. Butt! Butt!! Butt!!!*"

The news logo danced onto the screen again, and the theme song blared as six hands pulled Dennis out of the picture. A toilet paper commercial started to roll, then disappeared, and the logo zipped back on.

Five seconds later, co-anchor Colette Morgan materialized in Dennis' chair. With beads of sweat-logged makeup glistening on her forehead, she read a hastily prepared statement from a script on the desk in front of her.

"That wraps it up for tonight, folks. We'll see you tomorrow for the latest and greatest news stories. I must apologize for the confusion, but everyone here, including anchorman Dennis Hedlund, just learned… a few minutes ago… that his son Richard… Dick… is one of the shoplifting stooges… I mean, suspects. We extend our best wishes to both of them and hope everything comes out all right… in the end."

She looked over at someone off-screen to her left, and then faced the camera, struggling to stop her tight, vibrating lips from exploding into a snicker.

Logo. Theme. Commercial.

Air and Gem bounced up and gave each other a high five as they yelped in unison. "Yes!"

"As you sow…" Gem began.

"So shall you reap!" Air finished. "You taught us that, Papa."

"What goes around…" Papa began.

His girls finished together. "Comes around!"

Gem raced up to her room. "I gotta tell Tiger."

Papa raised one brow and eyed Air.

Air winked back.

ANGEL

Taller Wider Bigger

During his mental assessment of The Ridge, the hectic state of affairs today, and a future that now clashed with his past, Angel had drifted off.

He woke to the cabin attendant's seats-forward, trays-up speech, and peered out the window at Washington, DC, the capital of the world in too many minds. It struck him as a tad old-fashioned compared to the elegant artistic architecture of skyscrapers in Dubai, Abu Dhabi, or Hong Kong. A bunch of short, stodgy white buildings and one square, phallic monument squatted on the horizon below. He'd read somewhere that "by law, the DC skyline is low and sprawling." So was the CIA or an iceberg. Seven-eighths under the surface, like his own private world in The Ridge. Flying lit him up and fired his passion, yet he lived in a wormhole.

Something's got to change. No, someone's got to change. Me. Theoretically, wormholes are passageways between a black hole and a white hole. Let's make that reality.

Right now he needed rest and a body recharge, especially if he took this "life or death" mission. The past weeks had been relentless. He'd envisioned today's vacation as an undisturbed cycle of couch-potato naps and snack attacks. At least, during his battle with the hit-morons, he got the exercise he'd probably have skipped.

Inside, he heard his grandmother Dao's voice.

My grandson, make it happen. You can manifest what you need in life. You are both the sender and the receiver. Ask for what you want and it will come to you.

This didn't pertain only to major goals and dreams. It worked for everyday moments. If he wanted a parking spot in front of a building, he got into "parking consciousness." Calm his mind, feel his heart, visualize it, and ask his guides for exactly what he needed. Grandmother had told him, "Your spirit guides get bored just loafing around. They want to help, but if you don't ask, they won't."

He'd experienced her doing it with the weather. She'd get angry, and the wind would pick up or lights flicker, like exclamation points at the ends of her feelings. One day everyone might be worried and moan, "Storm's coming. We'd better not go fishing." But Grandmother Dao would say, because somehow she knew, "It's not going to rain. It'll pass." The storm would pass and they'd catch fish.

As the plane landed at Reagan National Airport, Angel entered his private "Manifestival," as he liked to call it. He didn't have to close his eyes, or meditate, or do any hocus-pocus whoha. Just focus, be specific, and give thanks.

I need to relax and sleep soon. I do not want to see Administrator Victoria today. The meeting should happen tomorrow for the greatest good of all. Thank you. Om shanti, om shanti, om shanti, om.

Angel eagle-eyed the other passengers as they gathered their belongings, plodded down the aisle ahead of him, and filed into baggage claim. As usual, he had a plan.

Step one: invisibility.

If possible, he scoped out who he was meeting *before* the meeting. He wanted to be hidden in the middle of a group, or with someone, an innocent hostage who didn't know they were being held.

In the walkway from the plane to the terminal, a silver-haired lady stopped and struggled with her rolling suitcase. Wearing jeans, T-shirt, and an Atlanta Braves baseball cap, Angel was merely the boy next door, the antithesis of a secret commando. Leading with a cherubic smile, he approached his target.

"Howdy, ma'am. My name's Angel. Can I give y'all a hand with that? Looks like your suitcase wheels ain't cooperatin' at all."

"Why..." She studied his dark radiant eyes. "Why, yes. I can't seem to get it to roll."

"Mind if I take a gander?" He kneeled down and tried to spin the wheels free, although even if he fixed it, he was going to roll it.

"You said your name is Angel?" she asked cheerfully.

"Yes, ma'am. I try to live up to it. And you?"

"Monica. Angel is a divine name. Everybody needs one now and then."

"It's no problem for me to carry your bag for you, Miss Monica, but y'all got a problem with your wheels. We both must be goin' to the same place."

"If you don't mind... thank you so much!"

Angel talked and walked close, as if she were his semi-deaf grandmother. "Is someone pickin' you up that can help you with this? Or are you takin' a cab or bus?"

"My friend couldn't come today, so I need to find a curbside taxi."

"Fancy that. So do I."

Angel pulled down his cap an inch and leaned into Monica, listening to her life's short story. They sailed past the waiting crowd behind the metal railings at security. Glancing over her padded shoulders and around her feathered hat, he scrutinized every other being in the room. He spotted a man holding a hand-written sign: Angel Phoenix. Angel hated that—his identity announced to the entire neighborhood in the capital of the world.

We should've set up a name like Amos Keetoe or Herb Uttsbig. Why wasn't I thinking? Oh, yeah. We were playing.

He recognized the sign man's face from his photo on the web. It was Deputy Jonathan Skipper.

Well, well, well! Dep'dy Jon! Right stocky fellow. He could use that butch haircut to scrub crusty eggs off a fryin' pan. Catch you in a few, Dep'dy.

Angel escorted Monica to a taxi, helped her into the seat, rolled the case back to the trunk, and skipped back to the window. "Your wheels are workin' fine now. Maybe they only needed a rest. Good luck, Miss Monica. It was my pleasure to lend y'all a hand."

She fumbled with her purse. "Please let me give you something. I've got some cash in here somewhere."

"Thanks, but no thanks, ma'am. Your smile brightened my day. And no amount of money could buy that." He tipped his cap and left her beaming out the taxi window.

He walked down the line of parked taxis until he found a bored young longhair who looked as green as his cab. Angel opened the door, sat next to him in the front seat, and quickly scanned the driver's laminated photo ID taped amongst an array of Rasta stickers. Angel switched accents from Southern Man to Universal Dude.

"Hey, man. How you doin' today?"

"Mellow," the cabbie said, his pupils dilated caverns. The taxi had a hookah bouquet. "Where you goin'?"

"I'm Angel and I gotta a deal for you. I just got off a plane and my buddy's waiting inside for me. I snuck by him because I wanna have some fun. I'll give you ten bucks to lend me your cabbie hat for five minutes. Here's twenty. When I return with your hat, you give me back ten. If I don't come back, the twenty's yours, but that won't happen, cuz Dude… I do not want your hat. You might not get another customer in this line for a few minutes, and maybe my buddy and I could use a ride, too. What d'ya say?"

The slightly baked driver raised his eyebrows and fingered the twenty-dollar bill. "Why not? Hat's too fuckin' hot, anyway."

"Thanks, man." Angel got out, then stuck his head back through the open window. "How much is your hat worth, anyway?"

"This morning? Wasn't worth shit. Right now? Twenty bucks… if I drive away."

"You gonna do that?"

"Nah. Ten's good enough."

Angel put up his palm. "Gimme five…" They smacked hands. "… minutes."

He ran back into the terminal, snuck through the dwindling crowd and sidled up to Jonathan. Angel Cabbie spoke in Nonresident Alien from under the brim of his new used hat. "Hey, Mister! You need taxi?"

"No, thanks." Deputy Jonathan didn't even turn his head.

"You sure?" Angel begged, tugging on the cuff of Jonathan's sleeve. "I give you discount. Turn off meter. Where you go?"

Jonathan looked down to the top of a cabbie hat on top of a kid. "I don't need one."

"Okay, mister, but I do odd jobs, too. You want special deliveries? I give you clues, Colonel Mustard…" Angel raised the brim of his hat and smirked.

"Son of a bitch," Jonathan swore with a smile. "Angel Phoenix the Fifth? Sixth? Twenty-third?"

"I told you on the phone, sir," Angel started as a cadet, switched to a Pokeberry Ridge native, and finished somewhere in between. "I'll see y'all before y'all see me! It's good to meet you, Deputy Jonathan Skipper."

"Nice to meet you, too. Thanks again for coming on such short notice. Classy hat. Is there a taxi outside with a driver in the trunk?"

"Five-minute rental. Have to return the hat before he runs out of air."

"Do you have any other luggage?" Jonathan asked.

"This is it. Backpack and one carry-on. If you don't have wheels, I do have a cab waiting."

Jonathan gestured toward the exit doors. "Truck's in the lot. I've got a special handi-cop sticker so I can park close. I needed an excuse to get out from behind my desk before I set fire to it."

"Sounds like we may have to flip a coin to see whose day was worse. I hope you don't mind, but I have to make a quick phone call, and I don't want to use my cell. How about if I return the hat, make the call, and meet you in front of that exit in ten minutes?"

Jonathan glanced at the door where Angel had pointed. "That'll work.

I'll be in a forest-green Ford Explorer."

"Just in case, what's your cell number?" Angel asked.

"You want to write it down on something?"

"I'll write it in my mind. I lose paper, but in spite of what other people say, I haven't lost my mind yet. See you in ten."

ANGEL TRADED THE HAT WITH THE CABBIE FOR HIS TEN BUCKS, found a pay phone, and called his pseudo-friend at FBI Headquarters.

"Bernie! It's your guardian Angel. Are you in the office or out officerin'?"

"In and out." Bernie had trouble giving only one answer. "What's up, Angel? I haven't seen you for about a thousand hours."

"I had three unexpected visitors at my house today. I don't have a house anymore, but the sheriff has the visitors. By the time I was close enough to them to ask their names, they were paralyzed, but looked more northern Colombian than northern Georgian. Maybe you could send someone to check 'em out."

"I'll see who's assigned to that area or let the Director know," Bernie offered delicately without offering his help. "You have any idea who they are?"

"Not yet. My security cameras might have recorded the attack, but I'm off the grid for a week or so. You may be the only FBI guy who knows where I live… or where I lived. So, would you mind contacting Sheriff Donny Dillon in Pokeberry Ridge today, if possible? He's a good man, but this is not a local matter."

"Okay, I will," he replied evasively, "if I can reach him."

"Thanks, Bernie, you're the man. Actually, I think you are the man. One more question. Did you happen to write my cellphone number on one of my business cards and give it to anyone lately?"

"I might have. I don't remember." Bernie wasn't a completely bad person, despite the fact that he had scales, no legs, and slithered through the grass. One or two times in his life, snake Bernie might have helped other people even more than he helped himself.

"Hmm… Bernie, what did it mean when I said, 'Don't give out my number to anyone unless you call me first,' and you said, 'Okay, I won't'? Did you get me mixed up with all the other Angel Phoenixes you know?" Angel spoke calmly. He wasn't angry, and certainly didn't want the Fucking Bunch of Idiots mad at him. It helped to pretend he was talking on a playground with a kid who'd lost his marbles.

"I only gave it to Jonathan Skipper at the DEA," Bernie backpedaled.

"You can trust him."

"As much as I trust you now?"

"I thought maybe you could help him, and he could help you."

No "I'm sorry." No apologies from Bernie. He spoke five languages fluently, but hadn't learned those words in any of them.

"Well, I think I can trust Deputy Skipper, because he wouldn't tell me where he got my number, except that someone from the FBI gave it to him. And you're the only one around there who has it. I suggest we both think about who we gave my number to, and then we might accidentally stumble upon a clue. They knew where I was, and when I was there, and wanted my place to be in the 'final resting' category."

Bernie spoke in his when-will-this-fucking-conversation-be-over tone. "I'll do what I can."

"That's what I'm afraid of," Angel sighed. "Feel free to give out this number to anyone. It's a payphone at an airport. That's where I live now. Thanks in advance for any help. I'll call back when I can."

"Take care of yourself," Bernie said and hung up.

Good advice. He definitely knows how to do that.

Angel jumped into the Explorer, and Jonathan apologized as he pulled out toward the airport exit. "Sorry I missed you inside. I guess I was looking for someone—"

Angel finished his sentence. "Taller, wider, bigger, older, lighter, darker?" He'd been here a hundred times before. It used to bug him, but he'd learned to love the way he was. His size, shape, and color had saved his life and the lives of many.

"No offense meant," Jonathan said.

"None taken. I imagined you'd be shorter and thinner. I thought maybe the photo on your web bio was life-size, and with that cute little one-inch head, you'd probably only be about a foot tall."

Jonathan snorted out a laugh. "What if I were six-foot-three with a one-inch head?"

"I'd have taken the taxi that was waiting on me. Or put the cabbie hat on your shoulders so you couldn't see me."

Jonathan snorted again, braking hard, so he didn't take home a Honda as a hood ornament. "Angel, you have a big reputation to live up to and I suppose you grow inside people's heads."

"I spend a lot of time inside people's heads. Some are amazing; some only a maze. I wonder how they even get dressed in the morning."

"Size matters," Jonathan admitted, "but it's relative. I can push my kids on the merry-go-round, but I can't follow them through the tunnels. If I tried their slide, it'd collapse."

Now he's talking! Jon Boy's inside my head, reading me. "Just think of me as little Napoleon without the funny hat and the hand in his jacket pickin' lint from his navel… Well, I do have some funny hats. If you had a job that needed a fly on the wall, would you send in a hippo?"

"Unfortunately," Jonathan sighed, slowing for a stoplight, "that's kind of what we did. And why we need your help."

"You sent in a hippo and you want this tiny fly to get it out? Do you know how many flies it takes to lift a hippo? I'd need 5,000 helium balloons."

"I thought you said you've never lost your mind."

"Occasionally I misplace it," Angel confessed, "but I normally find it again—with my keys and socks that disappeared in the washing machine."

"I'd love to be in your head," Jonathan mused aloud, "and see what it's like in there."

"Downright dangerous. Too many people are already wandering around in there. Lots of microscopic rooms, wide-open spaces, and sliding doors. You'd need a detailed map. I didn't get one when they screwed it on."

The Explorer crawled along the roads through rush-hour traffic. Five o'clock on a Friday night in DC = Democratic Congestion.

"Angel, I have a proposition for you. Today didn't go the way we'd planned. Administrator Victoria is stressed up to her receding hairline. How about if we check into the hotel, get you some vittles, and I'll brief you on what's going on? We'll meet her in the morning."

Yes! Few believe it, but it works! Ask and ye shall receive. With his right hand hidden between his thigh and the truck door, Angel gave himself and Grandmother Dao a thumbs up as his recent wish became reality. "Deputy Do-Right, you are already in my head and may have noticed the steaming piles of shit in my living room. It'd be best not to inflict me on Victoria right now. When you hear about my day, you might feel better about yours."

Jonathan snaked into the left-turn lane. "Great, the hotel's only a few minutes away."

"Deputy, you said, 'How about if we check into the hotel…' I know you almost set fire to your desk today, but I think you should stay at home tonight. I never sleep with anyone on the first date."

"You need help," urged Jonathan.

"So do you. That's why you called. We're even."

As Angel stepped out at the Hilton, he noticed a pink VW Bug right behind the Explorer, covered with daisy and peace sign stickers.

That's the exact car Tiger drove Gem home in my dreams. Angel scanned the area expecting to see them standing on the sidewalk. *Maybe my own personal Gem is close.*

When Angel had finished registering at the counter and the perky blonde receptionist offered him the key card, he leaned over, read her name tag, and whispered, just loud enough for Jonathan to hear. "Shannon, if this guy behind me tries to break into my room tonight, who do I call? You?"

At first taken aback, she glanced from Angel to the burly but smiling man in the tan herringbone suit, obviously carrying Angel's bags, then back at his devilishly angelic face. "You could call hotel security or your mother, whichever one would make you feel more comfortable."

"My mother?" Angel stood up straight and looked from side to side. "Is she a guest, or does she work at the hotel? Please don't tell her I'm here."

"Have a nice stay, Mr. Phoenix. I'll let you know if I see your porter here sneaking up the back staircase."

"Much obliged, Shannon." He shook her hand gently as he took his key. "You never know."

As they walked to the elevator, an amazed Jonathan asked, "Were you trying to get her phone number?"

"Just warming her up, gathering clues. She works late. There's a back stairway. She likes me."

Jonathan punched the button."How do you know?"

"Her eyes twinkled. Her palm was damp."

"You need a good night's sleep."

"Yes, Mother," Angel said obediently. "I'm planning for the future. It's good to have productive contacts in DC."

"I think you mean 're-productive' contacts. So what would you like to eat? Steak 'n' taters 'n' grits?"

"That was Angel the First. Angel the Phoenix would love a solid burger and fries in a laid-back atmosphere where we can talk shop."

"I know just the place. Beaumont's Barbecue."

"Do me a favor," Angel said on the elevator. "Sneak up the backstairs later. Then I won't have to call Shannon. She'll call me."

RED

Bad News, Worse News

After the infestation of her office by that Bug creature, Red had barely slept. She felt violated. Psychologically raped. Bug was unnerving on his own, but his association with Baldev Ishwar Gupta amplified her anxiety.

Red's father had introduced her to Baldev several years earlier. Instantly she didn't trust his artificial smiles, nor the intimidating frowns of the two broad-shouldered bozos he employed as his human bookends. She never grasped exactly what his business, or what his racket was, but her father seemed to appreciate his help.

Three months before her Bug encounter, Baldev had phoned and asked to meet her, which she did. He'd presented his external agenda evasively.

"My dear Miss Admiral, if you ever desire to extricate yourself from this crop-dusting chore and do something more suitable for a ravishing woman such as yourself, please let me help you out."

She could feel his internal agenda burning hot and clear. *He wants the land and maybe me, too.* Red gave him several pieces of her mind regarding the importance of her industry and the right of a woman, specifically her, to do as she damn well pleased.

Her manliness evidently impressed him as much as her womanliness, and he invited her to his Thursday night poker games with the boys. She'd played before, but not for real. To the surprise of the veteran players, and to herself, she'd been born with a stone poker face, albeit a charming one, and no one could ever quite determine what she held in her hand or what skulked beneath those bewitching auburn locks.

She won. For a while. Then, as if someone had thrown an off switch, her luck vanished, though her deluded self-confidence continued betting. Her current debt was the final tally from only one evening when Baldev had graciously covered her losses.

But he hadn't thrown her a life preserver. He'd set his hook. Back fence talk taught Red that she was one of many snared on his multi-line trolling apparatus. From Baldev's ostensibly altruistic fishing yacht, he cast his lines deep, far and wide, and had battleships to reel in the catch.

Two months had flashed by in a medicinal blur, and Red lost track of time. She hadn't realized the debt was due. After poring over her finances and accounts for hours, she concluded that she could cover it. Several large clients paid in advance for her services, and their funds would be transferred to her bank on the first of the month… tomorrow. She rose and stretched, then went to wash away her worries.

Bug's malignant hiss slithered through her mind as she went into the bathroom.

Bruce Gandhi.

It was a long shot that he'd pictured her exactly the same way she'd pictured herself, but even a longer shot that this room—And which others?—had been bugged. Bug had even admitted he'd come to bug her.

All this harassment for a debt I'd certainly pay, with interest? A "client" and a "friend" who'd never before stiffed him?

Red swallowed hard and turned the tap. No water. *Now what?* She stomped to her office and buzzed Azeez.

"Yes, Miss Red?"

"I have no water. What's happening?"

"I was recently looking at the pumps and it is not working. I do not know about pumps, but I will call a plumber. I was just coming to see you. I have news."

"What kind of news?"

"Bad news," Azeez stammered, "and worse news."

"Brilliant," she said, flinging the folder in her hand onto her desk and strewing papers onto the floor. "That seems to be all we receive lately."

After cleaning up her mess, Red leaned against the window, staring into the hangar at her father's old bird, the yellow Tiger Moth.

Hmm. The kid in my dream was named Tiger and loved tiger swallowtail butterflies.

The yellow Caterpillar petrol truck next to it reminded her of the yellow shovel Cats and dozers from her drug-induced hospital visions, tearing apart the rainforest in one scene and demolishing a house in another.

Perhaps Dr. B was right about messages in those strange dreams of mine.

The moment Azeez stepped into the office, Red turned from the window. "Did anyone come into the compound last evening?"

"No, no. I did not see anyone, Miss Red."

"I had a visitor, here in this room, unannounced. A sinister visitor."

"I was sitting in my residence by the gate and watching, and Kamal was not barking."

In her honor, Azeez had named his bulldog Kamal, Hindi for 'red.' As for his guard dog skills, Red thought the bulldog was bullshit. Because of its somnambulant state, extravagant appetite, and bulbous body shape, she called the dog, in Azeez' absence, Log. The only thing Log successfully protected was his bowl of food.

Red's scrappy stray tabby cat had wandered in under the ever unaware nose of Log and lodged itself in her life. She tolerated it only because she disliked rats more than she disliked cats. Its personality matched hers: neither of them cared a whit about the other. In a moment of unconscious affection, Red might pet the cat, who would pivot, hiss, and scratch her hand. Likewise, the cat might accidentally cuddle up to an ankle of Red, who would pivot, swear, and flick the cat away with her foot. She called it Cat Astrophe, often shortened to Cat Ass.

"Check the entire perimeter fence," Red ordered. "Make sure the electricity is feeding it. I do not want this to happen again. Now tell me the bad news first."

"I am sorry, but I am not finding a doctor who will sign your physical examination for your pilot license renewal."

"Keep trying."

She had an alternative scheme in mind, involving forgery with a slippery man at the market, a necessary skill acquired when she was an apprentice to devious Danny Admiral. When certain tasks became difficult, he'd discover a clandestine pathway through the maze and would explain the steps to Red. She'd ask: "But Father dear, is that legal?" His answer: "Half."

"Now then, what's your worse news?" Red asked Azeez.

"It is most distressing," he moaned, twitching uncomfortably. "Perhaps Miss Red would like to be sitting down."

"Out with it. I doubt it's any of your doing."

"Then Azeez would like to be sitting down." He flopped onto the couch and folded his hands in his lap. "The general manager of Agro Farms called today canceling his contract with Admiral Aviation, effective immediately."

The news kicked her in the stomach. "What?"

"And Universal Foods as well, I am afraid."

Another blow to her brain. "What?"

"And I am not even wanting to say it… Anwar's Fruits and Vegetables is also canceling."

Her throat attempted to eke out another "What?" but failed. She leaned against the desk on liquid legs. "Our three largest accounts," she whispered, trying to catch the breath his words had knocked into the neighboring district. "Why?" she wheezed, then rose up and lowered her tone. "Why."

"All any of them would say is that they had decided to go with another company. They said thank you very much and were wishing you the best of luck."

"Another company." The tears of horror she had fought back into her heart seconds earlier now boiled up inside the red veins in the whites of her eyes. She spoke through clenched teeth. "What company might that be?"

"Aero Dynamic Enterprises, Miss Red," Azeez said weakly, expecting her to either flare up or break down.

"If I'm not mistaken, the same company that purchased our Cresco crop duster at the auction, yes?"

"Yes, yes. I am thinking that is the one."

"These three accounts all cancel on the same day, right before their monthly payments are due, the day after our sinister visitor slinks in." Red paused, staring out the window but seeing the shadow in her mind.

How many people does this Bug serve? Did he call on my clients, too? Who's pulling Bug's strings?

Her eyes narrowed as she turned to face Azeez again. "We have work to do or soon we'll have no work to do at all. First, call a plumber straight away. I can't function properly without a bath. Second, schedule an appointment for me with Mr. Verma at the bank tomorrow. I need a loan as soon as possible. And third… Wait."

She tilted up her head as she envisioned the Angel in her dream destroying his cell phone after the Cats had destroyed his home.

"Third, get two new cellphones and two new numbers, one for each of us. Then use your new phone to—" Red interrupted herself as she considered what she should not say in their potentially bugged environment. "To… to replace that old one you have. I'll call each of our clients and try to seduce them back into the fold."

Azeez scurried out, and Red took several deep breaths, searching through her mental closet for a pleasant phone voice to wear.

I've worked with these people for over a decade. They are friends. Or were.

She chose to call Anwar first, one of her first customers. In their win-win symbiotic relationship, they'd both prospered over the years. She sat at her desk and tapped the auto-dial for Anwar's direct line.

"Hallo?"

"Anwar, it's Red. How are you today?"

"I am fine. And you, Miss Admiral?"

She could feel that he was already nervous. "I was fine until I heard some sad news. Azeez tells me you wish to cancel our contract. How have we disappointed you, Anwar? Please let me know so I can remedy the situation without delay."

"There is nothing to remedy, I'm afraid. Your services have always been most excellent."

"Were my pilots not on schedule? Off their course? Have they delivered incorrect payloads?"

"No, no, Miss Admiral. They have been timely and careful as usual."

She could sense this gentle man was in the deep end of someone else's pool. He was treading water, trying to avoid an invisible shark, waiting to be saved by a dial tone. Fear strangled his voice, as if the shark physically had a grip on his throat... or was on the line.

"What is it, may I ask? Why, Anwar?"

"I am sorry, but another company has made us an offer we cannot refuse."

"We've worked together for over a decade. I will match any other company's offer and try harder."

"No, you cannot match their offer, Miss Admiral. I must go now. Thank you for your help and the best of luck to you."

"If you change your mind," Red said, stuffing her frustration underneath her sincere concern, "you know where to reach me."

"I am deeply sorry. Namaste." He saved himself with the dial tone droning in her ear.

Red's next two calls were a replay of the first. No one mentioned the name of the other company, and all three reasons were identical—"made us an offer we cannot refuse"—as if someone had told them exactly what to say. She didn't press any further because the conversations were useless to her and conceivably dangerous for them.

Fighting for her life had been business as usual for the past six weeks, and now she was fighting for her livelihood as well. The doctor's drugs may have deadened her pain and dampened her spirit, but they seemed to bolster her will to survive. She would not be trapped like that blue butterfly flattened on the rainforest floor in her dream.

Whenever confronted by a perplexing or alarming conundrum, Red asked herself this question: "What would Danny Boy do?"

She pictured his conniving smile, his tousled strawberry-blond hair, and his mischievous blue eyes. And heard his perennial boyish voice cackling,

"They don't call me the sly red fox for nothin'. You know the golden rule. 'Do unto others before they do unto you."

Mother Chandra, the Karma Queen, the incessant "you'll pay 1,000 times for every unkind thought, word, or deed" nagging wife, called it "the fool's golden rule."

Words from her dream Angel popped in next to her parents, seemingly siding with father Danny Boy, though Red didn't remember what had happened before or after Angel's quote, and took it completely out of context.

Evil spelled backwards is live, live, live.

She would have to live or die, guided by this mistranslated message from the universe.

MONA

Losing It

Backing out of her driveway onto the main road in her monarch-colored, red-orange Ranchero, pampered every day since she bought it in 1979, Mona saw a crop duster flying low across the adjacent field, a cloud of chemicals spewing from its wings. When it rose over the road a few feet from her roof, instead of rolling up her window, she stuck a wrinkled hand into the rushing air and gave it the finger.

Mona spotted Yves Draggon, her neighbor, plodding along the road in the afternoon heat, a mile from his house. She stopped and leaned out of the window.

"Dragonfly! Where are you off to today?"

"I'm buying groceries."

"The store's nine miles away, you know."

"No, no… no," he stuttered, pointing ahead, "it's just down the road."

"Yes, yes! *Nine miles* down the road." She spoke with a lilt in her voice to disguise the sadness she felt talking face-to-face with the body of an old friend who'd left his mind behind. "The last time you tried this, I had to pick you up at a bowling alley in the next county. Get on in here, Yves. I'm goin' there, too."

Yves sounded irritated. "You are going… bowling? I am not going bowling."

"Dragonfly, c'mon. Just get in the truck."

Yves and Camilla Draggon had been Mona's dear comrades for a decade. Together they'd laughed heartily, pondered life's mysteries, and toasted many a sun rising through the red wine mist. A mechanical engineering wizard, Yves could fix anything Mona managed to break with bits of this and that from his shop. He'd stop by with his toolbox and yell, "Yves dropping by!"

The last few years had devastated him. Eleven of his brothers, sisters, and cousins perished in a plane crash on their way from France for a Texas family reunion. Camilla succumbed to a vicious flu. A stroke stole the few shreds of humor and emotion left in Yves, and now Alzheimer's disease was walking him home to his final address.

To Mona, he didn't seem unhappy, just not there—somewhere else perhaps, in the past or in the future, reliving what he'd lost or marking time until it might return. She'd spent years as a nurse, several in hospices. Heartbreaking and warming at the same time, she'd cherished the opportunities to ease folks over to the other side. It was harder with a friend, but all those other folks had become her precious friends in the end.

At the grocery store, Mona waited as Yves sorted out his needs while having a one-on-one conversation with himself. As he deliberated over his frozen dinner options—Country Fried Beef Patties, Beer Battered Chicken, and Grilled Bourbon Steak Strips—the déjà vu dancer grabbed Mona and waltzed her away into another food store in another time in another town in Canada.

She thought of the three teenage boys in Canada sprinting down the aisle toward her, followed by an angry man. They toppled her cart and sent her sprawling on the floor. The man bent down to see if she was hurt, then rushed away. She pictured watching herself falling down on an evening TV newscast about the shoplifting incident.

Music blaring an in-store commercial tore her out of her reverie, and she turned to Yves, but Yves wasn't there—in body or mind. Like the teenagers in her déjà-vu dance, Mona headed for the storeroom in the back, where she found Yves standing still, staring at a stack of boxes. As she took hold of his arm and led him back into the store, she slammed into an unnerving realization.

I've never been to Canada. That couldn't have happened. Good lord, I'm as far gone as he is.

After paying the bill and herding Yves to the Ranchero, Mona raced toward home as her mind raced into dismay.

Her years on the fringes of life and death, her deep meditations, and her spiritual encounter groups had assuaged any fears of a dark hell dispatched by the grim reaper. She reveled in her perception of peace in "The Big Sleep" and often looked forward to fading away into the divine white light—whatever wonders awaited her around that cosmic corner. But the concept of dropping into the living limbo of unawareness and mental torpor she'd witnessed firsthand in Yves scared the hell right back into her.

After settling him into his kitchen with a beer-battered chicken in his oven, the timer set for twenty minutes, and milk and silverware on his table, Mona skedaddled home, mixed a wine spritzer, slumped onto her floral davenport, and phoned Sasha.

"Sasha Goldberg here, the world's oldest living realtor. How can I help you right now?"

"It happened again."

"What happened again?" Sasha asked, instantly concerned. "Did you disappear by fainting? Are you all right?"

Mona spoke as if she were reading her own obituary. "I'm losing it. My mind. Slowly but surely."

"We all are, sweetie. How about if we race together slowly but surely toward the finish line? Last one there wins. Tell Sasha what happened."

Mona related the whole déjà-vu event in detail, gesturing dramatically with her wine glass.

Once she'd finished her tale, Sasha asked, "But how did this happen before?"

"A while back, we were chatting, and I told you about the nice young man at the airport in Washington, DC, who helped me when my luggage wouldn't roll and then escorted me out to a taxi. Remember? His name was Angel and I said he was one of those guardian angels who appeared in my life, just like you."

"I remember… So?"

"Then I realized I'd never been to DC. Ever. It couldn't have happened!"

"So maybe you dreamed it."

"I wasn't daydreaming then, or today, and I don't remember dreaming about either of these incidents at night. It worries me that I don't know what's real and what isn't. I've had patients who couldn't distinguish between waking and sleeping, a classic symptom of an impending nervous breakdown, maybe Alzheimer's."

"Do you feel nervous?" Sasha asked.

Mona thought for a moment, gazing up the trunk of the palm tree in her living room. "No."

"Do feel like you're breaking down?"

"I'm not sure what I feel, but tomorrow morning I'm going to the clinic for a complete physical. Maybe a complete mental, too. If I'm losing it, I want to know why. And if you're not busy, I'd like to take you out to lunch afterwards, since I'm already there."

"You're already where? I thought you were at home."

"I'm already out to lunch."

They both laughed, but anxiety laced Mona's laughter.

"Quit beating yourself up," Sasha told her. "You're drowning your sorrows in a spritzer, aren't you? If I were there, I'd slip a Valium in it. Take a hot bath and relax, my young and healthy and dear Mona Lisa."

"Okay," she sighed. "See you tomorrow at noon."

She loved it when Sasha called her Mona Lisa like her Papa Marco used to do. She smiled and stroked Marco the shepherd at her feet.

"Are you going to tell me where we're going to meet or should we just wing it?" Sasha asked.

"Oh… sorry. How about Taco Bell on Buena Vista? I'm feeling a little Mexican. If I don't show up, I'll probably be wandering around with Yves trying to find nowhere."

"Taco Bell at noon it is. Now get a good night's sleep and dream about your elderly angel and a juicy bean burrito in your immediate future."

Mona followed Dr. Sasha Goldberg's advice and drew a bath, quite pleased with herself because she remembered to turn off the tap before the tub overflowed. She slipped into the soothing water and tried to recall every experience in her entire life, but that was like trying to fill the tub without a stopper in the drain. She thought she must have a severe case of déjà-amnesia-vu.

I have the distinct feeling I've forgotten all this before.

TIGER

Sweet Dreams

HIS CELLPHONE RANG IN THE DARK BEDROOM as Tiger was about to drift off to sleep. "Hello?"

"Did I wake you?"

"I don't think so… Gem? You're calling me?"

Gem lay in a pile of Navajo pillows, playing with the fringe on the one in her lap. "Is that okay?"

Tiger rubbed his eyes with his knuckles. "Maybe I am dreaming…"

"Tom, Dick, and Harry won't be bothering you anymore."

"What d'you mean?"

"They were arrested today at Foodfare. Channel Five aired a special report on them called 'Three Shoplifting Stooges.' Videos of it are going viral on the web."

"What?" Tiger lurched up on one arm. "Really?"

"You gotta watch 'em yourself. Some of your insect soulmates even helped the police catch Dick! No one needs to see my movie. The universe took care of it for us." Gem punched her fist into the air. "Thank you, Canada!"

"I'll check 'em out."

"Did hunchbacked Igor limp over to work in your laboratory tonight?"

"He's up there alone in the dark. Maybe he's building you a darkroom."

"Mmm," purred Gem. "I've got plenty of candles."

"I said I was sorry when I bumped into you today at school, but I'm not sorry anymore. That was the best mistake I ever made."

"Think you'll make the same mistake again, Tiger?"

"I hope so."

"I'll wear shoulder pads and a helmet."

"I'll get a bigger net."

"Don't let the dead bedbugs bite."

"I'll make sure their pins are tight."

"See you tomorrow, Tiger."

"Sweet dreams, Gem."

He set the phone on the pillow and watched its light pulse for a few moments… like a heartbeat. He pulled a pad of paper and a pen from under his pillow. Bathed in the pale azure glow of his cell phone's screen, Tiger let the words to the song floating inside flow out…

Sweet Gemini was passing by
With eagle eyes and battle cries
Then Gem and I were flying high
Two butterflies in endless skies

He put the pen and pad under the pillow, lay back smiling, closed his eyes, and said a silent prayer.

Dear God, thank you for today. If I've been dreaming it all, please don't let me wake up.

ANGEL

Vittles and Evaluation

UNDERNEATH THE NEON CATTLE BRAND OF BEAUMONT'S BARBECUE—a blood-red BBBQ inside a blue circle surrounded by flickering yellow flames—their tagline read "Upscale But Down Home."

Inside the restaurant, wild-west antiques and country music record albums staked their claims on the crowded adobe walls. Leather-padded seats caressed the weary buns of urban cowboys and girls. Spicy scents shot through sinuses. The air itself felt barbecued.

Angel and Jonathan took a booth in the back, relaxed, and ordered two beers—one Miller and one root.

"So, Deputy, you had a fiery day. What happened?"

"Well, you know the line. 'I can't tell you or I'd have to kill you.' I don't need to set fire to my desk. I can let the ones burn I've been trying to put out." Jonathan stared through the menu and into his heart. "Sometimes I want to 'just say no to drugs' and law enforcement altogether."

"I know how you feel, man," Angel sympathized with a cock of his head. "Half of me didn't want to call you back this morning."

"Thanks again for coming."

"So far it's been a pleasure. I'm now up to seventeen hours of vacation. Since you can't tell me about your day, let me tell you about mine. A few minutes after we talked this morning, three thugs with a shovel Cat, dozer, and an Uzi attacked my house. The house is history, and so is my car, but luckily I got to them before they got to me. I live at the Hilton now."

Jonathan's face turned the color of his beer. "Good lord! I feel better about me and worse for you. Any idea why?"

Angel took off his baseball cap, shook his head to fluff up his flat, hat hair, and began shaping his brim into the perfect curve. "I wish I knew, but at least they're in my buddy the sheriff's jail. Well, I think they are. I need to call him. I must admit I thought the DEA had it in for me when it happened right after our talk. Few people know where I live, or where I am, and cellphones are hell on invisibility."

"Trust me," Jonathan said, "it wasn't us."

"I know that now. And those cats had to have been there before you called. They were waitin' until...... I came outside, to make sure I'd be inside. Did you give my phone number to anyone else at the FBI?"

"No one. I only got it two days ago."

"I know 'F Bernie I' gave it to you. That's who I called from the airport. I'd told him not to give it to anyone unless he called me first, but Bernie often thinks Bernie is the only person in the universe. That cell is also history. I'll have to give you my new number and then kill you."

Jonathan bowed, his hands folded over his head. "Mind if I eat first? Last meal and a cigarette?"

"I'm just shittin' you. I'll tell you up front, Jonathan. I do trust you. I trusted you on the phone when we first talked. Miles don't matter. Energy does. I can feel people. It's hereditary. If I listen, pay attention, and believe it, my Angel Radar has never failed me. I wouldn't be alive and talking to you right now without it. But I didn't listen hard enough this morning. When I walked outside minutes before the attack, I knew something was shady, and I didn't act on it. I paid for my 'ignore-ance' with my house."

"How can I help? I could call someone."

Angel took a long drink of his root beer and gazed at a wagon wheel ceiling fan as he considered the offer. "Not now, thanks. The good news is these thugs were probably amateurs hired by an amateur organization. If 'professionals' had wanted this Angel to go to hell, a sniper could have done the trick when I came out on my porch. Someone is playin' out of their league. Bad guys' revenge on the middleman who helped the good guys. It's not easy to help these days. Too many gray lines between black and white. Okay, enough, Angel. All I'm tryin' to get at is, sometimes, like you, I want to 'just say no to thugs.'"

"I know what you're saying," Jonathan sighed. "I've been in the field. My trials now are about the men I send into the playing field and my responsibility for their lives. Let me give you a rundown on this job, and why you.

"Okay, but let's order first. My stomach's starting to eat me."

"I hear you... or maybe I hear your stomach."

"I haven't had a bite since toast this morning ,while not wanting to listen to your voicemail."

Angel opened the mammoth menu and set it on the table. It stood up by itself. Beaumont's thirty-eight-page, five-pound menu inside a bird's-eye maple hardcover with a buckskin binding had entrée photos beside trendy descriptions suffocating from acute adjectivitis and capital cancer. Angel started reading with the waiter standing over him, who was tapping his foot and concentrating on other booths filled with cowgirls.

"I'll have..." Angel poked the waiter with his menu to get his attention and gestured to a simple round burger at another table. "I'll have what they're having."

"This one?" the waiter asked, pointing at the menu.

"Sure, and some fries." As the waiter zipped away to tend two woozy cowgirls across the room, Angel tackled the description, reading it out loud from behind the menu. "US Grade AAA, Nebraska Range-fed, Charcoal-grilled, Beef Tenderloin Hamburger Steak, smothered with Lactose-light, Coastal Oregon Cheddar-Swiss-Colby Cheese, nestled lovingly on an Organically grown, Stone-ground, Whole Wheat Sourdough Bun, lathered with Madam Zell's Dijon French-Belgian Fusion Mayo-Mustard, and Special Reserve Heinz 57 Classic Catsup, while having intercourse with Uncle Adolf's Gesundheit Garlic Gherkin Pickles." He peered over the menu at Jonathan. "I might have exaggerated along the way."

The Deputy ordered the same as Angel after he got tired of reading page two.

"Maybe you should have your DEA boys check into whoever wrote this menu. They were definitely looped on something illegal. I didn't read about our fries, but they may be French-kissed by authentic Frogs as waiters play accordions and sing "Frère Jacques" until we've finished eating them—the fries, not the waiters. You know, I've always wanted to be a waiter, and have someone ask, 'I'll have what they're having.' I'd go over to the other table, take their food, and give it to my customer."

"You wouldn't last through your first shift."

"You're right. That's why I'm eating and not waiting."

"You're wrong. We're both waiting and not eating."

"You're right again, Dep'ty. Okay, give me the nitty-gritty. I've fought with three Cats today and my curiosity is about ready to kill another one."

"This is definitely classified info," Jonathan felt obligated to add.

"You think what I've been telling you isn't?"

"Same category. Don't worry, Angel. No one would believe me if I told them about you, anyway." Jonathan moved in closer and lowered his voice. "A year or so ago, Victoria got a call from a friend asking if this Barry Majors could work at the DEA. His qualifications were superb. Great physique. Legs and arms like a ripped bodybuilder, chest like a gorilla. Football, basketball, and wrestling star. High academics. Served as a Navy Seal. Gung-ho attitude."

"Sounds like my sheriff bud back in The Ridge," Angel said, his head hunched over next to Jonathan's.

"We took Barry in and ran him through training. He excelled, but we saw that his enthusiasm was a little overboard. His heart may be in the right place, but his brain's chock-full of ego… and 'success'—a relative term—so we kept him close to home.

"About a month ago, Victoria got another call from her friend asking us to give Barry a mission, to get him out and about. We sent him to work in Bangkok so he could get a taste of the real world. We didn't assign a specific mission, but he took on one of his own, with an unauthorized and much-too-personal interest in a minor drug lord by the name of Khun P.

"During Barry's time off in northern Thailand, he must have done some clandestine Laos sightseeing, because he disappeared for a few days. Then Khun P emailed us Barry's vacation photos. He's in a bamboo cage, haggard and scarred. Khun P wants a million bucks within ten days, or he'll bury Barry. 'Bury Barry.' Those were Khun P's words, not mine. That was two days ago."

"Brave bastard, this Khun P, takin' on Uncle Sam." Angel put both elbows on the table and rested his chin in his fists. "Khun P. You know what that means in Thai?"

"Khun means mister. P means ghost. Mister Ghost. We don't have a photo, only a thin file on him. We don't know much about his facility, but we know where it is. Another agent in Thailand who's been working on the case has local contacts in a nearby Hmong village. Khun P recruited villagers against their will, and they haven't come back home."

"If he moves to the USA," Angel joked, "Mr. P is not the best name to have. He'd be ridiculed to death."

"I'll let him know if I see him," Jonathan said, holding up his empty beer mug as their waiter whisked by.

"You can't see him because he's a ghost. Besides, I think you want me to meet him first. You want to send an angel into another lord's hell to steal from a ghost. Why don't you send in your DEA troops? The CIA or the Seals? Or my Marine kinfolk? If this is a 'minor' lord as you say, there shouldn't be a problem. Or pay off Mister Ghost. Isn't one life worth more than a million? I read on your website that you've got a three-billion dollar budget. That's 3,000 people at a million each."

Jonathan put up a finger as he made each of his points.

"Number One: The DEA is maxed out. Every team that could handle this is on assignment.

"Number Two: It doesn't look good for us to call in the competition to mop up our messes.

"Number Three: We don't pay ransom as a first resort.

"Number Four: Victoria's friend happens to be the vice-president of the US of A."

"Ouch," Angel said with a grimace.

"And behind door Number Five..." Jonathan raised up his thumb for the final point. "Barry Majors is the VP's nephew." Then gave it a thumbs down.

Angel's forehead hit the table with an audible thud. "Perfect. Pride and prejudice, politics and presidents, and takin' the piss outta P. Tell me, what is your Plan P that includes me?"

"Slip you in the back door to Laos from a mountain top in Thailand, you scope an extraction point, shoot us the coordinates, find Barry, create a diversion, get him out and to the point where a chopper will be waiting."

"How many soldiers in the Ghost army?"

"Not sure. Less than fifty, maybe."

"What the hell, Jonathan!" Angel locked eyes with him. "Not sure, less than, maybe? This doesn't sound like intelligence to me."

"We don't want you to fight them, just get Barry. There's a quote in your file, supposedly from you. You tell me if you really said it. 'I'm invisible, I can fly, and I save people.'"

"That's me—Angel Mouth. I'd put it on a business card, but it sounds too cheeky, like this menu here."

"You've already demonstrated your invisibility. The accounts in our file show you have rare methods of flying into remote areas undetected. You save people, and here's someone worth saving."

Angel got lively and deadly serious at the same time. "What do you know about Ghost Land?"

"Unfortunately, not much. Too many trees for the satellite photos to pin point specifics."

As he described Ghost Land, Jonathan built a map on the table with the bread sticks, napkins, silverware, Angel's baseball cap, and his beer mug for the water tower. "One road in, a water tower, a few large buildings, several small ones at the base of a ridge. We imagined you'll somehow fly within a couple miles through a wider valley to where it merges with the stream flowing through his compound. Our local contacts will stash supplies you'll locate with a GPS tracker once you're on the ground."

"I need to see the SAT photos and topo maps. And every other shred of info you have… before giving any answer." Angel punched the cubes in his root beer with a straw. "A Cat fight in my driveway is child's play compared to this. I'm considering a career change, but it won't help if my last job's a suicide mission."

Without a word, the waiter delivered their burgers and fries, which took up less room on the table than their descriptions on the menu.

"I thought we'd get a complimentary side of adjectives with our meal." Angel poked his burger with a fork. "Is yours nestled lovingly on your bun?"

"It looks slapped on to me. I don't think the cook read the menu."

The reality of the juicy medium-rare burger in front of him dragged Angel away from the half-baked facts about Ghost Land. "Are you sure Khun P said dollars? If he's in Laos, the currency is kip. The last time I was there, I exchanged $200 and became a kip millionaire. I blew 50,000 on lunch. Lonely Planet guidebook says, 'spend your kip before leaving Laos because it ain't worth Jack Shit anywhere else.' Those might not be their exact words. I couldn't even exchange it for baht in Thailand. They laughed at me when I tried at a bank."

"I've been there," Jonathan said between bites. "Kip is scratchier than toilet paper and worth less."

"What do you have in mind for a 'diversion'?"

"We threw around the idea of a GPS-guided missile or two. We're professionals, you know."

"Right. With a government full of so many Christian Right-to-take-the-life-of-whomever-we-deem-heathen, couldn't you get biblical with this? Swarms of locusts? A plague of boils? An army of evangelists sellin' the only good book door-to-door? No offence meant, just friendly frothing at the Angel Mouth."

"I don't trust the drones. You'll have to create something on your own."

"If you were even dreamin' of a missile, please cancel the concept, but add the cost of one or two to my paycheck." Angel filled his mouth with burger and pointed the rest of it at Jonathan. "I can see it now. If the missile doesn't fire, I'm up Shit Creek without a paddle. If it lands too far away and gives the Ghost a heads-up to something fishy, I'm up Shit Creek without a paddle or a canoe. If it lands on me, I'm angel vapor up above Shit Crater. If it lands on Barry, Mr. VP drags in Victoria, who has rewritten the classified file and washed her hands with blame remover."

Angel raised the pitch of his voice and put his hands on his hips like a spoiled rich bitch. "I'm sorry, Mr. Vice President, but some rogue DEA boys blew up your nephew and hundreds of innocent villagers. It's Deputy

Jonathan Skipper's fault. I never authorized the mission. I have his head on a platter in my purse."

Jonathan loosened his tie and shuddered. "I'll work on the locust angle."

Angel was full of himself and in command of his audience of one. "Now, if we were back in the President Clinton Erogenous Era, Victoria could have crawled on her knees into the Oval Office… naked. Wild Bill would've been glad to meet her halfway, under his desk. Once again, no offense meant, but please turn off the recorder in that DEA pin on your lapel. You're not in the Hillary Lunch Bunch crowd, are you? If so, could you ask her to help me? Have her give a speech in that valley I'll be flyin' through. Hot air rises."

Jonathan raised his beer mug. "Root beer going to your head, Angel? Since I've had three Millers and you've had two roots, I'm guessing you're either too tired, or don't drink alcohol."

"Allergic to it, I think. Break out in hives, feel nauseous, have to lie down. Superman and Kryptonite. I'd love to be able to drink like a normal person, but my body says no."

"You're not normal, and you're not missing much, except a beer belly." Jonathan patted his affectionately. "In the words of the philosopher Homer, 'Beer, the cause of, and solution to, all of life's problems.'" He drained his mug in one gulp.

"Did Homer suck down a few brews on his

Odyssey?"

"Not that Homer. My son's hero, Homer Simpson."

"Great reverse role model. Speakin' of heroes, Mister Deputy, I know I'm here to be checked out for that category. Half of me still wants to fail your test. But I'm also checkin' you out since this job is a matter of life or death—mine. So… would you mind takin' the short, but incisive, PBNJ Personality Evaluation?"

"Sure. I've never heard of it."

"It's very local. From my own personal zip code. Six quick questions."

"Fire away."

Angel laid out six fries on his saucer. He picked up one. "First question. You know what PBNJ stands for?"

"Anything other than peanut butter and jelly?"

"Excellent. First question correct." Angel dipped his fry in the ketchup and ate it. "That wasn't hard was it?"

"No."

"Second question correct!" He dipped another fry and handed it to Jonathan. "You're doing very well. Third question. You like peanut butter?"

"Love it."

"Splendid. You're on a roll. PB's good on a roll. Might even work on a fry." Angel looked at the third fry and then popped it into his mouth. "Fourth question. Do you spread your peanut butter to the edges of the bread?"

"Mandatory." Jonathan took the fourth fry and chomped it confidently.

Angel pointed at Jonathan with fry number five. "I am tickled. We're almost done. Fifth question. Do you pay special attention to spread PB into each of the four corners?"

"Of course."

"Beautiful," Angel said as fry five disappeared. "The sixth and final question. Do you execute the same precise techniques with the jelly?"

"Stupid question. There is no other option."

"Deputy, my man, few people have passed this examination so impressively. Let us break fry together." Angel tore apart the last fry and gave half to Jonathan.

"So you won't work with people who don't like peanut butter?"

"Plain butter is boring, but if their spreading is thorough, I will consider them. My probing test reveals personality traits regarding planning, procedures, and follow-through. When I see someone slap a knife full o' PB on a piece of toast, leavin' wide expanses of emptiness, I just want to snatch it out of their hand and smack 'em upside the head."

"Do you have any children, Mr. Phoenix?"

"Not yet."

Jonathan clasped his hands and looked heavenward. "Thank God."

"If I do, I'll respect their choice, but I wouldn't take 'em on a mission."

"You mind if I use your PBNJ Personality Evaluation with new recruits?"

Angel bowed his head. "I'd be honored. All royalties are waived."

"How's your dinner? You want some dessert?" Jonathan wanted to make sure he took care of every one of his potential savior's wishes.

"No room for dessert. The burger was bangin' and I'm particular about a burger. Everything here was splendiferous like their menu claimed. If we'd read the whole thing, I'm sure we'd have found that word. You still hungry?"

"Nope." Jonathan put one hand up to his chin and lowered the other into his lap. "I am full up to here and my stomach ends down here."

"If you don't mind, I'd love to drift into Angeland, sooner than later, back at the hotel."

"Don't you mean back to Shannon?"

"I tole you I was plannin' for the future, Dep'ty," Angel griped, slipping into heavy Southern. "Raht now my future holds a thinkin' cap, a nightcap, and a meetin' tomorrow with Capt'n Victoria."

Jonathan called for the check with the universal sign of writing on invisible paper with an air pen.

Angel whispered, "So what's Captain Victoria like... off the record?"

"She's a good, strong, devoted woman. She was in the field and survived. I'm glad to work with her, but I wouldn't want her job. She's a 'secetary' like you said, and the president at the same time. A desk and phone slave to politicians, the public, and humanity in general."

"Your website says she's responsible for 10,000 employees in the U.S. and sixty-seven countries. That's a lot of humanity. I wouldn't want her job either. I am not presidential material. If I were elected—President Fat Chance—I'd be the first one to assassinate himself."

Jonathan took a deep breath and then finished his beer. "Victoria only wants this situation to go away yesterday."

"Well, I look forward to meetin' her," Angel said sincerely, "but I'd like to see all your info before our rendezvous with the Big Cheesoria. Besides findin' out who the hell Angel is, she probably wants to hear a yes or no."

"You got it." Jonathan took the bill from the waiter and gave him a fifty as they stood up to leave.

"I'm assuming you're the leader of the gang on the playground, bein' the 'chief operating officer of the DEA, overseeing all enforcement, intelligence, and regulatory operations', and any angels summoned for assistance."

"You did your research," Jonathan said as they strolled toward the exit.

"I need to know the lay of the land and where the players live on it. But I think it boils down to this—we need to get a note from mother before we can go out and play."

"You're right, but don't call her mother to her face."

"Wouldn't think of it!" Angel threw up his hands. "How about Mom?"

"No."

"Ma? Mama?"

"No derivative of the M-word whatsoever."

Angel pleaded with arms out and palms up. "Not even Mumsy?"

Jonathan turned to confront him. "Do I have to surround you with a SWAT team during the meeting?"

"Cool. For a demonstration of my eccentric abilities?" Angel karate-chopped a potted plant near the door. "Right in her office? Are the walls titanium?"

"Actually," Jonathan confided, worried, and joked all at once, "I only wanted to meet you to get some referrals. Do you know anyone who can help us?"

RED
Six-faced

Danny Admiral, Red's father, grew up on the gritty streets of London, then served in the Royal Air Force where he fought no one during the Cold War in Europe, and later in Indonesia, no one else. Retired at twenty-three, he scraped together enough money to buy one second-hand Tiger Moth biplane and began cropdusting in England.

Red's mother, Chandra Desai, the daughter of a well-to-do Indian family, went abroad to England at age eighteen to study law, to escape from her parents' yoke, and to experience the wild western world.

Danny and Chandra met at an early Beatles concert in the Grosvenor House Hotel in London. She bought her ticket; he snuck in through the kitchen. She was dark, dazzling, and exotic; he was white, dashing, and deviant. It was genital love at first sight. Soon after, they married for divergent ulterior motives. His—she was rich and he wasn't; she'd become a lawyer and he'd probably need one. Hers—their union was guaranteed to piss off her parents.

They had fun in the beginning, but then the wedding ceremony ended. They drifted apart, imperceptibly, like continents. Baby Danielle Chandra Admiral, who evolved into adolescent Red, was the only glue that kept them stuck with each other for the next decade.

Danny worked in the air over dusty fields. Chandra worked on the ground in opulent offices. Her upper crusty friends treated him like a hired hand; his down-and-out friends were Chandra's clients at the legal aid clinic where she volunteered on weekends. Red learned things in private schools she didn't care about, and Danny supplemented both of their educations on the streets.

One day Chandra haughtily announced that she was returning to India with Danielle—whom she never called Red: "to rediscover my roots which have been rotting here in England." Chandra and Red sailed first class on a luxury ocean liner.

Since the law was after him and his lawyer was leaving, Danny followed.

He flew his Tiger Moth with a maximum range of only 300 miles, dusting and lusting and fertilizing tender sprouts with his own innate seeds in sundry countries as he hopped his way to India.

Red grew up as a battlefield in the middle of a war between England and India waged by her parents. It was impossible to please them both—she wasn't quite British enough for her father and never Indian enough for her mother. Though her parents ceased living and fighting under the same roof, they never divorced because of Chandra's aversion to societal shame, and their wedlock never stopped Danny from two-, three- or four-timing.

At age twenty-two, Red married her father, in the form of a handsome Brit illegitimately cast from the same mold, but it soon became clear that he only cared to colonize her. He didn't really want her, only what she had, plus everything she could get from anyone else.

A passionate American swept Red off her feet a few years later, for a few years, then stepped daintily out of the groom closet and admitted, "I'm sorry. I love you, but I'm gay."

For her third matrimonial mismatch, she married her mother in the form of a semi-wealthy Indian man, semi-arranged by Chandra and her parents in an attempt to salvage the reputation of their half-breed, twice-divorced, over-the-hill failure at the age of thirty-one. After three months of suffering under the fossilized cultural yoke of Mistake Number Three, Red realized that the women's liberation movement had slipped by him unnoticed, and perhaps bypassed all of India as well. At the end of one absurd year, she flipped a rupee to choose her options—lion heads, kill him, or corn sheave tails, leave him. She had to toss the coin seven times before corn sheaves saved his life.

Her entire Indian family, including every deceased ancestor from the past 5,000 years, promptly disowned her, which suited Red fine. She didn't like being owned, anyway.

These days Red felt alone, a lone dark foreigner lighter than the indigenous millions. Although her parents were both gone, their bullheaded spirits continued jockeying to bend her will to one side or the other. She'd always leaned toward Danny, and eventually built her fortress in his camp. Her mother had deliberately deserted her years before, and though her father had disappeared, she knew he hadn't left her by choice.

And today she sat alone at her father's old desk, wondering what the hell might be lurking around the next corner of her life. She'd gotten the bank loan, although she had to twist it out of Mr. Verma, whom she called Vermin, the same species as Baldev Gupta. A loan was a respectable way to sink their teeth into their victim's future.

Azeez knocked on the office door and poked his head in. "Miss Red? Are you presentable and free to be talking?"

"Come in, come in," Red said impatiently.

"I have gathered the informations you are wanting about Aero Dynamic Enterprises."

Recalling the macabre episode with Bug, she suggested they go for a walk. Once outside and away from the hangar, she confided in Azeez. "That sinister visitor I had might have concealed microphones inside the condo. He knew things that seemed impossible to know. Bug. That was his name. He works for Baldev Gupta and who knows what other vermin."

"That is a very truly odd name, is it not, Miss Red? And Mr. Gupta is a powerful man most definitely. I am hoping you do not make him angry."

"I owe him money, and I'll pay him back soon. You and I will only talk about these matters outdoors or on our new cellphones. Is that clear?"

"Yes, Miss Red, most certainly clear."

"Now what did you learn about Aero?"

"It is a very successfully prosperous business for the owner, Mr. Murakan Patil. He is thirty-nine and his money can buy whatever he is wanting."

"Ah, I do remember him. We didn't speak at the auction, but his crooked leer said it all. What kind of 'very successfully prosperous business' is this Murakan involved in?" Red liked the unschooled way Azeez formed his sentences and had never tried to teach him otherwise.

"His business is like his name. In Hindi, Murakan is meaning 'six-faced', but I am thinking he has many more than six. His customers have much money like him. They are parking their airplanes in his hangars and sometimes he is fixing them. They are chartering his airplanes. His pilots are flying people to other places or carrying their packages and luggages. Now Aero is crop dusting like Red Admiral Aerial Application with our old Cresco and two more shiny new airplanes."

Red and Azeez walked past the main hangar that held her—and the bank's—two newish but rapidly aging dusters that normally would have been in the sky over her clients' fields, and then they continued their stroll on the runway.

"Do you know how many people this Murakan employs?"

"A very many people. Pilots and mechanics and large guards and young women who are helping. He is like the ruler of everybody and everybody calls him Shri P."

Red stopped dead as that name triggered another one from her dreams.

Shri P? Hmm. Like Khun P, the drug lord in Laos that Angel was gunning for.

"Tell me, Azeez," she asked, already guessing the answer but not expecting to get it, "what are in the 'packages and luggages' that Murakan's airplanes carry to other places?"

"I most certainly am not knowing!"

He sounded offended, but she couldn't understand why. Perhaps because he, too, assumed it was contraband and didn't want any part of it, not even the asking about it. Whatever Red decided to do about the situation, she now knew she couldn't ask him to help or bring him into her confidence. She sensed his fear of Baldev Gupta, and it appeared to overlap onto Murakan… Mister P. *How does Azeez know everybody calls him Shri P?*

"Where did you learn all this? You haven't gone over there, have you?"

"No, no, I would never be doing that ever!" Azeez gestured with his hands, waving them toward the ground as if trying to make the dog Kamal stay in one place. "Much informations is found on the computer, on the internet. And I am asking people on my new cell phone like Miss Red requested very specifically."

"All right then. Is there anything else I should know?"

He spoke rapidly with his head down. "I will most assuredly be telling you when I am knowing it. Right now I am worrying about you and your diseases and your business which is in a faltering place and this very ungood Bug person and vicious Mr. P and owing money to Mr. Baldev Gupta is most absolutely dangerous and—"

She interrupted him by putting her hand on his shoulder. "Azeez."

Like a small child, he looked up into her eyes.

"It's going to be okay, Azeez. We'll get through this. Please, you have to trust me."

He looked down again. "Yes, Miss Red, I am trusting you. I am sorry I do not have more informations."

"You did fine. Thank you. That'll be all for now. Remember, tomorrow you must take me to get my weekly drug fix. At half-past twelve, I think."

"Yes, Miss Red."

Red watched him plod to the gatehouse, his arms drooping at his side, so unlike the normal, perky, upright Azeez.

She walked over to the Tiger Moth parked in the hangar, looked ardently up at the cockpit, and then spied her father's leather pilot helmet and goggles hanging on the wall, leftovers from his air force days and flight to India in the '60s. She took them off their pegs and put them on over the unauthentic, un-Red, red wig she'd purchased in the market. She stepped up onto the lower wing and opened the creaking door. Her old buddies, the round, black-and-white gauges on the dash, stared inertly up at her.

You old chaps must be bored stiff. We'll fly soon, but I want to feel you now.

Red went to the front of the plane, swung the prop back and forth to draw fuel into its cylinders, then reached over the lower wing to flip the magneto switches. She set the prop vertical, gave it the big heave-ho with her hands, and the Tiger sputtered to life. She climbed into the cockpit and closed her eyes, reveling in the exquisite vibration that soothed every cell to its core.

In an impromptu general democratic election, the vast majority of Red's individual body cells voted for immediate takeoff, damn the torpor, full speed upward. Unfortunately for the trillion cells in her heart, her bossy brain vetoed the nearly unanimous motion and tabled it to standing committees for further study.

In one chamber, the What in Bloody Hell Is Happening Here Committee, chaired by Reasonable Red, sat scratching its bald heads, perusing a slim file of facts and a swollen file of speculations, trying to determine the relationships between Azeez' worries: diseases, the business in a faltering place, the very ungood Bug, the vicious Shri P, and the absolutely dangerous Baldev Gupta, etcetera.

In another chamber, the What in Bloody Hell Should I Do Committee—chaired by Narcotic Red, composed of the invisible chemotherapy drug Lords of Depression, Mood Swings, Memory Loss, and Judgement Problems—sat silently but diligently working overtime.

In a third chamber, beyond the third dimension whose lively existence her brain denied, the Karma Committee—chaired equally by all members, composed of the zillions of decomposing bugs, birds, and beings Red had gassed intentionally or unintentionally—sat turning her Wheel of Fate faster and faster.

In the mundane control chamber sat the What Would Danny Admiral Do Committee, with Rambunctious Red as chairwoman and sole member. The action to be undertaken depended on the answers to the question, "Why would the successful and wealthy owner of Aero Dynamic Enterprise start a dirty, noxious sideline of crop dusting meant for the lower class when the rest of his business catered to hygienic high society?" This committee of one, approaching orgasm from the vibration of the duster's seat, envisaged Bruce Gandhi in the mirror, mirror on the wall of her memories until the explanations appeared.

He's greedy and despicable. He wants my business and my land. He was spawned in bloody hell.

The action required became apparent. Since six-faced Murakan's covert company slogan seemed to be "Eliminate the Competition," she would see his bet and raise it with Danny's golden rule: "Do unto others before they do unto you."

Unable to call upon the masses like Gandhi, she alone had been called upon to be Bruce, star of the movies *Diehard* and *Red*, to conquer evil with a small band of comrades. Red now had a goal in mind—blind to the fact that she was out of her mind—and a nefarious plan began clawing its way to the surface.

MONA
Itch with a B

On her mission to find out whether she was losing it, Mona arrived at the clinic at nine in the morning, finished by ten, and phoned Sasha.

"Sasha Goldberg here, the world's oldest—"

"It's me. I'm done. Can I come over to your condo now?"

"Hmm… if you promise never to paint a picture of me in this condition. If children saw it, they'd have nightmares. My face is lying on my vanity in jars, powder tins, and eyeliners. My teeth are glaring up at me from a glass."

"I promise. I'll pick up a couple of cappuccinos and a bag of decadent pastries on the way. You can wear the bag over your head."

Thirty minutes later they sat across two coffees and a stack of Danish rolls on the white rattan table on Sasha's redwood patio overlooking sculptured gardens. Scattered around the azure swimming pool, several burnt sienna snowbirds baked in the sun like self-basting turkeys, stuck to their plastic lounge chairs. Smoke appeared to be rising from a few of the bodies. Sasha had managed to reassemble her face, but one surprised eyebrow was longer than the other and slanted diagonally upwards.

"Well, that was quick." Sasha peered over the rim of her cup. "Do they perform express exams with magic machines at our clinic these days?"

"I asked for a complete physical," Mona said, "but the receptionist said they had no openings for a month. I must admit I got a little snippy and said, 'Splendid. By then I might have to be carted in for an autopsy.'"

"Good one, girl."

They toasted with cappuccinos and clunked paper cups.

"She was kind enough to squeeze me in to at least talk with a doctor. The nurses then determined that I was breathing, my heart was beating, and that I'd gained weight and lost height. I meditated for a half hour on grim photos of diseases posted on the office wall until the doctor walked in. I was astonished how young he was! I wanted to ask him if he'd send in his mom or dad."

Sasha shook her head in amazement. "Must be the same one I saw last week. His entire personal experience of aging from egg to today looked to be about fourteen years."

"I told him about my episodes and worries, but soon realized I've probably forgotten more about Alzheimer's than he'd ever learned. He said I should see a specialist, of course, then handed me a brochure and gave me a web address for more information. Criminently, forty dollars for ten minutes, a brochure, and an address!"

"I know what you mean, but what does 'criminently' mean, anyway?" Sasha asked.

"Mama used to say it. I think it means… I don't know… criminently. If she ever said an actual swear word, she was sure lightning would strike her. When she got angry, she'd yell, 'Itch with a B!'"

They both chuckled. Whenever something disturbing happened to Mona, Sasha had the power to flip it over and make it fun, without really doing anything. Unlike others, she listened, responded, and stayed on track. Most people, especially older folks, would ask, "How are you feeling?" Then after a two-word answer—"Fine, thanks"—they'd be off and running at the mouth. "Well, my gallbladder is the size of a basketball and my daughter's goiter is having a child of its own and…" on and on and on, ad nauseum.

"This did make me feel better." Mona flopped the brochure on the table in front of Sasha. "It talks about seven major Alzheimer's symptoms and compares them with normal age-related changes. Even though they don't know much about it, Alzheimer's is a serious, stand-alone, deadly disease, but aging is just… well… aging."

"Let's see what it says here." Sasha donned her thick specs, opened it up, and started reading out loud. "'Number One. Memory loss that disrupts daily life, especially forgetting important dates or events, needing to rely on memory aids, asking the same thing over and over again…' Hmm…" Sasha gave Mona a puzzled look. "What did you say criminently meant again?"

"Criminently."

"What did you say it meant?"

"Criminently…" Then Mona got it and threatened Sasha with a half-eaten Danish roll. "Stop it!"

Sasha shook her head. "I'm gone, Mona, definitely gone. Luckily, I have you for a memory aid. Okay…" She read on. "'What's a typical age-related change? Sometimes forgetting names or appointments, but remembering them later.'"

"See? That's us!" Mona feigned optimism as the doubt crept back in. "We forget, we remember… well, maybe not for a few weeks…"

"Did you say you were coming over today? When will you arrive? Did you say your name is Criminently?"

"Stop it, Sashaheimer's. What's Number Two?"

"'Challenges in planning or problem-solving. People with Alzheimer's may have difficulty following a plan or working with numbers, such as keeping track of monthly bills.'"

"Then I was born with Alzheimer's," Mona surmised. "Math was my worst subject."

"Do you make occasional errors when balancing a checkbook?" Sasha asked, her eyes on the brochure.

"Yes, and the whole process is a pain in the assets."

"Me, too, and I run a successful business, for God's sake. We're still in the category of typical age-related change, and right now, this old body needs a change of location. Let's go inside. It's cooler in there."

Sasha's living room had a stark, Zen look with cushioned industrial furniture and futuristic lamps, not the decor anyone might imagine in an eighty-five-year-old widow's home. One wall was carrot orange, another ultramarine blue, the rest alabaster white, a color scheme that never would have entered Mona's artistic brain. Somehow it worked exquisitely.

On the wall behind the steel dining table hung the largest work Mona had ever painted: an extreme close-up of a red-orange monarch butterfly perched on the luminescent red, orange, and yellow bloom of a Mexican milkweed plant with the deep blue Rio Grande River curling into the distance. The butterfly itself measured five feet across. Near Mission, the Rio Grande was more dirty brown than deep blue, but in Sasha's commissioned artwork, it was ultramarine to match her wall.

Although her furniture was metal and Plexiglas, the odor of Lemon Pledge wood polish perpetually permeated her condo. Mona thought Sasha might have misread the label and used it as an air freshener spray, but never dared mention it.

Once ensconced in two chairs that looked painful but comfortably cradled buns, Sasha continued their personal assessment. "All right, then. Number Three. 'New problems with words while speaking or writing. People with Alzheimer's may stop in the middle of a conversation and have no idea how to continue.'" She paused and gazed at the brochure for a few seconds... then for a lot of seconds... waiting.

"Stop it!" Mona poked her in the side. "Stop stopping!"

Sasha grinned dementedly, her cheek wrinkles rising like porcupine quills around her mouth, then read on. "'They may not use the right word, or refer to things by the wrong name, like calling a watch a hand-clock.'" She glanced over the rim of her glasses. "I love the name hand-clock. I'm going to start using it."

"If I have a problem," Mona said, "it's not using the wrong word. It's blabbering too many of 'em."

Sasha read on silently before mumbling. "Uh oh."

"What? What is it?"

"We're definitely guilty as charged in Number Four. 'Confusion with time or place. People with Alzheimer's lose track of dates, places, and the passage of time. They may forget where they are going, where they are, or how they got there.'" Sasha looked up at Mona while pointing at the brochure in her lap. "Each of these symptoms has a picture by it. There's a photo of us next to Number Four."

Mona let out a snort posing as a laugh, then tried to stop grinning and look funereal. "What does it say about regular aging? Any hope for us?"

Sasha brightened as she read. "'A typical age-related change? Getting confused about the day of the week but figuring it out later.' We're good to go. Number Five here covers trouble with visual images and eyesight. Ha, we're artists. Do you have any problems, as it says here, 'determining color or contrast'?"

"Not at all, but does it include seeing incidents that couldn't have happened?"

"That's your internal ethereal sight. I can only draw what I'm looking at, but you, Miss Mona Amazing, can paint what you see as well as 'visual images' from another universe. It's a gift, not a symptom. Number Six is 'difficulty completing familiar tasks at home or at work.' You take care of your little estate and Yves next door, and me too, for heaven's sake. You may have A.D.D. but not Alzheimer's. Number Seven though, we have to talk about."

"What's Number Seven?" Mona raised her eyebrows and her upper body followed. "I didn't get that far."

Sasha read slowly. "'The moods and personalities of people with Alzheimer's can change. They can become confused, suspicious, depressed, fearful, or anxious.'" She paused, took off her glasses, and with sweet compassion gazed into Mona's eyes. "Look at yourself, honey. Anxious, confused, suspicious of yourself." Sasha sighed a warm sigh. "It's not Alzheimer's. It's fear. And what you fear is not here. I know this because I've been there and fear has done that to me. One day we both may have Alzheimer's, but not today. Maybe it's creeping in, but we're bounding along ahead of it through whatever is left of this life. Aging is a… let me quote your mama now, an 'itch with a B.' And to be more specific, without any difficulty choosing the right word, it's a fucking bitch. It's no surprise to me how you feel, and I'd say it's absolutely normal… well… as close to normal as you or I will ever be."

Mona couldn't speak because the tears welling up in her eyes were also dribbling down her throat.

Sasha handed her a napkin, leaned in, and spoke quietly. "It's all right, honey. Today, let the fear flow away in your tears. And tomorrow, you'll start chanting a new mantra. It's ancient, from a recently discovered stone tablet written in Hebrew. Quite simple. Easy to remember." Another pause. "Now say it after me… Fuck fear."

"Fu…" Mona's soft sobs flipped over into a dainty guffaw as she bawled Sasha's mantra. "Fuck fear!" Her tears melded with her spittle and squirted onto Sasha's shoulder. "I'm sorry," Mona squeaked, dabbing her napkin on Sasha's blouse, then blurted out, "I don't know if I'm laughing or crying!"

"Do 'em both," Sasha said. "You need each one." She brought over tissues and a glass of spring water. "Here, honey. Dry your tears and replace them with some water."

"It feels like a bubble burst inside of me. You're right, Sasha. Fear of something that's not even here. I try to forget about fear, but it seems to have a mind of its own."

"I think there's one more fear lurking in there. Number Seven Point Five. You're a caregiver, always have been, always will be. Maybe you're afraid other people will have to take care of you, because that's not normal for you. But think about this. Remember how good you feel when you take care of someone else? Let that feeling sit in your heart for a spell. If you have the right people in your life, that's exactly how they'll feel when they take care of you. When you give a caregiver the chance to give, it's a gift to them. Like me, for instance. I didn't do much, but I tended to you today and now I even feel better. When the time comes that you need help, let it happen."

"You're right again," Mona said with a shudder. "The thought of being helpless is terrifying."

"I agree with you. But unless you're hit by a truck or blown to bits by a bomb, you're going to need some help along the way."

"Nice thoughts. Have any other cheery ones?"

"I prefer to exit quickly. Take me when I'm happy. Let joy be the last moments of this life, so I can carry them onto the next." Sasha checked her watch. "Now I'm sorry, ma'am, but your appointment is over. I've got to help someone find a home. Let's see, two and a half hours at forty dollars per ten minutes. At standard clinic rates, you owe me six hundred dollars."

"Can I pay you with paintings?" Mona asked.

"Sure, paint me a realistic, life-size, $600 bill."

"I can do that. You mind writing out my prescription mantra for me?"

"If you can't remember that, girl, we should review the list of Alzheimer's symptoms again. Now let's see what you're going to forget to take with you."

They gathered up Mona's things, and Sasha escorted her to the door.

"Thanks so much, Dr. Goldberg. I feel much better. Inspired inside. Ready to head home and finish a piece for that gallery show next week."

"Good luck, sweetheart. And here's my final diagnosis." Sasha pulled Mona in for a tight hug and whispered in her ear. "Neither you nor I have All-Zheimer's. Just Half-Zheimer's."

TIGER

Death and Rebirth

During the night Tiger flew around his neighborhood, all over the school, and to faraway places he'd never been—not as a butterfly, as Tiger.

He concentrated on lightness and slowly lifted himself off the ground, then just stood there, upright and airborne, grinning, no flapping required. He put his head down and dove, soared under power lines, then rose above elm trees. Traveling faster than retinas could catch, he swooped through the school's front entrance and over students' heads in the hallways. Some kids felt a passing breeze. If anyone saw a shadow go by—or thought they saw and dared not admit it—no one recognized him. It was the closest he'd ever gotten to whatever the word ecstasy meant. He flew out of the school, across the great plains, over the ocean, over pyramids, over rainforests.

A strange sound in the room stirred him from his dream. Tiger woke, already exhausted but elated.

Thank God, it's Saturday.

As the images and feelings of flying faded, he heard a soft buzzing across the room. Something vibrating.

What is it? A mouse chewing?

Slipping out of bed, Tiger followed the noise to his table. Impaled through the back with a long, thin pin stuck into a Styrofoam board, a white-lined sphinx moth frantically flapped its wings. People often mistook them for hummingbirds since they're about the same size and hover above flowers, motionless in the air, sucking nectar from the blooms. This one's wings were a blur of terror.

"OMG!" Most of Tiger's internal organs dropped into his ankles, leaving his heart to beat alone in a hollow cavity. After he'd taken Gem home the night before, he'd mounted the specimens left in his killing jar. One had come back from the dead, or never quite made it there. Tiger could almost feel a sabre-sized pin in his own back, skewered through his heart.

He gently pressed two fingers on its wings and pulled out the pin. The sphinx moth rose, faltered, and careened into the wall with an audible thunk. It fell to the floor, flailing and bouncing, trying to catch the air. Gruesome memories pounded into Tiger.

It was like the dove trapped in their living room, slamming into the walls and the picture window, its beak clicking on the glass. Or Mrs. McIntyre's chicken running around the farmyard with its head cut off, spurting blood like a fountain.

It's hopeless. What can I do?

The answer came in his next memory—the night a deer ran out of the woods and smashed into their car on the highway. Tiger had watched his dad through the rearview mirror, his arm rising and falling with the car jack in his hand, terminating the jerking doe's suffering.

Tiger opened his ethyl acetate bottle and splashed fresh killing fluid onto a washcloth. Cupping a hand around the sphinx, he lifted it off the floor and wrapped it in the cloth. He knew butterflies and moths didn't have noses. They sensed smells with their antenna but took in air through tubes on the sides of their abdomen. After too many excruciating seconds, its death throes were done.

Tiger crumpled into his chair, experiencing whatever the words wretched and miserable and despicable meant, from the inside out. No tears came. He felt dry. Brittle. Shattered. His wondrous flying dream the night before,as Morpho had ended in a cruel nightmare. This flying dream ended in brutal reality.

I'm sorry. I'm sorry. I'm sorry, Sphinx...

He buried his throbbing head in his damp hands.

For giving him a slow death instead of a fast one?

Two voiceless voices murmured in his head.

Forgive me. I knew not what I was doing.

Now you do, and it's done. Your insect collection is finished. He is the last victim. Honor him.

In the bathroom, Tiger found white cotton batting in the medicine drawer. He folded the moth into it and tied an orange ribbon around the soft shroud. He went out back and buried it between the exposed roots of the box elder tree, where the moth's worm cousins could be nourished by its remains. A present for the Earth to honor the sphinx who had passed.

Honor the sphinx with a song, Tiger said to himself, or heard his soul speaking.

He sat in his decaying sandbox next to the tree, rewinding his life and playing it back. Years ago, he'd set up battlefields here, armies of plastic soldiers, planes and tanks, then blown them up with firecrackers.

Tiger remembered the sphinx moths that had delighted him since he was a tot. He'd always loved them, with their black-white-and-cream-colored, pointed upper wings above the rose-pink swath on the underwings. In his recent dream, he'd hovered just like they did.

White-lined makes sense, but why the name sphinx?

Tiger had the itch to write something, but he didn't know what. He went up to his room and surfed the web to learn more. He looked up "sphynx" and only found sphynx cats. Big-eared and hairless, they looked more like shaved rats. He realized he'd spelled "sphinx" wrong.

Finally landing on an appropriate page, he read what the web said: "In Greek tradition, the sphinx has the haunches of a lion, the wings of a great bird, and the face of a woman."

Okay, it's a she. Hmm. A lion, and that's close to Tiger.

"The Egyptian sphinx is typically shown as a man."

Okay, fine. It's both.

"In the Greek version, she's treacherous and merciless."

"The Egyptian sphinx was viewed as benevolent."

Okay, good and bad again. Depends on who you ask.

For some reason, the Greek version drew him in. "Then god Ares sent the sphinx to guard the city of Thebes…"

Sounds familiar. Gem and Air are both Aries.

"…where she asked every passerby the most famous riddle in history: 'Which creature has one voice and yet becomes four-footed and two-footed and three-footed?' She strangled and devoured anyone unable to answer."

I don't know. That sphinx would have killed me.

"Oedipus solved the riddle: 'Man—who crawls on all fours as a baby, walks on two feet as an adult, and then he uses a walking stick in old age.' Bested, the sphinx devoured herself."

Drama queen. Seems like banging her head on the wall would have been enough. Oedipus. Smart guy. Who's he?

Tiger felt better. His mind and heart wandered along a new path in search of a song. He surfed further.

"Oedipus represents two enduring themes of Greek myth and drama: the flawed nature of humanity and an individual's powerlessness against the course of destiny in a harsh universe."

Okay, that's me and my sphinx today.

As Tiger read more about Oedipus and the gods, he began to understand the phrase, "It's Greek to me."

A voice inside spoke again. *Don't write history. Write your story. It's not about the sphinx. It's for the sphinx.*

Tiger sat silently and let it evolve. He picked up his guitar, and it picked him up. It took hours, but the words came, and the music followed. It had taken years… for Tiger the caterpillar to develop, his cocoon to break open, and his wings to sprout. One metamorphosis was complete.

Take the time to dream
Picture where you'll go
Think of who you'll be
It starts before you know
Get out of the way
Put your pride aside
Focus on today
Find your guide inside

Look the lion in the eye
Take hold of the tiger by the tail
Go for a joy ride
Look the lion in the eye
Who cares if you fail?
At least you tried

You're afraid to fail.
So you never start
You never make the sale
You never get the part
As the saying goes
Be an old has-been
Not a never-was
You'll feel better when you…

Look the lion in the eye
Take hold of the tiger by the tail
Go for a joyride
Look the lion in the eye
Who cares if you fail?
At least you tried

ANGEL
Impossible Dreams

On the way to the Hilton, Jonathan tuned the Explorer's radio to an oldies-but-goldies station. Synchronicity reared her universal head, and out of her mouth came "The Impossible Dream" blared by singer Jim Nabors—Gomer Pyle from the TV town of Mayberry. Angel thought Mayberry and Pokeberry Ridge were pretty much twin towns. He never liked Gomer's operatic style with a southern twang, but he loved the song.

Jonathan negotiated the Friday night traffic as Angel rested his head on the side window and drifted back to The Ridge, where heavy traffic meant meeting two dogs and a pickup truck while driving into town.

"This song is like the DEA's war on drugs," Jonathan said. "It's impossible, but someone's got to do it. It's like trying to get rid of termites. I read that a typical colony has a million mites. And in one acre, there are forty more colonies. You burn one drug lord and ten sprout from the ashes. You can swat them, stomp on them, and gas them, but the only way to get rid of them is to die and leave them behind."

Angel turned and put his hand on Jonathan's shoulder. "All you can do is try, man."

"It reminds me of a recurring nightmare I had as a kid. I was in an endless forest. For some reason, I had to label every tree by tying a red ribbon around each trunk. I'd start, but knew I could never finish. I didn't know what it meant, or even considered that it meant anything. But now I think it was a harbinger of what my life has become. My task is to end a war on drugs and I can't do it."

"You're right. It's kinda like this song. You ever heard Luther Vandross do it?"

"I don't know… maybe."

"You need to." Angel pointed at the radio on the dashboard. "This Jim Nabors sings the words, but Luther breathes life into them. 'To fight the unbeatable foe, to run where the brave dare not go.'"

Then Jim took over with the last verse.

And the world will be better for this
That one man, scorned and covered with scars
Still strove with his last ounce of courage
To reach the unreachable star

Angel leaned back in his seat until the last note faded away. "I call this song 'The I'm Possible Dream.' Adds a little hope to the task."

"I may not win," Jonathan sighed, "but I'll keep trying. I hope you'll be on my team."

"I'm already on your team, bud. Tomorrow I'll figure out if I'm fit to play in this game."

It was only seven thirty p.m., but it felt like a hundred-and-seven thirty. Both men needed to crawl back into their caves and squat alone by the fire.

Jonathan stopped the Explorer in front of the Hilton and apologized in advance. "I'm not going to sneak up the backstairs. Can you handle Shannon by yourself?"

"Will you forget about Shannon already?" Ángel insisted. "She'll have to handle herself tonight. What time should I be at the DEA stronghold?"

"How about nine a.m.? I'll have the files ready for you. Can I send someone to pick you up?"

"Thanks, but I'll get there on my own. Maybe take a swim and sauna. Find some scrambled eggs and a sweet cup o' java. Life is too short for bitter coffee, boring soap, and bad eggs. The simple things gotta be good."

"Okay. I'm sure you're sick of me saying this, but thanks for coming. You've had one heck of a day, maybe thirty of them in a row."

"I try to look at life as one day in a row, Deputy. You made this one a good one."

Jonathan stretched out his arm for a handshake, the social substitute for the hug some guys can't ever give. "In the immortal words of Dirty Harry, I hope tomorrow you 'make my day.'"

Angel took his hand and gave it a firm shake. "I'll do my best." He opened the truck door, started to get out, but spun back to Jonathan. "One more extra credit question in the Personality Evaluation. If you're on an escalator or a movin' walkway at the airport, do you stop and ride, or do you keep walkin'?"

"I keep walking," Jonathan said. "Good exercise, and it gets me where I'm going faster."

"Me, too. You scored an A-plus. Thanks for the dinner and the ride. And thanks for puttin' me up… or should I say, thanks for puttin' up with me?"

"Both. See you at nine."

"Sleep well or else." Angel shut the door and headed toward the hotel.

He nodded politely to Shannon as he passed the desk, punched the ninth-floor button, and waited for the elevator—alone as usual. The doors slid open, Angel stepped in, and the doors closed behind him. He was surrounded by himself in a minuscule funhouse of mirrors on every wall. Whichever direction he faced, an infinite number of Angels stared back. He thought of Morpho in the swarm of blue morpho butterflies from his dream and flapped his arms. Then he pictured Morpho and his mate coupled in the rain under the umbrella leaves.

Will I ever find my mate out there, somewhere over the rainforest?

Angel believed in the dream. Sometime, somewhere, it was real. In the jungle, maybe, but not in this concrete one.

Tiger found his Gem, and he wasn't even looking. It'll happen when it happens. Ask for it, let it go, and it will come.

He stuck his plastic key card in the slot four different ways before the green light glowed above the knob. All rooms seemed the same except for different cards at the H-word hotels—Hilton, Hyatt, Hampton, Holiday Inn, Howard Johnson, Homestead instead of home, hundreds of homes away from home, wherever the hell that was.

Angel pulled the curtains aside and tried to open the window to coax fresh, authentic air into the room. Not even locked, not even a real window, only a pane of glass.

What a pain in the ass. Look but don't feel. Do they think I'll jump out and kill myself? Throw the TV out and kill someone else? Humph. I guess both are likely in DC. I'm sure the Hilton's only worried about their TV.

He flicked on the tube, scrolled through 487 stations, stopped at The Knitting Channel out of sheer amazement that it even existed, and shut it off. A steaming shower removed today from his skin. While planning how to sneak the plush H-monogrammed bathrobe out of the hotel in his backpack, Angel slipped it on and settled into the plush H-monogrammed chair. Although beyond burnt, he dug out his phone and called Sheriff Dillon.

Donny didn't recognize Angel's new cell number displayed on his phone. "Hello?"

"Chris here."

"Chris?"

"Chris P. Critter."

"Angel, my man! How you doin'?"

"The name says it all. You?"

"Fit and fiddlin'. Where you at, bud?"

"If I told you, you'd have to kill me." Angel furrowed his weary brow. "Wait… I got that mixed up."

"Well, wherever you go, there you are," Donny said. "I hope there is treatin' y'all fine."

"I'm gonna fall asleep in thirty-seven seconds and I'll call you tomorrow, but I wanted make sure you're okay."

"I am. I picked up your trash."

"Are they all alive?" Angel asked.

"Bruised and bundled up in my jail cell after a tour of our fine clinic."

Angel sighed and eased back into his Hilton throne. "Good. I don't think I've ever killed a man, but I didn't see every one I left behind."

"They were tryin' to kill you, man."

"Maybe they were only trying to kill my house."

"I've heard this before. 'Maybe they had a bad childhood'."

"I'm sure they did," Angel agreed. "Thanks for the help today. Sorry to throw this in your lap."

"They did the throwin', bud, not you. And I got a big lap for buds. Hit the sack, Angel. Sounds like you got half a leg to stand on."

"Talk to you tomorrow, Sher'ff Bud," Angel murmured, just before his speech degenerated into only vowels. He dropped his cellphone on the table and flopped face down on the bed—twenty-four hours after he'd done the same thing the night before. Home Sweet Wherever.

Maybe I should… turn off the lights… and… zzz.

RED

Nine... Eight... Seven...

"Your drugs have strapped me onto a roller coaster." Red clung to the side of the bed as Dr. B removed her IV and checked her heart after her weekly chemo treatment. "One minute I'm up, then I'm down, then I'm upside-down..."

"That is certainly not pleasant, but normal," he said, searching for a report in her medical file, "although each patient has a unique experience. I have received results from the lab tests on your cells—"

Red raised one hand to stop him and made the motion of zipping her lips closed with the other. "Azeez!"

Azeez stood outside the door, only feet from the bed. One swivel and he was in the room. "Yes, Miss Red?"

"Will you please fetch the car and wait on me under the canopy in front of the hospital?"

"Right away, Miss Red."

Red turned back to Dr. B. "He doesn't need to know everything. He's worried enough as it is. You were saying about the tests?"

"Yes, the lab report from your biopsy, I am sorry to tell you, does not show much improvement in your condition." Dr. B pulled up a chair and sat in front of the bed. "I suggest we try chemo for two more weeks and then consider radiation therapy."

Red deflated visibly, gazing past Dr. B into the room. Every visit the walls seemed dingier, the window curtains dirtier, the fluorescent lights darker.

"Have you ever heard the song 'Born Under a Bad Sign'?"

"No, I do not believe so. Why do you ask?"

"One line from it is, 'If it wasn't for bad luck, I wouldn't have no luck at all.' That's the way it's been lately, B. My water pump's dead. I have no hair, just an orange fright wig. A bloke broke into my condo, a substantial debt is due, my three largest clients bailed, and now this..." Her sentence trailed into a deep sigh as she slumped backwards on the bed.

Dr. B pulled his chair closer to her. "Good luck can appear at any moment. We have other treatments that have proved most successful. You have been on a long, hard road already, but you must keep going."

Red's face was as flat and expressionless as the wall. "I have been keeping going, B… downhill."

"I am not a joke teller, but sometimes the wisdom in humor is good medicine. I will try to do justice to this story I once heard. A doctor had diagnosed his patient and asked, 'I have bad news and worse news. Which would you like first?' The man said, 'Give me the worse news.' The doctor said, 'You have cancer.' The man swore and asked, 'So what's the bad news then?' The doctor replied, 'You have Alzheimer's disease, too.' The man smiled and said, 'Oh, that's not so bad.' The doctor asked what he meant. The man said, 'Well, I could've had cancer.' Then he asked, 'What should I do, Doc?' The doctor said, 'Go home and forget about it.'"

Red sat up and chuckled. "Jolly good, B, but don't give up your day job for stand-up comedy."

"I most certainly will not. The wisdom is in the forgetting. When we focus on the fear and on the negative thing itself, we make the fear stronger and the negativity grows. When I am riding my bicycle, if I focus on the large rock in my path, I will hit the rock. If I focus on the way around the rock, I ride safely by. So I say to you, forget about the rock and concentrate on positive things."

"I see what you mean." Red relaxed with the thought. "I do have a project that will demand my attention. Maybe you've heard it, but here's a short one for you, and I'm no comedian, either. After finishing his lab tests, a doctor said to his patient, 'You have cancer and only about ten to live.' The shocked patient said, 'Ten what? Years? Months?' The doctor continued counting, 'Nine… eight… seven… six…'"

Dr. B let out a subdued guffaw and covered his mouth with his hand. "Oh, my goodness! I would never tell that one to any of my patients."

"The wisdom?" She raised up her index finger. "It can always get worse."

"Or better." Dr. B exhaled, his eyes fastened on hers. "We shall both hope for the best. Do you have any questions?"

She had a throbbing blob of questions, but only three wormed their way onto her tongue. "Have you ever heard of Baldev Ishwar Gupta? Or met him? Or Murakan Patil?"

"Baldev Gupta, the gangster, or as they say here, 'goonda'? This Baldev I have heard of, but would most definitely not want to meet. I do not know the other name."

"Goonda." Red narrowed her eyes while adding a mob of other questions to her list. She'd never heard anyone refer to Baldev as a gangster, but it fit like a black rubber glove.

"It is odd you should ask today, because a detective for the Public Prosecutor dropped by two days ago and mentioned him. He asked me about your mother, Chandra, and her auto crash on the bridge. I am aware you two had become distant, but I assume you know that she too, as Public Prosecutor, had been on the trail of local crime kingpins. This man said new evidence had come to light, and his department is reopening several cases. It seems that other officials and citizens also died in so-called 'accidents' that might not have been accidents."

As she heard this news, a wave of nausea washed over Red. A chest X-ray would have shown her heart an inch lower than usual, but she forced her face to remain rigid. "I'm too woozy to even think about that now. I must be off. I'll see you in a week, I suppose?"

"One week as usual. Oh, one moment." Dr. B reached into his smock pocket, took out a slip of paper and gave it to Red. "I have the name and phone number of a spiritual advisor a friend recommended most highly."

"Thanks, B. I'll look into it. I've been wondering about the messages from those dreams of mine."

"Please call me anytime if you are not feeling well."

Right. That's most of the time.

When Red entered the mold-green corridor, she glimpsed the back and leg of a slim man in black slink into a room on the right, twenty yards ahead. *Bug! Here?*

With cold sweat itching her spine, she walked warily down the corridor to the amplified sound of her heels clicking on the marble floor. As she approached the door where she'd seen him disappear, a thin maintenance man dressed in black coveralls rolled a garbage cart into the hall. He smiled and nodded his head. Red paused to lean against the wall.

Focus, woman. There wasn't even a rock in your path.

Azeez was standing by her red Mercedes under the rain-stained canopy when she walked out the main entrance. He opened the door, and Red slid into the back without a word. After a few minutes of creeping along in the mash of vehicles, she pulled a hip-flask bottle of Glenfiddich single-malt scotch whisky from her purse and tipped it up.

Through the rearview mirror, Azeez' ever-watchful eyes spotted the upturned bottle. "Miss Red! You should not be drinking after having these strong drugs!"

She lowered the bottle in a flash. "You're driving and not drinking. I'm drinking and not driving. It's legal and helps keep me awake and alert. We have things to do before we get home."

Wild honking from behind snatched her attention. Red looked around and spotted an auto rickshaw driven by a thin man in a black beret. She turned back, slumped down in the seat, and glared at Azeez through the rearview mirror.

"Stop the car. Up ahead." She pointed to the side of the road. "There."

"But Miss Red, the traffic..."

"Just do it! Pull over by that roti cart!"

The moment Azeez managed to stop, Red jumped out of the car, ready to confront Bug in the auto rickshaw. As it passed on the right, she saw it wasn't him—again—only another three-wheeled taxi of death driven by one of the thousands of aggressive, skinny drivers in hats that millions try to avoid. Her dizziness returned. She stepped weakly toward the roti cart. The banana roti aroma smelled luscious rising above the street sewage air. She ordered two.

Azeez sat iron-faced in the car. She brought over the hot rotis wrapped in white paper, got in the back seat, and dropped one on the front seat next to Azeez as he wedged his way into the traffic.

"I bought you a banana roti." It wasn't a peace offering. It was a bribe. "I want to drive by Aero Dynamic Enterprises on the way home. It's not far out of the way."

Azeez stiffened and raised his voice, becoming someone who was not Azeez. "We should not be doing that, Miss Red! It is most assuredly not a good idea!"

Red lurched toward the front seat, pointing at him with her roti. "Who are you working for, anyway?"

Both of Azeez' feet hit the brake pedal and the accelerator at the same time. "What are you meaning who am I working for?" Azeez shouted. The Mercedes bucked ahead like a muskrat caught in a trap chained to a tree. "I am working for no one!"

Red was livid. "That seems to be the case here. You are obviously not working for me. You are telling me what to do. Is that the reason I give you a salary? Perhaps we should switch roles. You can pay me and then tell me what I can or cannot do."

Azeez shifted his tone down a gear. "I am just thinking that it is not a good idea—"

"I am not paying you to think! I am paying you to drive!" Her voice softened, but still steamed past her lips. "When I want your opinions, I'll give them to you. We both know where Aero is. Now take us there."

She leaned back, sucked down another hit of scotch, unwrapped her roti, and took a bite.

Azeez drove in silence.

As her dander dissipated and she stared at the back of his head, Red and her conscience accused each other of over-reacting. It was the first argument she and Azeez had ever had. Lately he looked older than his young thirty years, almost haggard.

Red thought back to the day her father, Danny, had coaxed a scruffy fifteen-year-old urchin off the streets and offered him a job. One arm around Azeez' shoulder, Danny grinned and announced in the living room, "Look what followed me home."

She dredged up a few red cells of compassion in the back seat. "I'm sorry I raised my voice. I'd like to blame it on you, or the drugs, but I can't decide which one, so I'll have to take it."

Azeez' shoulders lowered an inch. "I too am most sorry, Miss Red. I should not be telling you what to do."

"We'll drive by Aero once so I can have a look at their operation. Now eat your roti. You're too thin. And if you have any black clothing or a black beret, don't ever wear them around me."

She finished her roti and dozed through the clamor of the traffic until Azeez stopped the car on the roadside.

"Miss Red, we are almost there. Aero is right around the next corner."

Dragging herself from a dead slumber, Red slid over to the window and rolled it down. "Please drive slowly without attracting any attention."

Aero Dynamic was adjacent to Delhi Indira Gandhi International Airport, and a myriad of vehicles cruised through the area. As they neared the compound, she crouched low in her seat, peering over the door like a bad child spying on the neighbors over the fence.

Through the dusky light, beyond Aero's parking lot, Red could see several buildings and hangars in a row lining the runway. A sturdy mesh fence surrounded the compound, though she couldn't make out any security cameras. Straight ahead of the main drive, her former Cresco was parked with two other dusters in a hangar, open in the front to the roundabout at the center of the grounds, and in the back to the tarmac. Workers fueled one duster and filled another with chemicals. Aero's main offices sat to the left and right of the roundabout.

People walked about, but she noticed no "large guards" as Azeez had mentioned, because the large security guards with binoculars were in a secure, concealed area, watching a red Mercedes convertible glide by lazily.

Red quivered with excitement as she inhaled every shred of information she could gather. She was acting out her dream Angel's business card. This was unquestionably "on-site research" for an "odd job" in preparation for "special deliveries" in the near future. Her attack plans thundered in her head. *It's time to meet the slippery man in the market and score the necessities.*

The countdown had begun.

MONA
The Truth Be Told

For months she'd put off painting one memory in her *One Life* autobiography collection—one unforgettable day, decades earlier, that she had alternately relished and repulsed. Mona wanted to display it in her upcoming exhibition at the Real Rio Art Gallery during the Texas Butterfly Festival in Mission, but needed help recalling the details. Mona knew she'd told her penpal about it and sifted through the letters stored in her filing cabinet.

Since they were twelve years old, Mona Arcade and Zarita Flores had written at least once a month, sometimes more often, always in longhand, always on paper, for sixty-one years. Each had shared her entire life with the one constant friend who'd lasted through all their individual turmoils, but the two women had never met.

Zarita was Mona's living diary. Before writing her first letter, Mona bought carbon paper so she could send the original and still keep a record of her thoughts and feelings for herself. So far, she'd saved over 700 of her own letters. And over 700 of Zarita's.

After locating the one describing that extraordinary day, Mona removed the drawing of a face from a frame on the wall. With smudges and a checkerboard of fold marks, the yellowed paper appeared to have been carried in a back pocket for years. It had, and in wallets and purses, until it needed protection under glass from the elements, sweaty fingers, and tears. Mona sat in front of a bare canvas with the letter and the drawing in her lap.

Dear Zarita,

You could never imagine what happened to me yesterday, so I guess I will have to tell you. I knew someday my parents would tell me the truth, but I didn't know it would be like this...

When Mona finished reading it, she sighed like someone starting a marathon, gazed at the drawing of the face for a few moments, and picked up her brush, a magic wand enabling her to transcend the present—her own personal time machine. Mona mentally dialed in one Sunday morning in Wisconsin when she was fourteen.

With broad, aggressive brush strokes, she enshrouded the sky in black and blue and drifted back and inside…

MONA KNEW SOMETHING WAS UP. The evening before, her papa Marco had come home heavy. He and Lily went for a walk with Chipper the cocker spaniel, but she wasn't invited. Her mama had told her, "We'll eat soon, but first Papa and I are going for a little stroll."

Mona's Saturday night cribbage sessions with Papa routinely included three games as he sipped one tin cup of brandy, pausing as he shuffled the cards to spin another yarn. Last night's session had been one quiet game and three tin cups. Marco and Lily hit the sack early, but their hushed voices crept underneath the bedroom door for another hour.

Today the crisp morning was bright and serene, but church wasn't on the agenda even though no one felt sick. After the solemn meal and clean-up, Marco came into her bedroom, nervously snapping his suspenders. "C'mon into the living room, Mona. We're gonna sit for a while and chat."

Mona followed her papa out to the couch he'd fashioned out of maple logs and pine boards when he built the cabin. She and her mama leaned back on the cushions.

Marco pulled up an armchair and took a seat in front of them. "In a couple of hours, Mona Lisa, your grandfather's coming to visit."

"Grandpa Hans? Is Grandma coming, too?"

"No, no. A grandfather you've never met. But first, your mama has a story to tell."

Lily moved closer and held Mona's hands, giving them a slight squeeze. She looked into those brown eyes she loved and began slowly. "I've wanted to tell you about the day you were born for a long, long time. It was a cold Sunday night, and I was working late at the hospital. A woman came in, alone, very sick and very pregnant. She could barely walk. The doctor wasn't in, so I took her into the emergency room and let her lie down on the bed.

"Her name was Angela. She said she knew she was dying, just like her mother had twenty-one years before, when Angela was only one-year-old. Her father had moved on a few months before she was born, and she was raised by the other migrant workers near a little town in southern Missouri where they all planted, weeded, and harvested crops on local farms."

Mona sat spellbound, finally getting answers to questions she'd wondered about for years.

"Angela didn't remember her mother or her father, but eventually heard her own story from the kind workers who took her in as family. I could see the baby wanted to come out, so I got everything ready while Angela moaned in pain and pleaded with me to take care of it. I told her I'd do everything in my power to grant her wish and fifteen minutes later… I held you… Mona…" Lily's tears brimmed up to the edges of her eyes, as did Papa Marco's. "I held you in my arms, a beautiful child of God, delivered to make the dream come true that your papa and I'd wished for years. We couldn't have a child ourselves, but had to wait until you were sent from Angela's womb right into our lives." Her baby-blue floodgates opened wide, and she threw her arms around Mona.

Marco rested his wet face on Mona's shoulder and put his arms around both of them.

"You didn't grow inside of me," Lily whimpered, gently rocking back and forth, "but every moment since then you've grown up as our beloved daughter. You are our angel, our gift from heaven and from your mother, Angela."

"Oh, Mama, thank you for telling me," Mona cried. "Now I've got two mothers."

The trio of tears embraced itself in silence and soft weeping for a few moments. Marco got up and brought over a dish towel to soak up their emotions.

Lily's hands acted out the role they'd played that day. "I laid you on Angela's chest and raised her up so she could look at you. My left hand was on your neck and my right hand on her back. She smiled at you, and you went quiet. Her pain seemed to vanish… and then she slipped away, I think as happy as she could have been at that moment. I sat there, tears streaming down my face just like now, with one hand on life and one on death."

Marco joined them on the couch and put his arms around Lily's waist as he took up the story. "Yeah, I came to pick up your mama a while later, and she told me the sad news about Angela. I sure felt bad, but my heart sang cuz our prayers had been answered. We stayed at the hospital all night, feelin' kinda like Mary and Joseph starin' down at baby Jesus. I was thinkin' maybe those three kings from Orient Are might walk in."

A few of the tears turned to snickers. Shoulders relaxed.

"So we adopted you legally as soon as we could, and you've been our own joy ever since." Lily took a piece of paper out of her apron pocket and handed it to Mona. "Your mother asked me to give you this when you were old enough to understand. It's a letter to you on the back of a picture of Angela, drawn and signed by your real father, Carlos Mariposa."

Mona raised her wet red eyes. "Papa is my real father, the best papa in the whole world! And you're the best mama in the whole world!"

The trio started shedding tears again.

"You betcha, sweetheart, and you are the best daughter in the whole world," Marco blubbered. "But now ya have another mama and papa who are outta this world."

Mona looked down at the drawing in her hands. It was good. Her father had sketched and shaded with a pencil almost as she did. She could see herself in Angela's face, as if she were gazing into an aging mirror made of paper.. She turned it over, experiencing her birth mother's handwriting for the first time, and read the letter to herself as Marco and Lily watched intently.

My dear child, a boy or girl, I may never know,

I am afraid I will be gone soon to join your father. He was killed a few weeks ago in a tractor accident. I hope you find good people who will take our place in your life, like the good people who helped me in mine.

Like you, I never knew my parents. My father was gone and my mother died before I was one-year-old. Why? I keep asking myself, but we don't always understand the ways God works his wonders. But I truly know there is an important reason for you to survive.

I pray every day that you will live a long life with those you love and do not pass so quickly like your grandmother and me. However many days you have, live them fully and from the heart.

We will be together again, someday, somewhere, in some form, maybe as a butterfly. That is my name. Maybe that's what I will be.

Love forever,

Angela Mariposa

During the past two years, Mona had learned a few Spanish words from Zarita. Mariposa meant butterfly. She whispered her mother's name in English, caressing the words with her lips. "Angel Butterfly."

"Yesterday Lily met Angela's father at the hospital," Marco said, "your grandfather, and he's comin' to visit."

Lily had felt a knot in her stomach while speaking with this grandfather at the hospital, though she scoffed it off thinking of the intense emotions his appearance and what he told her had brought to the surface. Her next words were hell to drag out, but she pressed on, taking Mona's hands in hers once again.

"His name is Ernesto Guerro, and he told me something that made me more afraid than I've been for fourteen years. He said his wife, your grandmother—her name was Angelica—had told him that your great-grandmother, Liliana, died soon after Angelica was born in Texas. I know it's confusing, but the facts are simple. Your mother, your grandmother, and your great-grandmother all died around the age of twenty, and no one seemed to know why."

Mona couldn't quite take it all in. "Liliana is like your name, Mama."

"It sure is, pumpkin. Only God knows, but maybe that's why we're together today. The doctor here had no idea why your mother died. He said it seemed like she'd died of old age, even though she didn't look old. I tried to find more information or cases like this, but came up with nothing. Your papa and I have worried for years that it might happen to you, too, and it tore us apart every time we thought about it. That's why we didn't tell you all this until today."

"But I feel fine," Mona assured her. "Maybe it's only a coincidence. Doesn't that mean things happen at the same time by chance for no reason?"

"Yah sure, you got it." Marco said, resting a hand on both of their knees. "And it's not gonna happen to you. You've always been a healthy one, and you're gonna stay that way."

"In times of trouble, we've often been comforted by Angela's words." Lily spoke them like a prayer. "'However many days you have, live them fully and from the heart.'"

"We wanted to give you a butterfly name then," Marco said, "so we wrote down some we knew next to our last name—buckeye, viceroy, copper, nymph, monarch—but none of 'em sounded too ladylike. Then we looked at that list again and 'Monarch Arcade' jumped out at us. And whatd'ya know? Mona was the first letters of monarch and a girl's name. Mona Arcade. When you say 'em together, there's our girl and one of our favorite butterflies."

"Hmm, I never noticed that," Mona mused. To her, everything felt just the way it was supposed to be. "No wonder it's my favorite butterfly, too! I'm so glad you told me. I did notice I didn't look like you. Sometimes I thought maybe I was some freak of nature."

"I hope you understand why it took us so long to tell you." Lily's tears were ready to take over again. "We wanted to, pumpkin. You were never a freak, and we never cared that you looked different than us, and you were always beautiful... all ways."

Marco took out his pocket watch from his coveralls. "Alrighty then. Only an hour till this Ernesto comes." He eased towards the door. "Best get my chores out of the way." Translated into Marco language: "That was more than enough for me. I need some time alone."

Mona didn't have much experience with death—Marco's mama's funeral, her shepherd Shadow, and Billy, the boy at school who never came back. It seemed to her as if they were just somewhere else. Right now she was dying to write Zarita. Mexico had always fascinated Mona, and this information put the pieces together.

I look Mexican, and my real relatives probably came from there. Mexico is in my blood.

She went to brush her hair and put on a church dress because that seemed like the right thing to do. She wasn't really excited, only curious.

As Mona peeked through the living room curtains, a rusted truck inched along the driveway and stopped near the cabin. It looked like a refugee from a junkyard that had never seen better days. Round Ernesto stumbled out, his round head surrounded by smoky-gray rumpled hair that might have been styled with farm implements. She watched her papa shake his hand and listened as they knelt to meet their cocker spaniel, tentatively wagging his stubby tail.

"This here's Chipper, man's best friend," Marco said. "In fact, if any man's got a snack in his hand, he's already his best friend."

Mona slipped from the window and stood close to her mama as the men came through the door.

"Ya already met my wife Lily," Marco said, stretching both arms around his family. "And here's Mona, all dressed up pretty as a picture."

Ernesto extended his fat hand and grinned, showing his dull khaki teeth with two silver-capped canines like blunt fangs protecting his incisors. "¡Hola, Mona! Hello! I am so happy to meet you!"

Mona put out her hand to shake his, but he yanked her into his jelly belly. "Give your abuelo a big hug."

She winced, but did it, and then backed away. His clothes smelled like the greasy black garbage pails behind the schoolhouse. "I guess it's nice to meet you, too," she said warily. "Why are you here?"

Her question surprised everyone. Lily excused herself to get some refreshments; Marco grinned proudly, and Ernesto spoke quickly, too quickly.

"I am here lining up jobs for other migrant workers. I am too old to work in the fields, so I work for everybody in my truck. Some men and I were talking about old times, and it made me wonder what happened to the daughter I never knew and led me to the hospital to find Lily and learn about my granddaughter. She was nice enough to invite me out to see you."

"Are you from Mexico?" Mona asked.

"No. My parents were. A little village across from Laredo, Texas."

Lily brought in the lemonade and snickerdoodle cookies, and Mona got quiet as the grown-up small talk started.

Ernesto paid little attention to Mona, or to anyone else. His eyes didn't look at anyone straight and kept wandering about the room. After ten minutes, Mona could see he was itching to leave. Ernesto asked if Marco would show him around outside, which he did, and she followed.

On the way to his truck, Ernesto turned to Marco. "Maybe I can take Mona out for lunch sometime?"

"Hmm … we'll see… if Mona wants to… maybe."

Ernesto got into his truck, and the engine clanked into action. He shouted out the window as he backed out. "I am so happy to meet you, Mona."

"You already said that," Mona replied, stony-eyed.

"Adios." Marco tipped his head. "Say goodbye, Mona."

"Goodbye."

They didn't talk about Ernesto's visit or past issues for the rest of the day and went about life as usual. But later on, Mona overheard her parents whispering while washing the dinner dishes.

"I don't trust him," Lily said.

"Yah… I don't either," Marco agreed. "The way he kept lookin' round was like he wanted to steal somethin'."

"And he was half-crocked. Make sure every door is locked tight."

"Yah sure. Tight."

It was a school night and a workday tomorrow, so everyone went to bed by nine. Churning the facts and feelings of the day over and over, Mona's mind wouldn't let her sleep. Thunder rolled earnestly in the distance.

She got up and padded toward the door in her Winnie the Pooh flannel pajamas, with her red Ray-O-Vac flashlight in hand, and Chipper at her heels. She flipped on the bare yellow bulb outside, unbolted the door, walked on the stone pathway, and into the outhouse.

While sitting on the wooden seat in the dark, Mona thought she heard a yip from Chipper. Opening the outhouse door a few moments later, she expected him to bound up to her, but he lay motionless on the grass next to a fleshy thigh bone. She took a step and leaned down near Chipper.

A calloused hand clamped over her mouth from behind, and another wrapped around her chest, yanking her upright. Mona tried to scream "Mama!" but only the letter M escaped through the tightening fingers.

"Don't you make a sound, or I will hurt you."

She instantly recognized the hoarse voice. And the drunken breath, like opening a jar of rotten dill pickles. *Ernesto!*

Lily bolted up in bed, ears and eyes straining to pierce the darkness. She jabbed Marco with her elbow. "I heard something. Out back. Check on Mona."

Marco's body sprang from under the covers before his brain clicked on. He lurched through the door and across the cabin to Mona's bedroom. Seeing she wasn't there, he called her name as he ran toward the back door. He grabbed his Remington double-barrel shotgun from its mount over the door frame and cautiously stepped outside.

"What in tarnation?"

In the dim amber light, Marco saw Mona trapped in the plump arms of Ernesto, one hand holding the razor-sharp hatchet from his wood pile under her chin.

"Put the gun down shlowly or the girl getsh hurt," Ernesto demanded, his slurred words crawling over his lips. He moved the hatchet up an inch.

Marco's hot blood seethed into every muscle fiber. "If there is one scratch on her, I will skin you like these varmint pelts hangin' here on the wall."

"Drop it," Ernest growled, his portly torso tipping to one side. "Thish girl'sh mine."

Two multi-veined tongues of lightning tore across the sky, illuminating the entire area.

Mona spotted another man rushing around the corner toward Marco with a log raised over his head and tried to shout, "Look out, Papa!" Her words stuck in Ernesto's palm and the log fell on Marco's head. A deafening crack of thunder shook the ground as he collapsed in a heap.

Startled, Ernesto relaxed his grip for a moment and Mona jerked away.

A split second later, from inside the cabin, another crack rent the air. A rifle slug shattered the windowpane and tore through Ernesto's left shoulder, knocking him onto his back into the shattered glass. Another crack and another bullet tore into the other man's thigh and sent him sprawling.

Mona saw the back of a third man hightailing it through the woods as Lily charged through the door with her Browning deer rifle aimed at Ernesto's head.

"If you move, it will be the last one you'll ever make." The timbre of Lily's words was rough, their tone abysmal, as if spoken by the Divine Mother of the Universe, coursing with pure love and pure hate. "I'm a nurse and save lives, but I'll make an exception for you." Without turning her head, she spoke calmly to her trembling daughter. "Mona, pick up your papa's shotgun and point it between that other man's legs, right below his stomach.

Don't get close to him. If he moves, pull the trigger."

Mona picked up the gun and did as she was told. The thunder and lightning continued their volleys as the drizzle revived Marco. He held his head and struggled to his feet. The two assailants groaned in agony, but dared not move.

Lily stepped closer to Ernesto. "The only reason you are alive is because I am not an evil demon like you. I shot you exactly where I aimed. It could have been three inches to the right... through the middle of your heart... if you even have one."

Marco took the shotgun from Mona and hugged her with one arm. "Are you all right, honey?"

"I'm okay, Papa. Mama saved us."

"She sure did. I taught her how to use an ax, but she taught me how to shoot. She won the grand prize for marksmanship at the county fair." He tilted his head and smirked. "You don't wanna mess with Mama. Now go call the sheriff, pumpkin. His number's right next to the phone."

While Lily covered both men with her rifle, Marco dragged the second man over to Ernesto, took off his leather belt, coiled it around both of their necks, and cinched their heads together.

Mona burst out of the door. "Sheriff Oddmund said he'd try to get here in an hour! He apologized."

"An hour?" Marco huffed. "Good for little or nothin', that man. We're gonna have to make damn sure our varmints don't wanna move. Now Mona, bring those two chairs over here and set 'em back to back."

Marco tied both men's hands together behind their backs using deadbolt bowline knots from his Boy Scout days as he mumbled to himself. "Jeez Louise. Never thought I'd have to use 'em for this."

Prodding them with his shotgun, he herded the two men into the chairs, lashed their arms to the wooden staves with wire, and took off their boots. "You won't be needin' these where you're goin'."

Lily taped bandages on their wounds to stop the bleeding and over their mouths to stop their whimpering. Chipper came back to life, limped over to his mugger, lifted his leg, and marked his territory on Ernesto's bare foot as Marco kept chatting with his mute captives.

"I don't even want to know what you boys had in mind. If I knew, I might want to save the sheriff some trouble and stick the two of you in the root cellar to rot until spring." Marco put a log on each chair seat under the men's knees, raising their feet off the ground about five inches. He tied a rope to Ernesto's right ankle, stretched it diagonally under the chairs, and looped the other end around the other man's ankle. "Comin' into our home, eatin' our food, and then sayin', 'This girl is mine.'" He took two metal-toothed, thirty-inch-wide bear traps off the wall, pried them open, set the springs, and placed one under and around each man's feet. "After leavin' your own daughter thirty-some years ago?" He shook his head. "You are somethin' else."

Marco put another trap on the ground to the side of the men so they could watch his demonstration out of the corners of their eyes. He set the trap and picked up a three-inch-thick branch from his stack of firewood. "Now you boys watch real close here. This is what'll happen to your legs if you decide it's time to move."

He tripped the trap with the branch. The steel jaws slammed shut and snapped it in half. The bound brothers shuddered.

"You two varmints can think about life in prison until the sheriff gets here. We're gonna get out of this rain, sit by the warm fire, and pray you'll be behind bars, quick as a wink." With a smirk at the captives, Marco ushered his family into the cabin and slammed the door.

Mona had almost finished her painting, but paused to study the images her memories had created. Floating in the center with a brilliant ivory veil covering her entire form, a faceless goddess Kwan-yin dominated the scene—the protector of women and children, the Chinese fertility deity with the power to grant children to couples worthy of them.

Two branching trees of lightning blossomed through the blue-black sky behind her like gossamer wings. On the ground to the right lay the shadowed bodies of a dog and a man.

From Kwan-yin's outstretched arms, a golden ray flowed across the canvas, enveloping the monarch butterfly on a woodpile. In the middle, another lily-white angel, poised with a cocked bow in her hands, glared up at two arrow-pierced ravens dropping from the sky as a third flew on.

Holding her father Carlos' drawing of her mother in one hand, Mona meticulously painted the face of Angela as the face of Kwan-yin. In the lower right-hand corner, she signed her mother's name, Angela Mariposa, underneath the title.

"Demons Vanquished, Wishes Granted, Northern Wisconsin, 1955."

ANGEL
Ghost Land Plans

FIFTEEN MINUTES BEFORE NINE A.M. Angel arrived at the DEA Headquarters in DC and meandered up to the gatekeeper behind the info desk. If she wasn't already on the cover of a beauty magazine somewhere, he'd consider publishing one of his own.

"Mornin', darlin'," he crooned. "How are you today?"

"Fine, thank you!" She smiled through her stiff bouquet of silky brunette hair adorned with a wireless headset. "My name's Darla, but darlin' is close enough."

"I know. I cheated. I read your name tag. I think I talked to you on the phone yesterday."

"Maybe. So many people call."

"Name's Angel Phoenix and I'm here to meet Deputy Jonathan Skipper."

Darla reached down to press Jonathan's line. "I'll let him know you're here."

"Before you call him, can I ask you a question? This sign says it's the Information Desk."

"Sure. Ask away."

Angel raised a finger and pointed around the lobby. "Do these people here have any idea how beautiful you are?"

Darla's personal gates flew open and fell off their hinges. "Why, aren't you the sweet mouth? Thank you!"

"Just tellin' it like it is," Angel said, raising one eyebrow a quarter inch.

She rang Jonathan, her eyes stuck on Angel. "There's an Angel here to see you, Mr. Skipper. Can I bring him up personally?"

"I'll be right down," Jonathan replied. "You're the gatekeeper, Darla. Stay at your post, please."

Three minutes later Jonathan strolled up to the desk in his Saturday casual clothes: no suit, no tie, long-sleeved plaid shirt, khaki pants, and Hush Puppies. Leading Angel down the hallway, he asked, "What did you do to Darla? Her voice sounded sweaty on the phone. I think she's in heat."

"Yes, she is hot, inside and out. I'm just planning, remember? Gettin' the lay of the land."

"I think you mean getting laid in the land," Jonathan said, still imagining last night's encounter with the receptionist at the Hilton. "Were you up all night? You're early."

"Nope. Right on time." Angel slipped into a little Southern speak. "If ah ain't early, ah'm late."

Jonathan took his Energizer Bunny by the arm and led him round a corner. "Your room okay? Find your coffee?"

"I was a log for ten hours. Steamed off the bark in the sauna. Caffè latte'd over Wi-Fi. I am juvenated again."

"Juvenated? Is that a Southern word?" Jonathan asked, pinching his eyebrows together as they walked.

"It may only be an Angel word. How could I rejuvenate if I hadn't juvenated once before? So is gruntled. If disgruntled means unhappy, gruntled must mean happy. Today I am juvenated and gruntled."

"Now I understand why you don't need to do drugs. You were born with them." Jonathan punched in a security code on the wall pad and opened the windowless door. "Here's my mission control room with the maps you wanted. The satellite photos are on the big screen and in the files on the table over there."

"Nice playroom. What time do we meet Mom?"

"She's on call. So is the SWAT team if you use the M-word."

"Just agree with everything I say during the meeting, or Mum's the word," Angel threatened. "One hour here and we'll have made up my mind."

They sat down across from each other at a spacious circular Plexiglas table. Jonathan showed him the location of Ghost Land on the topographic map revealing the surrounding terrain. "Here's the mountain ridge I mentioned. This wider valley stretches to the stream leading up to Khun P's place and Barry's cage."

"Ah, ha. Phu Chi Fa." Angel leaned over the map and smiled at the vision of it in his mind. "I vaguely remember goin' there when I was a kid. Stunning views into Laos from Thailand. Back then I didn't consider jumpin' off the cliff."

"So what are your jumping-off and flying options?" Jonathan asked. "Your file mentioned a squirrel suit. I think I've seen them in movies, but thought they were only special effects."

"Squirrel or wing suits are special… and effective. Absolutely exhilarating. You don't officially fly—you glide. You swoop. You become the soaring, diving hawk." Merely talking about them got Angel excited. He had to stand up and get a little closer to the sky. "They were inspired by flying squirrels who glide using folds of skin that stretch out from their bodies to their front and rear feet," he said, creating the suit with his hands on his body. "The suit expands with the wind and you look like a flyin' air mattress."

"I'd need a king-size mattress," Jonathan admitted, "and a new set of nerves."

"You are height-and-weight-challenged for a squirrel suit. Like you said, size matters. And landscape size matters. You have to plan two rather important stages besides the gliding: starting and stopping. You need at least a 500-foot vertical drop to build enough speed for your suit to grab the air and several thousand more down and ahead for the flight—three feet down for every one ahead. Easy from a airplane."

Angel leaned over the map and pinpointed Phu Chi Fa. "This Phu Chi Fa valley doesn't have enough space, down or ahead. You can reach speeds of 200 miles per hour during the glide, so you deploy a parachute to land. A squirrel suit here would be a suicide suit… a suiticide."

"So what can we do?" Jonathan asked. "I think it's the highest peak in the area."

"Paragliding is the way to go. Strapped into a wide kite that fills with air like the suits. Easier lift-off, slower glide, and more control. Distance record for them is 500 kilometers. With a stiff wind, I could cruise over to Bangkok."

Jonathan folded his arms on his formidable chest. He didn't know if he liked what he was hearing or not, and the wrinkles on his forehead conveyed his confusion. "So this mission depends on the whims of the wind? We don't have time for more than one go at this."

"Whatever we decide here, the weather may veto whenever we get there. On the right day, I should be able to get off the ridge and then rely on Lady Luck for a landing. A rice field? The river? Does Mister Ghost have a swimming pool?"

"I'll email and ask him for a brochure," Jonathan said, trying to slip a little levity through his uneasiness. "Last resort, hike in, I guess."

Angel turned around the chair, straddled it, and rested his chin in his arms on its back. "Here's my take on the best-case scenario. Glide like a bat out of heaven at dawn, park, and locate your local's baggage claim holding my cached supplies courtesy of the GPS. Take the rest of the day to sightsee in Ghost Land and then set my surprises that night. Spring Barry from his trap just before the following dawn, sprint to the exit as the sun rises and symphonic music fills the valley, then have an American breakfast back at the DEA office in Thailand."

"You're making it sound like a holiday. What's the worst-case scenario?"

"It's pissin' rain, your locals pawn my luggage, Barry's not there, python strangles me, etcetera. We could write an entire appendix of etceteras. Maybe you should just kill me now. Save money in the long run."

Jonathan fished for the yea he wanted to hear. "Do I detect a desire to give it a go, to at least stand on the mountain that morning and feel the weather?"

"Let me be alone with these files and the SAT photos. Getting in and out is dicey. Finding Barry is a crap shoot. The whole concept might be full of shit. Could you please fetch me a cup of coffee and a jar of peanut butter?"

"Will do. Take your time." Jonathan left the room with fingers crossed, in search of anything that might help sway this angel into his field.

Angel stared at the slim stacks of info. Nothing in the DEA file shed light into the corners of this conundrum. The SAT photos showed hazy shapes in the mist like a low-budget horror flick. He thought he might have to take off his shoes and play the eeny-meeny game with his toes to decide whether to go and save, or stay and be safe.

Then he heard the Devil whispering. *"Don't do it."*

Angel closed his eyes and leaned back in his mind to listen. Sometimes these dialogues were only irritating circles, but often their insight yanked him off the barbed-wire fence of choice that he was straddling. At least he had someone to talk to, even if it was only himself. "Why not?"

"I don't give a damn."

"You never do."

"Barry dug his own grave. The DEA gave him a shovel. The Ghost provided the dirt. It's just the way it is."

"He just wanted to be a hero. Peer pressure from his hotshot family."

"He just wanted to be an ego. Peer pressure from his hotshot human race."

"That's all you are, amigo, an ego."

"Angel baby, we were joined in holy union, remember? Till death do us part. I'm your better half."

"You're my bitter half. I'm the sweetener."

"You could die over there. Not so sweet."

"Doesn't sound so bad. Then I wouldn't have to talk to you anymore."

"What would you do without me?"

"I could just be myself."

"You can do that now, Angel. Go get him. Bring him home."

"What? I thought you said, 'Don't do it.'"

"I'm learning. I was being the Devil's Advocate. You've taught me a thing or three, you know."

"Are you on drugs or somethin'?"

"I'd like to be. You won't let me."

"Whatever. I'm goin'. You comin'?"

"Hell, I'm already there."

RED
The Slippery Man

Today I'm going to be invisible. Red felt charged for a change. She now had a goal requiring forward motion instead of reeling backwards, struck repeatedly by bad news. As her plans had percolated at night during those elusive moments where slumber melds into half-consciousness, pieces of her recent mystifying dreams floated by like trash and treasures in a stiff wind. "I'm invisible, I can fly, and I save people." She could certainly fly and was trying to save herself, Azeez, and her business, her father's legacy. And invisibility was part of her strategy—hiding in plain sight.

Though half Indian, Western dress was her norm. She liked India, but loved England. Red's brain was definitely British; destiny had planted her feet on Indian soil; her heart flopped around in between. She preferred looking down on India, whether standing tall on the ground in a business suit or soaring through the sky in jeans and a flight jacket.

Few had seen her in a sari, which she imagined would disguise her entire persona. Mother Chandra had taught her the complex wrapping steps for one of the eighty different styles—the nivi—made popular by Bollywood stars in the 1930s. In the past three decades, Red had a only worn a sari once, at a masquerade ball she attended with her second husband. He went as a twenty-eight-year-old white, USA Nehru, and she, a tall glamorous version of Indira Gandhi with red locks cascading to her shoulders.

Now, standing in front of her full-length mirror, Red stared forlornly at her face, shrunken during these weeks of chemo, a gaunt semblance of those days gone by—her bald head on a stick neck above protruding collar bones and anorexic arms like a runway model. Stuffing away sorrow and the tears it nearly spawned, she dragged herself back to the task at hand.

Wearing the matching petticoat and tight, midriff-revealing blouse, Red gazed at the nine-yard, red-and-black sari folded on the floor. She thought of the fun they'd had donning their costumes that night with their mutual companion, Scotch. Chase had commented, "You're going to use the whole nine yards?"

During the wrapping, pleating, and folding process, he'd suggested they switch outfits. A year later, with two bruised hearts, they parted. He genuinely adored Red, but had an inner urge to pursue a more homoerotic lifestyle with a twenty-something Indian lad.

How could I have missed the clues? Graphic designer, organic gardener, and gourmet chef; tidy, energetic, compassionate, able to arrange flowers and furniture. Chase Youngman... even his name said it all.

Red knew the first step: tuck the plain end of the sari into the petticoat waistband and wrap the cloth around her lower body. The pleating task consistently befuddled her.

Blimey! Eight-and-a-half yards left?

She pleated and pleated and pleated, then tucked again, finally draping the leftover fancy end of the fabric under one arm and over the other shoulder. She stepped back to take in her work, and the entire sari slipped off, leaving Red ankle-deep in a pool of cloth.

Oh, blast it. I need the instructions. And Scotch's help.

She retrieved him from his home in the liquor cabinet. Clutching Scotch in one hand, she unfolded the crumpled "How to Wear an Indian Sari" directions she'd saved.

"Hold sari so shorter distance goes from waist to floor and long end can be wrapped around. Then, start at one end and tuck corner of fabric into petticoat at left hip, wrap around behind, over right hip, past navel, and around again until reaching navel. Beginning from tucked-in end, make pleats about five inches deep, about seven to ten pleats that fall straight and even, then tuck them into waist to left of navel making sure they turn left."

Mother, help me!

Red polished off Scotch and scanned the rest of the directions. It said something about pins. She rummaged through drawers until she located them, though they weren't the safety kind. She struggled through the steps, puncturing skin several times, the red sari absorbing her blood.

This must be how those butterflies felt in my dreams when Tiger mounted them with those long pins.

Fifteen minutes later, all the parts appeared to be in the right places, and fabric flowed from shoulder to floor. As she draped a red scarf over her head and around her mouth and neck, wishing it were her departed hair, Red spied the note at the end of the directions which should have been at the beginning. "Wear your high-heeled shoes to get accurate length."

Bollocks. Damned if I'm going out barefoot.

She donned her heels, fetched Scotch's twin, and started over again.

Finally dressed successfully, with a flamboyant beaded purse at her side, she walked past the red Mercedes familiar to friends and clients, and delicately climbed into the scarred pickup truck, only stabbing herself with a pin in the stomach once. The truck was the workhorse of Red Admiral Aerial Application, moving waste or building materials from here to there and transporting poorly secured chemical barrels from storage to dusters. The scorching sun had baked the paint on its bonnet into flakes. Spillage had scored its chrome bones and eaten through the skin of its bed. It looked like a burn victim. She drove to the steel mesh entrance gate and honked.

A shocked expression tormenting his face, Azeez hopped out of the gatehouse. "Miss Red! What are you doing?"

"Open the gate, Azeez," she commanded.

"But Miss Red, I am the person to be driving you. I am not liking that you are driving and I am even more not liking that you are driving this most dirty old truck."

"Right now you should be opening the gate and closing the gate and staying here and minding the chemical warehouse in case a customer comes in. It's the only income we seem to have at the moment."

"But Miss Red—"

She spoke emphatically, shaking her head side to side and up and down like Azeez. "If you are not opening the gate most immediately, I will be ramming the gate most expediently, and then you will be welding the gate in the hot sun most uncomfortably."

Sometimes she had to speak his language to pound in the message.

Deflated, Azeez pressed the button to open the gate. As she passed, he pleaded, "But what place are you going to, Miss Red?"

She ignored him, and he watched her drive off. As usual, watch dog Kamal sleeping at Azeez' feet didn't watch.

With no air-con, the truck became a roasting oven; the torrid breeze through the window, a hell-fan. Wet with sweat and with humidity clogging her lungs, Red fought fatigue and continued her mission.

Two blocks from Khan Market, she found a parking spot on a busy thoroughfare, then drifted through the river of saris streaming into the sea of stores and stalls. In the middle of the street, women shoveled wet cement into a monster hole large enough to swallow a sacred cow. With ten adobe bricks balanced on top of their heads, women shuffled across rickety plank bridges on construction sites. In grimy trucks, women perched on garbage bags, their brightly colored scarves trailing behind like pheasant tails. Clean women dressed elegantly doing the filthiest of chores.

Life throbbed around Red in the sprawling market, its cobblestones smoothed and shined after decades of transferring their rough edges to the calloused feet of its customers. The balloon peddler scraped his fingers rhythmically on the rubber to turn heads—crrryck, crrryck, crrryck—one of thousands of the market's singular heartbeats.

As Red strolled, her fingertips caressed supple pashmina shawls in stalls. Sellers behind packed carts bargained heatedly with buyers over the price of incense, saffron, umber and vermilion powders, flashy bangles, and perfume bottles imported from the next aisle over. Their voices intertwined with the shrill sound of movie theme songs belting out of a lamppost loudspeaker.

The stench of sewage seared Red's left nostril as the savory fragrance of chicken vindaloo wafted into the right. Whining dogs scuffled over scraps of paper that once wrapped around rotis. Watchful crows let out piercing caws, then dove into the fray to score morsels dropped from the mouth of a mangy goat. None of this fazed the turbaned Sikh with a white beard stretching into a curl in his lap. He seemed to have been squatting on his woven mat for centuries, silently hawking his scrappy selection of wares.

Red turned down another bustling lane to the slippery man's shop. The professionally printed sign hanging from the eaves read, "Travelers Treasures" above a hand-painted banner touting, "We By And Sell Evrything."

She passed stacks of backpacks, cases of used books, and racks of clothes lining the archway leading to the main salesroom. The shop walls were filled with fierce Chinese dragons, fat laughing Buddhas, and gilded images of Brahmin gods and goddesses brandishing swords like those jutting from circular stands below on the tiled floor. A stone Jesus staked to a wood cross stared helplessly at shoppers sorting through the menagerie of icons. Here she could buy whatever deity, demigod, or demon she desired.

Red opened the door in the corner. "Namaste, Shri Lochan." She bowed slightly, pressing both palms together, fingers touching one another and pointing upward.

The slippery man, Ganesh Lochan, sat behind his heavy-duty handlebar mustache, a huge hairy caterpillar crawling across his lip. It split his face in two. His yellow-white eyeballs with black irises and blacker pupils hovered above his stache like vacuum cleaners sucking in infinity to sell it. His bottom row of yellow-white teeth hid beneath his gold upper dentures. He appeared perplexed by this tall personage in front of his desk. Though he catered to anyone with rupees, Ganesh's clients in this office weren't women in saris—they were men in suits.

"What can I do for you?" he asked in Hindi, barely disguising a tone insinuating, "What are you doing here, woman?"

Towering behind him and his leather-padded chair, an eight-foot bronze statue of the Hindu god Ganesha with five elephant heads and ten arms—the Lord of Success who ensures triumph in human endeavors—gazed down on his namesake.

Red answered in English as she pulled the scarf back from her mouth and neck. "Shall I speak with the god or the man? I need to remove an obstacle standing in the way of my success."

"Miss Admiral!" Ganesh switched to English. "I did not recognize you! You are looking so… so Indian today."

"My better half," she lied with a smile. "How are you?"

"I am well and prospering, thank you. And you? How is your business?"

"Up and down. Flying and grounded. I need a document signed to keep me in the air." She took a file from her purse containing previous medical examinations and the current one requiring forgery or a slippery doctor's signature, and dropped it on his desk. "Perhaps you can help me as you have in the past."

"You like oolong, I think, yes?" Ganesh asked as he stood.

Red nodded yes, side-to-side, Indian style.

Ganesh shouted to a worker, then closed the door, and flipped through her papers. "It shouldn't be a problem. When do you need it, Miss Admiral?"

"Two weeks will be fine. It's not as time-sensitive as my other requests."

Ganesh sat, lit a clove beedi cigarette, and took a drag. "What might those be?"

"I need three players for a theatrical piece I am producing. A female and male WASP and an Indian man, none of them from Delhi, players who know their way around the law as you do."

"I am assuming you mean the white Anglo-Saxon Protestant kind and not the annoying insects."

"I find them all annoying," Red scoffed. "I don't care about their religion, only their ability to be white and act wealthy. The Indian man must have a brain and be able to portray their chauffeur. He'll also need an untraceable driver's license to rent a limousine."

"What sort of theater? A play for the public?" He blew a smoke ring to the side. "I didn't know you had such talents."

"It's a private production, and as you've mentioned before, you needn't know about your clients' activities."

"I see," he said, sucking in another hit from his beedi. A knock on the door signaled tea. An employee delivered a green porcelain pot, and Ganesh poured two cups. "And when do you desire these players?"

"Soon… as soon as the rest of my plans are in place. One day for a meeting, two short days of dress rehearsal and performance, three days total."

"With millions milling around, the Indian man is easy. And you may be in luck regarding the others. Two of my associates are visiting from the south. A German couple, Dietrich and Toma Sheppard."

"You've come up trumps with the tea, Ganesh, but I said WASPs, not German Shepherds."

His grin flashed his gold fangs. "I see you haven't lost your bitter wit, Miss Admiral. They are acrobats and actors who once traveled with the Titali Circus… until their extra-curricular activities left an obvious trail. Both about forty and very fit. Perhaps they'll suit your needs."

"I'd like to meet them, but don't tell them my name."

"That can be arranged." He stubbed out his beedi meticulously. "When?"

"When you can deliver my last request," she said, eyes glued on his, "three IEDs."

Ganesh raised his teacup and took a sip. He didn't quite believe what he'd just heard. "Begging your pardon, but are you sure you do not mean IUDs, Miss Admiral?"

"Not funny," she said gravely. "I don't suppose I'm speaking with Dr. Ganesh, am I? IEDs, Improvised Explosive Devices. Small, adhesive-backed, and remote-controlled."

"Special effects for your play? Or do you plan on eliminating infidels?"

"Remember, my respectful Shri Ganesh, you don't need to know. But if you must… If the audience doesn't like the play, I'll blow them to bits."

He laughed courteously, aware of the rising price tag for his services. Ganesh worked both sides of any religious war, every side of all business wars, and in between personal ones. The slippery man in the middle greased everyone's palms with everyone else's grease and relaxed on an unsoiled pile of cash in the end.

"Seriously now," Red said, "the actors will deliver the special effects and leave town."

"Please wait here for a moment and enjoy your tea." He opened his closet door, then turned to the right and opened another door to a stairway leading up.

Red's eyes widened as a déjà vu drifted in. *A secret laboratory upstairs? That's like the Tiger kid in my dreams.*

Ganesh returned a New Delhi minute later with a ring-bound set of 4x6 snapshots, his homemade brochure on IEDs. He explained the various kinds—explosive, chemical, biological, radiological, incendiary—and their alternative methods of detonation—wire, radio, cellphone, infrared, or victim-triggered. With her tea in one hand, Red became engrossed in the photos and delightedly chose her selection as if she were ordering holiday gifts from a department store catalog.

Once she'd concluded her shopping, Red rose to leave and scrutinized the statue of Ganesha. "Thank you for your time and your help, Shri Lokan. And your strictest confidence. It appears you do indeed have ten arms stretching into ten dimensions like your namesake behind you. I wonder how many heads you have?"

"Only one, the head of my valued customer," he said humbly. His words hit the floor with a splat, like spit.

"I'll call you." Red walked to the door, opened it, and then turned. "Please don't call me," she said, securing her scarf around her nose and mouth.

As she strolled past the used book cases in his 'Travelers Treasures' passageway, a title caught her eye: *Stranger in a Strange Land.* She grabbed it off the shelf. *This book was in my dreams. And I've always felt like that. Strange.* A guerrilla warfare handbook sat right next to it. She bought both of them.

Backtracking her way to the truck through the throngs of shoppers, Red spied a short train of three men in shiny black suits—one bulky engine in front, one armored caboose at the end, and one passenger car in the middle, Baldev Gupta. The goonda and his goons.

He passed within an inch of Red but didn't see her, didn't turn his head. Beneath her scarf, she smiled with wild inner satisfaction. Reveling in her invisibility, she didn't consider why Baldev might be there, on the same path to the slippery man she'd taken moments before.

Another message ignored. Another nail in her destiny.

MONA
Art Attack

"Oh, my!" Mona exclaimed in a whisper as she savored the array of butterfly creations in Mission's Real Rio Grande Art Gallery.

This first white-walled, track-lit room held entries for the annual Texas Butterfly Festival Photography Contest. Through the wide door, she could see a huge chainsaw butterfly sculpted from a tree, and a flock of swallowtails crafted entirely from yarn, fabric and paper stretching from floor to ceiling. She'd delivered her *One Life* collection of paintings earlier that week and was proud to be part of this multi-genre artistic tribute.

On the afternoon before the opening, only a handful of people milled about. She crossed the room to a photo of a fir tree scratching the blue sky with its branches. Countless monarchs clustered like fall leaves in a pile melding upwards into a congested mass of wings blanketing the bark, as if they were all cells of the same organism. Transfixed by the image, she barely heard the husky voice behind her.

"My wife, Beatrice, took this one."

She hadn't noticed the young man standing there when she walked up to the photo, even though he was six-foot-four and built like an Olympic weightlifter.

Mona didn't even turn her head, but spoke reverently. "It is beatific… rapturous… almost sacramental. Where on Earth did she take this?"

"At the El Rosario Monarch Butterfly Preserve near her hometown," the voice replied. "Ocampo, Mexico."

That caught her. She turned to see the silver end of his bolo tie at eye level, then raised her head toward his kind face and dark hair trailing down to his shoulders. "I want to go there."

"Well, you should then. It's amazing. Hi. My name's Antonio Vega."

"Mona," she said, resting her petite hand on his mammoth palm. "Nice to meet you. Are you always this tall?"

"Ha!" His laugh seemed small coming from his big chest. "Yeah, for the past few years."

"Tell your wife she has a gift, and her photo is a gift to us all." She looked back at the image and shook her head. "Talk about being in the right place at the right time."

Still bewitched by the monarchs, Mona searched for her collection and wandered through the next room into a third area. It hung on the far wall: ten paintings, each about thirty by forty inches, including the oak frame. She was already imagining painting something similar to that mesmerizing monarch photo. Her short bucket list—Mexico—now had a subcategory: Ocampo. She swiveled slowly to take in the other works of art in the room: the abstract sculpture, more fiber art, the woodcuts, the…

On the wall directly across from her collection, she beheld a kaleidoscope of iridescent colors creating designs, but not butterflies. She walked over to inspect them closely. Her heart clogged with horror. Whole butterfly corpses and body parts, glued or pinned together in patterns or pieces of other forms, were packed into the frames. Scores of detached blue morpho wings in a meaningless geometric spiral. Red admirals, yellow sulphurs, and buckeyes mashed together into an abstract grave. Tears gushed up from her soul.

Heaven have mercy!

There were hundreds, perhaps thousands of them. She despised barbarous collectors who captured insects for sport to mount on their walls like repulsive moose and lion heads. She loathed scientists who thought they had to kill to find out about life. Most of those people kept the insects' bodies intact, but this brutal artist must have been hacked from the same tombstone as that infamous serial killer from Mona's home state of Wisconsin, Ed Gein, who fashioned trophies, belts and lamp shades out of human skin.

She could feel one of her familiar fainting spells overtaking her, but halted it with steel resolve. *If I am to disappear, I'm taking my paintings with me.* She marched over to her paintings, took one off the wall, and held it under her armpit as she reached for another.

A sharp voice cut across the room. "Mona Arcade! Cease 'n' desist this instant!" The gallery owner, Barney Beaton, a walking stick, rushed over in a tight black jumpsuit and purple ascot. He plucked the painting out of her hands. "What're y'all doin' to my gallery?"

"I will not have my paintings in the same room as that goddamn morgue of murdered butterflies over there!" She flung her finger in the direction of the opposite wall.

"Y'all signed a contract, remember? These here paintings are mine for ten more days."

"Your goddamn contract can burn in hell, along with you. I am removing my collection from your vile exhibition." She wrenched her painting out of his hands and turned to rescue another off the wall.

Barney grabbed her around the neck and shoulders from behind with his bony arms, trying to subdue the crazy woman. His forearm pressed on Mona's windpipe.

Fear diluted the adrenaline pulsing through her body. She started to slip toward the floor.

Barney felt a fleshy vice grip on his collar as he was raised above the floor until his toes barely touched the tiles. With his other hand, Antonio caught Mona and eased her onto the divan under her collection.

"You little piece of shit!" Antonio held Barney with both hands locked onto his ascot and jumpsuit, a foot off the floor. "You have two choices. Either you help this woman remove her paintings from your gallery, or I will gladly fling you through the picture window behind you. And then I will walk back to my office at the Mission Chronicle to write my feature article on your opening called, 'Ghastly Real Rio Owner Attacks Elderly Artist.' Choose now!"

"Don't hurt him," Mona gasped.

As Barney experienced weightlessness for the first time in his life, he flopped around, struggling with the strength of a Raggedy Ann doll. "Ah'll he'p 'er," he cried. "Put me down. Ah'll he'p 'er!"

"Wise choice." Antonio let Barney fall into a heap and leaned down to Mona. "Are you okay?"

"I think so. Thank you. What a wicked man."

Nervously glancing around the room, Barney dragged himself up and brushed off his jumpsuit.

"He'll be our servant for a while. I'm going to see that your paintings are safe and sound and out of here. Do you have wrappings to protect them?"

"Yes, each one of them has a special box."

As Barney tried to slink out of the room, a five-fingered anvil pressed down on his shoulder. "Get the boxes these paintings came in, please," Antonio demanded. "Immediately." He turned back to Mona. "Can I give you a ride home?"

"No, no." She waved her hand weakly. "I have a truck, a Ranchero. I can take them."

Antonio smiled down at her. "I didn't realize the Mona I met earlier was Mona Arcade. Angela Mariposa. I am honored to meet you and offer my assistance. My wife and I have admired your work for a long time. We've got one of your calendars in our apartment."

"Well, thank you again. You are a kind… and a strong man. I try not to think vengeful thoughts about anyone, but I must admit I did enjoy seeing Barney suspended above the floor."

"How far do you live from here?"

Mona wiped the sweat from her brow with a hankie. "Not far out of town… in the old Frank Lloyd Wrong house."

Antonio's eyes sparkled as he sat next to her on the divan. "That place is amazing. We've wondered what it's like inside. It's so wonderfully weird on the outside."

"I'll have you over for dinner to repay you for your spontaneous bodyguard duty."

"If I might be so forward as to ask… I can see you're still a bit shaken, so may I please drive you home and help you unload these paintings? I've been wanting to meet you. I'm a writer, and the inspirations for your paintings must be fascinating. It'd make a great story."

"You don't look like a writer."

"Is that good or bad?"

"Neither," Mona smirked, feeling comfortable next to another artist after her battle with an artificial owner. "Most writers I know only lift pens, not people."

"Beatrice is picking me up on her way home from the hospital, but I know she'd love to meet you, too. I can drive your Ranchero and then come back with her in our car."

"The hospital? Is she sick?"

"No, no. She's a nurse. She works there."

"Well, if you're sure it's not too much trouble. I'm still a little rattled."

"Super. You just sit and relax. The slave and I'll take care of your artwork."

First Antonio rang Beatrice on his cell phone, then boxed and loaded Mona's paintings in the Ranchero while having a terse one-on-one with Barney. "I still have to write about your opening, for the artists and their work, and for my job, not for you. But since I have some compassion, which you seem to lack, I won't mention this incident. You have anything to fill up that blank space?"

"Ah've got a bunch of kids' butterfly drawin's Ah can put up," Barney mumbled. "Ah'd 'preciate it if this don't get out 'n' about."

"You know this town. Pretty hard to keep big mouths from flapping." Antonio walked out the door, still talking."Maybe your old hardware biz suited you better. Nuts and bolts. You certainly are one of those."

A few minutes later Beatrice pulled up, smiling and waving from behind the wheel of their maroon 1990 Celica with one gold door and a sandblasted front panel. Mona wondered how Antonio and his broad shoulders and his mighty arms and long legs could all fit inside it.

Beatrice jumped out and hopped over to Mona, brown eyes beaming and black hair bouncing. "I'm so glad to meet you! We were talking about you at the Butterfly Center yesterday and imagining some of your artwork gracing the wall where another exhibit used to be."

"Well, I'm glad to meet you, too. Your dashing husband saved me from the grip of a wicked man. He said you're a nurse, but do you work at the Center, too?"

"No, only a volunteer, but I love it!"

She reminded Mona of her mother Lily, the nurse with bubbling enthusiasm for the things and people she loved, but Beatrice looked like pictures of Mona herself in her twenties.

Mona pointed toward the back of her Ranchero. "Ten paintings are right there without a wall. If the Center wants them, they're packed up and ready to hang."

"Really? I can't wait to tell them!"

Antonio gave his wife a squeeze. "You follow us, okay, honey?" He opened the passenger door for Mona, then stuffed himself into the driver's seat. "Wow. Nice set of wheels you got here. 1977?"

"1979. My thirty-five-year-old baby. Had her since she was born."

"Eight years older than me," he said, pulling away from the curb. "I'll be very careful with the old baby."

Mona settled into the seat. It felt good to ride instead of drive. "You don't sound like you're from around here."

"Nope. Pennsylvania. Bea and I met in Ohio during college. Two Latinos too far away from home. We moved here about five years ago. You're from up north too, right?"

"Originally northern Wisconsin, then Minnesota, Iowa, and Missouri, finally here for twenty years. I never liked the cold and kept moving south."

"Did you know the Real Rio Gallery used to be a hardware store? When I first moved here, I went in to buy some wire. While I was hunched over a shelf, I heard a voice ask, 'Can ah he'p you, ma'am?' I stood up, turned around, and looked down at this skinny little face going crimson. It was Barney. He stuttered and apologized, 'Um… Sorry, sir. Um… I thought y'all were a woman. Yer hair…' So I say, trying to make a joke and comfort the guy, 'No problem. I thought you were a man, but you're wearing an apron.' That didn't work. Maybe he thought I was making fun of him."

Mona just listened, lost in his story and her memories. She felt safe and secure. It took her back to her cribbage games with papa Marco, when he'd shuffle the cards and spin tall tales, and time would drift by unnoticed.

"Then he asks all suspicious cuz I'm a long-haired freak, 'What are y'all lookin' for?' I ask, 'Do you have any wire?' He's clueless and says, 'Pardon?' Then I enunciate, 'Wire. Do you have any why-er?' But his face is a blank board. So I make wire in the air with my fingers and stretch them out into a line. I talk real slowly. 'Why… Er… Thin metal string to wrap around stuff.' He shouts, 'Wahr! We got wahr! Raht ov-ah he-ah!' The more I exaggerated Northern, the further I got from Southern. 'Wahr!' At least he understood my sign language."

"Great story," Mona said. "You should write it down and frame it."

"You know, Barney even looks like he's made out of wire. And boy, he was just as persnickety back then. Everything was in its place at Barney's Hardware Store. His unspoken motto was, 'The customer's always right… right messy. Know what y'all want, pay, and git out.'"

"Hardware to art. That's a stretch."

"Walmart moved in, and Barney gave up a few months later. But I think it was a way for him to crack open the closet door and take a step out."

By the time they reached Mona's house, she was beat, but her mind teemed with ideas. Beatrice pulled in behind the Ranchero and the three of them chatted in the driveway.

"Why don't you leave these paintings in the truck bed?" Mona asked. "I'll take them over to the Center tomorrow… if they want them. You let me know." Mona wrote her phone number on a scrap of paper and gave it to Beatrice.

"Okay, I'll call them up. Your place is phenomenal. We've never been this close to it."

Antonio grabbed Bea around the waist with one hand and pointed with the other. "Look at all the butterflies. And so many monarchs. No wonder you live here."

"This area's smack dab in the middle of one of their migration routes," Mona said. "Monarchs from all over the country pass through here on their way south."

"A bunch of 'em winter right near my hometown in Mexico," Beatrice said.

"Ocampo."

"How'd you know?"

"Antonio told me. You'll have to come out soon for a homemade dinner and a tour of this unique homestead."

"We'd love that," they both chirped in unison.

"If you ever need help around here, let me know." Antonio pointed over to the house. "Looks like those fallen palm fronds need to come off the roof."

"They do, they always do," Mona said. "That job's never finished until you're dead, like laundry. Thanks for the offer, thanks again for everything." She took their hands into hers. "Now this old body needs a rest. I'll see you both again soon. Sooner than later, I hope."

Mona waved to them as they backed out, her friend Sasha's words echoing in her mind. *"When the time comes that you need help, let it happen." Hmm. Antonio and Bea are like my parents... or the kids I never had.*

ANGEL
Meeting with Mom

Jonathan strolled back into the mission playroom with a cup of coffee in each hand and vending machine snacks tucked under each arm. "Here's your java, but no jar of peanut butter. Will a pack of PB crackers do?"

"Yes, let's do it," Angel murmured. His eyes were glazed as he tried to steer himself back from another dimension after his conversation with his devil.

"Do what?" Jonathan asked, not quite following. "PB?"

Angel's internal autopilot handed over the controls. "Sure, PB. Pick up Barry. Book my flight. Assemble the weapons."

Jonathan grinned like a little birthday boy who'd gotten a gun that shot rubber slugs instead of only popping out a cork on a string. "It's a go?"

"Go for it." Angel's mind landed, and he hopped up from his chair. "I'm ready to meet Mom."

"Stop that!"

"Where's Mumsy's office?" Angel peered down the hallway. "Maybe she'll spank me."

"Hold on! Sit." Jonathan put his hand on his shoulder, dragged him back, and sat him down. "Relax. Finish your coffee. Eat your snacks, and wait until I call Mother. Shit! Now you've got me saying it!"

In the anteroom of Victoria's office, Jonathan introduced Angel to her secretary, an attractive black woman with blonde hair, plus a little magenta on the split ends. Angel thought there must be drugs involved.

"Selena Ambrose. Angel Phoenix." Jonathan's eyes and hands went back and forth between the two. "Angel. Selena. Is Victoria alone?"

Selena corralled Angel's eyes but spoke to Jonathan. "She's waitin' on y'all."

As Angel rested his elbows on Selena's desk, Jonathan took hold of one arm, led him away, and stopped a yard before Victoria's office door. "You're the one in heat. Do I have to put a leash on you?"

"Leather with spikes."

"Your odd job just got harder. I want you to bring back Barry's cage, too, so I can put you in it."

"Selena is an 'administrator's secretary'?" Angel asked. "Isn't that redundant? The déjà vu identical twins?"

"I think I liked you better when you were tired."

"Two cups of coffee." Angel hung his head. "I overdosed on drugs at the DEA."

"Take a deep breath and let's do this."

"Okay. One more thing." Angel leaned close, cupped his hand by his mouth, and whispered to Jonathan. "Remember. Don't call her Mother."

Jonathan's eyes rolled back into his sockets. He knocked on the half-open door and poked his head in. "Angel's here. You have a few minutes?"

"Do come in." DEA Administrator Victoria Lionel spoke from behind her monumental, intricately carved walnut desk. It had a woman's feel, but she manned it like a tank. Hard, dark-brown hair framed a fifty-something-year-old face buried beneath bulletproof makeup. She didn't rise, but delivered a volley of words from behind her bunker. "Welcome, Angel Phoenix. A living legend. I've heard so much about you and am glad you came to visit us."

"I'm honored to meet you, ma'am," answered Angel, once again the perfect gentleman. "I respect you for taking on this humanitarian challenge in a drugged world and making it your life's work."

"Well, thank you, Mr. Phoenix. Please have a seat." She opened the thick classified file on her desk.

Angel took the power seat right in front of her desk. Jonathan sat off to the side.

Victoria spoke as if she were giving a speech to a TV camera. "Our challenge is rewarding as well as intimidating and frustrating. Eliminating drugs from the world is like trying to empty a bucket of water while standing ten feet under the sea."

So far Angel imagined she'd said every one of her words a thousand times before, in exactly the same order. "That is a succinct analogy, Administrator Lionel, but makes it sound hopeless. The war may never be over, but I know you've won some major battles along the way."

"I'm hoping you may be able to help us with an important one. Deputy Skipper speaks highly of you, and the accounts in your file are almost unbelievable. I must admit that I thought you'd be—"

"Taller, wider, bigger, older, lighter, darker?" Angel had been ready for this one. With both hands on his knees, he leaned in closer to Victoria's desk, as if confiding in a buddy over the hall water fountain. "Ma'am, people often have an image in their minds of what they think they'll see when they meet me. I'll bet you hear the same thing." Angel slowed his pace and lowered his voice into a slight Southern accent. "I would've thought the administrator of the DEA would be a…" He waited for her to finish the sentence.

"Man." Victoria scowled. "How right you are."

"It used to bother me too, but not anymore." Angel leaned back in his chair. "I know who I am, what I can do, and I have the freedom to choose who to do it with. I think it's high time women were in the back room power offices. Men have brought this world to the brink of I don't know where. Did they forget where they came from? Om, the sacred sound and symbol. It's right in the middle of womb, right in the middle of home, and at the end of atom and Mom. How does 'man' begin? Ma."

The silence was religious. An ash dropped from a cigarette would have hit the floor with a resounding crash. Jonathan sat like granite.

After three elongated seconds, Victoria's somber expression relaxed into a smile. "How refreshing!"

"Men seem hell-bent on finding their 'om' in gloom, doom, and tomb. Mankind? I don't think so. Womankind, yes. Man-unkind."

Victoria raised both eyebrows. "Can I arrange for you to speak at the United Nations?"

"I'm sorry, ma'am, if I might have overstepped my bounds. I am sleep-challenged. Yesterday I imagined being self-confined for a week in my bed at home to recover from last month's work."

"No, no. Go on," Victoria urged, shaking her head. "I needed those words. Thank you."

"Okay, ma'am." Angel turned and spoke to Jonathan, but had captured Victoria's full attention. "Related to this topic, something occurred to me after we talked last night." "You and I were talkin' about Khun P meaning Mister Ghost in Thai. But I got to thinkin'… and maybe you've already considered this. Khun doesn't only mean 'mister.' It's a unisex title of respect in Thai, so Khun P could be Miss or Mrs. Ghost. I heard you don't have a photo nor run into anyone who's seen him… or her. Most drug or thug lords have egos the size of the Pacific Ocean but this one chooses to be secret. Why? Could be a sideline of a business… or a government. Mister Ghost might be Khun Alter Ego of a Deputy Prime Minister. This situation's already dicey, but there could be a whole 'nother set of dice under the table."

"I hadn't thought of that," Jonathan admitted. "We've hardly time to think since the photos of Barry arrived."

"Mr. Phoenix," Victoria broke in, gesturing to the file on her desk, "now that Mr. Skipper has briefed you on the facts, you can understand what a delicate state of affairs this is."

"Yes, it is, and please call me Angel. Friends don't call friends 'mister.' My real name is Chris. I picked up Angel and Phoenix along the way, two cities I lived in as a kid. A lot easier for folks to pronounce than my given name—Christopher Worthington Sengtavisouk. Innocent people have been rushed to the hospital to get their tongues untied. Under my name on credit cards, it said, 'Continued on the other side.'"

Victoria hesitated, mentally trying to translate what he'd just said. "Well, Angel," she said, trying to keep control of the conversation, "your reputation does fit the task. Our file says you can fly, you are invisible, and you save people. Barry needs saving. The VP needs saving. We need saving. Will you help us?"

"I tell you this, ma'am, I will try. It may be a delicate situation for you, but for me, it's a sticky, sharp, slippery one... a can of worms in a cactus patch in a hellhole. But as you say, ma'am, it seems fittin' you should send in an angel to outwit a ghost. Now I don't really believe he or she is invisible, but I have medical proof that I am."

"What do you mean, Mr... Angel?" Victoria asked, perplexed, but her curiosity lit.

"I went into a psychiatrist's office once and talked with the nurse for a bit. She rang the doctor on the intercom and said, 'Sir, there's a patient out here who thinks he's invisible.' The doctor said, 'Tell him I can't see him right now.'"

The elongated seconds returned while Angel's tiny group of two spectators tried to sort out truth from fiction. He thought Victoria might be one of those people who laughed three times at a joke. Once when she heard it because everyone else laughed, then when someone explained it to her, and once more when she finally got it.

Victoria chuckled, cracking her makeup. "Jonathan, you'll have to put that in his file."

"The more time you spend with Angel, the more he grows on you," Jonathan replied. "Like a puppy, or mold, depending on the moment."

Victoria tapped her pencil eraser on the desk. "Do you boys have a plan of attack?"

"We do have a plan," Angel stated confidently, "but it's like puttin' together a jigsaw puzzle without the picture on the cover of the box. We've given it the code name Beaumont's BBQ. BBBQ—Bring Barry Back Quickly."

Jonathan shot him a pseudo-glare. "I didn't hear about that."

Angel turned in his chair to face him. "You know I like to make up stuff, Skipper. You'd probably call it somethin' humdrum like Jungle Storm."

"Personally, I liked Double-T Poop. Takin' the Piss out of P, pardon my French."

"Which one of those words is French?" Angel wondered out loud.

"Would you boys like to be alone for a while?" Victoria asked impatiently.

They both looked down like two scolded children concealing double smirks.

"Sorry, ma'am. The Skipper and I are just gettin' on too famously. I met him in a dream a while ago, but don't fret, I won't tell the press what he did."

"We'll go with Operation Barbecue," she pronounced and wrote it in pencil in the file. "That's what will happen to us if this mission fails."

"Ma'am, since we're discussin' names, let me ask you one question, please." Angel leaned in again and widened his eyes a bit. "How should I address you? Miss Lionel? I know you're married with a family, so Mrs. Lionel? Administrator Lionel is long and sounds so secretarial for a woman in your position. Fearless Leader? Help me. I'm just tryin' to be proper."

Victoria smiled at Angel puppy. "Just call me… Mom."

Jonathan somehow kept his jaw from plummeting into his lap.

Angel's invisible wings unfurled. "Okay, Mom. And outside your inner sanctum here?"

"Victoria will be fine." She glowed inside, proud of her new personal yet professional role.

"I like the name Victoria. You couldn't be where you are today without being a victor."

"You do have a way with words, Angel. I'm sure you'll find a way to bring Barry back to us."

"That's what I do, and I'll do my best. It's been a distinct pleasure to meet you, Mom, and I hope to see you again before I leave. I'll have to stay another night for more planning in Jonathan's playroom. I'm makin' a list of what I'll need: battleships, nuclear weapons, karaoke machines for diversions, large amounts of cash and prizes—"

Jonathan shepherded him out while looking back over his shoulder at Victoria. "Don't worry. We're cutting him off coffee immediately. I'll try to drain off some of his energy to recharge our cellphones."

Victoria resumed her administrative voice. "Good luck, gentlemen. We only have seven days until the ransom is due."

In the hall outside her office, Jonathan pulled Angel into a corner. "Who are you?"

"You said I was a son of a bitch when we met at the airport. I should have complained to Mom. So where was your SWAT team? I used the M-word."

"She said it *first!* How did you do that?"

"I planted a seed and watered it. She let it grow, and we all harvested," Angel said smugly.

"Have you considered going into politics?"

"I'll go with Mark Twain for the answer." Angel raised one index finger. "'Suppose you were an idiot, and suppose you were a member of Congress; but I repeat myself.'"

RED

Due Day

LATE MORNING SUN FLICKERED THROUGH THE SHEER CURTAINS, but the brass reading light on the headboard of the bed still burned. On Red's Persian rug, a US Army Guerrilla Warfare Handbook rested half-open, standing on the half-circle of its stiff pages. One dead soldier—an empty Glenfiddich bottle—lay face down on the nightstand.

Red's cheek itched. Still asleep, she scratched it with one hand. Her forehead tingled. Climbing out of her drug-and-alcohol-enhanced coma, she lifted both hands to her face. Something tickled the inside of her nose and her ears. Her eyes went from slits to full disks as she saw the cloud of insects coursing around the room, bashing against the windowpanes, crawling on every surface.

She wobbled out of bed, whisking winged ants or termites or whatever they were off her shoulders, arms, and nightgown. This had happened at the beginning of the rainy season, but never this time of the year. Flinging open her armoire, she snatched a shawl and a pair of Aerial Aviation coveralls and stumbled into the living room/office, bracing herself on walls and furniture along the way.

As she reached for the intercom button to call Azeez, her new cellphone rang. She grabbed it, looked at the screen but didn't recognise the number, and set it back down. She leaned against the desk and closed her eyes, summoning her sanity and strength. Without voicemail activated, the phone kept buzzing.

She picked it up and shouted into the phone. "Hello!"

"Miss Red." The voice sounded dead. Or deadly.

"Yes. Who is this?" she demanded.

"Baldev Gupta."

Two of the three molecules of strength she'd summoned fled, tripping over each other as they left. "I was just preparing to ring you," she said, hoping her impromptu cheery voice would mask the lie. "Today is due day, I know. I have your money. Will you please give me your bank account number so I can transfer it?"

"I did not lend you a transfer. I lent you cash. And that is how I expect to be paid."

Cheeky bastard. "Fair enough," Red said, stifling any terse words that might hinder resolution of this sticky situation. "I will withdraw it and bring it to you."

"Bug will be picking it up, depending on your acceptance or rejection of a proposal."

"Begging your pardon, Baldev," Red and her remaining strength molecule replied, clutching onto each other for support, "but I don't want that vile creature on my property ever again."

"He's already there," Baldev grunted and hung up.

Red whirled around expecting to see that thin grin floating in the dim light of her desk lamp like the last time Bug had appeared in the room, but it was daylight and he wasn't there.

She tip-toed toward the bathroom, looking under and around anything that might conceal the skinny imp in black. As she passed her desk, the intercom blared. She twitched, glanced nervously behind her, then slammed her hand on the button. "What is it?"

Azeez' voice squirmed out of the speaker, professional but tinged with fear. "Miss Red, there is a Mr. Bug here to see you."

"I'll be there in a few minutes." Regardless whether Bug could hear her or not, she barked, "I do not want him in here, period."

"Yes, Miss Red."

Retrieving presentable clothing from her besieged bedroom was out of the question. She went to the bathroom and donned her coveralls. As she wrapped the shawl around her hairless head, the realization struck her.

Where did Baldev get my new phone number? I've hardly used it. How many eyes and ears does he have?

A tide of anger and resentment rose inside Red. She took a slug of scotch from the decanter on her liquor shelf and stomped toward the gatehouse to send the weasels back to the holes from which they had crawled.

A practical but nondescript brick building, the gatehouse held the decades-old, four-screen security system, a gray metal desk and two ottomans in the front office, and Azeez' quarters in the back. There had never been a break-in or a theft. Who would steal an airplane or a barrel of noxious chemicals? A jet-black Bugatti C16 Galibier sat outside the gate, silently staking out the grounds.

Red took a deep breath as she entered the gatehouse. In the far corner of the room, as far away from their visitor as possible, Azeez tried to comfort bulldog Kamal whimpering between his legs.

Bug pulled over a chair and eased into it, his lip curled into a smug smile. “How are you, Miss Red Admiral? You are looking rather… rather plebeian today. Not much like an owner, only a worker.”

“I’ve always been an owner and a worker, both jobs that I love. Titles are meaningless. Better than being a slave doing the dirty work for a quasi-king.”

“I am thinking Miss Red Admiral must have gotten out of the wrong side of her bed today,” Bug retorted, “or perhaps the wrong side of the womb so many years ago.”

“Azeez, pour a cup of tea for our pest, pardon me…” Red scowled at Bug. “Our guest. Then, fumigate my bedroom. Like our Bug intimated and I assume already knows, my bedroom is swarming with his relatives.”

Bug remained still, silent, his smile set in cement.

As Azeez delivered the tea to the low table in front of Bug’s chair, Red placed two serving bowls and a spray can of Baygon Insect Killer next to it. “How do you like your tea? With milk, sugar, or poison?”

Overhearing her remark as he walked out the door, Azeez winced, relieved to be going anywhere this very ungood Bug was not.

“Oh, Miss-chievous Red Admiral,” Bug chided as he took his tea, reveling in the repartee, “trying to kill the messenger! Such a nasty way to treat the delivery man carrying a gracious proposal from your benefactor, Baldev Gupta. He is offering you another option besides paying your debt in cash.”

Red sat on the ottoman across from Bug, raising her teacup as if in a toast. “What? With an arm? A leg? My firstborn? You’re out of luck. I don’t have any children.”

Ignoring her, Bug removed a legal document from his satchel and placed it on the table in front of Red. “Baldev is willing to cancel your debt, and the interest, if you allow him to buy Admiral Aerial Aviation and the land on which it sits.”

“This isn’t between you and me. Why hasn’t he approached me personally? We spoke on the phone a few moments ago, but I wouldn’t call it a conversation.”

“Baldev Gupta is a man of few words. He is a man of action on many fronts.”

Red wondered how many fronts, backs, sidelines, and underhanded dealings that included. “My land is not for sale. This business is my life and my life is not for sale, either."

"But Miss Red Admiral, you must admit that your business is failing. Your planes are owned by the bank and now another building is mortgaged."

Once again, Red was amazed. *Who are these people? How does everyone seem to know everything so quickly?*

Bug continued in his pseudo-sympathetic style. "This offer gives you the opportunity to extricate yourself from the imminent crash of your lead balloon and start a new life—free and clear—with plenty of funds."

"Plenty of funds, you say," Red said with a smirk. "What might his offer be?"

"Thirty million rupees… in cash."

Red threw back her head and laughed. "Ha! Either the man is off his trolley or seriously deluded, or perhaps both. The land alone is worth twice that amount."

"Let me ask you one question, Miss Red Admiral. To whom is it worth twice that amount… besides you?"

"At this moment, I don't know," Red admitted, not backing down an inch, "but I can put it on the market and let the bidding begin."

"My dear Miss-informed Red Admiral, there may be other things you do not know as well." Bug leaned back on his chair with no trace of his former sneering smile. "Like the fact that Baldev owns all the land surrounding yours and has most impressive plans for this area. With only those facts in your over-inflated brain, how many people do you imagine would dare bid against a man of such stature as Baldev Ishwar Gupta? To block his path? To be completely boxed-in, or shall we say, imprisoned by his power and influence? Think again, Miss-ing the Big Picture Red Admiral."

"Then we will be neighbors across the fence. I promised Baldev I'd repay my debt in cash today. He said you'd pick it up. I'll meet you at three in front of the Standard Chartered Bank in the Citi Plaza." Red stood, picked up the document, ripped it in half, and threw it into the trash basket. "I shan't have my life torn apart over a loan freely given! A debt I am ready and willing to pay! Cheers to you and your ruler, Mr. Bug. See you at three."

Red reached for the door, but Bug grabbed her elbow, jammed his sharp fingernails to the bone, and commanded, "Sit for a minute, Miss-guided Red Admiral, and learn."

"Now what?" Red protested feebly as her lone molecule of strength waved a white flag, collapsed, and died.

"A short demonstration of your situation, since my words seem useless." Bug twirled his black hair with the fingers of his left hand and pointed between her eyes with his right. "You fly, yes?"

"Yes," she whispered like a child spanked.

"Yes... you... fly..." he murmured, concentrating on his left hand. He yanked a strand of hair from his own scalp, then deftly tied a loose knot, creating a tiny noose on the end, and set it on his knee.

"Yes... you... fly..." Bug stared at the sugar cup for a moment, then as fast as the tongue of a toad, his right hand flashed toward the table, plucking a house fly out of the air as it left the cup.

Red was transfixed.

"Yes... you... fly..." Relaxing his grip, feeling the vibrating prisoner with his curled fingertips, Bug removed the fly by its wings with his left hand, smiling with sick pride. He picked up the knotted hair, slipped the noose over its eyes and head, tightened it, and grasped the strand by the other end. The fly rose up and flew in circles above his hand.

"Listen and learn," Bug hissed, pointing at the fly. "You... fly. The hair... Baldev. The hand... Baldev. Me... Baldev. The land... Baldev. You are on a short leash, chained to Baldev. He decides where you go, what you do, and when you do it."

He rose to leave with the tethered fly still buzzing and circling in the air. "I will see you at three and take your petty cash to Baldev. A baby step toward your future."

Red barely breathed.

"We don't want your firstborn. You are the firstborn. The only born. So hardheaded, like your Danny Boy and Mommy Chandra. You think you can see the future, Miss-taken Red Admiral. I will show you the future where these baby steps of yours lead."

He snatched the can of insect killer off the table and sprayed the fly. It wavered, then dropped straight down and hung motionless at the end of the strand. Bug opened the door, stepped out, then turned and flipped the hair-hung fly into the room.

"I know you're out of red locks, Miss Bald Admiral. Keep this black one to remind you of me."

MONA

One Thing after Another

Beatrice phoned Mona at nine in the morning to tell her the National Butterfly Center would be "pleased as punch to have her collection brightening their walls."

By ten, after a lengthy session in her bedroom deliberating over which flowered frock to wear, Mona went outside to water the golden marigolds and chrysanthemums in the front yard, then left the hose watering a large clay pot overflowing with periwinkle blooms. She glanced at her Ranchero filled with boxed paintings and strolled over to the carport.

I guess I might as well deliver these now.

She drove the few miles to the Center and chatted with its manager while volunteers carried in her paintings.

As she pulled her Ranchero under the carport at home, Mona remembered she hadn't checked on her ailing neighbor lately, and decided to drive over to Yves' house after going inside to the bathroom. She left the Ranchero running with its door open, but strolled in her thoughts, picturing the monarch swarm photo that had titillated her at the gallery.

By the time she completed her deep-seated meditation on the toilet, it was past lunchtime. She whipped up a batch of Jiffy Corn Muffins, spooned twelve dollops into the cups of her metal muffin pan, and put it in the oven at 400 degrees. With a glass of lemonade, Mona eased herself onto the davenport next to the massive palm tree trunk in the center of her round kitchen-dining-living room.

I want to paint. but I don't know what.

Bea's image haunted her as if it were a dreamy scene from her past—or one in her future. She'd said to Antonio at the gallery, "I want to go there," but those five words didn't convey the primal urge in her gut that had formed them. Four words would have: "I am going there." She didn't want to recreate the photo, but the its elements felt so familiar. Seeing Beatrice's youthful face when they met was like gazing into a mirror fifty years ago.

What is it? Something from my twenties?

Mona needed her memory aids—the years of monthly correspondence with her pen pal Zarita. She walked out to her studio, opened the filing cabinet, and sifted through the carbon copies of her own letters.

Her twenties had begun as she was finishing nursing school in Minneapolis, Minnesota. After working at a hospital for too many years, she got fed up with five months of winter, a frozen nose, and frost-bitten toes. She moved 250 miles south to Des Moines, Iowa, where she treated overweight natives who supplemented their corn-on-or-off-the-cob with corn-fed pork and corn liquor.

As Mona thumbed through the years, words popped off the top of one letter—"horrible, horrible thing"—followed by a string of exclamation points she was prone to use to express joy, despair, or any other strong emotion. She took out the letter and began to read.

Dear Zarita,

A horrible, horrible thing happened last week!!!!! I was at the laundromat after I finished the late shift at the hospital. My boyfriend Derrick had dropped me off and left to pick up a pizza. No one was there but me. I sorted my clothes, you know, dark and light, and put them in two washing machines.

Three guys come in, high on something, and start talking to me, not in a nice way. They wanted me to go home with them!!! I try to say, "No way, Jose," and suddenly one of them grabs me and growls, "Then we'll do it right here." The next second they all have their grubby paws on me and drag me back to a laundry folding table, lay me down on it, and one of them rips off my sweater!!!! I'm thrashing around and yelling but they hold me down tight.

Derrick bursts through the door, almost breaks it down, and runs at us shouting some war cry at the top of his lungs! He's big and had just come back from Vietnam, shell-shocked, paranoid, sweet but battling nightmares inside. These other guys looked like green farm boys that might have wrestled a pig, or done whatever else they do with them here.

Derrick picks up the guy holding my sweater and throws him headfirst over a row of dryers. Another guy charges him, but Derrick grabs his arm, chops it, and flings him aside. I heard his bone snap!!!! The last guy heads for the door, but Derrick trips him, flips him over, and starts pounding his face with his fists, over and over!!!

I'm freaking out and screaming, "Stop it! Derrick! Stop it, stop it! You're killing him!" I jump on him and try to hold his arms back, but he shoves me off. Now I'm fighting the guy who's saving me!!!!!

He finally stops and says, "Let's get out of here," grabs my arm and starts dragging me to the door, just like the other guys who grabbed me and dragged me to the back!!! Now I'm screaming at Derrick, "Let me go! I'm a nurse, for God's sake!!! If I were at the hospital, I'd be the one treating them in the emergency room!"

The first guy hadn't moved and had a gash on his head. The second guy held his arm and moaned. The third guy lay there motionless in a pool of his own blood. Derrick says, "Let the bastards suffer." I stomped over to the payphone and called an ambulance while he sulked in the corner.

I'm sick of this place!!!!! I got so, so depressed. I broke up with Derrick. How could I ever trust him again?!!! I quit my job. Now I know what they meant in Minnesota when they joked about what Iowa stands for. Idiots Out Walking Around.

I packed up all my stuff and moved out of my apartment. When I finish this cup of coffee, I'm flying back to Wisconsin to visit my parents and sit on the shore of Lake Superior until I decide what to do with my life. I'm going home!!!!

Mona set the letter in her lap and stared out the window, beyond the horizon, beyond today.

That's it.

She walked over to her easel, dabbed her brush in the sky-blue oil paint and swept it across the blank canvas, sweeping herself back in time.

WEARING HIS RED PLAID FLANNEL SHIRT AND PRESSED BLUE JEANS, Papa Marco waited for his twenty-seven-year-old, five-year absent daughter at the gate—waving, grinning, unable to conceal the fact he was ready to jump out of his skin. Mona gave him a hug that nearly collapsed his rib cage onto his pounding heart. He picked up her bags and carried them out to a newish, bluish, two-door Rambler American.

"Where's Chester?" she asked.

"The ol' truck's happy at home. We needed somethin' smaller, better gas mileage. I don't haul much around anymore 'cept your mama and me." Marco gave her a one-armed side hug. "I'm so tickled that you're here, my Mona Lisa."

During the ride home, Mona's emotions sprang to the surface the second the small talk slipped away. The whole laundromat scene and her depression and her frustrations and her fears gushed out with her tears.

Marco apologized for not having wipers on the inside of the windshield, too. He patted the front seat next to him. "C'mere here and sit close, sweetheart." He put his arm around her as he drove the twenty miles to their cabin. "I'm so sorry this happened to ya. I think man is the cruelest creature on Earth," Marco sighed, "especially macho men. Yah… when I was in Germany during the big one, it was hell. Young bucks killin' young bucks that looked just like them, prob'ly their relatives way back when. If the world had been smart, they'd've sent the women over. There wouldna been any fightin'. They'd've hunkered down and talked about it, made a big dinner together, and done some quiltin' afterwards while they solved everyone's problems."

"Thanks for listening, Papa. I'm just glad to be home to see you and Mama and the woods… and the lake."

"Well, my little butterfly, you can stay as long as you like, even longer than forever."

It was Sunday, but Lily wasn't home. As head nurse at the hospital, she didn't own her own time anymore. The log cabin smelled as organic and inviting as ever. Marco said he needed a little shut-eye, so Mona went outside and took a deep breath of the fresh fall air, teeming with that woody, mossy, untamed fragrance she adored.

She hiked down the hill to the beach through the flaming red-yellow-and-orange maple trees lining the trail. White-spotted, red toadstool mushrooms waited for toads under the arching ferns. Shiny red wintergreen berries danced with the tiny leaves swinging them above the forest floor.

Mona stepped from the narrow path into the realm of Lake Superior, the world's largest freshwater lake—an inland sea. On the ivory sand and iron-stained clay shore, powerful waves had scattered white driftwood as far as Mona's eyes could see. Mammoth tree trunks, their bark peeled off by the seasons, lay like sun-bleached dinosaur bones.

She'd forgotten about the ladybugs. Red flowed and flew everywhere. Every fall billions of them gathered on the shore, on the driftwood and on the trees, rivers of crimson-and-black dots running along their white trunks, a cosmic convention of minuscule Volkswagen beetles with six legs instead of four wheels. One-spotted, two-spotted, eleven-spotted, twenty-two-spotted—Mona had spent days counting the different kinds during her childhood.

She lay on the sand, head resting on a rock pillow, and watched a one-spot crawl up her finger. Beyond her hand, legions of ladybugs sunned themselves on the dead arms of a fallen tree, now overflowing with life. Beyond the tree, the lake horizon melded into the azure sky. An inner peace settled over Mona, one speck of a being, one spark of energy amongst the infinity surrounding her. No fear, no depression, not apart—a part of the whole.

Mona gazed up into the blue to the north and felt as though she were floating, pivoting, turning to fly south. She'd had a similar eerie sensation on the plane when it took off to the south of Des Moines and then curved around to the north. She'd thought then, or only felt, I'm going home, but this is the wrong direction. Now in the northern land she adored, that feeling grew.

It's great to be home, but this isn't home anymore.

The words Mona's birth mother Angela had written in her letter faded up in her mind's eye. *I truly know there is an important reason for you to survive.* Whatever that reason was, it wasn't here, and that felt all right.

MONA HELD HER BRUSH HANDLE IN HER TEETH as she reveled in the painting her hand had created. Like Beatrice's monarch photo, countless black-and-red beings swarmed on a tree touching the blue sky. Beatrice had been standing and looking up, but Mona had been lying down, looking out over the lake. Her painting captured that scene with one addition—a lone monarch lifted from the universe of ladybugs and flapped south.

She signed it, "Superior Communion, Wisconsin, 1968," then leaned over to rouse shepherd Marco, lounging by the door. "C'mon, boy. Let's go get you some food."

As they walked to the house, Mona noticed the rays from the setting sun reflecting off the road. The pavement looked wet, but it hadn't rained. She went around to the front of the house and stood on the shore of the newly created Lake Mona, spring-fed by her hose, still gushing into the clay pot now wallowing in four inches of water. Under the carport, waves lapping at its rear tires, the Ranchero purred with its door open, waiting for a driver.

She turned off the truck and the hose, feeling like an idiot out walking around, and went inside through the front door. A burning odor lingered in the room, like a campfire still smoldering.

The corn muffins!!!!!

The stove was too hot to touch. Mona donned her mitts, removed the pan from the glowing oven, and dumped the damage into the sink. The muffins weren't burning any more since they'd been reduced to their essential element—inert carbon. Twelve Jiffy charcoal briquettes.

She grabbed the kitchen phone and rang Beatrice.

After Mona's call, Beatrice plunked down across from Antonio in the dining nook of their cramped one bedroom, living room, bathroom, not-enough-room apartment. The chaotic life of the family next door vibrated the far wall and echoed into the room. Kids shouted over a game show on the tube. Dogs and parents barked. The faint smell of cigarettes wafted through the vents.

"I like Mona. She's got a funny sense of humor."

"What do you mean?" asked Antonio, his head buried in his laptop.

"Her first words on the phone were, 'It's Mona. Remember me?' I said, 'Of course!' Then she said, 'At least one of us does. I have trouble remembering me.'"

"She is getting on, you know. Must be over seventy."

"When I asked her when we should come over for dinner, she said so seriously, 'Yesterday.'"

"She said that?" Antonio's head flipped up from the screen. "That is funny. Did you tell her we were already booked for the past?"

"Exactly what I said. Great minds think alike!"

They high-fived each other.

"Then she asked me, 'How about right now?' I laughed and told her tomorrow would be fine, and asked what we could bring. She said, 'Everything.' I laughed again and asked if we could borrow her Ranchero. She said, 'No problem, but you don't need to bring anything. I have more than enough for all of us.' I guess she meant she had enough food."

"She's a sweet lady, and I'm glad we met her. Let's bring her a present. She really loved your monarch photo in the gallery. You have another print you could give her?"

Bea's eyebrows jumped up and bumped into each other. "I do!"

"I know she'd love it. She told me to tell you that you have a gift and your photo is a gift to us all."

"Well, that's so nice of her," Beatrice purred.

"Who'd have ever thought one of your butterfly photos might be hanging in the house of Angela Mariposa, Angel Butterfly? It's like a dream come true that we never could've dreamed in the first place!"

ANGEL
The BBQ Checklist

In the mission control playroom, Angel and Deputy Jonathan Skipper hunched over the pieces of the puzzle—maps, photos, weather statistics, Khun P's classified file, and peanut butter snack crackers.

"I hope you didn't mind me callin' you the Skipper in front of Mom."

"No, many people do," Jonathan said. "I was captain of the rowing team in college. It stuck."

Angel popped a snack cracker into his mouth. "The title of deputy seems beneath you. Tin badge. Deputy Barney Fife of Mayberry. Middle mismanagement. I know you are the skipper who sails this ship. Mom's only the general sittin' onshore. Jonathan is a fine name, but Skipper fits better."

"Call me whatever you want. I'm sure you'll have a few four-letter names for me by the time this is over."

Angel was coffeed-up and keyed in after their meeting with Victoria. "Now that we have an official mission moniker and a hall pass, let's plan this undertaking vigilantly to make sure I won't be calling you my undertaker." He paused, then changed course. "What a weird word—undertaker. Sounds like the devil diggin' from the bottom up."

"Angel, you think too much. Try one thought."

"You're right," Angel agreed. "I gotta break the thinking habit. Feel with the heart instead. Did you know that the heart in a baby develops before the brain? It's not just a slave pump—more like a mini-brain communicating through nerves, waves, hormones, and electromagnetic fields. It learns, remembers, feels, and controls the body on its own. You can live if you're brain dead. When your heart dies... game over, man."

"Are you talking Scientology, theology, or mythology?" Jonathan inquired, intrigued.

"Apology. Sorry for ramblin' on. You started it with the 'think' word."

"Wrong," Jonathan corrected. "You started with the 'undertaker' word."

"Oh... yeah... right again. Out of my mind... again."

Jonathan leaned back on two legs of his chair and put his hands behind his head. "Keep talking. I think we're on the same page. And I do enjoy The *Book of Angel*, read by the author himself."

"Well, I'm just talkin' plain ol' biology here." Angel stood and paced around the table. "This isn't new-age mumbo jumbo. Reputable doctors have proven this stuff with their magnificent machines. I love readin' solid data confirming what poets and mystics have written for centuries—if they weren't burned at the stake." He bent down and looked under the table, then around the room. "Skipper, you have a soapbox for me to stand on?"

"Why? Are you trying to brainwash me?"

"Yeah, me and TV. In this case, I believe what I've heard because I've experienced it in my own way. The heart's electric field is about sixty times greater than the brain's and can be detected anywhere on the surface of the body. The heart's magnetic field is more than *5,000 times stronger* than the field generated by the brain and can be measured many feet away from the body, in all directions. I'm sure it's the main receiver in my Angel Radar. My brain's only the processor, a computer with too many bugs in it."

Jonathan spoke softly to his pacing, hyperactive partner. "Angel?"

Angel stopped and turned toward him. "Skipper?"

"I've got a new name for you."

"What? Professor Shuthefuckup?"

"No… Strangel."

"Strangel." Angel said it like he was petting a kitty. "I like that. I consider it a compliment."

"Strangel in a Strange Land. Sounds like you."

Angel flashed him an A-OK sign. "Now that is a great book."

Jonathan folded his hands in prayer. "Bible."

"Valentine Michael Smith," Angel mused, its main character alive in his mind, "born and raised on Mars, before turnin' God upside down on Earth."

"When I mentioned we're on the same page earlier," Jonathan confessed, "I almost said, 'I grok you in fullness.'"

"That's because, not only do you *compliment* me with the name Strangel, we *complement* each other. Two peas in a pod goin' after Khun P. Okay, one more did-you-know, and then back to busyness. Did you know that Robert Heinlein's publisher made him cut down his original 220,000 words in *Stranger in a Strange Land* to 160,000 before they'd print it? Almost one out of every three words? I'm tryin' to do that in my life."

"It's not working."

"I only said *trying*." Angel sat back down at the table. "Now, work. In case we need have secret chat on phone, is BBQ good enough you?"

Jonathan feigned exasperation. "Strangel, would you please send Angel in here?"

"I tried to cut out one-third of my words."

"You sounded like a Thai taxi driver trying to speak English." Jonathan got as serious as he thought Angel would let him. "Okay, then. On unsecured phone calls, BBQ is our codename. Barry's the burger. Buns are the buildings in the compound. Fries are the opposition. Extraction point is the relish. If something goes wrong, we're in a pickle."

Angel was in his element now, especially since the element on the line was his life, and he was planning with a man who spoke his language. "Charcoal briquettes are the fireworks for my diversion. Corn cobs are what I'm gonna stick up your ass if my charcoal briquettes and grillin' utensils aren't in the neighborhood before I get to the buns. And I don't want bloody catsup or anything red at this barbecue. It's a rescue mission, choreographed like a holiday display for everyone to ooh and aah over. I don't need much, but let's make a list and check it twice, so I won't be naughty to anyone who's nice."

Jonathan had fetched a notebook as Angel spoke. He slapped it on the table, sat down, and licked his pencil lead. "What do you want for Christmas, my boy?"

Angel pointed at the photo of Mister Ghost's compound. "Who knows what's where in this SAT pic, or what'll go down at dawn on P-Day, but I'd like to take out the water tower, maybe a generator, disable some vehicles, and knock down a few trees to trip the Ghost Soldiers' legs."

Angel had to stand up again and move around the room as he moved around in his mind. "So… Number One: Can you rustle up eight or ten remote-activated C-4 explosive packs, each about a pound and a half? I need to slap 'em on quick and detonate at will. Timing. It'll save the lives of Barry and the bad guys."

"I'll let you know ASAP," Jonathan said as he scribbled.

"Number Two: I'd like a roll of det cord because it does wonders on its own with tires and trees."

"That's easy."

"Number Three: Find out what the Ghost Soldiers wear. I doubt they wear uniforms, just camo shit. I want to look like them. My face and size are standard for the territory, but the costume must be complete. Get Barry some boots, socks, camo pants, and a shirt. He could be naked in that cage, and you don't want your boy coming home with lacerated feet and genitals after our jungle trek."

"I'll try," Jonathan half-promised. "I don't think our elderly village contacts have cell phones."

"Well, Santa, get your elves over there and talk to 'em face-to-face." Angel put his hands on the table and stared at Jonathan. "This could be the key that makes it or breaks it… and you can substitute the word *me* for *it*."

"I'll do my best and make my men do the same," Jonathan promised.

Angel resumed his pacing. "One more, Number Four: a small pistol with a silencer as a last-resort disabler if I need to nail someone in a sensitive spot. I've got several non-lethal ways of putting bad guys to sleep."

"Shouldn't be a problem."

"The C-4s and det cord need to be in the ground cache, the clothes and gun on me when I glide in." Angel stopped to think for a moment. "I can take my canopy and other toys on the plane."

"I'll get you a secure phone to shoot us the extraction coordinates before and then rendezvous time later. And GPS bugs for you and Barry, so we'll know exactly where you are every step of the way."

They batted ideas back and forth like doubles tennis teammates, trading volleys on the practice court before Wimbledon.

"I'll fly to Atlanta and be in Chiang Mai by Tuesday morning, meet your ground crew, and get to Phu Chi Fa in the afternoon. That only gives your elves two days to gather my gifts. Can they do it?"

"They have to," Jonathan said, "or they'll get a lump of burning coal in their stockings."

"The Ghost gave you the ten-day ultimatum last Wednesday, right?"

"Correct."

Angel took off his baseball cap and ran his fingers through his hair. "We're cuttin' it close,"

"What else can I do?" Jonathan asked.

"What about your agents in Thailand? I've gotta save one already. How many other gung-ho-hum Barry types you have over there?"

"Don't worry. Barry was a special case, not a special agent. I sent him there so he could learn from some of the best men we have."

Angel forced his legs to let him sit down. "Okay. Who's my main man?"

"Doug Anderson."

"Doug and her son?" Angel threw up his hands. "You're joking. A transvestite with a family? We've already got Bury and now we've got Dug. They both sound like undertakers."

"Strangel, you'll have to go with your heart on this one. Doug's heart and soul is in his work. If I left the DEA, I'd recommend him for my job."

"I've gotta write a book about all this shit. It'd have to be published after I've been buried, so everyone who'd want me dead couldn't kill me."

"How about if you book your flights and I contact my elves in Thailand?"

"Okay. Do you think we should tell Mom, now that we have the picture on the front of the puzzle box?"

"We should. She gave us verbal permission, but I'd like to have her physically sign off with a signature. I keep thinking about my barbecued head on a platter in her purse."

"You run around with your head cut off and then let's do lunch. How 'bout Thai food to acclimate my innards for this mission?"

"Fried chicken feet, crickets, and giant water bugs?"

Angel's whole body shuddered. "I said acclimate, not decimate."

"You know what they say in Thailand. We eat anything with four legs except a chair, and anything that flies except an airplane."

Angel put a hand on Jonathan's shoulder. "My stomach's motto is… 'just say no to bugs.'"

RED

Scarlett O'Hare

THE LAST TWO DAYS HAD BEEN RELATIVELY TRANQUIL since Red's apocalyptic encounter with Bug and the fly. The afternoon following their meeting, she arrived in front of the bank at three p.m. to find him parked by the curb, glaring out his side window of his Buggati.

After withdrawing the cash, Red approached his car, her eyes livid slits, and handed him a manila envelope containing two million and twenty thousand rupees. Neither of them said a word. Bug's glare fixed on Red, he rolled up his window and crawled beside her for ten yards as she walked away. Then, with a throaty roar, Bug lurched into the street, showering Red with dirt and pebbles from his tires.

When the dust cleared, she noticed the pink VW Bug covered with peace signs and daisies on every body part except the windows. Red rubbed her eyes in disbelief.

What's this? The pink bug from my dreams? Am I going mad? Hmm. Maybe it's a good omen. Tiger and Gem were both fine and dandy. Maybe their luck with rub off on me.

Yesterday, two pilots had dusted several client's fields, and rupees trickled in for a change. Azeez installed deadbolts on doors and windows in Red's quarters. Cat Astrophe caught three rats and left their tails on the welcome mat to impress Red and scare those who'd escaped her claws. Baldev's loan had been paid; Aero Dynamic would pay dearly for their deeds; business should soon be normal.

A facade of income, safety, and mundane activity lulled Red into a false sense of security about the slippery path she'd chosen. From one shaky stone to another, she stepped blithely through her river of intrigue, oblivious to the reality it was a mile deep and lined with quicksand.

Today's tasks were straightforward: stop at the Khan market to pick up her forged medical evaluation and special effects for her imminent production, then meet her tentative cast of characters.

At first, Ganesh was cordial but cool behind his desk, though he warmed when her initial cash payment greased his palm and his personality. Wearing white gloves, he opened the metal box containing the three bombs and casually explained the arming and cellphone detonation procedures to Red, as if teaching her how to start a car.

Red reached toward the box.

"Stop!" Ganesh took another pair of gloves from his pocket."Wear these. No fingerprints anywhere."

"Of course." She put them on with the air of a seasoned terrorist, despite the fact that her trembling hands caused her to nearly drop one of the IEDs. "What if someone dials a wrong number—this number? Are my performers history?"

"No chance. Each device has a special built-in decoder. You punch in three more numbers after you hear the ringtone: one… three… five. That triggers the vibration… then… boom."

"How do I know they'll work? I doubt you'll give me a demonstration."

Ganesh gave her a do-you-think-I'm-an-idiot look. "Have the documents I've provided in the past worked for you?"

"Yes, but they didn't have to explode later on."

"If my wares didn't work, I have clients who'd dispose of me in a heartbeat… my final heartbeat."

"Where do I meet my auditioning actors?" Red asked.

"Two o'clock on the Athpula Bridge in Lodhi Park. I told them they're meeting Scarlett O'Hare."

"Very creative. Red Airport. I'll use it if I have to change my name after this venture."

As Ganesh closed the box and helped Red tuck it into her bag, he spoke gruffly from his heart, a hardened place where compassion was an unwelcome guest with excess baggage. "Be careful, Red… I miss your father when I see his spark in you. Devious Danny. He had many… shall we say… innovative ideas." Ganesh grinned, showing his picket fence of perfect gold teeth. "But where is he now?" He snapped his fingers as his smile flipped into a frown. "Gone. Not even a spark. We all must accept our karma and live with our destiny. Will that be your fate as well? I am hoping not."

"If I follow in my father's footsteps, I might find him along the way. No one seems to know for sure what happened to him." Red's tone went from irritation to venom in a split-second. "The police are a bunch of crooks. When I find whoever is responsible for his disappearance…" The steel look in her narrowed eyes finished her sentence.

Ganesh paused with a knowing look in his eyes, contemplating whether to reveal things Red did not know, then guided her out the door with his hand on her shoulder. "I doubt you'd take advice from one such as me, but consider this. Your real enemies are within. Anger, hate, and revenge. Perhaps you should try to conquer them first. You might live longer."

She turned to watch the door close in her face.

He's right on one count. I won't take his advice.

MONA
A Wild Hair

Beatrice and Antonio were due for dinner in a few minutes and Mona had five questions to ask them before she could spring the big one. The only thing she trusted about her memory was the fact that it took unscheduled vacations, so she wrote five words on her palm with a pen.

Kids. Pets. Smoke. Meat. Quiet.

As Mona walked out onto the half-moon, redwood deck that wrapped around the front door to the bedroom wings on each side of the house, they pulled into the driveway. Marco loped over to the car and greeted them like old cronies. Beatrice jumped out, stretched out both arms, spun in a circle, and pranced up to the deck.

"Hi, Mona! Mmm, it smells so fresh out here. And so quiet. I love it! Thanks for inviting us!"

"You're very welcome. I'm so glad you could come."

"We're trying to save money by living in a teensy-weensy apartment. The people next to us smoke all the time, and it stinks up our space. Their kids stomp around screaming and make us glad we don't have any. Their TV blares day and night. Their dogs howl. The only pets we have are three plants, but they don't make a sound. We have escaped to heaven!"

"Well, it's heaven on Earth to me," Mona said, secretly checking the words on her palm. Four questions answered. One to go.

"Hello there, Mona," Antonio said, taking hold of her hand. "Have you recovered from the horrors of your art attack?"

"It's in the past, which I have a hard time remembering anyway. And thanks to you two, my *One Life* collection is now hanging peacefully at the Butterfly Center."

"Your house looks so intriguing from the outside." Beatrice bubbled. "Antonio wanted to write about it and the guy who built it. Frank Lloyd Wong. What a great name!"

"I thought it was Frank Lloyd Wrong, just silly wordplay because it's so odd. I'd love to hear more." Mona motioned toward the door and started walking. "Let's go inside and get some refreshments first. I'm having a red wine spritzer. Water and fermented fruit. Same thing butterflies drink. I've got Coke and Sprite and orange juice and maybe a couple of antique Tecate beers in the fridge."

Beatrice followed her into the house like a hungry elf. "When in heaven, do as the angels do! I'll have a spritzer like you. Wow, it smells good in here! You're so kind to go to all this trouble."

"No trouble at all. I eat at home and get exactly what I want. I eat out, I settle for substitutions. We're having a spinach nutmeg quiche, pumpkin cumin soup, and a salad, half from the market and half from the yard."

"That sounds super. I was going to tell you we don't eat red meat or pork, just chicken and seafood once in a while when we go out… but I forgot."

"You forgot, eh? You'll fit in just fine here." *Hmm. Five questions answered without even asking. Only the big one left.*

"Please sit down and make yourselves at home. Antonio, what would you like to drink?"

"An antique Tecate would be great. The colder the better." He spread out his arms, palms up like a minister addressing the congregation. "Will you look at this, Bea. A circular living room. And here's the tree Flank saved."

"Did you say Flank?" Mona asked as she leaned into the fridge. "I thought Beatrice said it was Frank."

"Depends on who you ask. This house was built in the early 1970s by Mission's wealthy Asian-American, Frank Lloyd Wong. He pronounced it Flank Royd Wong, so that's what a lot of the locals called him… Flank. His father was a gentle Chinese man and his mother a redneck Texan. Folks say he embodied both his parents equally in his schizo personality."

"Keep talking. I haven't heard any of this." Mona handed him a frosty bottle. "One semi-frozen beer for you. Your spritzer's on its way, Bea honey."

"Thanks for the brew," Antonio said, raising it to eye level. "It's a great story. I wish I'd met him so I didn't have to rely on hearsay. I guess his army stint in Vietnam split him apart even further because he'd essentially fought a war with himself: East versus West. Came back with a Purple Heart for a head wound and a real broken heart. When he got back home to his speck of dry ,caked land, he turned on his water faucet and black crude spurted out. He tore down his shack and put up an oil derrick."

Mona delivered Bea's spritzer and eased down next to her on the davenport to listen to Antonio's story.

"An old guy I met who knew him pretty well said that Flank never married cuz he already felt like a couple. Not gay, not straight, just self-sufficient.

He spoke fluent Mandarin and rip-roarin' Southern and carried on conversations with himself in both languages, complete with each of his parents' unique mannerisms. Flank built this house to honor both of himself—one half like a 'Remember the Alamo' fortress stretching squarely to the west and the other like a graceful wooden structure flowing to the east. He'd had enough killing in the war, so he left this palm tree of life sprouting through the center, a reminder of the oil well that made it all possible."

Antonio took a long draw on his Tecate as he gazed up at the tree reaching out through the ceiling and then finished his story.

"He died young. His friend said Flank was bored with himself and fed up with the rest of humanity. This house became one asset of a trust fund he'd created to help poor children of any multiracial background."

"He donated the land and a bunch of cash for the Butterfly Center, too," Bea added.

"Goodness sakes," Mona said. "I am honored to live here. My realtor friend Sasha told me that during the short time it was on the market, most folks who viewed the house thought they'd go insane living here. No manicured lawn. The tree grows up through a hole. Bugs get in. It sounds like Flank was delightfully bonkers when he built it, and now I'm continuing the bonkers tradition. A toast to Flank."

Bea and Antonio echoed her. "To Flank."

Two wine glasses and one bottle clinked.

"I think I'm a little like Flank," Mona mused. "Self-sufficient. Never met a man I could live with or one that could put up with me. My grandfather held a hatchet to my neck and tried to kidnap me with two other thugs. My boyfriend almost killed three guys who tried to rape me and those experiences kind of killed the concept of a man in my life. If anyone got ideas, I'd take a paintbrush out of my purse and tell them I was already married to Art. I didn't imagine then Art's full name would become Arthur Rightus."

Nurse Bea's smile drooped into a frown as she realized by Mona's sigh it was a serious joke. "Is your arthritis bad? You seem to get around okay."

"Oh..." Mona said, looking down at her knees. "It's not so bad. When Mr. Pain is your constant companion, it's best to make friends with him. He reminds me I'm alive and makes me look forward to when my soul won't have to drag around this old bag of bones."

A few moments of silence sat with them until Mona tried to raise herself off the davenport but didn't quite make until Bea helped her up.

"Let me show you the rest of Flank's creation," Mona said, her raised eyebrows coaxing her lips into a grin. "Over here is the 'graceful wooden structure flowing to the east.' You *are* a writer, Antonio. I just call it my bedroom."

Mona led them around the palm tree atrium and slid open a pair of mahogany doors with hand-carved dragons in bamboo groves. A multi-angled room stretched out from the center of the house like a wing of a being, not of a building. The ceiling sloped down to intersect a bank of eight windows facing east, presenting a panoramic view of the Rio Grande River valley.

"This room would make me want to rise and shine!" Bea said as she bounced over to the windows.

Mona soaked up their oohs and aahs. "Look at this bathroom over here, you two—a work of art in tile. Besides the huge sunflower shower head on top, there are three more spouts down each side wall."

Antonio peered into the stall. "Looks like you could either shower under a waterfall or battle a horizontal rainstorm."

They sauntered over to a door on the other side of the bedroom, and Mona let them peek in. "This may be the most beautiful and largest storage closet in the world, tainted with boxes I carted in twenty years ago and haven't touched. I mainly live in the round, living-room-kitchen or in my studio. The rest of the house sits idle, waiting for someone else, I guess."

"So what's in the Remember the Alamo area?" Bea asked. "More stuff?"

"You'll see, and then you can decide."

As they walked by the wide-open windows on the south wall of the main round room, the afternoon breeze flavored the room with eucalyptus and mesquite.

"What's that hut out there on the bluff?" Bea asked.

"That's my studio. We'll go out there in a bit." Mona led them to another pair of black walnut doors serving up a scene from the Battle of the Alamo.

"Awesome," Antonio sighed as he ran his hand over the carved horses, soldiers, and cannons. "This wood is so smooth it almost feels soft."

Mona rolled open the doors and let them walk into the expansive adobe-walled room with an eight-foot, diamond-shaped skylight in the ceiling. She pressed a button on the wall, and the translucent skylight receded into the roof to reveal a deep blue sky and billowy white clouds beginning to absorb the ruddy shades of dusk.

Antonio stared upward as his mouth dropped downward. Slipping off her sandals, Bea hopped onto the four-poster bed and gazed up at its white lace canopy.

Mona pointed to a door beyond the foot of the bed. "There's an empty room over there. Could be for storage or an office. Your bathroom's over there. It's big and butch and the tub has jacuzzi jets."

"Our bathroom?" Bea asked with a bewildered look. "Are we spending the night?"

"Not tonight, since these rooms haven't been cleaned properly since my last guests a few years ago. But let's sit a spell and talk." Mona drew back the brocade curtains covering an archway leading to a sitting room with windows from parquet floor to ceiling, a cottonwood table with leather-backed chairs, and a cowhide sofa facing the sunset. "You two nestle into that loveseat there."

"Sweet! Cushy and creamy," Bea purred as they plopped down and she swung her legs over Antonio's. "I could spend a few hours right here."

Antonio was somewhere between dazed and dazzled. "This isn't the way I remember the Alamo."

Mona sat at the table and held up her open palm. "You've already answered five of the questions I scribbled on my hand. Kids. Pets. Smoke. Meat. Quiet. I've got one more."

"Ask away," Bea said.

"It's sudden and radical, but what the heck? Artists get a wild hair and have to let it grow. How would you two like to live here, in this Alamo wing, and share the rest of this splendid heaven with me, rent-free?"

ANGEL
Checking in and out

Info Desk Darla, a blissful smile floating above her shoulders, watched Angel stroll through the lobby. She waved, silently praying the angel would ask her another question, any question, bus routes, classified DEA secrets, the price of tea for two in China, phone numbers, hers in particular, exact directions to her apartment written in lipstick on her handkerchief.

Angel waved back, but went outside in search of unconditioned air that hadn't shuttled in and out of a thousand lungs, sat squat-legged on the grass near a fountain, and rang Donny back in The Ridge.

"Sher'ff Dillon… The Alien."

"Angel, mah man! How y'all doin'? You yourself again?"

"Sleep's a tonic. Been runnin' on thirty-nine winks, but I'm almost back."

"To The Ridge?" Donny asked, hope in his voice.

"No… back to Angel. 'S'ap'nin', dude?"

"Well, yer cats are still in the bag. Y'all won't believe this, but the driver's name is Van Hitmann."

"You are shittin' me!" Angel took the bait and jumped to his feet.

"The other two are Tommy Gun and Vic Timm."

"You're learnin', Sher'ff." Angel was proud of his apprentice word playmate.

Donny spoke nonchalantly now, ready to deliver his next carefully crafted list. "The driver's name is Rex A. Ford and the other two are Lou Dickruss and Stuart Pid. We call him Stu… Pid."

"You take home the trophy in this round of the Name Game. Had too much time on yer hands lately?"

"Yesterday was wild as a peach orchard hog," Donny proclaimed. "Litter pickup and three citations! One for perpendicular parkin' in a river, one for illegal parkin' on top of a Honda, one for assault and battery of a house. No way to keep the life and times of Angel Phoenix off the front page of *The Ridge Gazette*."

"Well, if it ain't on the front page, it'll be on the back cuz it's only one sheet of paper," Angel scoffed. "Weekly."

"I don't have 'em with me," Donny said, serious now, "but yer thugs had plain Tom, Dick, and Harry names. All three on bright, shiny Florida driver's licenses. Looks like they were stamped out the same hour on the same day."

"I don't know who sent 'em, but they're Sunday drivers." Angel paced, his feet pounding out his words on the pavement. "A trained assassin coulda put me on my ass permanent-like with a rifle at fifty yards. I wish you coulda been there when I took 'em down and wrapped 'em up in duct tape. You'd have sat on the sidelines, laughin' yer ass off."

"Tag team like the good ol' days?"

"Didn't last that long. Two were out cold in minutes. With me barrelin' down on him in the shovel Cat, Van Man freaked and blew his whole wad of bullets in five seconds. Reminded me of that video game, Premature Ejaculation. You put in yer quarter and the game's over."

"Haw!" Donny guffawed.

"Then you can't play again for twenty-five minutes."

Angel heard the knee slap punctuate Donny's laugh.

"Y'all crack me up." With a new lilt in his voice, Sheriff Donny confided, "FBI's drivin' in from Atlanta tomorrow."

"Good." Angel missed the cue and plunged ahead with his own agenda. "Did an agent by the name of Bernie call?"

"No one called. I called them."

"Bernie is halfway between a piece of work," Angel grunted, "and a piece of shit."

"I don't think I wanna meet Bernie," Donny said, then slipped back into his let's-get-personal voice, "but Miss FBI Agent Caroline Livingston is comin', and she sounds like a looker."

"How does a looker sound, Sher'ff?"

"You know… breathy."

"That could jus' mean big lungs perched over a big belly," warned Angel.

"Speakin' of big lungs and everything like that, Georgeann Taggart at the bank asked about you. She had that look in her eyes."

"What look?" By now, Angel had walked half a mile around one fountain.

The Sheriff started singing. "The look… of love… is in… her thighs."

"I thought you said her eyes."

"It seemed to travel down yonder."

"Not interested. I prefer natural blondes, not bottle blondes. Her peroxide locks look like they'd snap off in yer fingers. And I cain't tell whether her two outstandin' features were made by the good Lord or Silicon Industries." With all the body language flying out of him, anyone watching might have thought Angel was the poster child for the dangers of drugs. "Besides, she's a head-and-a-half taller than me, and twice the weight of my mother. Imagine David and Goliathena walkin' down Main Street. I don't reckon we could kiss and make love at the same time without a visit to a chiropractor the next mornin'."

"Well, ain't you the snarly one today?" Donny declared, nailing Angel to a wall.

"I am so sorry, Donny." Angel slumped down on the fountain edge like he'd been smacked upside the head. "Please forgive me. I am not quite here yet and I will be far gone tomorrow. Right now I think I'm runnin' on coffee fumes. It's just that I've met so many women who are attractive on the outside and perfect at their core, but not the match for this picky bastard. Not *the one*. When you see our teller, tell her I said, 'Hey.' She is a friendly one, but my heart says friends forever."

"I feel ya, bud. I'm standin' right there beside you, right now. Any idea when you might be home?"

"No," Angel took a deep breath and let it out slowly as he talked. "And right now, the 'home' word is a little vague. I'm not invisible anymore, and you know I need that. Good luck with Miss Caroline. I'd be honored if my house sacrificed its life to bring joy to my best bud. You take care, Donny Dillon. I'll ring you when I can."

"Call me if you need anything, Angel buddy. C'mon back now, ya hear?"

Angel meandered into the DEA building, dragging his heart behind him. Donny is a kind one of a kind. I can feel him from here.

After he'd booked his flights and printed out the receipts with the help of darlin' Darla, Angel walked into Jonathan's office—a working office with tables, files, photos, and paper tools of the trade spreading into every corner. Unlike the arrogant DC chambers with a moat of pretentiousness surrounding a barren desktop, where power brokers sign clandestine contracts during secret tête-à-têtes, this room said, "Come in and have a seat. I live and serve here. I'll get your job done, but let's get on it. I've got fifty more waitin' in line."

"How's it goin', Skipper?" Angel asked, turning the brim of his baseball cap to the back.

"As good as it gets on a Saturday afternoon in America and a Sunday morning in Thailand. I think it's handled for now, but it'll be a 24/7 task soon enough."

"I booked my flight to Thailand. Here're my itineraries and receipts for yesterday and tomorrow. I wouldn't mind gettin' reimbursed like you said on the phone. With short notice and alterations, it's a chunk of change."

"Great," Jonathan said, tucking the receipts into a file. "I'll send these through the system and transfer the funds if you give me your bank account number."

"Darla wants all my numbers and wants me to have all of hers. I have a personal favor to ask."

"No, Darla can't come with you. She's only qualified to use a phone and push buttons that she had to color-code with stickers of stars, hearts, and panda bears."

"I had the opposite in mind." Angel spoke a little softer—serious and sincere, one bud to another. "Can you get me outta here? I'd like to eat and pretend I'm a tourist for a while. My mission prep consists of relaxin' and sleepin', cuz my day begins tomorrow at 3:45 a.m. and I'm not sure if that's early in the mornin' or late at night. Then time turns into miles and miles of miles and miles. I won't hit another bed for forty-some hours, only a blob of minutes before my solo flight at dawn on P-Day."

"That suits me fine," Jonathan said. "I'd like to spend a Saturday night with the family before they forget my name. What d'you want to do?"

"If it's okay with you, I'd like to go to the Smithsonian's Museum of Natural History to see one exhibit. Their website showed an enticing 'green' restaurant, rated four-stars with no hearts or panda bears."

"Roger that. Ten minutes and I'll meet you in the lobby."

"How 'bout if I meet you here instead? Darla seems to degenerate into a fruitcake when I'm around. I'm afraid she'll sprain her damn face from winkin' and grinnin'."

"I see," Jonathan grimaced. "A sprained face. That's a pricey workers' comp payment."

"I'm gonna to say bye to Mom," Angel said as he drifted out the door.

An old hand at the DEA after five hours in the building, Angel found Victoria's office straightaway. Secretary Selena let her know he was there.

"Hi, Mom. I stopped by to say goodbye." Angel plunked down in the chair in front of her desk and set his baseball cap in his lap. "No… See you later. Sounds better."

"Did you two get it all worked out?" Victoria asked in her professional voice, though her smile made it personal as well. She'd dealt with hundreds of agents, but during their first meeting this odd angel had touched her like no other.

"As much as we could from here. Time-difference, time-sensitive, time to fly on planes and by the seat of my pants."

Victoria put her papers to the side and gave Angel her full attention. "You can count on Jonathan on this end. He knows what he's doing and cares about the people he does it with."

"The one thing the Skipper and I didn't talk about is what Mister Ghost is expecting. We're in a time bind and won't spring Barry until day eight. I'm hopin' he thinks he's in control, and his million'll be in his pocket on day ten."

"Well, we're ahead of you on one count," she said. "That's what we've communicated via email. We're playing meek. He's expecting an exchange rendezvous at a location he'll tell us on day nine."

"If all goes well, we meek will inherit the Earth."

"Good luck out there, Angel. Many lives are depending on you in many ways."

"I have a favor to ask of you, but I'd guess it's already in the works." He leaned back, balancing on the chair's two rear legs. "Yesterday I had an incident at my house and the house didn't survive. The perpetrators are in the clink, but I don't know which part of my past they crawled out of. You know what it's like in this biz. Help one, get hell from another. I know this is a hush-hush operation for the DEA, but I want to make sure the name Angel Phoenix stays in your file, written in invisible ink."

"What operation?" She knitted her brow, then smirked.

"I dunno," Angel murmured, gazing off to the side. *She's fast. Been around the block, the globe, and the back hallways of Washington.*

"Sorry to hear about your house, but I'm glad you made it. Mum's the word on all ends. No one wants this to go anywhere but away."

"I do appreciate it. There's nothin' wrong with bein' a secret hero for one person. Three's triple the pleasure."

"I hope to see you when you come back."

"I'm not sure when that'll be." He moved closer and rested his elbows on her desk. "I'll visit my mother in Laos. She's got a laid-back B&B near Luang Prabang. I don't see her enough… never have. Right now home is where this heart is," Angel said, laying one hand on his chest, "goin' from one mother to another. You can thank her for me takin' this job. I don't think I'd have gone to any other place. No coincidence you called. It's exactly what should have happened."

Every time Angel spoke, he took a few more steps into Victoria's heart. "Please give your mother this message from me. 'Thanks for having Angel.'

You keep in touch."

"Ha. Do I have a choice?" He slapped his palms on her shiny desktop, pushed himself up, headed for the door, and paused in front of a monarch painting on the wall. "Beautiful piece of art you have here."

"It is, isn't it? By a woman named Angela Mariposa. I think she only paints butterflies."

"I kinda feel like this monarch today, the only one that migrates thousands of miles from home and back again. Maybe that's why I'm goin' to Asia."

"Well, home or not, don't you disappear on us."

"I'm sure the Skipper'll stick a GPS inside my assets. When this is over and done, I'll have a ceremonial burning of it on the beach. See you when it's meant to be."

"You're a good one, Angel. Thank you so much for coming… and going. Go get him."

He met Jonathan in the hallway, walking out of his office. As they entered the lobby, Angel veered away from him toward Darla at the Info Desk.

"You are a sweetheart, darlin' Darla." Angel took off his cap, lifted her hand, and kissed it. "Thanks for all your help. If I don't see you again, have a nice life."

For the first time today, perhaps for the past month, she couldn't locate one word that was willing to step off the tip of her tongue.

Angel turned and went out to the parking lot.

Outside, Jonathan asked, "How was her hand?"

"Damp and vibratin', bless her heart. She was speechless. And her pretty press-on lash almost flew off her lid with that final wink."

RED

Calm before the Swarm

Once she'd picked up her goods from Ganesh, Red drove to central Delhi's ninety-acre Lodhi Park to scout her prospective cast. Sipping from the ever-present flask in her purse, she sauntered to the rendezvous spot, the sixteenth-century Athpula Bridge. Its ancient brick arches spanned a pond dotted with pink, white, and yellow blooms stretching above lotus leaf island chains.

Taking a cue from her dream Angel, she wanted to see her actors before they saw her, so she'd once again wrapped herself in a sari, plus a black scarf covering her head and her face below the eyes. She had no problem spotting one short Indian standing with two tall Germans and scrutinized them from across the bridge walkway. Wearing the proper outfits, Dietrich and Toma Sheppard would fit the wealthy couple role. She crossed the walkway and leaned against the railing next to them.

"Pleasant but crowded. Let's talk somewhere else."

Dietrich turned like a startled cat. "You are Scarlett O'Hare, I trust?"

"Yes, you can trust *me*," Red said, "but can I trust *you*?"

"I believe so, and also my wife, Toma. You'll have to decide for yourself about Hari here. We only met him five minutes ago."

Blond-to-brown-haired Dietrich could have led a safari in his Vasque hiking boots, khaki shorts, and shirt. Blonde-to-auburn Toma wore the uniform of a beach bum in Goa: plastic sandals, a white yoga blouse, and a flowing skirt sewn from a patchwork of motley fabrics. She was quite fetching, and her lengthy locks made Red long for the past—and for the future when hers would return. With his silk Nehru shirt and pressed black pants, Hari only needed a limo to become a chauffeur. They were all around forty, but Hari looked fifty and the Sheppards looked thirty.

"Tell me more about your job experience while we stroll," Red said. "My production needs players who don't shrink from intrigue and risky business. I hear you were actors and acrobats with the Titali Circus?"

"Acrobatic clowns would be more appropriate," Toma replied. "Exploding cars and selzer bottles, on the ground and on the high wire."

Beneath her scarf, Red grimaced as she led them off the bridge toward the park's Butterfly Conservatory. *Thank you, Ganesh. Two German Sheppards who used to be clowns.*

"It worked perfectly for our extracurricular activities. The audience never saw our faces during the show." Three silk scarves appeared from nowhere as Dietrich talked and walked and juggled them. "We'd fleece the native townies with a shell game or magic tricks on our time off." He plucked a rupee coin from behind Hari's ear and handed it to him. Hari's eyes went wide. "Relax, man. It's only a rupee. You should take better care of this." Dietrich returned his leather wallet as Hari patted his back pocket in disbelief.

While they traipsed across a manicured lawn shaded by massive chinar and eucalyptus trees, Toma chimed in. "We'd case the local joints in towns during the day and score other treasures at night." She turned her head to Dietrich and yelled, "Ladder!"

The next moments were a blur. Standing to his side, she flipped her bare right foot into his right hand as he raised it and her whole body. Toma's left hand went to his head and her left foot to his shoulder. Dietrich then grabbed a foot with each hand, straightened his powerful arms, and thrust Toma above his head. In five seconds, they'd become thirteen feet tall.

"C'mon up, Hari. I can hold you!" Toma shouted.

"Impressive indeed," Red said, "but please restrain yourselves! We don't want to attract attention now or later." She turned to Hari. "And what about you? Any special skills?"

"Nothing like them! I am more useful standing around and driving. I have been working as a security guard for most reputable and most disreputable establishments, although I too am doing other activities. My friends call me 'The Robbing Hood' because I take from the rich and give to the poor…" He pointed at his chest and smirked. "Me."

"Dietrich, I'm puzzled by your speech," Red wondered. "Most Germans I've met speak better English than Americans, yet you seem to use some sort of hybrid."

"I think we speak, as they say in the USA, a 'Heinz 57 variety.' My teachers were British. Toma and I met at the Ringling Brothers Clown College in Florida."

"A great place to study weird people," Toma added. "Ventriloquists singing duets with their red rubber noses. A Volkswagen Bug might pull up and thirty-six people would get out."

Dietrich took hold of Toma's hands, bent forward, and lifted her a few inches off the ground. "We toured with an avant-garde circus through Georgia and Mississippi. They spoke a whole 'nother English than we'd learned in school."

Toma served up some Southern. "I ain't drankin' no more of yer farn likker, specially Rooshin vodka."

"Y'all're mahty raht about that." Dietrich returned her volley. "You should'n oughta have another one."

"I reckon we all might could go over yonder."

Dietrich and Toma both burst into laughter.

Red smiled, but winced inside. *Doesn't sound wealthy or WASPish, but I'll have to trust they've got it in them.*

Once they'd walked to a secluded spot next to the Butterfly Conservatory gallery and sat at a green concrete picnic table, Red decided to let them in on the logistics and see if they'd accept her offer.

"A certain despicable business has sabotaged my company and must be taught a lesson. Your mission will only take a few hours over two days. Think of it as a play called 'Hiding in Plain Sight.'"

"In act one, Toma and Hari visit Aero Dynamic, posing as the wife and chauffeur of a wealthy man moving to New Delhi who needs a private airport to park his plane. While Hari takes note of the overall activity, Toma will, as you say, 'case the joint,' take the tour, be the dazzling prospective client, and plan where to hide three small devices in the hangar.

"In the second act, the three of you return with a special delivery. Dietrich will be the leading man, the rich client and the distracter, while Toma plants the adhesive-backed explosives. Then your roles in the show are finished, and I'll take care of the rest later. You alert me of your success, leave the city, and Bob's your uncle."

Three brains mulled over the facts while their bodies sat still. Dietrich was the first to speak.

"What about security guards and surveillance systems?"

"I've only seen their compound from the road. Those questions will be sorted after your research on day one. If you think it can't be done, we'll cancel act two."

"So day one is completely legal," Toma asked, "like checking out a hotel room before checking in?"

"Is visiting the competition illegal spying? No. What do you say, Hari?" Red asked.

"I am only the note-taking driver." Hari's head bobbed side to side. "I am most certainly in for act one."

Out of the corner of her eye, Red had been watching an elderly tourist with a cane meander closer to them.

Standing next to the fence surrounding the Butterfly Conservatory, the woman cheerfully addressed the group. "My, my! Isn't this a grand undertaking? Look at all these lovely butterflies!"

Red stood and scowled, positioning herself between this intrusion and her three actors. "Yes… this is a lovely spot," she snapped. "However, it's our private spot, and you can find your own spot… somewhere else."

"Oh… I see," the woman said, her eyebrows backing up and away from Red's biting words. "How antiquely British, and as I think you might say… cheeky. Your costume doesn't fool me." Turning to depart, she continued her chastisement. "Do you ever wonder why we Americans and these delightful Indians wanted folks like you to leave both of our respective countries?"

Waiting until the woman was out of earshot, Red dismissed the incident and focused on Toma. "And how about you, dear?" Red moved closer, touching her arm. "You are indeed a beautiful woman. Surely you can charm their pants off."

"Why, thank you, Miss Scarlett." She curtsied. "I'm game if Dietrich's game."

"I'm not sure if I like the 'charm their pants off' part," Dietrich muttered.

"I was attempting to speak American," Red grumbled. "I used to be married to one. He charmed my pants off and then decided he was gay."

Dietrich stood and smiled, then sighed as he paced around the table. "All right. Toma's game. I'm game. For the first act only. We'll see about the second. Sounds a little tricky to me."

"Brilliant. Red handed Hari a slip of paper and an envelope full of rupees. "You'll need to pick up your fake driver's license and bogus plates for the limo from Ganesh. Here's the phone number of a man who'll rent you a limo with only a cash deposit. Toma, pick out your jet-set costume. You're the actress. I'll trust you to decide what to wear. And Dietrich, here's a new cellphone and my number. Only call in an emergency." The gray semi-liquid poop from a myna bird fell on Red's head and dribbled down her scarf. "We'll meet here in two days at four p.m. to finalize the plans… in the limo at the main entrance."

Three more mynas swooped low and more poop splattered on her shoulder. Not knowing what it was, Red tried to brush it off with her hand, then looked down at the gooey mess on her fingers.

"Ow!" Dietrich shouted, followed by a shriek from Toma as bees landed on their arms and necks, stinging immediately and swarming around the four of them. A flock of rock pigeons joined the crapping brigade as the clandestine cadre broke apart, slapping themselves silly.

"Bloody hell!" Red screamed, ducking and covering her whole face with the scarf. "Leg it! Meet me in two days!"

They scampered along the fence with several mini-forces of nature in winged pursuit. A small audience of butterflies floated above the migrating three-ring circus of bees, birds, and human beings.

As they bumbled past, the elderly woman waved. "Have a nice day! Heading home to England, I hope?"

MONA

Worker Ant and Queen Bea

After Mona had sprung the big question about whether they wanted to live with her and share the house, Antonio and Bea became frozen statues. Brain waves ceased waving. Sensitive audio equipment may have been able to capture the sound of blood screeching to a halt. Mona's words were far beyond anything they could've imagined coming from her mouth.

Mona knew the symptoms of shock. "Okay, you two. Breathe. Blink. Move your fingers."

"I'm… overwhelmed." Antonio looked like a deer blinded and paralyzed by car headlights. "I… I don't know what to say."

"Selfishly, I could use some help around here. Before I'd move into a square box in town, I'd climb into a rectangular one in the ground. The house is in good shape, but something always needs fixing. You offered to take those palm fronds off the roof. Imagine little ol' me trying to do that! Criminently… I can't even lift the ladder. I need a worker ant. Worker Antonio. And my memory isn't what it used to be, but then I'm not really sure if I remember it was any better in the past. Right before I called Bea to invite you two out here, I'd been painting in my studio for six hours while the hose I stuck in a pot created a lake next to the Ranchero idling with its door open as the oven inside baked twelve muffins into charcoal briquets."

Bea's brain shifted out of park. "When you told me on the phone to bring everything, you weren't joking, were you?"

"No, just stunned. That experience was a clear message that it's time to ask for help. Advertise for roommates? I felt you two had been sent to me before I'd even asked. And I firmly believe everything in our lives—and everyone—appears for a reason. We see it or we don't. Meaningless coincidence doesn't exist."

Antonio took a step out of Flabbergastland. "I don't know how many times we've driven by and said, or thought, 'Wow. Imagine living there…' But that's about as far as it got. Never to the wishing or dreaming stage."

"You can save money. You've got your smokeless peace and quiet. Your pet plants will be surrounded by thickets of their relatives. There's a fenced garden plot in the back where you can grow whatever you want."

"We used to grow tomatoes," Bea said. "Much tastier than the rubber ones at the grocery store."

"I don't think I'm hard to live with, but I had a few questions that you answered without knowing it." Mona held up her palm again, pointing to each word as she spoke. "I love children, but I'd rather they live somewhere else. Smoking is acceptable if it's outside, preferably in the next state. Pets are fine, unless it's some creature like a six-foot rattler that might slither into my bedroom."

"I am not a snake fan," Bea said, stroking Marco at her feet, "but I do love dogs!"

"If you were bad people, Marco would've showed me the moment you arrived the first time. I cook him some chicken once in a while, but I can barely handle the smell of a slab of frying red cow flesh. I'm a lacto-vegetarian with a few eggs thrown in for protein. You two and Marco can eat your chickens after they're dead. I'll stick with eating them before they're alive."

Antonio shook his head in amazement. "You're serious about us moving in, aren't you?"

"I'd say dead serious, but this is more about life—all our lives. I don't need an answer right now. Give it some thought." She put her hands on the table and pushed herself up. "I'm going to put the quiche in the oven, and then I'd like to show you my studio."

Leaving Antonio to wander through these new possibilities, Bea followed Mona to the kitchen.

"My dear husband may not be much help in the remembering department. When he starts writing, he's gone… lost in another world."

"Now that's a blessing and a curse, isn't it? When I paint, I'm gone, too. Your monarch photo took me somewhere familiar, and it took me hours to figure out where."

"Oh, I forgot! We brought you a present!" Bea took the print from her canvas briefcase and handed it to Mona. "Antonio told me what you said, and now you have one of your own. We didn't have time to frame it."

"Mmm…" She slipped on her Mona Lisa smile. "This stirs my soul, it does. One day you must take me to this spot… to this exact tree. Thank you so much. It's already hanging in my heart, but now we'll mount it on the wall."

Mona set it down reverently, put the quiche in the gas oven, and glanced at the antique clock on the wall, the one her papa had nailed to their cabin wall seventy years ago. "No timer on this ol' thing. You'll have to help me remember to take out the quiche."

Bea had her wrist up, ready to set her multi-function Casio watch. "That's easy. I'm a nurse. I put in and take out stuff all day. How long?"

"Forty-five minutes... You know, my mama was a nurse and so was I, but those are stories for another day." Mona picked up the photo and fetched her walking stick. "Let's go out to the studio."

After retrieving Antonio still fantasizing in the Alamo, they strolled outside as Mona rambled on.

"Not much upkeep when your yard's a field. My neighbors call my wildflowers 'weeds.' They try to get rid of insects, and I attract them." She caressed a leaf as if it were a cuddly bunny ear. "Monarchs love these milkweeds. Without them, they'd be extinct. I started a little foundation called Monarch Aid and donate five percent of my painting sales for research and planting more of these so they have food for their southern migration."

"Monarch Aid," Antonio repeated, squinting his eyes and nodding. "Mona Arcade. I hadn't noticed that monarch was part of your name. And I've wondered why you sign your paintings Angela Mariposa."

"My birth mother's name. Never met her. *Another* story for another day. You told me you wanted to write an article about the inspiration for my paintings. That's today's story."

She herded them into the studio, a narrow adobe cottage with windows facing the river in front of her easel, a porcelain work table with chairs behind on the left, a storage room and filing cabinets to the right. Mona set Bea's print on the easel next to her painting.

"Bea's photo inspired this recent piece I created. I call it Superior Communion. It's similar to a scene I remember on the shore of Lake Superior with millions of red-and-black ladybugs on a sun-bleached fallen tree. Bea snapped her monarch image looking up at the sky, but I was lying on the beach, looking out at the lake."

"That's wonderful! So lifelike." Bea said. "Our butterfly images are like twins. Not identical... fraternal."

Mona talked as she walked to her filing cabinet and took out a stack of letters. "I couldn't remember exactly what the familiar image was until I checked through these—pretty much a complete history of my life." She dropped them onto the table in front of Antonio. "My Mexican pen pal Zarita and I have been writing monthly since we were twelve. Over sixty years. I have every one of her letters and carbon copies of mine—almost 1,500 letters. She's an archeologist specializing in Maya culture. Antonio...

you're a writer and I think you like to write about people. Here's a book waiting to be written. Maybe called *Two Lives*. If you care, you can write it."

Antonio gave Bea a sideways, sheepish look as he stumbled out of speechlessness once again, then raised his eyebrows and face to Mona. "I… ah… I'm honored you'd even consider me."

"Do you see any other writers here? No? Then you're elected." She took a letter off the stand next to her easel and handed it to him. "Here's the inspiration letter for this painting. When I thought of Bea, I saw myself in my twenties, so I sifted through what I'd written back then. That gallery incident triggered something else in me, a horrible experience I'd shoved underground… the last time I was physically attacked." Mona paused as the feeling seeped back in. "An attempted rape that tore me out of Iowa and sent me home to Wisconsin to lick my wounds. It was great to be back near the lake with my parents, but it wasn't home anymore. I felt that home was somewhere south, as I always had, and kept moving in that direction. Now something about Bea's photo feels like home, and I want to find out why."

"Well… I sure look forward to reading these letters. I've never even heard of a sixty-year pen pal."

"No hurry. No deadline. If your writing's like my painting, it's like gardening. You sow, and you water, but the plant grows in its own time."

"You are so sweet to think of him," Bea said. "I think being a reporter is beneath his abilities and nowhere near his passion, but it does pay the bills."

"I have another little idea for you, Bea honey."

"What is it? I'm all ears!"

"Years ago I got fed up with bowing to almighty doctors trying frantically to save lives that should have been sent gently on their way to the other side. I started a personal home health care business and people were standing in line… well, sitting in wheelchairs and lying in beds. Lots of older folks in Mission need care and don't have many options. My neighbor Yves is struggling with Alzheimer's, and tending him is getting to be too much for me. The Silverstones down the road are looking for help. My eighty-five-year-old friend, Sasha. Me, for that matter. A home care business could be a part-time venture at first and a career before you know it."

"I've thought about it," Bea said, "but I don't really know how to do it."

"Are you an RN?"

"Yeah."

"Then you're perfectly qualified. You only need the will and the way. I was doodling today and thought of one way."

Mona tore out a sketchbook page and set it on the table. To the left, a cheerful cartoon bumblebee wearing a nurse cap with a red cross and a stethoscope hanging from its neck. To the right, bold letters across the top with three points underneath:

Queen Bea's TLC
On-site Healthcare
Special Services
Odd Requests

"Mona, you are such a genius!" Bea was beside herself—drawn on the page and standing next to the table. "This is like a dream come true."

"You think about it, honey. If you want it, you can make it happen." Mona turned, walked to the easel, and gazed at Bea's photo, talking softly to herself. "This scene hypnotizes me. Is it a dream? Or… Is it real…?" She stood still, transfixed, utterly unaware of Bea and Antonio hunched over the table and whispering behind her.

A few minutes passed. Then they rose, and Antonio spoke to Mona's back. "Okay. We're in.

Mona's body drifted around, her face blank with a light's-on-but-no-one's-home look.

"We'll be three wild hairs living together. Bea and I feel so privileged that you even asked us."

Mona responded vacantly. "Asked what?"

"To move in here with you!" Bea exclaimed, her arms outstretched to the sides. "We can do it as soon as you like. We'll have to give our landlord thirty-days notice, but if you're serious about no rent, we can come anytime… even this weekend."

Mona's eyes stared at them, her mind focused on somewhere else, another place, another time. "What on earth are you talking about?"

ANGEL
Morpho's in Town

An enormous stuffed tusker greeted Jonathan and Angel inside the Smithsonian National Museum of Natural History lobby, a three-storied rotunda crafted from white marble floors, walls, and columns.

"If you're not starving, let's check out one exhibit first," Angel suggested.

"Sure. Which one?"

Angel pointed to a four-foot monarch butterfly model hanging on a marble railing between two columns. "Lately, butterflies have been on my dream agenda."

"I've always enjoyed watching butterflies," Jonathan said, following Angel up the stairs, "but I don't know anything about them."

"Me, too, and me, either. The only things I know came from my dreams or on the web today. I wouldn't have asked you to come with me if you hadn't mentioned that dream you'd had as a kid. Some folks never remember them, or say they mean nothing, but I know they're messages from somewhere."

A massive sign and photo of a moth welcomed them into the exhibit—"Butterflies: Masters of Disguise."

"See that?" Angel asked, walking up to the sign. "They're callin' me by name. That's an Atlas moth there, the largest in the world. I saw it in a dream two nights ago and checked it out on the web. The facts from the dream were true."

"Is that life-size?" Jonathan asked. "It could carry me away."

"Nah. Their wingspan's about twelve inches. Imagine that in your hand." Angel led him past several displays until he found the blue morpho butterfly previewed on the Smithsonian website. "This one was the star in the dream I had right before you called yesterday morning. I was this butterfly, and my name was Morpho. I came out of a cocoon, flew around, ate, mated with my sweetheart, and died." Angel gestured to another butterfly across the walkway. "And this one in my next dream, or the same one. I don't know which. A tiger swallowtail. I was a kid named Tiger who collected butterflies. Then a real tiger swallowtail visited me on my porch right before the attack. Caterpillars, the yellow metal kind, wreaked havoc in both dreams, but I ignored the message."

Jonathan stuck to him like a spy, listening intently to *The Book of Angel.*

"There must be a skipper butterfly here somewhere," Angel said. "It's what *you* were in my dream the night *before* you called, but I didn't realize it until later on."

"I'd help you look, but I don't know what I look like."

"Ah, here you are! The silver-spotted skipper. I tried to net one of these when I was Tiger, just like you were tryin' to net me for this mission. Right after I got one, three neighborhood bullies attacked me in the dream. Right after you got me on the phone yesterday, three thugs attacked me in real life. Coincidence? No way. In-your-face synchronicity."

"I love coincidences, but I'm not exactly sure what synchronicity is."

"You're not alone, but let's table that talk until lunch."

Jonathan bent down to scrutinize the skipper butterfly mounted behind the glass. "I'm not very big."

"Neither am I, remember? So what's it say about you?" Angel asked, trying to see over his shoulder.

Jonathan read the description on the display card. "Skippers are stocky with a large head, a chunky body, and short, strong wings."

Angel poked him in the side like a high school bud. "Look in the mirror, Skipper, a full-length one."

"It also says I'm a powerful, rapid flier and have a nervous disposition." Jonathan Skipper stood up and looked down at Angel. "Victoria would agree with that part."

"Didn't I tell you on the phone yesterday you were nervous as a dog in a roomful of rockin' chairs?"

"Well, you've amazed me again. Which one are you? The blue morpho?"

"We'll get to that," Angel promised, "but first, listen up. There's a warnin' for you on this sign. Says here, 'Skipper butterflies can be difficult to identify without killing them to dissect their genitalia.'"

"Thanks for letting me know." Jonathan put both hands over his crotch. "Now I'm going to have nightmares."

"I think your haircut should be a dead giveaway without killing you."

"I'll put a certificate from the doctor on my office wall. Okay, Professor Phoenix. Which one are you?"

"I'd hoped there'd be a peanut butterfly, but no such luck. So I looked up Angel and found a whole bunch of angel wing butterflies called nymphalids.

It's a huge family with 4,000 species and that gives me a shitload of choices. That big monarch when we came in. The red admiral. The painted lady... sounds like Victoria. And 'what a coincidence,' some folks would say, the blue morpho butterfly. And..."

Angel paced through the exhibit until he found one. "The question mark. Today I choose to be this angel wing butterfly, cuz that's what my life feels like—a big question. See that tiny white question mark on its underwing? Its scientific name is downright otherworldly. 'Polygonia interrogationis.'" Angel went Southern. "Zat sound like my bidness card? On-site research?"

"Are there any called Washingtonia interrogationis?" Jonathan asked. "They could be the CIA."

"Let's see what else it says here." Angel followed the words on the card with his finger. "'Male question marks find females by hanging on tree trunks in the afternoon. They may chase other insects and even birds.' Skipper, I'm just readin' the words here."

"Darla and Shannon must be the birds, but did you just call me a tree trunk?"

"It did say skippers were stocky. Check this out. 'Question mark caterpillars must find a host plant; they then eat leaves and live alone.' That's me in Pokeberry Ridge, my host plant. I am a lonely cat livin' alone in my burrow. And now, this worm needs to eat."

"I'm ready. Lead the way. You've got the map."

Angel kept talking as they walked. "Do you happen to know what 'pee sua' means in Thai?"

Jonathan had to walk forward, then sideways like a crab, to listen to and answer Angel. "Like Khun P, 'pee' is ghost. 'Sua' is shirt, or clothes, I think."

"You're right, literally 'ghost clothing.' But 'pee sua' together means butterfly in Thai. What's happenin' right now? You're sendin' an angel wing butterfly wearing ghost clothing into a big fuckin' question mark to steal from Mister Ghost."

"It sounds like a fairytale," Jonathan said. "You do need to write a book about all this. *The Book of Angel.* A twenty-volume set. I'd buy it."

"Cool. I'll sell four. You, my mother and father, and my buddy Donny in The Ridge."

As Angel sat down in the restaurant and picked up the menu, the signs kept coming. "Skipper, what'd I first tell you I wanted to eat after we finished workin'?"

"Thai food?"

"Well, it's right here on the menu." A simple joy radiated from Angel. He didn't feel as if he had a halo; he felt as if he was a halo. "I'm getting the Pad Thai I thought about today, and I got to see the butterflies I dreamed about yesterday, all in one pretty present. See? You can manifest what you want in life. Don't forget that."

"I brought your soapbox in the truck, Strangel," Jonathan joked. "Should I get it for you?"

"Sorry, Skipper." Angel rested his palms flat on the table. His hands were tired of talking. He continued in a softer, introspective voice. "Here I am tellin' you what I'm tryin' to tell myself—lookin' in a mirror and talkin' to me. You caught me at a unique time in my life. I'm on a precipice, ready to jump. I love to fly, but I want to know where I'm going. I see so many signs pointin' the way, and the direction's still not clear. I'm a man who's not sure what to manifest."

"Forget about it. I'm just giving you half the hard time you give me. I think we're leading up to a reading from *The Book of Angel, Volume S* for synchronicity."

"You're a kind man. I would've told me where to stick my soapbox."

"Let me take a shot at it." Jonathan pulled up his shirt sleeves and adjusted his collar as he gathered his words. "Synchronicity is a coincidence that means something… like there's a reason it happened. How'd I do?"

"Very well," Angel complimented him, happy Jonathan wasn't a member of the "oh, isn't that odd" club. "Here's a simple, real-life example. My sheriff bud took a bullet in the arm in Georgia at four in the morning, and five minutes later his phone rang. His mother, 3,000 miles away in Seattle, asked, 'Are you okay, Donny Boy? I felt something scary.'"

"I wouldn't call that a coincidence. I'd call it love."

"People can call it what they want. It's a connection beyond space and time. Energy. Synergy. Love synchronized in both hearts. Synchronicities are those special moments when our imaginary border disappears between in here and out there…" Angel's palm moved from his heart to an open gesture at the universe. "During those connections, like in dreams, messages bleed through other dimensions outside of time. You can listen to them or ignore them. Your choice."

"I think I'm starting to grok you in fullness," Jonathan said, a bulb lighting in his brain, powered by the heart.

"Isn't that odd? You quote your bible, and it's Angel's bible, too. What a coincidence!"

"When I think of all the coincidences you've mentioned, I'm beginning to get it."

"Since we've just been in Bugville, let me tell you a story from Dr. Carl Jung, the guy who coined the term synchronicity. He even chatted about it with Al, that Einstein guy who had similar feelings, like the law of relativity."

"Now there's a meeting I'd like to have been at. Hanging around with Carl and Al."

"Me, too. So Jung had a patient stuck in her brain. He felt like it was a dead end, but hoped, in his words, 'something unexpected and irrational would turn up' to shake her loose. The woman shared a dream she'd had the night before, where someone offered her a pricey piece of jewelry, a golden scarab. The moment she told him, they heard tapping on the outside of the window. He opened it and a gold-green scarabaeid beetle flew into the room. Jung grabbed it, handed it to her, and said, 'Here's your scarab.' It was the key that unlocked her brain jail and shifted her perception, making her receptive in a new way."

The waitress delivered their food, and Angel picked up his chopsticks and dug in. "So Skipper, you think it's a coincidence you're sending me to jump off Phu Chi Fa ridge to save Barry, right when I'm thinking of jumping ship from The Ridge? Pokeberry Ridge?"

"I'm not sure what to think anymore," Jonathan sighed. "Since our conversation this morning, I'm just trying to think more from the heart."

"Well, you can't go wrong startin' from the heart."

The meal was good and green, as the website had promised. They talked about dreams in general and their own personal life dreams. Angel had found a kindred soul in a most unlikely place. And he'd almost talked himself out of returning Jonathan's original call.

"Skipper, I am glad you made the call, and I am glad I called back. I wish you were comin' with me."

"I would definitely like to." The cock of his head and the slight grimace on Jonathan's face showed those three words to be true and from the heart. "But it's just not in the DEA cards. I thought about it, but I'll have to do what I can from here."

"I understand. Just sayin'. It'd be great to have you there."

Both men ate, chewing on that thought, until Angel broke the stillness with a subject change.

"The flip side of the messages you receive are the ones you send out, the ones that manifest the choices you make. I have a feeling I'm goin' on this journey for a completely different reason than your mission. I don't know what it is, but I'll find out along the way. But right now," Angel lied, "I need a men's room."

He walked across the room, pivoting toward the cashier when Jonathan wasn't watching. He paid the tab, came back to the table and spoke with fatigue dripping off his words. "I'm sure traffic's a rat race now, but would you mind takin' me back home to the Hilton? This caterpillar needs to climb into the cocoon before the wings take me away. And I'm sure your family's waitin' on you."

"Let's go," Jonathan said, reaching for his wallet.

Angel put his hand on Jonathan's. "This one's on me. Already taken care of. Let's not make it our last supper."

They drove in silence most of the way, each man digging deep into his own life. Of the million words they wanted to share, at that moment, there were none left to say.

As the Explorer pulled up to the hotel, Angel pointed at the doorman on the steps. "Will you look at that guy? His toupee looks like a roadkill tryin' to crawl off his head. What's the motto this man should have?"

"Motto?" Jonathan asked, squinting at the doorman.

"I'll give you a hint. Just say no…"

Jonathan had to think for a second. "To rugs."

"Bangin', Skipper. The PBNJ Evaluation never ends, you know. Why don't I ever eat escargot?"

"Just say no… to… slugs."

"You could get a job as a mind-reader on the side. Just keep readin' mine and take care of me while I'm gone. I'll take care of you and yours."

Jonathan spoke slowly, sincerely. He'd sent many men onto the playing field, but had never felt quite like this. "Good luck out there, Angel. Be careful. Call me when you can if you need anything. It has been a great pleasure to meet you… and an education."

Angel opened the door, then turned to Jonathan. "Get out of the truck."

Jonathan raised his eyebrows, got out, and walked around the SUV to the sidewalk.

Angel put his hands on his skipper's bulky arms and looked him in the eye. "Never say no to hugs. Gimme one, buddy."

Heart to heart—or Jonathan's heart to Angel's neck—they embraced with the required hearty male pats on the back to distract from the actual hug.

Angel strolled up the steps, lost in thought, but could not resist the storm that hit his brain. He had to turn once again and catch Jonathan as he stepped into the Explorer. "One final question, Skipper."

"Hit me," Jonathan challenged. "I'm ready."

"What if your main man in Thailand tells me to do somethin' I don't wanna do?"

Jonathan smiled as he read Angel's mind. "Just say no to Dougs."

"You are smokin'!" Angel gave him a thumbs up and bounded into the hotel.

RED

Act One

SHE'D HARDLY SLEPT THE LAST TWO NIGHTS, visualizing and mentally directing the production she couldn't perform in or even attend. Red's nerves were frayed like hair with severe split ends. If she'd had any hair left, she'd have pulled it out.

Once again wearing a sari and scarf, she got out of her short, dirty company truck and walked toward the only long, white limousine parked at the entrance of Lodhi Garden in central Delhi. An elderly chauffeur with a full, curly gray beard, dressed in a white uniform and gold turban, stepped out of the driver's side. Red stopped short and looked around for another limo.

A familiar voice emerged from the living mannequin in front of her. "Good day, Miss Scarlett."

"Hari?" Red asked, surprised.

"At your service," he said, bowing slightly.

"You're looking quite dapper today."

"Is dapper a good thing?"

"Jolly good," Red said. "Most dashing."

As he slid open the door for her, Red saw an exotic woman lounging in the rear, legs stretched out toward the front seat facing her. "Toma? Not Dietrich, I'm sure. You've chosen your costume well."

"Oh, bless your sweet heart. You are too kind. Thank you so much, Miss Scarlett." Toma delivered the line with an elegant drawl, then donned a beige wide-brimmed, floppy hat that matched the sash around the waist of her low-cut black dress, and batted her ample lashes at Red. She'd transformed her blonde hair into jet black locks tumbling down to her bare shoulders. On her neck hung a pearl necklace, a spoil from previous exploits.

Hari climbed in behind Red, sat facing the rear, and poured three glasses of soda water from the bar on the side wall of the limo.

"Quite fetching, I must say," Red said, resting a hand on Toma's knee. "Beautiful as an innocent butterfly flitting through their compound. Have you written your script and memorized it?"

"Off the cuff suits me best. And my name isn't Toma. It's Melanie, married to my handsome sugar daddy, Mason Butler. We're in the import/export jewelry trade and live in Atlanta."

"Brilliant. Where's Dietrich?"

"He's not in the first act, so he's running around the city somewhere," Toma said. "He'll meet us later."

"I wish I knew more about the layout of Aero Dynamic, but the crop-duster hangar is just beyond the roundabout at the end of their drive. I think they park clients' planes down the runway to the left."

"Don't worry your precious little self," she assured Red in southern speak, then flipped back into Toma. "I'll figure it out. This is business as usual for me."

Red sipped her water, wishing it were her buddy Scotch and water. "I imagine there must be a toilet in the duster hangar. After your tour of their facilities, perhaps you could delicately venture to the loo while checking out locations for three fist-size, adhesive-backed explosives. Chemical barrels or a gas tank? I don't know. We'll discuss what you learn later."

"Let me get this straight now," Toma asked. "I'm only looking around today, then coming back with my husband who arrives later on. Correct?"

"Spot on. Your next visit will be the day after tomorrow on Gandhi Jayanti, a national Indian holiday celebrating Gandhi's birthday. I doubt many people will be working or flying, but Aero's like an executive airport, so they'll have to stay open. Please let them know you'd like to return then."

"Well, it sounds easy. Anything else?"

"One more task." Red dug inside her textile purse and handed Toma a small cloth bag. "Here's a tiny camera I can control from my cell phone. Don't touch it with your bare hands. We want no fingerprints. Pull off the plastic strip and stick it to a wall, under a fuse box, somewhere I can see what's happening in the hangar. I want to make certain that no one gets hurt… only things."

"Okay," Toma said. "I'm ready to go."

"How about you, Hari? Any questions?"

"I am only driving and watching, but I must know where to be driving."

"Silly me. Of course." Red extracted a dog-eared map from her purse, unfolded it, and set it on his lap. "I've circled the location here… near the Indira Gandhi International Airport. Have you been there before?"

"Years ago," Hari said. "It must be in the same place."

"Just keep your eyes open. I've never had a real chauffeur. Do you sit in the car? Walk around? Smoke?"

"I will be standing still and tall next to the limousine," Hari pronounced, raising his chin an inch, "ready and waiting for my mistress' commands."

"All right, then." Red leaned toward Toma. "When and where are you meeting Dietrich?"

"When we finish and I call him. Where? You tell me."

"The Hangar Bar at the airport Holiday Inn is quiet and dark."

"The Hangar Bar. That fits with our little escapade, doesn't it?" Toma said with a grin and looked over at Hari. "You know where it is?"

"No, but I am a professional driver, watcher, and finder. It is a Holiday Inn. The sign must be a big green H."

Red reached for the door, but Hari's hand got there first and opened it.

"Good luck to you both. I have a few things to do. By six p.m. I'll be at the Hangar Bar. Dietrich has my cell number." Red started to walk away but turned back. "By the way, Aero's owner is Mr. Murakan Patil, the man responsible for sabotaging my business. If you meet him, be on your toes. He's a dodgy one."

MONA

Time and Matter Destroyed

Before the knocking began, Marco padded over and sniffed the crack under the door. As the years piled up on Mona's davenport, the soft innards of its cushions had hardened and migrated toward the edge, leaving crusty indentations in the middle. Mona tried three times before raising herself high enough to balance on two feet and then hobbled over to open the door.

Queen Bea wore a pastel party dress and held a blue Samsonite suitcase in one hand, a white paper bag in the other, and a toothbrush behind her ear. Her worker Ant sported a loud Hawaiian shirt under a hefty backpack and carried his laptop bag over his shoulder, a bucket of sponges, cleaning fluids, and a bottle of Merlot, plus a juicy bone in his hand. Marco was already licking it and drooling on Antonio's sandaled feet.

Bea's smile stretched beyond her face on both sides. "Hi! Remember us?"

"Of course I do," Mona said. "Aren't you the young couple spreading God's word door-to-door? I just don't remember which god."

"She's Mormon and I'm a Jehovah's Witness," Antonio joked. "We're here on a membership drive. This year it's a head-to-head competition."

"C'mon in," Mona said, extending a hand into her world. "All gods and goddesses are welcome here. How long will it take you two to learn you don't have to knock on the door of your own home?"

"We tried the knob, but the door was locked."

"Now that's dangerous. I'm not sure if I still have a key. I've hidden and lost many of them outside. You'll probably stumble over them in the yard."

Bea held up her white bag. "Veggie Chinese, as promised. Where should I put it?"

"Let's put it in our stomachs. I'm famished." Mona set the bag on the antique dining table and sat down in front of it. "Antonio, I didn't complete your tour last time. The paper plates are on the top shelf in the far cupboard, but I need a stool to reach them. Would you mind?"

"Glad to." He touched her shoulder. "You sit tight."

Bea pulled up a chair. "And how are you doing, Mona?"

"Three days older than the last time I saw you and definitely feeling it."

"Pain? Are you sick?" Nurse Bea wanted to rush to her rescue. "What are you feeling?"

"Actually..." Her eyes brightened as if gazing into her soul. "I'm feeling quite well."

The incident in her studio during their previous visit had bothered Mona at first, when she had no idea what they meant about moving in with her. She'd told them it was a joke, pretending she'd forgotten, but it had nothing to do with a loss of memory. It seemed to Mona that she'd dropped into some sort of spontaneous meditation. And the more she replayed the experience, the more she wished it would happen again.

As she had stared at the tree swarming with monarch butterflies, Mona felt she entered Bea's photo, the actual location of the photo—Mexico's Snowy Mountains Range. She felt the delicate wings of other monarchs brushing against her. She heard the rustling of countless wings, legs, and antennae surrounding her. She smelled the leaves and sap from the sacred oyamel fir. No words could describe it because there were no words in her mind at the time, only sensations, like a baby who'd recently entered this world from another.

And it felt beyond good. Not even good—simply beyond—and she wanted to stay there. When she'd turned to face Antonio and the foreign sound of words, she may have looked like she was lost in that limbo land between consciousness and unconsciousness, drifting back from slumber, but from Mona's point of view, it felt as if she were falling back asleep, not waking up.

Antonio laid out the plates and chopsticks, set the white cardboard boxes of sesame noodles, stir-fried broccoli, and egg foo yung on the table, then poured everyone a plastic glass of Merlot. "You like my shirt? The volume control is the third button down."

"You both look handsome and happy," Mona cooed.

"This weekend feels like a honeymoon vacation," Bea said, raising her hands above her head. "The start of a new life for us."

Savoring the Chinese fare, they chatted about possible plans for Queen Bea's TLC home care business and Antonio's desire to write the *Two Lives* book, about dogs, the weather, mundane aspirations and lofty dreams—stuff that makes up conversations among old friends.

Once they'd emptied the boxes and filled their stomachs, Antonio announced, "I have news. Well... a chance to make *you* the news, Mona."

"Me? News? I'm old news."

"I pitched the idea of a feature story on you and your *One Life* collection of paintings to the Mission Chronicle, and they bought it. But they want it soon, as a follow-up to the Butterfly Festival. What do you think?"

"How soon?" Mona asked.

"Tomorrow."

"Then we'd best start now. At my age, sometimes I have to hurry. Not much time left."

Bea started to clear the table. "I'll take care of this and then clean the Alamo. You two can work."

As he laid out his vision in words, Antonio took his laptop from its bag and powered it up. "They'll print a large color painting on the front page, maybe two more black and whites plus a shot of you on a continuing page. I'll use photos Bea took of your paintings at the Butterfly Center. I've learned a little about your life and your creative process, but which one of these would you like to feature in the article?"

After he'd scrolled through the ten paintings on his screen, Mona said, "It's got a quirky name, but how about using the one called 'Buck Ministers Fully'? You know what that means?"

"No. Who's Buck?"

"Richard Buckminster Fuller. I heard him speak at a college when I lived in Missouri. I can honestly say that he changed my life."

"Ah, yes, Bucky. Inventor of the geodesic dome and author of *Operating Manual for Spaceship Earth.*"

In Mona's painting, hundreds of butterflies, but only one monarch was in her rendition of the audience at Bucky's presentation. A short, balding white man with thick black-framed glasses, dressed in a suit and tie, stood on stage with his arms stretched out and up. Behind him, instead of a curtain, a pitch-dark, star-studded universe receded into infinity with a larger-than-life Big Dipper constellation to the left, an atom-like solar system with electrons for planets to the right, and a gigantic translucent baby in diapers dwarfing the tiny man in the middle of the stage.

"I think you should give your readers more of a message than just some babble about me."

"Okay… you relax and talk. I'll listen. My laptop will record every word."

Mona closed her eyes, summoning that day, and spoke without opening them. "I was thirty-seven. It was a chilly spring evening in Springfield. I knew nothing about Buckminster Fuller except the geodesic dome he invented, whatever it said on his lecture poster, and maybe a quote of his. 'There is nothing in a caterpillar that tells you it's going to be a butterfly.' The auditorium might have seated 1,000 people, but only a handful came.

"He walked out on stage and never stopped walking… back and forth, as if he was talking to each one of us. I don't remember his exact words, but first he said something like, 'Thank you so much for coming. I'm eighty-three and I won't be around much longer, and I've learned so much that I'm so excited to tell you about.'

"You could feel that he cared. He was like a little kid all hyped up about Show and Tell in class, you know, 'I got a new toy atomic microscope and some meteorites and look at my keen ant farm called Our Galaxy!'

"He went on and on and on, stretching my brain beyond its limits. At one point, I felt like the left and right sides of my brain were trying to trade places inside my head, as if they were swimming through each other like two schools of fish in the ocean. I remember trying to remember as much as I possibly could, but that was like trying to carry away a bunch of bowling balls without bags. Impossible! I *hate* that I did this, but I left during intermission so I could hold on to some of the treasures he'd already given me."

Antonio pressed the pause button on his laptop. "Super. You're doin' great. Just keep sayin' it like it is in your own words."

"Okay. Hit it. I am back there again. I will never, ever forget that day."

"Recording. Go for it." Antonio sat back with his arms behind his head.

"I only remember three treasures Bucky shared. Number one: time. He said most of us think of time as a linear series of events, or as lots of things happening at the same time. I'm sure you've seen the Big Dipper, seven stars twinkling in the night sky. You look at your watch. It's eleven o'clock and the Big Dipper is happening right then… for you. Fact is, each of those stars is millions of light-years away, but not the *same distance* away. One's fifty million light-years away, some eighty, and two over 100… million… light-years away.

"So… bear with me here. I'm not Bucky. At eleven o'clock, one moment in time, you are watching seven non-synchronous events that began millions of years apart and millions of years before you were born, when the light left each star. He said it's possible some of those stars may not even exist anymore! They may be dead. We may only be seeing the light from when they were alive. Bucky destroyed my entire view of time right there."

Mona poured another glass of wine and drank half.

Antonio hit the pause button and sighed, "Whew," but Mona was on a mental roll and continued rolling, so he pressed the record button again.

"Number two: space. And something that occupies space: matter, which can be solid, liquid, or gas, but let's just talk about the solids. Like this table. It's solid." She rapped it with her knuckles. "You can see it and feel it. It's hard. I think Bucky stamped his foot on the stage, right before he destroyed my entire view of matter and space.

"Then he says, 'all matter is 99.999999999'—I don't know how many nines—'percent space.' Every atom in existence, with its little electron planets flying round its little proton-neutron sun, is pretty much like our solar system. He didn't say it like that. I did. Calculate the amount of matter compared with space in every atom and you get your 99.99-whatever percent space. So… this table is pretty much nothing. Maybe its internal forces make it hard, but a table is mainly… times a few million… nothing.

"Maybe he didn't say 'nothing.' Maybe he said ether or spirit or vacuum, I don't remember. But we human beings, a wolf pack of nothing, are so wrapped up in things, it's pathetic. You tell me what matters."

Antonio pressed pause again. "Well… your words definitely matter to me, even though they're nothing… and you're nothing, like me. Well, you are nothing like me…"

"See what Bucky did to me?" Mona held up her hands as if she were offering him something invisible. "Now he's doing it to you. I couldn't think straight for months, but he did make me focus more on space. Seemed reasonable. There's so much more of it."

"I might have to ask Hal if this article can take up the whole issue."

"I don't know how you'll translate it into Mission speak," Mona said. "I've been trying to condense these ideas for years, and they only keep expanding." She picked up her wine and toasted to Bucky wherever he was in the universe. "Okay. Are you ready for the final memory? I know you're glad I've forgotten the rest of them."

"Standing by…" Antonio started recording. "Shoot."

"Number three: gravity, which helped me understand why, as a young child, I thought I could fly. Bucky asked us if we knew why little babies drop stuff off their highchairs. They pick up a spoon, they stick it over the edge of their tray, and drop it. You pick it up. They do it again.

"They're not trying to harass you. They just haven't been *matter* for very long. Before they were born, they were *spirit*. No mass, no gravity. They expect the spoon to stay in the air where they put it, like the good ol' days before the womb, before they squirted out onto Earth.

"I *completely* felt that as a child. I knew I could fly and had flown before. I'd only forgotten how to do it." She finished her wine and then set the glass firmly on the table. "There you have it. The inspiration for that painting. To me, it's worth a million words, but I cut them down to a thousand."

Antonio closed his laptop with one hand while running his other through his long dark hair. "Some artists arrange fruit in a basket and paint it. You transform a multi-dimensional universe onto a flat canvas."

"Sounds impressive when you say it, but I really only paint these images for me. *One Life* is merely one elderly woman's memoir. Now that I think back, Bucky reminds me of me now. Both of us immersed in our final Show and Tell. Old characters in the twilight of life, acting like kids from the dawn of life, each about the same distance from two opposite ends."

"I turned off the laptop, and now I'll have to write that down," Antonio complained. "Every shred of kidding aside, this will make a great story. Thank you. I'll have to process it for a while and add a few Mona factoids tomorrow. You mind if I check and see how Bea's doing?"

"No, no, go," Mona said, slipping into the formless ether. *Matter doesn't matter. Time doesn't exist. I love the freedom I have to space out. I'm on my way home.* Then her mind became still.

A few minutes later, Bea and Antonio returned from the Alamo as Mona drifted back to Earth.

"We were wondering about the house rules for the appropriate direction of the toilet paper rolls," Bea asked very seriously. "We drape the end over the back so it falls tidily behind the roll by the wall."

"No, honey," Antonio corrected. "It must drape over the front of the roll, toward the person."

"You're mistaken, sweetheart," Bea disagreed. "It's always over the back."

"I'm sorry," Antonio insisted with his hands on his hips, "but it's over the front."

"The back," Bea parried, raising her voice.

They both faced off, pointing index fingers at each other.

"Front."

"Back."

"Front!"

"Back!"

Mona's eyebrows jumped upward.

Suddenly Bea and Antonio cracked up and bent over with their hands on their knees.

"Sorry, Mona," Bea said. "It's a little game we play to remind ourselves to lighten up. At Antonio's brother's wedding, the bride and groom had major issues about toilet rolls, and we witnessed this exact argument… twice."

"Surprisingly," Antonio added, "they're still together."

"How long?" Mona asked.

"So far, three weeks."

"Well, it doesn't matter here. I keep my rolls in a wicker basket. Pick them up with a finger in the tube and turn them whichever way I want. I use the dispenser on the wall as a shelf for the books I read in the bathroom."

ANGEL
Paralyzed

As his vision slowly swirled into focus, Angel saw blurry bars above. His eyes rolled to the right… bars. To the left… bars. He was in a cage—a bamboo cube six feet by six feet by six feet. Squinting, he looked beyond his boots through more bars lit by the flickering flames of torches mounted on a jagged rock wall. He was flat on his back in a cage in a cave.

Groggy, Angel tried to lift his head, but it didn't respond. He tried to turn over, raise an arm, and move his legs. No luck. He was paralyzed, as if he'd taken one of his own tranquilizer darts in the neck.

Where am I? How'd I get here? I… I can't remember.

The steamy air smelled moldy. Rancid like dead rats. He tried to yell, his tongue a dead slab in a dry mouth in a locked jaw. Groans writhed out of his throat. Only his eyes were alive, swiveling back and forth, up and down.

Hearing voices and faint footsteps echoing in the distance, Angel summoned every shred of strength and will, lurched to one side, and succeeded in lifting one shoulder one inch before dropping back onto the canvas cot.

Ragged silhouettes traipsed in, a yard beyond his feet and the bars. Gaunt men leaned over and leered at Angel, yellow rotting teeth stinking as they taunted him. Their foreign words were familiar, but he couldn't understand them. The men, maybe ten of them dressed in olive-green camouflage fatigues, congregated to the left of the cage near a split wood door. The top half swung open, and they lined up in front of the lower door. It was payday.

Help me… Help me…

No matter how many times or how hard he tried to speak, "help me" only eked out as "hhhh… ehhhh… eeee…"

The men near Angel knew he couldn't move and continued to devil him like a caged animal. None of them jabbed him with their swords or threatened him physically, just pointed, poked their fingers, and harassed him. The scorn in their smiles set fire to one leg, and Angel kicked a boot toward their faces. It passed through the bamboo bars—not through the spaces between the bars—through the bars. And through their heads, as if the bars and heads, or his boot, were merely a mirage.

The faces rocked up and back in laughter, larger than life, too big for their bodies, lurid grins suspended in the air.

I'm dreaming.

Paralysis dreams had plagued him before. Right now he wasn't thinking about the past, but in that moment in this nightmare, Angel realized he was asleep. And he knew if he could roll over on his side, he'd wake up and slip into the real world. Like a bulldozer plowing through brush, words from another dream—Tiger's song—shoved their way into his chaos of thoughts.

Look the lion in the eye
Take hold of the tiger by the tail
Who cares if you fail?
At least you tried, you tried, you tried…

The stupor subsided a notch as his conscious mind reconnected with his muscles. Angel kicked both feet through the bars at the cluster of torsos, flopping on the cot like a beetle on his back caught on the dirt in a butterfly net. His lips began to form consonants around his strangled vowels.

"Way… wake… mmme uhhh. Wake… me… up!"

He wailed, again and again, the words sluggish in his mouth. The cage melted away. The sounds and sights of the men disappeared. With a surge of semi-comatose adrenaline, he flipped over on his side, panting and blinking.

Somewhere above the Arctic Ocean at 33,000 feet, Angel stared at the startled Asian woman in the reclined Global First-Class seat next to his. He smiled meekly and apologized in three languages. "Sorry. Khow tote khrap. Sumimasen."

Angel flicked his seat upright and concentrated on the dim ceiling lights so he wouldn't drop into the horror again… yet. His shaman grandmother Dao had said many times, "If you can't face your fears in a dream, how will you conquer them when you're awake?"

She'd taught him a method of meditation and Buddhist protection chants to help him venture back into his nightmares. During school in Arizona, he'd picked up lucid dreaming techniques to consciously direct and control his visions while unconscious. After his Muay Thai kickboxing sessions at a temple in Thailand, Angel studied with a guru and practiced yoga nidra, or dream yoga, a state between wakefulness and sleep that opens deep phases of the mind. Sometimes his mixture of these methods worked.

Angel reclined the seat and ran the nightmare by again, wondering if it were a mental fabrication of Barry in his cage at Mister Ghost's, or some message from the universe, or an unresolved issue in his psyche demanding attention. Then he let his grandmother's ancient chant fill and still his brain, repeating it silently, over and over…

Nahmo poo tai ya nama pata japa gasa oo ah mah oo

Visualizing the dingy cave in his dream, Angel relaxed his entire body, step by step—each toe on his left foot, the arch, the heel, the ankle, the calf, the thigh up into his hip. The same with his right leg and both hands and arms. He could feel the hum of the airplane and the pressure of the leather seat on his back slipping away. He relaxed the front of his groin, stomach, and chest. Then his spine from lumbar to shoulders and into his neck, jaw, and mouth.

As his final thoughts meandered away to the beat of his chant, they marveled for a moment that even his tongue could carry the tension of the day, and he relaxed it. And his nose, ears, eyes, and the top of his head. Then Angel drifted into the darkness, into a semi-aware meditative sleep.

Once again, he lay on the cot. The cave was quiet. Torch flames flashed on the walls. He swung his legs to the floor and looked around. It was a tunnel, not a cave. Far to his right he could see a tiny spot of light, perhaps the distant opening of the tunnel.

Angel walked toward it, twenty-some yards, his fingers stroking the cool damp stones to feel the way, but the spot didn't expand into an entrance as he got closer. He reached a dead end. A thin shaft of light shone through a small hole in the wall that appeared to have been made by a bullet. He leaned down and peeked out with one eye.

Sunlight glinted off a swarm of rifle slugs hanging motionless in the air, their tapered heads pointing directly at Angel. An army of translucent soldiers faded in and out of the background fog.

Turn around. Head the other way.

Shuddering, he shuffled back down the tunnel toward another blue-white light shining through the split door. Angel eased it open. A bank of entangled vines and creepers blocked the exit, but he squeezed through the web of vegetation into a clearing. Moonlight and its shadows waltzed on the foliage below as the trees swayed in a breeze seasoned with the spice of night blooms.

Angel stepped onto a narrow path nearly reclaimed by the jungle. Gazing up at the full moon, he glimpsed a human shape in the fork of a tree, a dozen feet ahead and up, facing away from him, and ducked into a thicket of broadleaf plants. Crouching low, he inched forward to get a better view. The figure wore a black ninja suit, not camo clothing like the men in his previous nightmare.

Is that me up there?

Suddenly the ground vibrated… No, the Earth trembled. Trees switched from swaying to shaking. He grabbed a sturdy horizontal vine on his right to steady himself. The ninja in the branches cried out and fell into the underbrush. Angel felt pressure on his shoulder and whirled around to confront the assailant.

"Sir… Mister… Excuse please… We experience bad turbulence."

Shifting his eyes from one dimension to another, with his right hand clutching the armrest and his left wrapped around her wrist, Angel peered up at the stewardess through the mist in his mind.

"Sir, we are preparing to land. Please raise seat to upright position and fasten seat belt now."

RED

Nowhere to Go

After meeting and directing her cast of two for act one, Red sat in her beat-up truck and watched the limo pull away. She'd lied. She didn't have any 'things to do.' Except wait. Wait for them. Wait for the cancer to retreat. Wait for the chemo fatigue to subside. Wait for the red hair to return on her head. Wait for the weight to lift off her heart. And have a conversation with a shot of single-malt scotch.

Red gazed at the worn, cracked dashboard and thought of the good ol' days with daddy Danny Boy. He'd named this truck Spencer, after Spencer Tracy, his favorite actor. Danny had always been the director in their productions; she a mere player. It was much easier back then.

She looked at her watch 4:00 p.m.

What do I do now? If I drive home in this traffic, I'll have to turn around and drive another hour back to the airport.

Three months earlier she'd have climbed into her Tiger Moth, soared into the clouds, and her sorrow would have been sucked right out of her. She wrenched Spencer into gear and headed to the Holiday Inn to shack up with Scotch.

The Hangar Bar was a long and narrow cocoon, like the limo, but with an arching corrugated ceiling and dark paneled walls, mirrored bar on one side, mellow yellow-padded chairs and tables on the other. The sallow light set an opium-den mood. It was empty at 4:37 when Red strolled in and ordered a Glenfiddich single-malt, neat.

She and Scotch sat at a table next to the far wall, but he disappeared the next moment. She summoned another, determined to savor him, to revel in his fruity pear nose and subtle oak taste. She finally slowed down while reminiscing with Scotch the Third.

Red thought of her dream Angel. He was friendly to most everyone, but only had two friends he could talk with and share the underbelly of his life—the Sheriff and the Skipper. Red was unfriendly to most, but also had only two friends: B, an old doctor, and Azeez, a young servant. But they weren't real friends like Angel's buddies—partners who felt his core and accepted who he really was. She sighed as her tongue caressed Scotch. Somehow she felt closer to the imaginary Angel than anyone in the real world, as she, a babe in this covert crib where she'd imprisoned herself, haphazardly modeled her mission after his. The emotions swirling round her heart funneled into one simple fact: Red just wanted a friend to talk to.

She looked at her watch—5:04—and raised her index finger. The bartender brought over Scotch the Fourth. Her dilated eyes wandering around the room, Red relived the only other time she'd been at the Hangar Bar, to meet a prospective client who didn't show. Like tonight, she'd been conversing alone with Scotch, had looked up, and there was Chase Youngman, her second husband. They'd kept in touch once in a while but hadn't seen each other in a decade. She'd been successful then and had played the part. They'd chatted for an hour, comfortable and close.

Chase and I were like Tiger and Gem. On the same wavelength. That was two years ago… Three? Four? Or was it only a dream?

She found Chase's number and pressed the call button. As she counted seven rings, Red tried to rest one elbow on the table, but it slipped off.

"Hello?"

She knew it was Chase. "Are you still gay?"

"Who is this?" he asked.

"Your former wife."

"Red…"

She heard a warm sigh on the phone. "You didn't answer my question."

"Yes, yes, still gay, still happy I'm gay."

"Damn." She devoured Scotch the Fourth, signaling for another.

"Are you all right? You don't sound so good."

"You know, Chase… you are the only man I ever loved."

"I'd hoped you'd meet someone better than me."

"Met a bunch… a bunch of idiotsh," she slurred.

Chase knew Red and knew what she was doing. "I'll bet you're having intercourse with your old buddy Scotch."

Once again, she ignored his words. "Maybe I loved you becaush…" Her tongue staggered around the syllables. "You were more'va woman than me."

"Don't say that. You are an absolutely divine woman and always will be."

"I thought I was with you."

"You were! It was my fault. I didn't know who I was back then."

"I'm not beautiful anymore."

"What's going on, Red?"

"Everything'sh going wrong."

"Surely not everything." Chase listened for a response, but only heard labored breathing. "Talk to me, sweetheart," he crooned.

"Someone'sh killing Admiral Aviation, I'm not shupposed to fly, I had a brain tumor, they operated, chemotherapy shtole my hair. I'm bald, Chashe, bald as a billiard ball. Red'sh gone…" A tear or two fell on Scotch. "I think I'm dying."

"Good lord, Red. I'm so sorry to hear this. You're not dying. Things'll get better. Hell, they have to. Sounds like they can't get any worse. Where are you and Scotch now?"

Her tongue moved like a banana slug on tacky asphalt. "Hangar Bar where you 'n' I lasht met."

"I remember. That was a good night. Let's get together again. I'll be out of town for a few days, but when I get back, I'll call you."

"I need help, Chashe… a friend."

"You have one. Me. Can you get yourself home?"

"If I can't, I'll shtay here. Thanksh for talking to me."

"I'll see you soon, Red. Please take care of yourself."

For a minute she sat entranced by the silent cellphone stuck to her ear, then lifted one heavy arm and stared at her watch… 5:47. Reaching over clumsily, she misjudged the distance to her glass and knocked Scotch the Fifth off the table.

Damn it. If I don't get home now, I'll be on the floor, too.

Her cell phone rang. Red looked down and saw at least three of them, then picked up the real one on her second try. Scotch crept up from behind, slithered through her spine, and shattered her cerebellum with a lead pipe. She pressed one button and nothing happened. She pressed all of them with both thumbs.

It was Dietrich. "Miss Scarlett! We are on our way!"

"I'm shick. Can't meet now. I'm… I'm shorry."

"Can I help you somehow?"

She struggled to hold the phone to her ear. "No. Going home. I'll ring you 'n the morning."

"That's fine. If it makes you feel any better, everything went as planned today. Camera's mounted. Act two scheduled in two days. Toma even said she had fun."

"Good, thanksh. Musht go. Tomorrow."

Red put the phone down, signaled the bartender for the check, and rested her forehead on the table as the Hangar Bar spun around her. She didn't know how many drinks she'd had and couldn't focus on the bill, anyway. Her numb fingers rummaged for rupees in her purse and slapped a wad onto the table.

She located the autodial button for Azeez at home, pushed it, and prepared to sound competent.

Azeez answered immediately. "Red Admiral Aviation."

"Asheesh, my good friend! Why aren't you here?"

"Miss Red!" He could sense immediately she was off. "Where are you?"

"Here… I already shaid that."

"Please tell me what is wrong, Miss Red? Are you ill?"

"Shick 'n' tired 'n' mosht pished. Come get me. I'm leglessh."

This had happened before, but not for months. "But where will I be picking you up?"

"I'm barely shitting at the Hangar Bar. In Holiday Inn airport. Come."

"I am coming straightaway. Please be drinking water and nothing else."

Red's arm fell and dangled at her side. The phone dropped onto the bench. The rest of her body followed.

In a dither, Azeez arrived forty-five minutes later and scanned the bar—no Red. The bartender pointed toward the lobby, where Azeez roused her from a divan in the back corner. Sleep and no Scotch had partially revived her. With an arm over his shoulders, Red wobbled to the Mercedes and crumpled onto the rear seat.

Azeez knew from experience that it was neither the time to ask questions, nor to even speak, nor to worry about the company truck left in the parking lot—just drive.

Red attempted to steer her whirling thoughts and emotions toward the mission at hand, a task as useless as trying to redirect a cyclone with a feeble whisper. *Act one sorted. Soon all will be well. Two days to act two.*

Three weeks earlier Red had felt a physical kinship with two bald warriors, *Die Hard* Bruce Willis and Mahatma Gandhi, and had privately chosen her personal moniker, "Bruce Gandhi."

In selecting the national holiday, Gandhi Jayanti, as the auspicious day for her explosive production, Red had been unaware the United Nations General Assembly adopted a resolution in 2007, ironically, declaring that Gandhi's birthday shall be the International Day of Non-Violence.

Another message overlooked, not from the universe, but from her own neighborhood.

MONA
Downhill

A NEW NOISE IN THE DISTANCE CREPT INTO MONA'S EARS. A crunching, rumbling sound. More disturbing than the noise itself was the fact that she felt the ground vibrate. She walked out onto the back deck to investigate and saw Bea at the picnic table spread with papers, Marco lying at her feet, and gazed beyond them across the yard. A fresh breeze carried the bitter odor of gasoline into her world.

On the next property fifty yards to the east, a horde of Caterpillars—not the kind she cherished—were butchering the land and devouring its perennial organic attire, including the white-bloomed milkweed and its orange cousin butterfly weed that Mona and her cohorts had planted to attract and sustain monarchs. Dozers, trucks, shovel Cats, and tree harvesters were about to devour the field and forest, the precious landscape that had been her horizon for a decade.

She shook her head as her heart sank.

There goes the neighborhood...

While Mona stared at the cedar elm, sugar hackberry, and Rio Grande ash woods, whose days—maybe only hours—were numbered, she seemed to float above the scene as the trees metamorphosed into rubber trees, palmetto and walking palms in a deep green jungle. Encircling a majestic 200-foot kapok tree with a few flaps of her iridescent blue wings, she gazed down at Caterpillars driven by human specks with insatiable appetites for the fruits of the rainforest and the rocks and minerals below.

The scene below changed to Caterpillars razing a field behind a house in a small town, to a Cat dozer and shovel truck destroying another house in a mountain forest, and finally to a Cat petrol truck exploding inside a wide, flat building.

Hard at work on her day off, Bea paid no attention to the carnage and greeted Mona cheerfully. "Good morning to you, Mona! Sometimes I still have a hard time believing I'm sitting here on Angela Mariposa's deck writing stuff on my Angela Mariposa calendar while I'm living in her house and watching the butterflies right here on this page flit through her yard!"

Snapping out of her reverie and confronted by Bea's everlasting upbeat personality, Mona didn't have it in her to be a cloud of doom by sharing her despair. "What stuff are you writing, honey?"

"I'm making a schedule for all the people who need home care..." Exasperation seeped into Bea's enthusiasm. "And trying to figure out how to be in many places at once."

"What's that saying?" Mona asked. "Be careful what you dream. You just might get it."

"Yeah. Or be careful what you wish for. It just might come with a vengeance. They're all sweet folks, but they need more than healthcare—house cleaning, fixing meals, running errands, helping them read their pill bottles. Can you believe how puny the instructions are on medicine bottles? I can barely read them myself."

"They're a blur to me," Mona agreed. "I have eye drops to help my vision and trying to read the label makes it worse. One of these days, I'm going to accidentally pick up a bottle of super glue."

"Don't say that!" Nurse Bea paused as her heart took hold of her words. "You know, most of them just need someone to talk to."

"You're right. Sometimes I find that a receptive ear heals more than medicine. Silence goes deep where a pill can't reach."

Months of activity had been packed into a few weeks. Queen Bea's TLC grew wings and took off. Bea printed business cards using Mona's artwork with handwritten taglines and a phone number, a powerful testimonial to the aging friends Mona had called. Now Bea's cell buzzed incessantly, and after meeting her, prospective patients succumbed to her infectious personality. They were hooked and had no choice but to notify their friends.

Antonio had dived into Mona and Zarita's letters, planted a vegetable garden, and transformed the empty Alamo room into a home office for their new ventures. His article in the newspaper on the inspiration for Mona's paintings was well-received, though a few of the local Christian Right became convinced she was the Heathen Wrong. In Mission, located in the bowels of the Sun Belt—or Bible Belt, or Gun Belt, depending on the shade of red on the resident's neck—anyone talking about spiritual matters had best refer to, and thank regularly, Jesus.

One of Mona's quotes jacked up some folks' religious hackles into spikes. "We are all God and she is all of us."

A young couple, Melvin and Melvira Southerland—perhaps attracted to each other by their multi-directional teeth or their familiar status as second cousins—staged a protest against Mona in front of the Butterfly Center where her paintings hung. With their two exuberant children, Mary and Joseph, they paraded back and forth for three days, shouting at passersby and waving their hand-scribbled signs:

"God ain't a she! He's a he!"

"Angela is a devil amongst us fayathfull."

"Ubstain from her piantings!"

A Brownsville TV news crew filmed the fiery family, and several stations ran the story with tongue-in-cheek anchors proclaiming:

"The devil casta spell on my spellin'!"

"Let us all ubstain from gramma'!"

"What's that there rule? 'I' before 'a' except after 'p'?"

On the day of Barney's attack on Mona at the Rio Real Art Gallery, a visitor had recorded the deed on his smartphone and posted it on Facebook. It went viral, inciting a Texas-style backlash against the gay community. Mona felt horrible and had called Barney to apologize for her actions. With a hint of thanks in his voice, he said, "What's done's done. Ain't no closet big enough to hide my hide now."

Bea swished a rolled-up paper at a couple of curious wasps that wouldn't leave her alone. "Go away! Git!"

"They won't sting you unless you sit on 'em," Mona advised, stroking Bea's shoulder. "Neither will honeybees unless you're standing in their beeline from the flowers to the hive. Give me a minute. I'll save you."

Mona went into the kitchen, returned with a plate of over-the-hill apples, and set it on the other end of the deck. "Come and get it, boys!" she shouted to the winged ones and then joined Bea at the picnic table. "Now give *them* a minute."

"Thanks, Mona. Hope it works. I get stung, and I've got a sore mountain on my skin."

"You're sweet and pretty, but rotten fruit's much more attractive to them. I can only think of one time seeing wasps or bees attack people. I was at a butterfly conservatory in a park and tried to strike up a conversation with four folks—two Indians and two foreigners. The Indian woman got snippy and told me to go away, but I could tell by her accent that she was British. A little later, a flock of pooping birds and a bunch of angry bees chased them away. I remember yelling at them as they ran by. 'Have a nice day. Heading home to England, I hope?'"

Elbows on the table, Bea had leaned in close, resting her head in her hands. "Where'd that happen? With Indians around here?"

As Mona searched for the answer through her filing cabinet of life, she realized this was another of her strange experiences. "No… not around here. In India. New Delhi."

"Wow," Bea said, "the other side of the world. When were you there?"

"Never been there…" Mona replied with that faraway look that Bea had begun to notice during these weeks of living together. "Never set foot outside the USA."

"I don't understand. You think it was a dream?"

"I don't think so, nor do I understand." Mona closed her eyes. "In my mind, the experience is real. In reality, it's not. Maybe it came from space… the ether… Call it what you like. Beyond time… past or future lives."

Mona told Bea about chatting with her friend Sasha and relating an incident in a Canadian grocery store, and another at the airport in DC, both places she'd never visited.

"These visions used to scare me, like Alzheimer's had taken control, but it's not that. And now I'm intrigued." Mona sat with her thoughts for a moment, toying with the end of her waist-length, black braided hair. "I have a confession to make."

"What is it?" Bea leaned across the table toward Mona.

"That night I asked you two to move in, I told you I'd made a joke when I said, 'What on Earth are you talking about?' It was no joke, nor did I forget that I'd asked. I was somewhere else, specifically inside your painting. No… inside the swarm of monarchs on that very tree in Mexico. It felt wonderful. I was there, and I wanted to stay there. I wasn't dreaming… it felt more like an awakening."

"You mean like meditation or enlightenment? I've tried to meditate," Bea said, spinning her eyes around, "but I can't seem to stop my mind from wandering in circles."

"For some folks, meditation takes years of practice. Others I've met seem to have danced off with the spirit at birth. I don't really know what enlightenment is, only what I've read. White light? Eternal peace? That's not what these visions are." Mona pushed herself up and climbed over the picnic bench attached to the table. "There's more. Let me get my sketchbook."

After reliving the cosmic inspiration she'd received from Bucky's lecture during her interview for Antonio's article, Mona had decided to focus on space, since it was ninety-nine-point-whatever percent of everything. She'd always wanted an official, sparsely furnished meditation area and felt badly that her spacious storage room overflowed with matter that didn't matter, ninety-nine percent unused and useless to her.

Not only spacious, its decor was space. Its outer glass block wall diffused light onto the other three—a panoramic mural of the solar system Flank had commissioned an artist to create. On the eastern wall, Father Sun dominated the black background with Mercury, a speck of gray, and Venus, a spot of orange, in the foreground. On the middle wall, the sea-blue, pea-green Earth, its little brother red Mars, and a gigantic cream-salmon-brown-striped Jupiter. On the western wall, a ringed yellow Saturn, with frozen aqua Uranus and cobalt Neptune floating beyond. Pluto hid among distant star clouds, a shadowy beige grain of cosmic sand on the invisible horizon.

Mona had sorted through decaying cardboard boxes filled with the past, and carted clothes, dishes, books, and other dust magnets to Mission's Goodwill store.

With Antonio's help, she'd fashioned a simple three-tiered altar from adobe bricks and pine boards, then filled it with treasures gathered during the past seventy-three years—an Ojibway feather dream catcher from Wisconsin; a bronze Saraswati, the Hindu goddess of wisdom, music, art, and nature; a jet black obsidian globe resting on a wooden tripod; her threadbare teddy bear and a faded photo of pen pal Zarita at age twelve among a clutter of agates gathered from the Lake Superior shore.

In the middle of the second tier, she'd set a framed painting she'd done of Buddha, Jesus, and Mohammed, relaxed and casual, arms on each other's shoulders, as if they were buddies hanging out at a coffee shop. Front center on the top tier sat a stone replica of the round Maya calendar mirroring the circular yin-yang rug on the floor.

Retrieving her sketchbook from the meditation room, Mona passed the kitchen counter and noticed a letter with a Mexican stamp.

Hmm. A little late this month.

Letters from Zarita, the methodical archeologist, arrived like Swiss clockwork. She wrote them on the last day of the month and posted them on the first of the next. Letters from Mona meandered into Mexico at routine but irregular intervals. She picked up the envelope and tucked it under her arm on the way to the deck.

Opening her sketchbook, Mona laid it on the picnic table in front of Bea. "Look at these images I've encountered in meditation or arbitrary moments during the day. I don't know where they're coming from."

Bea studied the pencil drawing of a small hand slipping a large butterfly into an envelope; on the facing page, two teenagers, a boy in a baseball jersey and a white girl in African native dress, riding in a pink VW bug.

"Are these part of your *One Life* autobiography?"

"No, not unless it were called 'Someone Else's Life.' I have no idea what they mean." Mona flipped to the next page. "This one looks like a huge cocoon hanging by ropes from a dead tree! Go figure. And what's this?"

"A building blowing up? A weird building." Bea bent down with her finger on the sketch. "It's got a curved roof here, like an airplane hangar. Maybe this is a runway."

Mona nodded her head. "Could be. I've never seen anything like it." Turning the page, she confided, "This next one disturbs me. A woman in a hospital bed next to a blank window… and a monarch floating above her."

Mona had used a dull pencil to sketch the woman with a hazy unrecognizable face, her arms stretching out and up to the monarch drawn with pastels, red-orange and black, as big as the reclining body below, blurred as if landing or taking off. Above the bed hung a wall clock with numbers but no hands.

Bea didn't want to ask it, but did anyway. "Could this be your *One Life* collection in the future? You… or your monarch spirit rising toward heaven?"

"Perhaps. But I don't want to kick the bucket in a hospital."

Bea's cell phone buzzed on the table. She picked it up, looked at the number, then at Mona. "It's Yves next door."

"You'd better get it. No telling where he might've wandered off to. Say hello from Mona and let me know if he remembers who I am. I've got a letter from Zarita to read."

Mona picked up her sketchbook, the letter, and her carved walking staff, and made her way toward her studio with Marco at her heels.

Ever since receiving her first letter from Zarita at age twelve, Mona had sat on the same silver maple stool Papa Marco made for her, facing south toward Mexico as she read her friend's words. Mona still had the stool, wizened and weather-beaten, now in the shade of the cottonwood tree next to her studio on the bluff overlooking the Rio Grande.

She rested her staff against the trunk and sat down, facing southeast toward Teapa where Zarita now lived, and set the letter on the sketchbook in her lap. Glancing down, she furrowed her brow. The handwritten address was different than before, similar Zarita's first letters, written in the script of a young girl without the curly cues and flourishes one adds with age—definitely Zarita's handwriting but each individual letter seemed to tremble. Mona noticed the return address had been written by a steady hand—another person's hand.

Now Mona began to tremble. She fumbled with the envelope as she slid her finger under the flap, took out the letter, and unfolded it. Shaky words filled the stationery stained with watermarks and dried tears blurred the sentences.

Halfway through the words, Mona's tears pooled under her lids, then overflowed. As they fell and hit the ground, so did Mona's numb body, seemingly in slow motion, her head cushioned by the bushy grass at the base of the cottonwood, her arm across the drawing of the bed-ridden woman in her open sketchbook, Mona's braided hair streaming through the green blades like black blood.

ANGEL
Home Is Where?

Random turbulence ruled the remainder of the fourteen-hour flight from Atlanta to Tokyo. A mischievous god seemed to control the 747 and its passengers, many sitting rigid with eyes shut and a light green pallor on their faces, praying the roller coaster ride would end soon. Their world would wobble, then fly steady before plummeting thirty feet in a second. Angel rather enjoyed it. The stewards managed to serve a meal, which he thought folks should pour straight into their barf bags to save one step. As the jet wrestled with the weather, Angel played the reflex game with a full water cup and didn't spill a drop.

A woozy man across the aisle watched him. "How you do that?"

"Relax, be aware, and go with the flow." Angel demonstrated as he spoke with both hands. "The plane goes down, your cup goes up and vice versa."

The man did fairly well until the next plunge. The plane dropped suddenly, as did his hand holding the cup, leaving a blob of orange juice suspended in the air above his head. He caught it with his lap.

As the 747 continued to shake and shimmy, Angel replayed his paralysis dream, but didn't have to think too hard to get it. *I'm in a cage I made for myself. My underground safehouse is like a cave. I'm just one of those soldiers lining up on payday.*

He needed a new direction, away from the line of fire, but couldn't break out of the tumultuous career he'd chosen fifteen years earlier. He was addicted to flying, and work gave him the means to feed the beloved monkey on his back. He'd succeeded in his life's mission, one that had always felt like a predestined calling—to serve and to save those in need—but these days, it didn't sit right in his soul. *Maybe it's time to save myself… Morpho loved to fly but didn't last long. He relied on instinct alone. No intellect. No experience. Tiger changed. He loved collecting butterflies, but the killing finally tore him apart, made him stop. My dream served up his song to help me.*

ANGEL'S NEXT SEVEN-HOUR FLIGHT ON AN AIRBUS TO BANGKOK was smooth, silky like Asian skin, and traditional Thai clothing. Stepping out of the terminal's conditioned air, Angel breathed deeply and let an audible sigh slip out of his smile. "Ahhhh..." *Feel that thick, humid air. You can almost roll it between your fingers.*

The sweet smell of jasmine, the perfumed blooms of potted lilawadee trees, and the bouquet of the tropical atmosphere masked the fumes from the crush of honking buses, tuk-tuks, and taxis. These Southeast Asia sensations always stirred dormant emotions in his chest, as if his nose, eyes, and ears connected directly to his heart. Only one word could describe them all. Home. Angel hadn't lived in Asia since childhood in Laos, but every time he'd visited for business or pleasure, his love for the land grew deeper, wider, stronger. He could feel that his internal compass no longer pointed north. It was stuck on southeast.

After thirty-odd hours of flying and layovers, time had fallen off the clock. Midnight in Bangkok only meant he had a six-hour dose of now before his short flight to Chiang Mai. After checking into the Novotel near the airport, he savored the nighttime coos and cackles of birds in the courtyard, jacuzzied the sweaty miles off his skin in the hotel room, and curled up on crispy clean sheets.

The next morning during his eighty-minute hop, Angel acted as naïve as a twenty-one-year-old and as seasoned as a thirty-three-year-old globetrotter could be, and made friends with three young female travelers, his ticket to invisibility once they'd landed.

Chiang Mai's airport was white, compact, and unassuming. Wearing a T-shirt and jeans, a baseball cap shading his eyes, and three Dutch girls taller than he veiling his profession, Angel cruised by the expectant crowd of friends, relatives, drivers, and one heavy man stuffed in a white shirt and tie who couldn't have passed for anyone but an FBI or DEA agent... except for the flat-brimmed Stetson hat. *Must have a mold to stamp out these guys.*

Angel bid adieu to his companions and circled back behind Doug Anderson, his new main man for the mission. He spoke from beneath his baseball cap.

"Mister... you need hotel? Nice guest house? Good company?"

Exactly as the Skipper had done in DC, Doug didn't even move his head. "No, thanks. Mai ow, khrap."

"I know beautiful place. Cheap for you. But I no have car. Phu Chi Fa. The mountain reaching for the sky."

A surprised Doug turned, his weather-beaten face peering down, and stuck out a beefy hand. "I'll be damned. Angel Phoenix. Welcome to Thailand!"

Doug's fingers reached all the way around Angel's hand. "Glad to be here. DEA Doug, I presume?"

"Nice to meet ya. You must be beat."

"I'm okay. Four flights, forty-one hours, fourteen naps."

"Truck's out front," Doug said, pointing at the exit. "Can I carry one of your bags for ya?"

"Thanks, I got 'em. Need to wake up my muscles." As he followed Doug, Angel read him from behind. *Six foot three, bowlegged, worn cowboy boots, uneasy when dressed up, limping from an old injury, once fit now failing, fifty going on sixty.*

They climbed into the nut-brown Ford Explorer, the same SUV Jonathan drove except for the color. Doug asked, "What'dya need before we hit the trail? Ride's about six hours depending on weather and traffic."

"Doug, my man, while I've been eatin' plane food, and I mean plain boring food, I've been dreamin' of a hot plate of holy basil chicken followed by a dish of mango and sticky rice. How 'bout hittin' a day market?"

"Sure you don't wanna sit-down diner?"

"I don't need fancy, just authentic. Real Asian markets are scarce in the US of A."

"We'll find one on the way," Doug said, pulling away from the terminal. "You know, I thought you'd be..."

"Taller, wider, bigger, older, lighter, darker?" A little too much sarcasm crept through Angel's fatigue. "Which one, or all of the above?"

"Take a pill, bud," Doug chuckled. "Jonathan told me to say that to get your goat."

Angel's lips rose into a one-sided smile. "You got the goat by the balls. Sorry, man. You have no idea how many times I've heard that line."

"I read your file. I think you're the only soul in the world who'd take this bitch of a job *and* has what it takes to make it work."

"We'll see, maybe I'm the stupidest soul in the universe to even try."

"Won't find a 300-pound jockey on a racehorse." Doug wove through the crazy mesh of motorbikes zipping by in any lane, going in every direction. "And in this part of the globe, you're already in disguise."

This guy's okay. He's like the Skipper's country cousin. "The thing about bein' small is that it disrupts the large ego. Mr. Big looks down on this little Angel and thinks, 'No problem. This one's nothing.' He lets down his guard, givin' me a two-second edge, and it's game over for him."

"I hear what you're sayin'. There was this short kid on my college basketball team. Scooter Jenkins. Maybe five-six and fit as a fiddle. The skinny giants paid him no mind. He'd dribble 'em to death, sometimes slidin' right between their legs. When he got a clear shot, it was a damn bucket ev'ry time."

"The Marines taught me a bunch of combat techniques, but then I studied Brazilian jiu-jitsu in South America, Krav Maga from an Israeli dude, and Muay Thai here on the isle of Koh Pan Ngan."

"You get around, don't ya?" Doug turned off the teeming street into the parking lot of a sprawling street market.

"I watched a ton of Bruce Lee movies." Angel raised his folded hands in respect and gratitude. "He was the master who wove many disciplines into his own brand of street fighting. Different styles give me a multi-edge." Angel kept talking as he got out of the truck—more room to speak with his hands. "Let the giant think I'm doin' the Muay Thai dance, then all of a sudden his ass is on the grass, layin' on broken bones. Jiu-jitsu means the 'supple yielding art' in Japanese, but I say it means the bigger they are, the harder they fall."

"Grub's over there," Doug said, pointing at the plastic tables and blue stools surrounded by food stalls.

During his instinctual 360-degree surveillance of the parking lot, Angel's eyes locked onto a rack of olive-green camouflage fatigues in front of a quintessential Thai whatever shop displaying a disheveled array of goods—orange highway cones, used TVs, and banana bunches from the owner's backyard. "Doug… What color camo did you get for us to wear?"

"Oh, brownish, I guess. Yours are in the truck. Barry's are stashed in the jungle waitin' for you with the rest of the supplies on your wish list."

Before Doug finished his sentence, Angel was striding toward the shop. Doug's lanky legs strained to keep up.

As Angel neared the racks, he recognized the exact color and pattern worn by the leering men in his dream cave—a knock-off camo with pixelated leaves and splotches. "Green's what I need. Brown's fine for Barry." *You can take that answer or leave it, Agent Man. I don't have the time nor the desire to get into any metaphysical mumbo jumbo right now.*

They bought the fatigues, then take-away food served in foam trays and plastic bags from a couple of stalls. Angel would've loved to eat his way through the market, relishing the odors of everything he'd eat later, but he was on a mission. The magical camo message had revved him up and slammed him into gear, although riding through Chiang Mai with Doug's sparse comments eased him out of his future and back into the present.

As a kid, Angel had visited Chiang Mai—the "Rose of the North"—but he and the city had both evolved over the years into bustling, energetic beings. Global progress and the tourist industry had changed the cityscape from traditional to international. Tour buses bigger than many natives' hovels ruled the roads and parked wherever they damn well pleased. Modern hippies strapped to backpacks—a bit smaller than an armoire but heavier—lumbered along in search of lodging. English billboards touted Tiger World, elephant parks, five-star hotels, and McDonald's. In spite of the blatant commercialism, Chiang Mai's inherent charm still shone through—sparkling temples adorned with stone dragons curving up stairs to golden Buddhas; the square moat with water fountains surrounding the old city guarded by the crumbling remains of walls built eight centuries earlier; an 88-year-old grandmother pedaling a rusty bicycle on the way to visit her 108-year-old parents.

I need to come back here...

A half-hour later they were out of the city, climbing up one of the mountain ridges circumcising the flat Ping River plain where Chiang Mai lived.

Doug's straight arm hung over the steering wheel like it was a cattle fence. "Aren't you gonna eat?"

"Good idea. Had to chow down on the scenery for an appetizer first." Angel took out his assorted food containers and balanced them on his lap. He attempted to open the plastic bag of holy basil chicken, sealed with a red rubber band by a vendor using a complex series of mystical twists and knots, a sleight-of-hand trick that food vendors perform in two seconds. Angel struggled with the bulging pressurized bag, finally punctured it, squirting the sauce and a wrinkled basil leaf onto his white T-shirt. "I shoulda put on that camo before tacklin' this bag. How the hell do you get into 'em?"

"I dunno," Doug smirked. "I've tried with every tool on my Swiss Army knife. None of 'em worked. Try one of your kung fu moves."

"How'd you get into the drug biz over here?" Angel asked through a mouthful of sticky rice. "You talk like you're a down-home cowboy from out west."

"Once was. Born in Durango. Married a gal from Denver and became a cop. Saw too many kids divin' into drugs, crackin' their heads open in the shallows or dyin' in the deep end. Instead of pickin' up bodies in the background, I headed for the front lines and the DEA kept sendin' me forward. You can have Bangkok, but I feel at home in Chiang Mai. It's kinda like

Denver with a mountain wall to the west. You just look up and know which way you're walkin'."

Angel held up a mango slice skewered on a plastic fork. "Wanna bite? It's bangin'."

"Ate right before I picked ya up, thanks."

"You know this Barry Majors?"

"Met him once or twice. Polite well-heeled hulk."

"So he went off on his own private crusade? Any ulterior motives? Any way he's in cahoots with Mister Ghost?"

"Not smart enough or stupid enough." Doug's eyes roamed from the road to Angel's. "Off the record, he's a half-pint cowboy with a ten-gallon hat. Big Daddy Megabucks and Big Vice Uncle in the Big House. Barry Boy don't care about this job. He's just bidin' time, tryin' to be a damn hero along the way."

During the next five hours they passed over more mini-mountains, wound round a thousand rice fields, through a small city, several smaller towns, then tiny villages, the population diminishing as the miles multiplied. Whenever they stopped to stretch, Angel scrutinized the sky, the clouds, the wind. Not only would the weather influence the entire mission, its fickle whims could cancel the operation right on the starting line—the summit of Phu Chi Fa at dawn.

"You been to Phu Chi Fa before?" Angel asked.

"Couple times as a tourist. Purty spot. Didn't consider jumpin' off."

"Ever go at dawn?"

"Nah. Lazy vacations. Midafternoon, maybe."

"You know the weather's a crapshoot this time of the year," Angel sighed, "with dice loaded in favor of Mother Nature."

"I know, bud. You could look it up online, but do better lickin' your finger and stickin' it up in the air. And ya never know what's round the next mountain curve."

They'd begun the steep climb up the range bordering Laos. Doug concentrated on the narrow pavement, a series of tight S-curves strung together like snakes biting each other's tails, until they reached the ridge road and turned toward Phu Chi Fa. Rice paddies had given way to forty-five-degree cabbage crops sloping back down to the Thai landscape below.

Finally able to take one hand off the steering wheel, Doug pointed to the drop-off inches beyond the shoulder on his left. "How the heck do these farmers plant, weed, and harvest on this incline? Looks like one wrong step and you're down in the valley."

"Velcro boots?"

"Maybe. Or their own personal gravity."

Angel's mind shifted ahead a few hours. "The cliff at Phu Chi Fa's straight down, great for liftoff, but then there's a maze of ridges down to the Mekong. I've looked at the sat photos and topo maps, but I have to see in person. Dawn may not be the best time to begin this op."

"You're callin' the shots, Angel. I'm just doin' anything I can to make it happen."

"Travel sites talk about a 'blanket of fog.' The sun looks like it's risin' over a white ocean of mist in the photos, and that's not a place I care to land. I won't have an autopilot or a lit runway."

"I hear ya, bud. We'll mosey up to the cliff first thing when we get there." Doug checked his watch. "Should arrive about two p.m."

"There's another thing I'm concerned about." Angel pressed his forehead against the Explorer's tinted side window, weighing each element that could tip the scale from success to fiasco. "Sightseers write about gettin' up hours before dawn and trekkin' up to the top, tour guides, Hmong hilltribe kids posin' for tips. Sounds like a goddamn circus to me. I want no word o' mouth makin' its way to Ghost Land before I get there. If I'm gonna survive this, I need to be invisible and a big fuckin' surprise."

They drove in silence the rest of the way, the superb scenery barely softening the tension building inside both of them. Careers, reputations, and two lives were staked on the front line ahead.

RED

Small Medium, Large Omen

The morning after her numbing bender at the Hangar Bar, Red felt as if her leaden head were pounding inside a sealed Ziploc bag. Life had become a suffocating burden. Everything about the past seemed better than the present.

God help me. What do I have to do today?

She stumbled through the list in her mind.

Pick up the truck, call Dietrich, watch the spy camera, suffer through chemo, exist.

Pulling her aching body into a sitting position, Red saw the slip of paper Dr. B had given her with the name and number of a spiritual advisor.

Devika. Little goddess. I need to talk to someone.

She called and made an appointment for Scarlett at eleven. Red had grown to like the name because it highlighted her feminine identity, and she often felt more like a man than a woman. Scarlett wore a sari. Red wore pantsuits, a flight jacket, or Admiral Aviation coveralls.

She plodded to the toilet to wash, a task she'd mastered without looking at the foreign face in the mirror, though she cringed when her soapy fingers slipped across her hairless scalp.

Red dressed in a casual salmon sari she'd recently purchased more suitable to her style—less fabric, less wrapping, less time to become invisibly Indian—until she spoke.

She buzzed Azeez on the intercom.

"Yes, Miss Red."

"In fifteen minutes I'll need a ride to get the truck."

"How are you doing today?" he asked.

"Foggy, but the mist is lifting."

"Are you feeling all right to drive?"

Red let a three-second silence communicate her answer and sour mood. "Azeez, just be ready in fifteen minutes."

"Yes, Miss Red."

As he drove the Mercedes with Red in the backseat staring out the side window, Azeez knew he shouldn't ask, but couldn't help himself. "Miss Red, why are you being so Indian lately and wearing a sari and driving our most undignified truck?"

"Because I don't want to be recognized," Red snapped, "and have to explain my appearance to anyone I know, including you right now."

"I am sorry to be asking, Miss Red."

Steady on, girl. It's Azeez, your friend. "Pardon me, Azeez, but I am stressed. And last night, overwhelmed. Thanks for bringing me home."

"You are most welcome, Miss Red. You know drinking and chemo—"

"Azeez," she said sternly.

"Yes, Miss Red."

After their taciturn trip, Azeez parked next to the company truck in the Holiday Inn lot, hopped out, and opened the back door for Red. "It's Thursday. Shouldn't I be driving you to chemotherapy at the hospital?"

"Last week Dr. B said he'll be trying a new method of treatment, and he's out of town today." It wasn't a lie. B was out-of-town and her final chemo session was today, sans Azeez. She thanked him for the ride, pulled away in the pickup, and phoned Dietrich.

"Guten Tag, Miss Scarlett. Are you feeling okay today?" Dietrich asked. "You seemed ill and out of it last night."

"Better. I admit I was quite sloshed. Scotch crept up from behind. I'm sorry to miss our rendezvous."

"Should we meet up today?"

"I'm afraid today is full, and I'd rather not discuss our little surprise on the phone. I'll be remote viewing today and tonight, and we can plan our outing tomorrow. Say ten a.m. in the parking lot as before?"

"Ten it is," Dietrich agreed.

"Dress the part. Your wife was smashing yesterday."

"She always is. We'll be ready."

"Cheers." Red's mood swung upwards. She'd reveled in their clandestine chat and felt a morsel of morale return.

The way to Devika's wound through the maze of skinny streets in Old Delhi. Weaving around hoary men, their sinewy legs straining on the pedals of cycle rickshaws, Red felt as if she were traveling into the past.

Devika's two-story shop, clean and inviting, stood out from the other stores housed in timeworn dwellings, their chipped and faded plaster revealing brick skeletons. As Red opened the front door, a brass bell tinkled above her head. Thick with the essence of frankincense, the room held a myriad of spiritual icons and ritual accessories on wall shelves and covering the display table in the middle.

A tiny woman wearing a white cotton peasant blouse and fisherman's pants emerged from a passageway in the rear. She thought they might be about the same age, but Red felt worn and this Devika looked reborn, timeless. She bowed and greeted Red warmly.

"Namaste. You must be Scarlett."

"Namaste. Thank you for seeing me on short notice." Red looked into Devika's kind face and wondered how this woman could see her at all; her left eye gazed fixedly to the left, four feet to the right of Red.

"Time is only now, and my time is now yours. Please come into the prayer room."

Devika lead Red through beaded curtains into a larger space with a short round table encircled by stately statues: Durga the warrior goddess, riding a tiger and brandishing weapons; Lakshmi, the goddess of wealth and prosperity, seated on a magenta lotus blossom; the dark mother Kali Ma, goddess of creation, preservation, and destruction, with a garland of human skulls representing the elimination of the ego; a sleeping Buddha reclining on his side, tranquil and detached from the desires of the world. The room was painted shiny gold with a universe of religions replicated on its walls—a cross, the Star of David, three archangels, and a circular yin-yang symbol floating like a black-and-white planet on the ceiling.

Red felt small, surrounded by gods and goddesses taller than she. "Are you a Hindu, Brahman, Buddhist… or… I see a cross and angels… or a Christian?"

"I am…" Devika began, crossing her legs in the lotus position at the low table, "as we all are, all of these modalities. All the spokes of a wheel lead to its center. If I must distinguish myself, I am a medium, somewhere between the spokes. Please sit across from me."

As Red sat on the round cushion, legs to the side, visions of crystal balls and floating tables drifted through her mind. "A medium, you say? Do you talk with dead people?"

"No. Some call me a psychic. Others call me insane. I see and feel and hear things others cannot, though everyone has the potential to do the same. A mundane scientific meaning of medium resonates with me: an intervening substance or agency for transmitting or producing an effect." Devika smiled, one eye sparkling, the other gazing at the wall or off into another world. "Just think of me as a happy medium."

Transfixed by the shimmering silver bindi on Devika's forehead, Red wasn't sure what to do or say next in this completely foreign situation. "How much will this… this talk, reading, whatever it is… cost?"

"Whatever you wish to donate." Devika pointed to the envelopes next on the table between them. "Now please close your eyes… or not… and focus on why you have come… or what it is you would like to explore… and rest your hands on the table, palms up."

Eyes halfway shut, Red felt like a naughty peeping Tom. She had to see what was going on.

Devika chanted several stanzas, some that Red recalled hearing her mother Chandra used to call upon and honor deities. She placed her palms lightly on Red's, but only for a moment. Devika's cheeks raised and tightened, scrunching her closed eyes into narrow wrinkles as she jerked her hands up and away, tipping her head and shoulders to the side as if avoiding a blow on the temple.

"What do you see?" Red asked, eyes wide open and alarmed.

Devika sat silently, relaxing her muscles, formulating sounds to describe what she'd seen and sensed, then spoke with closed eyes.

"You came into this life with heavy karma, and your actions have heaped more weight upon it. Dark entities are attached to your body and swarming all around it. I feel sadness and anger and revenge coursing through you. You are strong and stubborn, caught between conflicting worlds: male and female, black and white, love and hate. If you seek revenge, dig two graves. If you do not change direction, you will end up where you are heading."

Red couldn't have closed her wide eyes even if she were underwater, which is how she felt—drowning in Devika's diagnosis. Questions bombarded her brain, and she forced one out. "Where… where am I heading?"

Devika slowly opened her eyes and held Red's gaze with compassion. "I cannot predict the future. I can only see what is. Like a map, or perhaps a time compass pointing in many directions from now."

As much as she doubted anyone's paranormal abilities, or discounted Devika's perceptions, or denied her biting words, Red couldn't help but think and feel one reality. *This woman speaks the truth.*

Devika seemed to have read Red's mind. "I can only speak the truth. If that is what you seek, please speak the truth to me. Tell me why you have come and what you want to know. Talk to me."

Red's scarred heart softened, split open, and feelings flowed out with her tears. She spoke of the strange, confusing dreams, the kinship she felt with the imaginary Angel, the living nightmare of her failing business, her loneliness, her love of flying, and finished with a barrage of questions. "What should I do? What are the dark entities? What do the dreams mean?"

"Thank you for your honesty, Scarlett. You are what you are, neither good nor bad. But as Lao Tzu said so succinctly, 'When I let go of what I am, I become who I might be.' Your task is more about being than doing. Simply be love." Devika leaned across the table toward Red. "I can feel the love in you."

"Dark entities sound like a horror movie. What are they?" Red asked.

"They are the millions of souls of the flying and crawling creatures you have murdered and sent into limbo between living and dying. Like you, these entities are neither good nor bad, but they feed on you, like mosquitoes." Devika rose and went to a bookshelf by the wall. "Chanting, prayer, and meditation may help you. Apologize to these poor souls and ask them to continue on their journey home." She handed Red a thin pamphlet. "Choose the Sanskrit chants that resonate with you. The words and ritual may facilitate connection with the divine, but the intention in your heart is what the spirit hears."

"I suppose I can try," Red sighed. "I've never done anything like that before."

"Take one step at a time," Devika said, walking her fingers across the table like a little person. "Each one might reveal another path you couldn't have imagined before taking the first."

"What about my dreams? They felt so real, and the one with Angel keeps playing in my head."

"I believe dreams are combinations of the daily images we encounter in life, messages from other dimensions, and directions we are trying to communicate to ourselves. You have to sort the wheat from the chaff. Any butterfly dream heralds change and transmutation." Devika gestured to the Sleeping Buddha behind her. "Like the Enlightened One achieving nirvana as he died, like your Tiger went through a metamorphosis from a cocooned child into an adult when he stopped collecting and killing insects. I think you're like the Tiger in Chinese astrology. Unpredictable, always tense. Tempestuous yet calm, warm-hearted yet fearsome. Confident, but perhaps too confident sometimes."

"When you put it that way, I'm definitely a tiger."

Devika took Red's hand and led her to the wall of angels. "I feel Angel is the dream voice to follow, but perhaps you've misinterpreted some of his wisdom. He seems like a composite of the archangels on this wall. In the middle, Michael the Protector looks after us physically, emotionally, and psychically, his flaming sword slaying fear and unwanted entities." Devika stroked Michael's feet and trailed a hand across the wall to the next angel's heart. "Here's Raphael the Healer, Patron of Travelers on inward spiritual journeys. He's the friendliest of all the archangels. Look at him chatting merrily with the mortals!"

"He looks like my former husband. Is Raphael gay?"

"Probably bisexual," Devika quipped.

This tiny woman had forged her way into Red's heart, one fact or feeling at a time. Too much information perhaps, but though her words were beyond reason and logic. They seemed to make sense. She listened intently, watching Devika's eyes light up and long black hair bounce as she gestured at the images she adored.

"Gabriel the Messenger here is the only female archangel. Call on her when your body is full of toxins or negative thoughts and needs purifying, or to help you find and understand your purpose in life. She can give you direction to guide you through the changes ahead."

"My cancer. Can she cure it?" Red asked. "Can you?"

"I can neither stop the wheel of karma, nor reverse it. Perhaps *you* can slow it down, Scarlett. Your cancer is the internal manifestation of your external life. The killing, the anger, and the choices you have made are running wild inside like the entities surrounding you. Besides altering your being, there's one thing you can do a doctor friend told me." Devika recreated him with a silly grin, hands on her stomach, and voice a tone lower. "'Fill your body with fresh strong ginger tea.' He said it makes cancer cells go crazy and commit suicide!"

Red laughed along with Devika, comfortable and content. "Your English is perfect! Where'd you learn to speak so well?"

"My parents met while studying abroad in Boston and chose to stay in America. After graduating from college, I met India and chose to stay here." She pointed to her wall near the angels. "When I left America, they gave me this monarch painting by Angela Mariposa, an artist whose name means 'angel butterfly' in Spanish. Father said, 'Our butterfly from the West is migrating home to the East.' Perhaps today it's a portrait of Scarlett on her way home."

"Hmm, so lifelike." Red was riveted for a moment. "Somehow familiar." Glancing at her watch, she saw that the hour had slipped away. "I must be off. This has been most enlightening and uplifting. I'll come see you again."

"Please do. I hope my words have helped. Wait here for a moment. I want to give you something."

While Devika went into the next room, Red put too many rupees in an envelope on the table, hoping to show her gratitude again once she'd departed.

Devika returned to the prayer room, carrying an amulet in her palm. "I'd like you to wear this: a small Buddha in the Banishing Evil pose that signifies expelling demons, negative entities, or sickness. The beads of the necklace are carnelian, used by Buddhists for their powers of protection. Ancient warriors wore carnelian for courage and physical strength to conquer their enemies."

Her words about warriors lit a fire in Red's eyes.

"Carnelian wards off anger, fear, and depression, so you can look at the bright side of life. And it's a stone of love, red like your heart and the name Scarlett."

Red put it on immediately. "It's beautiful. I need all those powers right now!" As Devika took her hand and led her to the door, she promised, "I give you my word I'll start praying, chanting, and meditating in a few days, as soon as I finish one pressing task."

Devika took both of Red's hands into hers. "I can sense the severity of your task, so I will leave you with the words of the Buddha around your neck. 'Holding onto anger is like grasping a hot coal with the intent of throwing it at someone else. You are the one getting burned.'"

The quote hit home, and Red wished she hadn't heard it. "You must stop, Devika," she said, forcing a smile. "You've given me enough to hold on to already. The chemo has stolen parts of my memory as well as my hair."

"I'm just giving you more than your money's worth. One final thing," Devika said, grinning affectionately and pointing at Red's waist. "Although you wrap your sari to the right, you must turn your pleats to the left. Wise words from my mother. She taught me that right isn't always right and what's left might be right."

"Yes, Mother," Red said, a tad embarrassed. "I'll get it right next time."

And then she left. It was time to deal with the cancer in real time at the hospital. Walking toward the old truck, she felt lighter. The anchor in her chest had reeled up a bit, still heavy but not stuck on the ocean floor.

As she prepared to pull away from the curb, Red noticed a red car in the rearview mirror. Not just any car, a red Mercedes. Her red Mercedes. Parked twenty-five meters down the street. Red's newfound peace of mind fell to pieces, and rage took its place.

"Bloody hell! That son of a bitch is following me!"

MONA

I Am Another You

While listening to Yves ramble on the phone, Bea had watched Mona stroll out to the bluff and sit on her stool to read her latest letter from Zarita. Her contentment vanished as Mona collapsed onto the ground. She shouted into the phone.

"Yves! Mona needs help! I'll call you later!"

Bea clicked into emergency mode and sprinted down the path, personal panic displacing any detached professional manner learned in nursing school. Marco was leaning down, nudging Mona's shoulder with his snout. Bea knelt, felt for a neck pulse with one hand, and rested her other hand on Mona's thigh. "Mona. I'm here. Mona."

Scanning her body for injuries, she saw the letter on the ground. Three words jumped off the page: "I am dying." Though touching her heart, they eased her anxiety and solidified her diagnosis—shock. She shook Mona's leg. "Come back to me, Mona. Come back."

Mona's eyelids wavered, then she opened her eyes and looked up into Bea's face. "Zarita?"

"I'm Bea, Mona," she said. "You're home. Here with me."

"You look like Zarita," Mona murmured. "So do I. Three peas in a Mexican pod."

"How are you feeling?" Bea touched Mona's forehead with her palm. "You fell off the stool."

"I'm sorry. I faint."

"That's okay. I'm so sorry about Zarita. I looked at the letter, but only saw three words."

"'I am dying.' That's when I started to go down." Mona covered her eyes with her hand, and tears leaked between her fingers as her chest throbbed. "Oh, dear Zarita. I've never even met you!"

"I'll bet she was the woman in the hospital bed in your drawing. You felt her pain, Mona. She came to you. Or somehow… you were there."

Mona struggled to get up, wiping her damp cheeks with the hem of her skirt. "I must go there. I must see her. I have to get ready."

"Easy now. Let me help you. We'll go inside and get ready." Bea braced Mona as she rose to her feet, picked up the letter and sketchbook, and handed over her staff. "Put your arm around my waist. Let's walk together."

In the round living room, Bea fluffed up the throw pillows at one end of the davenport, helped Mona lie down, and brought a glass of cool water. "You gave me quite a scare out there."

"Thank you, Bea honey. Scared me too."

"What else can I get you?"

"Nothing. I'm feeling better now. But would you please read Zarita's letter to me? I didn't even finish it."

"Sure. I kinda feel like I know her a little already." Bea sat with Mona, perched on the edge of the cushions, the letter in her lap. As she read Zarita's wobbly handwriting, Bea pictured a pencil shaking in aged fingers.

My dearest Mona,

I hope you are well and happy. I enjoyed hearing about your new project in your last letter. Painting your autobiography! You are always so creative! I wish I could have come to see them in the art gallery.

I have news, not good news and not bad news, just news. I had a heart attack. I'm writing this at the hospital in Villahermosa, but I go home to Teapa tomorrow. You know better than anyone that I don't want to be here. I am dying. I know it. The doctor knows it and avoids it.

My mother had a big heart, but it had big problems, and she passed her genes on to me. I've been living with dying since I was born, like everyone. We're born each day and die each night. Some nights just last longer than others. Soon I'm going to see, no, to be the Galactic Butterfly.

I can't come to you with this old body. Maybe you are free to come to me. To come home and feel the roots of your ancestors. If not, I understand completely. You are already in my heart, as you have been since our beginning so many years ago. When mine gives way, it will live in yours. The separation between us will disappear, and we will be one.

You've made my life rich and fulfilled. I have cherished every word we have written. I cherish you. Thank you for being in my life, Mona Arcade, Angela Mariposa, my friend.

In Lak'ech Ala K'in.

Forever,

Zarita

P.S. My cell phone number: 52-999-478-2903

The tear-stained letter now looked as if it had been left out in the rain.

Between sobs, Bea had barely been able to speak the words. She put her arms around Mona as they wept and rocked together, life hugging itself.

"Thank you so much for reading it and sharing it with me," Mona said, stroking Bea's dark hair. "I must go to her as soon as possible."

"Yes, you must."

After a few quiet moments, Bea dried her eyes on Mona's blouse, then sat up, gazing at the letter. "What does 'In Lak'ech Ala K'in' mean?"

"'I am you and you are me.' It's a traditional Maya greeting, like 'namaste' in India, or 'mitakuye oyasin' for the Lakota tribe. When you offer this sacred greeting of unity, you place your hands over your heart."

"In Lak'ech Ala K'in," Bea repeated, hands on her heart. "That's beautiful."

Mona sat up and looked toward the kitchen. "I need some water… or tea… no, Merlot."

"I'll get it. You relax."

"Thanks again, Queen Bea. I have to call Sasha. Maybe the old girl will go with me."

With a wine spritzer in hand, Mona rang Sasha, and for a change, let her finish her standard greeting. "Sasha Goldberg here, the world's oldest living realtor. What can I do for you right now?"

"My dearest friend Sasha, you could come with me to visit my other dearest friend."

"Where?" It never took Sasha long to get with the program.

"Mexico," Mona said.

"Zarita. So you're finally going there. You've only wanted to do that for seventy years."

"Sixty-one."

"Hair-splitter," Sasha quipped. "When?"

"As soon as possible. Maybe the day after tomorrow."

"Zarita must be sick. You don't sound so good yourself."

"She's dying," Mona said, once again wavering on tears.

"Oh, no!" Sasha leaped into Mona's heart with Zarita. "I'm so sad to hear this. What happened?"

"Life… now death. Her heart's had it."

"We know it's going to happen our whole lives, to us, our family, our friends, yet it always comes as a shock."

"So what do you say? Can you come?"

"Mona, sweetheart, I would love to, but my family reunion is this weekend. I thought I told you."

"You did. I forgot."

"Four generations will be here. Daughter, mother, grandma, and… gasp… great-grandma Sasha. That 'great' word is so hard to get used to. I am so sorry, but I can't miss it."

"I understand. You can't. At least you can feel a little fuzzy in your heart knowing that I asked you."

"I do feel a little fuzzy. Thought it was the vodka."

"Can we get together before I leave?" Mona pleaded. "Maybe Thursday?"

"I'd like that. You let me know when and where. Can you feel the warmth from the hug I'm sending your way?"

"I do feel a little warm. I thought it was the Merlot."

"Call me," Sasha demanded in her mother voice, "if there is anything I can do for you."

In her mind, Mona saw Sasha's furrowed forehead and index finger wagging in the air. "I always do. Love you."

"You, too."

Bea had been listening while she cleaned up the kitchen that didn't need cleaning. She walked over to Mona and looked her straight in the eye. "I'm going with you."

"I'll be okay. I can make it on my own."

"No, I'm going with you," Bea said adamantly. "If I don't, I'll have a heart attack worrying about you, and you'll have to rush back to take care of me."

"But what about your job at the hospital?" Mona asked.

"You said that soon I wouldn't need it. You were right. They'll understand. They're in the living-dying biz."

"Neighbor Yves and your new Queen Bea patients?"

"They did okay without me for years. They can handle it again for a few days."

They heard a car screech to a halt in the driveway. Ten seconds later, Antonio burst through the door. "Mona! I got here as fast as I could. Are you all right?"

"Sad but fine. I have a live-in nurse, you know."

"I'm so sorry to hear about Zarita," he said, putting his arm around Mona and drawing her in. "Bea called me."

"Thanks," Mona sighed. "Me, too."

Bea had been staring at Antonio with her 'we need to talk' look. "I'm going to Mexico with Mona. I'm quitting my job."

Antonio was taken aback, but Bea's directness and commitment were traits he loved about her. "Okay…" His voice rose at the end to a tone between a question and a what the fuck is going on. "When?"

"When?" Bea asked, looking over at Mona.

"I haven't figured that out yet. Yesterday, if possible."

Bea handed Antonio the letter. "Babe, read Zarita's letter and you'll get what's going on."

Mona flipped through her sketchbook as Antonio sat at the kitchen counter with the letter, soaking in the love of this strong woman named Zarita. Bea leaned on his back, reading again with her arms around his shoulders. He'd read hundreds of her letters by now, and Zarita seemed like a friend he'd never met. When he finished, he shook his head. "I understand."

Bea gave him a kiss on the neck, then walked over to Mona resting on the davenport. "So what's this 'Galactic Butterfly' that Zarita's going to see or be?"

"It's a Maya symbol representing all the consciousness that has ever existed in this galaxy. All our ancestors: humans, animals, reptiles, fish, plants. The consciousness that organized all matter from a whirling disk into stars, planets, and solar systems. God, I suppose."

"Wow. Big meaning."

"So big the original Maya had no symbol for it," Mona added. "I don't think they even had a name for God. Just knowing the concept was good enough."

"I read a letter from years ago where Zarita talked about it," Antonio said, "and there was a picture of it. A circular pattern, black and white, with antenna-like shapes and almost a yin-yang swirl in the middle, right?"

"That's it," Mona said, sitting up, herself again. "I think the symbol was created later in blankets and stone necklaces. They thought butterflies were their ancestors returning for a visit in a physical form."

Antonio took his familiar storytelling position between Bea and Mona. "What amazes me is that the Maya were aware of the location of the center of our galaxy 2,000 years ago. And in the middle of the Milky Way, which looks like a whirling cloudy disk, scientists have verified there's another whirling disk, a massive black hole drawing in all matter and light, maybe creating other galaxies or universes on the other side or in some other dimension. It's beyond me, but not beyond the Maya."

"That's where we're all going sooner or later..." Mona said, "to start over once again. The Maya thought time was circular, not linear. That's what their calendar's based on. The world wasn't going to end in 2012... only cycle on to a new phase."

"If you ladies don't mind, I'd like to come with you."

"Hmm…" Bea said. "Well… okay."

"What?" Antonio looked alarmed. Or hurt. Like a little kid. "You paused. Is it women-only?"

"Just yankin' your chain, darlin'. What do you think, Mona? Can we stand him for a few days?"

"Hmm…" Mona scowled, then smiled. "Well… okay."

"I'll stay here and golf with the men," Antonio joked, his head down, then up again. "Wait. I don't golf."

"I'd be honored, but you're a working man." Mona got up and took hold of Antonio's elbow. "You can't quit on account of me."

"I have an idea for a story my editor might bite on."

"Well, your tickets are on me. I can deduct the expenses for guides on my taxes. I've got a few ideas myself."

"When I saw the Galactic Butterfly in Zarita's letter, I wondered if you'd ever painted it."

"I did," Mona said, refilling her glass half with Merlot, half with sparkling water. "I stared at the canvas for an hour and then realized it was already one little particle of that infinite butterfly. Anything I painted would just get in the way. I didn't feel qualified to draw God. I signed the blank canvas, *Galactic Butterfly,* and hung it up in my bedroom. It's still there. Reminds me of Papa Marco. When I was a child, he'd pick up the paper before I'd drawn anything and show it to my mama. 'Look it this,' he'd say. 'Mona drew a picture of a brown bear eatin' berries in a blizzard, but the bear ate all the berries, so he left.'"

Antonio loved to trade tales. "That reminds me of the story about the little girl in art class. The teacher asks what she was drawing, and the girl says, 'God.' So the teacher says, 'But no one knows what God looks like.' The little girl doesn't look up, just says, 'They will in a minute.'"

Everyone chuckled. His gentle humor had a way of easing sorrow into the past and people into the present.

"I have to ring Zarita and see if she's okay," Mona said. "Mail can take a week or a month to get here."

"I need to give Hal a call at the office."

"I'm gonna check flights on the internet."

Like three secret agents planning a mission, they all dispersed to their separate stations.

Mona settled into the davenport with her spritzer, praying Zarita was alive, well, and would answer. She held the phone to her ear. It seemed to ring forever.

Zarita answered with a whisper. "Bueno?"

"Zarita, dear. It's Mona."

"¡Oh, mi querida Mona!"

"You're alive."

"For a while," Zarita said feebly, then perked up, hope nourishing her spirit. "Are you in Mexico?"

"I am on my way." Mona spoke tenderly, yet resolutely. "I just received your letter. I'll be with you in a few days."

"I will wait for you."

"I'm so sorry to hear about your illness."

"What is, is."

"Are you still at home?" Mona asked.

"Sí. A nurse comes in."

"When you were in the hospital, were you lying in the corner with a window to the left of your bed?"

"Sí."

"Were the walls light green with a round clock hanging above your head?"

"Sí, but the clock did not work. Why do you ask?"

A chill went through Mona, a warm chill. "Ten days ago… before I knew you sick… on the same day your letter was posted… I drew a picture of a woman in a hospital. There were no hands on the clock. I didn't know the woman was you until today."

"I am not surprised. We are two wings on the same butterfly. When my mind stops thinking of you, my heart takes over, pumping day and night."

"Now you sound like a poet, not an archeologist."

"I am neither, only a dwindling flame."

"Poet again."

"Oh, Mona. Your words have charmed me for decades. To think I might see the sparkle in your eyes, feel your hand in mine…" Zarita's words became wet.

"Very soon." Mona had to swallow and take a deep breath before she could continue. "Get better now. Keep that heart pumping."

"When I realized my oldest and longest and best friend Mona was on my phone, my heart skipped a beat."

"Well, I'd better not call again," Mona teased.

"No, not a bad skip. A skip a child takes before it starts running a race."

"That's good. But remember that you're the official with a black-and-white flag, resting on the starting line. I'm the runner, on my way back to you at the beginning."

"Muchas gracias por haberme llamado."

"I know what that means. You've taught me well. I'll call you as soon as I know when my flight arrives."

"I feel happy and strong," Zarita purred, like the twelve-year-old she'd been when they first began writing to each other.

"I'll see you in a few moments. Stay happy and strong."

"I will."

Neither Mona nor Zarita wanted to be the one to say goodbye. In silence, in silent union, they each rested their phones on their hearts, silently chanting inside.

In Lak'ech Ala K'in.

ANGEL

Now or Never

At two p.m. DEA Doug drove past the accommodation area and up the forty-five-degree road to the viewing area of Phu Chi Fa. Vans and visitors had to park 300 yards before the cliff, but DEA agents had contacted the National Park Service and pulled a few strings. Behind the area roped off by the rangers, a handful of tourists meandered around with Hmong hilltribe children at their heels. The big show each day was sunrise over Laos, not sunset over Thailand to the west.

Angel stepped out of the Explorer and stretched, savoring the fresh mountain air. Smiling inside and out, he walked to the sheer cliff jutting into the vast Mekong River valley.

Thirty-three years earlier, somewhere beyond the curving horizon, he'd had his first encounter with Earth in war-torn Laos. His mother had helped save the lives of the people in his tiny village and his freedom fighter father. Angel now carried on the family tradition.

Far below, winding out of sight to the north and east, the murky Mekong slithered through the green-and-brown tapestry of fields and forests on foothills running down to the river plain. The sky was clear here and overcast there, the schizo breeze calm, then swirling from both sides of the cliff. An ominous cloud with rain streaks draining beneath bullied its way into the peaceful scene.

Onto this vista Angel mentally superimposed the image he'd seen of the sunrise, the "sea of mist" obscuring everything below except the tall ridges in the distance. He knew immediately there was only one option and let out a long, visible sigh. *Dawn tomorrow would be a disaster. Today I have a chance.*

Doug had been standing behind him, gazing over his shoulder. "Whatd'ya think?"

"It's now or never. I was lookin' forward to some shuteye, but maybe I can sleep-glide."

Doug saluted. "All righty, boss. Let's do it. Whatd'ya need?"

"I need all my bags over there," Angel said, gesturing to a stand of windblown trees. "I need fresh water for my canteen, the camo, the gun, the GPS locator, whatever device you have for me to send the extraction coordinates, and some help with the liftoff."

"Bags, pistol, and camo first," Doug suggested, already heading to the truck. Huddled under the rear hatchback, he opened the metal case and handed Angel the 9mm pistol. "Couldn't get a small semi-automatic like you asked for, but a Sig Sauer M25 should do whatever you want it to do."

"Sweet," Angel whistled. "Suddenly I'm a Navy SEAL."

"It's got a night sight, suppressor, light and laser, but no tweezers or corkscrew like my Swiss Army knife."

"This'll do just fine. Hope I don't have to use it."

"I need to get your electronic goodies from Nat at the lodge. She'll be your wizard in the tracking van." Doug tipped up his Stetson and ran his hand through what was left of his hair. "Those gadgets are not in my corral."

"It'll take me a half-hour to get ready. Go for it."

"How 'bout if I bring my Hmong friend up here? He owns the lodge where we're stayin', and Khun P has taken some of his relatives."

"If you trust him, Mr. D, I trust him. I could use someone to point the way in the real world instead of maps in my head."

Angel donned his camo clothes, filled the multi-pocket vest and pants with his toys, strapped on his ankle knives and the Sig Sauer, and then slipped into his nylon flight suit for protection against Mother Nature's thorny spots. First, he checked the packing of his reserve parachute, then spread out the thirty-foot rip-stop wing—iridescent ultramarine underneath and brown camo on top. To the riser straps on the harness seat, he attached the fourteen Spectra lines branching into 200 connections on the wing canopy, over 400 meters of line.

As Angel scrutinized the lines, Doug returned with two passengers and gadgets. "Angel Phoenix. Nat and Leej."

"Thank you, khap khun khrap, ua tsaug," Leej said in three languages, pumping Angel's hand. "Thank you for coming to help us."

"You're welcome, yin dee," Angel replied in two, not knowing Hmong except for "ua tsuag" he'd learned three seconds before, but wondered what the word "us" meant. I'm not here to save us, only Barry. He extracted his hand from Leej and extended it to Nat. "Professor Gadget. How are you?"

"Perfect. It's great to meet you." Nat squeezed his fingers in a vice grip. "We're counting on you."

Two inches taller than Angel, she had the physique of a gym teacher and the brain of a geek; her pale skin bleached baby-blue-white from indoor fluorescent bulbs and computer screens. She was all business, all loose ends tied up neatly like the tight brunette hair bun lashed onto her head, but Angel caught a flash of monkey business in her green eyes. "So your name's Gnat, like the annoying bug?"

"No 'g'... It's Natalie, like the alluring Wood or Portman."

She briskly explained the ins and outs of the electronic devices, protocols, and procedures, then in slow motion unzipped his flight suit and fastened a GPS bug securely inside his pants pocket.

Angel had the fleeting desire to secure something inside her pants, but beat it back down into his reptile brainstem.

"Here's Barry's GPS," Nat said, grinning. "Stick it up his ass for me. If it weren't for his antics, we wouldn't be here."

"I didn't pack any latex examination gloves." Angel put on his big brown puppy eyes. "Did you?"

Nat winked."Sorry, left 'em all at home."

Angel dragged himself from his future fantasy and turned to Leej. "You mind givin' me a tour of the land below from the cliff over here?"

"Yes, and I would come with you if I could."

"Sorry, pal. This butterfly only carries one passenger." Angel put a hand on Leej's shoulders and pointed across the valley with the other. "I've only seen the Ghost's location from SAT pictures and maps. I'll fly straight east to that ninety-degree curve in the Mekong, then north to that second valley. What do you think?"

"Yes," Leej agreed, nodding. "About twenty kilometers to the river, then maybe three north to your supplies and three more to Khun P's."

"I'm worried about that storm to the south. Which way does the weather normally move here?"

"The weather goes where it wants." Leej's eyes traveled up from the valley and into Angel's black pupils. "But the Butterfly Mother will help you on your journey."

"The Butterfly Mother?"

"Mai Bang, the creator. She will guide you."

Well, another butterfly fits into my dreamland just fine. "Okay, let's get this show on the azure road," Angel shouted, skipping down toward his troops. "This sharp cliff's too skinny for liftoff, and I don't wanna snag my lines. I'll launch to the right of it." Angel fastened the waterproof instrument panel and the gear cache's GPS locator to the flight deck pack and then clipped the pack to the foam-padded harness using carabiners. He pulled on his

Gore-Tex gloves and Reevu helmet and climbed into the harness as the breeze picked up from the left. “Doug, my man. Have that chopper ready before dawn the day after tomorrow. You’ll get your coordinates tomorrow and the extraction time when I figure out when it is.”

“I’m on it,” Doug assured him, patting Angel hard on the back. “Good luck, buddy. Happy trails!”

“Now if you three would raise the wing, one in the middle, one on each end, and run with me a few steps, I’ll be off into the wild blue.”

Doug, Nat and Leej took their positions twenty-five feet behind him and held up the wing.

Angel stood in the harness and jogged a few steps. His canopy cells puffed up with air, transforming into a smooth, curved wing shaped like an inverted canoe with a seated marionette hanging beneath on strings.

“Don’t forget to let go!” he yelled.

In five yards Angel lifted off the ground, backwards for a moment as the wind took over, then to the right, where the wind wanted to go. Behind him three fists raised in a victory salute, and the eyes of every Hmong child, park ranger, and tourist watched him shrink into the sky, a speck swinging from the thin crescent of a blue moon kite.

Whenever he flew off a mountain, Angel became his vision of Icarus from the Greek legend: no flight suit or canopy, only a loincloth over bare skin and feathers fastened to his arms with wax. His soul seemed to take control as he swooped down into the valley and let the updrafts lift him up. The colors of his paraglider brought Morpho to mind, sailing without flapping on the breeze, the wing’s ultramarine underside echoing the sky when viewed from below and its camouflage pattern on top merging with the ground when viewed from above.

Hmm. The same colors as Morpho’s wings, only reversed.

He thought of Tiger, who’d dreamed he was flying—not as Morpho, as Tiger himself—but right now reality far surpassed any dreams he’d ever had. These were the supreme moments of Angel’s life, though often tainted when merely a means to the beginning of a mission, where his menacing destination eclipsed the magnificent journey.

A stiff gust brought Angel back into his flight suit and his eyes from the horizon to the instrument panel.

10 miles out. Speed, 40 mph. Elevation, 6,200 feet. I’ll hit the valley in about fifteen minutes.

He flew as high as the changing thermals allowed, 1,600 feet above Phu Chi Fa where he’d started.

The smell of rain wafted into his nostrils as he looked at the internal side and rearview mirrors of his Reevu helmet, giving him a 360-degree panorama. The gray cloud to the south had darkened, its body expanding upward, bloating outward. It seemed to travel northeast, as if Angel and the storm were on a collision course. He knew the winds were treacherous from these cumulonimbus—"towering thunderclouds that scare you senseless." Major updrafts sucked air into its center, while the cool precipitation in the front spawned strong downdrafts.

Okay, Zeus. I'll race you to the finish line.

He pressed the accelerator bar under his feet, pulling down the leading edge of the wing, decreasing its angle of attack and increasing his speed. Angel's destination became clearer as he descended. Bending round the final ridge before Ghost Land valley, the Mekong below narrowed to a third its former width, beige sand and rocks on the banks, white rapids in the waterway.

Zeus, the god of the sky and weather, with thunderbolts as his weapon of choice, stretched over Angel's right shoulder, his breath stronger now, blowing the paraglider left like a leaf. With the god's spittle misting on his helmet, Angel tugged the right brake control line, folding one wing tip under to counter the force of the wind.

Once over the valley, just short of the blinking dot on the cache's GPS locator, he pulled in both wing tips, slowing his speed and tilting the paraglider down to avoid a stall. Like the blazing sun that had melted the wax holding the feathers to Icarus' arms, a stall could send Angel plummeting to his death.

Zeus was on him as Angel pulled the right brake and slammed his weight to the right, inducing a sharp turn into a spiral dive, like a corkscrew, the fastest method of descent demanding extreme skill and precision. As his downward speed doubled, Angel whirled out horizontally to the side of the paraglider, the front of its wing pointing directly at the ground. As he reached the lowest altitude possible to end this risky maneuver, Zeus' bellows suddenly shifted from updrafts to downdrafts.

Angel released his inner brake while pulling the outer brake and throwing his weight to the left, but the gale from above pressed relentlessly, collapsing his wing cells into floppy fabric.

He shouted at the heavens. "You fucking bag of wind!"

Angel swung below the flopping canopy in a pendular motion, frantically pumping the brakes to reinflate it. 1,300 feet up from ground zero, nearly in a free fall, he released his reserve parachute from the harness and strove to steer toward the center of the field below.

Affronted by Angel's epithet, Zeus unleashed a tempest of wind and rain, punctuated by lightning bolts, drenching the flimsy chariot, enveloping the infidel in his puny canopy shroud, flattening the parachute, and finally wrapping its lines around the limb of a dead standing tree.

With a final crash of thunder, Zeus cackled and marched on, leaving the mummy draped beneath the branch, hanging like a lifeless cocoon.

RED
I Spy, You Spy

Red checked the rearview mirror again to make sure she wasn't dreaming. The odds that another fifteen-year-old red Mercedes SL500 convertible sat on the same street in Old Delhi were beyond calculation.

It has to be Azeez.

Her fuse was lit and an explosion inevitable, but she didn't want the shrapnel to tarnish the serene scene she'd had moments before with Devika, nor expose the Wrath of Red to this sweet person to whom she'd just promised to chant, pray, and meditate. She eased away from the curb, her eyes glued to the side mirror to see if the Mercedes would follow. As she slowed at the intersection to turn left, it pulled into the street behind her.

All right then. Let's play your little game, whatever the fuck it is.

Red gunned Spencer, and though he clanked and complained, the old truck barreled down the next road. Three blocks later, she performed the same maneuver, turning onto a bustling thoroughfare, then again a mile ahead at the next major intersection, veering left into a half-finished industrial park. Her mind was racing faster than Spencer, as Red replayed the last few days of driving him. She'd noticed a red car in the rearview mirror on her way to Khan Market, but paid it no mind. She'd seen a red Mercedes in the parking lot of Lodhi Park and disregarded it.

How many other clues have I missed?

In front of a dilapidated warehouse on a back street lined with building construction, she parked on the left, scurried to the other side, and hid behind a pile of bricks and trash. A few seconds later, the Mercedes rounded the corner and crawled down the street.

Come to me, you fucking wanker.

As it drew closer, Red could clearly see Azeez in the driver's seat. When he paused next to the truck, she jumped into the street in front of the Mercedes, slammed her palms on the hood, and glowered at Azeez through the windshield. His dark face turned three shades whiter.

Red's rhetorical question began as a shriek and ended an octave higher.

"Now you are spying on me?"

Azeez' head poked out the window. "Miss Red, I… I…"

"Get out of the car! Now!" By the time he'd opened the door and swung his feet onto the pavement, Red was on him, livid, her face the shade of her name. She stood tall above him, one hand clamped on the roof, blocking his exit. "What in god's or the devil's name are you fucking doing?"

Azeez held his hands in his lap, his head down like a bad child sent to sit in the corner. "I am worrying about you… driving the old truck… your illness… you have changed into someone else… I am missing Miss Red."

Her eyes went wild, and her words dripped into his ears like acid. "Now you sound like that bloody Bug."

"No, no, no, no!" Azeez jerked his head up as if he were an innocent prisoner charged with manslaughter. "I am not at all like him!"

"You say I've changed?! Look what you've become! Are you my fucking nursemaid now? The GM of Admiral Aviation? A psycho stalker? "

Azeez' head almost dropped into his lap.

Red's sarcasm bit into his exposed neck. "No wonder we've had no chemical sales lately! The store's been closed, its manager out to lunch. What else haven't you done lately?"

"I am worried…"

"You said that already," she snarled through clenched teeth, her voice a low-pitched growl. "You followed me to Khan Market, did you not?"

"Yes, Miss Red," he confessed, shaking.

"You followed me to Lodhi Park, did you not?"

"Yes, Miss Red."

Her eyeballs like blinding spotlights in a dark interrogation room, Red grilled him, her ire escalating. "Whose car is this?"

"Yours, Miss Red." His eyes had locked onto his feet.

"Look at me, damn it!"

With a tight grimace, Azeez raised his head, cocking it to one side as if a slap were imminent.

"Who taught you how to drive?"

"You did, Miss Red."

"Who employs you?"

"You, Miss Red."

"Who gives you a place to live? Who feeds you?"

"You, Miss Red."

"Who saved you from the gutter fifteen years ago?"

Azeez squirmed. "Your father… Mister Danny."

"And what would Mister Danny do right now?" Red's fury diminished as she played it out in her mind.

"He would give me a walloping," Azeez whispered.

"And send you back to the streets where you belong."

Lightheaded from her barrage of rage, Red released her grip on the door and turned, leaning back on the side of the car for support. Words gave way to the racket of saws and cement mixers.

Azeez buried his head in his hands.

Red's memory of her father choked her throat before she could speak again. "Danny told me once, 'If you pick up a gun, don't use it as a threat. Shoot the gun.'" She swung around, her glare boring into his brain. "I will say this to you only once, Azeez. If you spy on me again… if you give me any more advice about drinking… if you do not perform your duties as an employee… I will fire you on the spot and you will be out of my life straightaway. Forever."

Azeez tried to say, "Yes, Miss Red," but only a feeble breath emerged, lost in the clatter of a jackhammer.

"Now take my Mercedes home and get to work."

As she pivoted to leave, he tried to squeeze out a sentence. "I am sorry, Miss Red, but I must… I… You…"

"What is it, Azeez?" While Red waited impatiently for his stuttering to reach a coherent destination, she glimpsed a trace of terror in his eyes, as if the teeth of some intangible demon were embedded in his throat. *A dark entity, like Devika saw swarming around me?* A cold wind on this steaming day shivered her vertebrae from behind, and Red felt the urge to hide. Or at least remove herself from his presence. "Tell me later then when you figure it out. I have an appointment."

As Red drove to the hospital, she could barely concentrate on the traffic, her mind a metronome clicking between anger and angst. The calm inspiration she'd felt at Devika's became a hot-air balloon shrinking in the sky.

She parked in Dr. B's spot and barged into the outpatient lobby, summoning the nurse from across the room. "Come to me, my Angel of Drugs. I'm ready for my final overdose. Let's get cracking!"

After two hours of restless slumber, she'd had enough. Red pulled out the IV needle and marched through the lobby, a frantic nurse following with an alcohol-soaked cotton ball and adhesive tape.

She sped to the nearest liquor store. While waiting for Glenfiddich to arrive from the back room, she noticed a subhead in *The Hindi Times* newspaper on the counter: "Reporter Investigating Crime Kingpins Missing." She bought a copy and drove home, sucking on Scotch in a paper bag. Azeez opened the gate. Red drove past him without a word or sideways glance.

Inside the hangar condo, she tuned her stereo system to the twenty-four-hour jazz station, flopped down on the leather couch in the living room/office, undressed Scotch, wadded up his paper shroud, flung it at the waste basket, and missed.

"Hair of the dog," she mumbled, toasting to herself. Inverting Scotch, she chugged a mouthful and wheezed. "Fuck chemo."

Red took the smartphone from her purse and connected to the remote camera Toma had stuck in the corner of the hangar at Aero Dynamic. At 5:17 p.m. workers walked through the scene lugging barrels of pesticides or fertilizers. She could make out a tank of chemicals near the side wall. A yellow Caterpillar petrol truck, exactly like the one she owned, fueled a duster on the tarmac in front of the hangar.

Business as usual. It'll be unusual soon enough.

Bored after fifteen minutes, Red picked up *The Hindi Times*, but couldn't make it through the missing reporter article, the next saga in the reopened case Dr. B had mentioned. It reminded her too much of her father's disappearance. She skimmed through the schedule of events celebrating Gandhi's birthday, once again talking to and taking in Scotch.

"Day after tomorrow they'll be reading about the fireworks display at Aero Dynamics."

Flipping through the international news, the headline "Instant Karma in Thailand" caught her eye. *Hmm. My dream Angel was off to Thailand...* With Scotch stuck into an armpit, she kicked off her heels, hiked up her sari, and lay back on the couch to read the article.

Bangkok (AP)—An Iranian man carrying explosives blew off his own legs and wounded four civilians Tuesday after an earlier blast at his house in Bangkok. A passport discovered at the crime scene indicated the assailant was Muhmood Shahzad from Iran. Security forces confiscated more explosives at a house where Shahzad was staying, Police Chief Panupong Pakpao said.

The violence started in the afternoon when a cache of explosives apparently detonated by accident in his house and destroyed the roof. Witnesses said two men quickly fled the residence, followed by a wounded Shahzad.

"He tried to flag down a taxi, but he was covered in blood, and the driver refused to take him," Pakpao said. "He threw a grenade at the taxi and ran away." The blast damaged the vehicle and injured the driver.

Police responding to the first explosion attempted to apprehend Shahzad, who hurled another grenade at them to defend himself. "Somehow it bounced off a tree and back at him, severing both of his legs," Pakpao said. "Sometimes the wheel of karma moves very quickly."

"What a bunch of fuckin' tossers. Blew up their own houshe." She slugged Scotch and scoffed, "Grenades bouncing back. Ha. I was leglessh drunk last night. Now he's really leglessh. Shoulda used shticky bombsh."

Red checked the spy camera again, but had trouble focusing on the small phone screen. At 5:55 p.m. a duster taxied into the hangar. The pilot sauntered away from the airplane, removing his jacket as if his workday was done. Red talked to him as he walked. "Go home now. I don't wanna hurt you, jusht your bird."

A half-hour and a half-bottle later, she fell deep into Red Land like the previous night.

Around seven o'clock, Azeez marched up to the hangar condo, determined to finish what he'd tried to say to Miss Red that afternoon. He knocked on the door. No answer; the only sound a saxophone wailing. He knocked harder. Drum solo. He eased the door open. The room smelled alcoholic.

"Miss Red?"

Azeez entered to see her sprawled on the couch, crumpled pages of a newspaper tucked around her neck and shoulders like an airline blanket that's too short. An empty Glenfiddich bottle lay in a puddle of scotch on the floor.

He tried to rouse her, gently shaking her shoulder. "Miss Red. Miss Red."

No answer from her sorry, saried body.

Slipping his hands under her back and legs, he lifted her up and carried her to the bedroom.

Red stirred in his arms, but didn't open her eyes. "Shcotch…? Zat you?"

"It is Azeez, Miss Red. Please stay sleeping."

"Asheesh…" she mumbled, "poor boy…" and then mumbled more, her words incomprehensible.

Azeez laid Red on the bed and covered her with a light cotton paisley blanket. He turned on the amber wall sconces, knowing she couldn't sleep in the dark since her recent daunting showdowns with Bug.

"Shcotch?" Red asked.

"No more scotch left," he said and sat on the side of the bed. "It is Azeez."

Red seemed to be dreaming, not talking to Azeez, talking to Scotch. "What'sh Asheesh doing? He'sh not himshelf anymore."

Azeez tenderly drew the blanket up to her neck and rested his hand on her forehead.

"He'sh shtalking me like I'm hish enemy. But he'sh the boy I never had… My son… What'sh he thinking?"

His body quivering, Azeez tried to blink away the moisture in his eyes.

"Maybe I should tell him I feel like he'sh my son. When I die, everything I have will be hish. I have no one elshe. Asheesh ish my will." Tears slipped out of the corners of her closed eyes and she became still.

In the living room, the Canadian pianist and singer Diana Krall crooned, "The look… of love… is in… your eyes… the look… your smile… can't disguise."

In the bedroom, two sounds merged. The rhythmic tick of the pendulum swinging in Red's father's antique grandfather clock on the far wall and the bottomless sobs pulsating from Azeez' chest.

MONA
Migration

THE SCENT OF ESPRESSO AND BUCKWHEAT PANCAKES seduced Mona into the kitchen at 7:30 a.m. Antonio, flipping flapjacks on the electric griddle, greeted her with a grin. "Mornin', Mona! Hal bought my story idea and gave me a week out of the office. I'm good to go."

Bea leaned over the counter, writing on a page in her day planner under a headline written in all caps—MISSION POSSIBLE. "I've put together a travel plan to Zarita in Teapa, fifty miles south of Villahermosa, where one of my cousins lives in a big house. I'm sure we can stay there if we want to."

"Bea has relatives all over North America," Antonio said. "Over 7,000 cousins alone."

"Forty-nine." Bea didn't look up from her planner.

"She has more aunts and uncles than most people have fingers and toes."

"Only sixteen."

"Their family slogan is, 'How can I miss you if you don't go away?'"

"You're just jealous," Bea said to him, her head still down.

"She's right. I'm the only child. My parents divorced when I was seven, then had a huge custody case in the courts. Neither of them wanted me."

"Better check out what he writes about you, Mona. He never lets facts get in the way of a good story."

Mona paused between them in the kitchen. "Did you two overdose on coffee? Too much sugar?"

Bea glanced up at her. "No, excited times ten. Except for a few hours in Matamoros across the Rio, we haven't been to Mexico for five years."

"I guess I'm excited too, but fragile underneath. I've never been there."

"Why not? You've wanted to go since you were a kid."

Mona sighed as she sat at the counter and sipped the espresso Antonio had set in front of her. "I think it's because I didn't want to tarnish the unique treasure Zarita and I created over the years. Everyone else bounded into the computer world, but we stayed with paper and pens and the past, like explorers in the olden days."

She paused, wondering if she'd said enough, but seeing their attentive faces drew her further into her fragile side.

"A special present came every month, wrapped up in stamps or stickers or sketches, maybe with a real photograph, a letter on new stationery, or handwritten around the columns in a newspaper. And in every envelope, feelings savored on both ends, written and read slowly... always with love... the love that sometimes falls away in quick conversation or when you're distracted by a friend's annoying traits. Maybe we've both been writing to our own illusions, but it's lasted for sixty-one wonderful years." Mona sighed again. "Sorry, long answer."

"What a nice way to put it," Bea said. "I think I get it more now."

Antonio brought over two plates of pancakes. "It reminds me of the couple who got to know each other on the web and finally met in person in a coffee shop. They talked a little and felt awkward, so they both got out their laptops and chatted online."

Mona chuckled and said, "Now that's pathetic. Judging by our conversation last night, the only reason Zarita and I would have trouble talking is if we became one large puddle of tears on the floor."

Bea rolled up her pancake and headed toward the door. "Thanks, babe, I'll eat this on the way. I need to get to the hospital early and find some folks to take my shift next week before I drop the bomb. Wish me luck."

Mona and Antonio wished out loud in unison. "Good luck, honey!"

Once Bea was out the door, Antonio sat next to Mona with coffee in one hand and a rolled-up jack in the other. "Your pancakes are divine," Mona told him. "Is your story idea as good?"

"I told the editor about you finally meeting your sixty-year pen-pal and that whole concept was news to him, fit to print."

"I've been thinking... I have a triple agenda. My bucket list used to be one word—Mexico—which really meant Zarita and exploring my heritage, my Mexican ancestors. Now the list is, in this order: meet Zarita, stand among the Maya ruins she loved so much near Palenque, and then experience that monarch tree near Bea's hometown. I want to do it all."

"Then you will," he assured her. "Or we will. We'll see what happens on the first leg."

"I don't think Zarita will last too long. She's ready to go home."

"Maybe you shouldn't even say that. Words become things. Thoughts become real."

"You didn't talk to her," Mona said, a bit miffed that her feelings had been squashed.

"I'd better be off. Nine-mile bike ride and I've got deadlines today." The frown on his face lifted. "And lifelines in the future."

Mona spent the day getting things in order with Zarita's words pounding in her heart and Sasha's words echoing in her head. *So you're finally going there.* No, the echo was only part of one of Sasha's words: final. As Mona wandered around the house, she felt as though it would be the last time she'd be doing some of the familiar, mundane things she loved. The last time she'd water her pots on the deck. The last time she'd stroll along the river bluff. The last time she'd play fetch the tennis ball with Marco in the yard. She felt wrapped up in a warm but scratchy blanket of excitement and sadness.

Maybe it's time to move to Mexico, to complete the migration I started so many years ago…

Mission had treated her well, but this mission on the horizon compelled her into the unknown. She was comfortable here, although every artist knows the cage of comfort can be the death of creativity.

At noon she got a call from Bea, mirth incarnate. "Mona! The deed is done! I told my boss just like it is and she gave me her blessing!"

"That's great, honey."

"She even said I could have my job again any time I want." Bea shape-shifted into a fast-talking travel agent. "I didn't have time to tell you this morning, but we should drive to Monterrey and fly to Villahermosa from there. Flights from Texas take forever! A three-hour drive to Monterrey, a three-hour flight to Villahermosa arriving around three p.m. And we get to see more of Mexico! You might have to trust me on this one."

"I do. Let's do it." Mona paused. "How do we do it?"

"I can book it on the internet. Saturday morning? We'd have to leave Mission about seven a.m. What'd'ya think?"

"Okay, Saturday it is. Let me know when you're certain and I'll call Zarita." Mona paused again. "Bea?"

"What?" She answered almost before Mona had finished saying Bea.

"You already sound like you're about ready to fly off a cliff, and this might put you over the edge."

"What, Mona? What?"

"After we have our time with Zarita, we're going to a Maya ruin to bask in its mystery—"

"Really?"

"And then you're going to take us to your hometown, Ocampo, on the way to that monarch tree in your photo."

"O! M! G!" Bea shouted. "Are you serious?"

"Calm down, girl. You're going to wake your patients… even the dead ones."

"I said this before. You *are* an angel, Mona. I'll see you later. I… I… I need to go and take a pill or something."

ANGEL
The Moon Comes Alive

An hour after the aerial battle with Zeus, Angel crept back to consciousness in his canopy shroud swaying in the sun. His eyes settled on the instrument panel twisted sideways on the flight deck pack above his lap. 4:11 p.m. A stationary red dot blinked on his GPS screen.

Battered, bruised, and disoriented, he was chilled to the bone, but sun rays filtering through the nylon began to warm him. Still half gone, Angel wondered whether this was real life, or he was back in his dream of Morpho emerging from the cocoon. He turned his aching head, searching for a way out. *Shit. No opening.*

Freeing his right arm from a snarl of line and straps, he reached down, pulled the knife from its ankle sheath, and sliced a slit through layers of wrapped fabric and canopy lines. Light streamed in, blinding him. He wrenched his body a few inches out of the harness. *Ouch.*

He poked his head out of the slit. Two old men in black, upside down, stood ten feet below on the upside-down ground, puzzled but grinning.

"Hello," Angel said weakly. "Sambaidee."

"Hallo," one man repeated, then rattled off unfamiliar words while the other man gave him a thumbs up.

They must be Hmong. "Please help me get down. Chuay duay..."

Angel tried a few more sentences in his multi-language of English, Thai, and Lao, maybe with Spanish and Japanese thrown in unwittingly. He tore open the canopy further and squeezed an arm through the hole next to his head like a baby escaping from the womb.

His rambling and hand-waving communicated something, because the men traipsed over to a stand of foliage ten yards away, threw off several branches, and returned carrying two boxes made from wooden planks.

Through the cracks, Angel's inverted eyes could make out shiny green duffel bags inside. He began to get the picture. *These are the guys DEA Doug found to haul in my supplies.*

They'd been expecting a tall white man in a fancy airplane, not a short

Asian in a space helmet riding a kite. The man's thumbs up might have meant, "Oh you lucky—or maybe divine—bastard! You crashed next to your shit!"

Angel had landed on, or been hurled to, the edge of the field he'd only guessed might have been his actual target. He remembered the parting words from Leej about the creator Mai Bang guiding him. *Huh. Zeus must work for the Butterfly Mother.*

They piled one crate onto the other, then Mr. Hallo stood on top and Mr. Thumbs Up crawled onto his shoulders. *They look eighty, but they're sturdy.*

Angel cut through the canopy and climbed down the human ladder. *GPS. Grandpa's Parcel Service.*

Both delivery men wore wide-bottomed black pants, half-sleeved embroidered black tunics, and sandals. They had a total of about twenty teeth, like yellow ducks spaced out randomly in a carnival shooting gallery.

"Ua tsuag, thank you," Angel said, bowing and giving each man a wai, like the respectful namaste greeting in India with palms pressed together under his chin.

Mr. Hallo straightened up to his five-foot-four height and pointed at himself. "Kuv nyob hauv Kong."

Angel assumed the man's name must be Kong and put a finger on his own chest. "Kuv nyob hauv Angel. Glad to meet you, Kong." Turning to Mr. Thumbs Up and raising his eyebrows, he asked, "Kuv nyob hauv…?

Thumbs Up smiled proudly, with a twinkle in his eye. "Kuv nyob hauv Kong."

Great. The Hmong twins are both named Kong. Maybe it's their last name. The Kong Brothers. With help from his new friends, Angel retrieved his paraglider, chute, and instruments, stuffed them into the harness which doubled as a backpack, then pried open the crates with his blade. Thawed sufficiently, he removed the flight suit to reveal his camo fatigues, received two more thumbs up, and returned them with both hands.

Strapping on his harness pack and gazing up the valley, Angel announced in English and Thai. "Okay, Kongs. Ow bai ban Khun P."

Exchanging nervous glances, but with a glimmer of hope that this Angel might be the savior who'd reunite them with their families, both Kongs understood the alien wanted to go to Ghost Land. Hallo Kong lifted one of the green waterproof dry bags onto his shoulders. When Angel reached for the other, Thumbs Up Kong snatched its straps and held on tight. His words were only tones to Angel, but his eyes said it all. "I am honored to help. I will carry this bag for you. Period."

Twenty-five minutes and a mile uphill through trees and underbrush later, the Kong Brothers made it clear that this was the end of the trail for them. They smiled, shook hands, patted backs, bowed constantly, and finally pointed to an overgrown path veering off into the jungle. Hallo Kong said something that sounded like "kilometer."

Hoping it wasn't ten kilometers or man-eating tigers, Angel said "ua tsuag" several more times and then schlepped off, a sixty-pound pack on his back and a full supply bag in each hand. An hour or so before sunset, he found a natural depression near the path covered with bird's nests and tree ferns. Sweat-logged, Angel stashed his gear and rested for ten minutes, but felt compelled to hike further. *I gotta see Ghost Land, pinpoint its location.*

Donning a camo hat, he trekked ahead along the small stream next to the path, forging his way through the dense undergrowth, invisible to any lookouts. Soon Angel heard the sound of motors and faint shouts among the bird songs and insect chatter. Crouching low, he crept the final hundred yards until he could make out a water tower above the treetops. Skipping ahead from bush to bush, he saw Khun P's compound from the side, not from above like the hazy satellite photos. It sat in flatland bordering the tail end of a ridge. A rutted road trailed up and off to the right.

Spotting a small rise where he might have a better view, he faded back and circled around to the left. When he reached the bottom of the rise, Angel crawled the last yards on his stomach through tall grass. Bending branches from a broadleaf shrub back and forth to avoid any snaps, he laid them over his shoulders and inched the last two feet to the top of the rise, binoculars in his hands and a lump in his throat.

Motionless under the leaves, he scoped out the layout and routines of Ghost Land. Daylight melded into dusk. The sun set below the tall ridge, and the full moon began to climb, imperceptible through the jungle behind him. Angel slipped backwards down the incline, crawled several yards, then rose up, eyes searching the ground for signs of his footsteps to lead him back to the path. At that moment, his Angel Radar, his sixth or seventh sense, beckoned him. *Look up.*

A silhouette in the forked branches of a tree—a dozen feet ahead and up, facing Angel—looked down.

Dressed in black like a ninja warrior, head hidden under a hood, the figure's feet rested precariously on each branch. Angel was momentarily paralyzed. *My dream. I'm living my dream. It's going to fall…*

The ninja lurched behind one branch, reached down towards an ankle, slipped, and fell into the bushes.

Angel felt no fear or anxiety. The figure had been gazing into Khun P's compound as he had just done. *It's dressed in black. The old men wore black. We're on the same side. I hope.* He stood still and watched.

The ninja thrashed in the bushes, struggling for freedom from vines, then popped up in a Muay Thai pose, dancing from one foot to the other. In place of boxing gloves, the ninja brandished a kyoketsu-shogei, a knife on a chain in one hand, and a kunai dagger in the other.

Angel spoke calmly. "Ua tsaug. Kuv nyob hauv Angel."

The ninja hesitated, the dance easing to slow rocking.

A yard to the right, the flared head of a king cobra rose from its nest in the tangle of leaves to a height of four feet, the rest of its twelve-foot body coiled below. Its forked tongue flickering, the serpent swayed, mimicking the ninja who'd disturbed it, ready to strike.

Angel's eyes widened as he raised one palm like a traffic cop and pointed at the snake with his other hand. "Ngu! Yoot!" *Cobra! Stop!*

The ninja's head turned slightly and froze.

Angel bent down centimeter by centimeter and picked up a long, thick stick, jiggling the end to the right of the cobra. The snake swung around, sank its fangs into the wood, then curled back, ready to lunge again. Angel retreated a few steps, coaxing the cobra's attention to the stick while motioning for the ninja to move left. As the cobra struck once more and clamped its jaws onto the stick, Angel flung it right and leaped left.

The ninja side-stepped away, eyes locked on the serpent, then with a high-pitched cry, dropped out of sight.

Angel raced to where the ninja had disappeared and peered over the edge into a ravine. A yard down the steep incline, one hand clinging to an exposed root, legs dangling over a fifteen-foot drop into the creek, the ninja hung—her hood askew, her oval Asian face finally uncovered, black hair streaming down her back.

"I'll be damned and hog-tied." Angel shook his head. "Ninja Girl. Hold on and no more screams." He belly-flopped onto the ground, locked his feet around a thin tree trunk, leaned over and grabbed her wrist.

"Who the fuck are you anyway?" she snapped in perfect English, a little too loudly, her feet scrabbling for a toehold on the steep bank.

Flat on his stomach, Angel jerked back in disbelief. "American. Mai pen rai. Don't worry. I'm on your side. This camo's a disguise. Be quiet. Ua tsuag." He pulled her up onto the precipice. They both lay on their backs, panting heavily.

"What the hell are you doing here?" the ninja asked.

"Rescue mission. We gotta get outta here. They might've heard your screams."

"I didn't scream," she growled, rolling over.

She is beautiful. Angel crouched beside her. "Where are your knives?"

"I dropped them in the ravine."

"Good thing you didn't have a gun. We'd probably both be dead."

Ninja Girl glared at him. "Follow me."

Mmm. Those eyes. "Yes, ma'am, ua tsuag," he said, snapping his hand to his forehead in a salute. "You lead so I can save you again."

"Shut up." She bounded off through the brush, vaulting over fallen trees and slapping foliage aside, then scampered down a scree slope to the bottom of the ravine.

Strong legs. Leaps like a black tiger. Darting in and out of the creek, Angel kept at her heels as twilight waned and the inky jungle closed in. The terrain leveled off, and the creek widened into a crooked stream. Ninja Girl slowed to a walk, leading him up to a trail pot-holed with hoof prints, the same path he'd been on before darkness had descended.

"What the hell are *you* doing here?" Angel asked, out of breath, playfully echoing her earlier words.

"Rescue mission," she barked, echoing his words, and squatted on the ground. "Let's rest here. We're out of the Ghost Zone."

"I like that." *I like you.* "The Ghost Zone. I've been calling it Ghost Land." Angel sat on a rotten log next to the path. "So, who are you rescuing?"

"My brother. Cousins. Family and old friends. You?"

"That's classified information."

"Bullshit," she scoffed. "You're here to get their latest catch. Big, burly, white guy. An idiot."

"You met Barry?" he grinned, surprised.

"No, but I saw him taken next to the road. He might as well have like, come in honking a horn and waving a flag. Put up a fight, but the army ants swarmed all over him. He fucked up my plans good."

"What plans?" Angel asked, completely captivated by this woman.

"I've been here for two weeks. I was ready to save my family, and everything changed." She paused and looked back toward the Ghost Zone. "But I'm ready to go in again."

Angel unstrapped his water canteen and handed it to her. "Been here from where? You sound American… even Californian."

"Bright boy," she said, almost smiling, and took a swig.

"Ua tsuag."

"Why do you keep saying that?" she asked, perturbed. "Do you speak Hmong?"

"Yes, I do," he announced, raising his chin and feigning arrogance. "Those are two of the seven words I know. Ua tsuag. Kuv nyob hauv. Mai Bang. Just learned 'em today."

"From whom?" His honesty seemed to soothe her suspicions.

"Two old Hmong guys who'd stashed my supplies and got me out of a tree."

"What are you talking about?"

"I flew a paraglider from Phu Chi Fa, a storm hit me, got tangled on a tree down in the valley. They helped me climb down. Both named Kong, the Kong twins."

Ninja Girl smirked, a knowing gleam in her bottomless brown eyes. "How'd you figure that out with your big Hmong vocabulary?"

"Simple. Both of them pointed at their chests and said, 'Kuv nyob hauv Kong.'"

"Their names aren't Kong." She handed the canteen back and flashed a wide smile as Angel took a healthy gulp. "Kuv nyob hauv Kong means, 'I live in the village of Kong.'"

Realizing the absurdity of his mistake, Angel guffawed, spewing water out of his nostrils, then pointed at his chest and wiped his chin on his sleeve. "Kuv nyob hauv Village Idiot."

"You remind me of a joke." Ninja Girl's pure white teeth and pure eye whites almost glowed in the dark.

"I dunno if I can take a joke right now," he wheezed.

"How do you know if a cow thinks your jokes are funny?"

"I give up. How?"

"Milk comes out of its nose."

Angel laughed, coughed, and choked again. "Stop! You're killin' me here."

She stood and gave him a few whacks on the back. "At our face-off today, you said, 'Kuv nyob hauv Angel.' Is that like, your name or where you live?"

"Both, I guess. Angel Phoenix. Angel as in Los Angeles, Phoenix as in Phoenix. I used to live in both cities. Yours?"

"Mani." She sat on the log next to Angel and stuck out her hand. "Maybe I'm glad to meet you."

"My pleasure." Angel took her hand and shook it for a few seconds too long. "A woman named Mani. Sounds very solid and a little schizo."

"Mani's a common name around here. Means jewel or gem in Sanskrit.

Or if you want to get Norse about it, Sol was the sun and Mani was her brother, the moon.

A mental truck slammed into his head. Dumbfounded, he gazed up at the full moon peering through the trees.

"What is it?" she asked, alarmed. "You look like you just saw a ghost."

"Mani... the full moon..." he whispered, then took a short time-out in his memories, finally daring to share them. "I saw you in a dream during the plane ride over here. I was standing on the ground and you fell out of a tree. It just happened again back there." Angel gestured up the path. "You were a black silhouette in my dream with the full moon rising in the background."

He pointed at the night sky behind her, and Mani turned to look. The full moon looked back.

Mani had grown up with spirits and stories and village shamans. She respected the messages from them and from dreams. "You said you knew the words Mai Bang. Do you know who she is?"

"The Butterfly Mother... the Creator. That's all. Before I launched off the cliff, a Hmong guy said she'd guide me."

Mani took the canteen out of Angel's lap and sipped as she told a tale from her childhood. "Mai Bang emerged from the heartwood of the sweet gum tree, but like, born at an unlucky time, it was hard for her to find a mate. One day she made love with the wave foam on the river and then gave birth to twelve eggs. Mankind hatched from the first broken egg. Other beings born from the Butterfly Mother's eggs were the Thunder God, a dragon, a tiger, a snake, and an elephant."

"I battled the Thunder God today." He sat like the Thinker stature, chin on the back of his hand, elbow on his knee. "I called him Zeus and yelled at him. He flung me down right by my cache of supplies." Angel paused, turning his head toward Mani. "Guess he was on my side."

"I was standing in a sweet gum tree today,' Mani added, "above the cobra. At first, I thought you were a snake in the grass."

"A few nights ago I had a dream about a kid named Tiger. And I thought you tore through the jungle like a tiger."

"So who's the dragon?" Mani asked, drinking in the canteen water, the myth, and this curious man.

"I dunno," Angel said. "Mister Ghost?"

"Could be. The elephant must be that Barry guy. He's built like one."

She wore the most charming smile Angel had ever experienced. He caught her eyes in the moon shadow of her brow. "I saw some wave foam in the Mekong rapids today."

"Maybe downstream a ways," Mani bet, seeing his emotions and raising him one. "Mai Bang, like all butterflies, guides people to their loved ones. She brought me here to save my family."

"Who's *my* loved one?" He already knew the answer in his heart. "Not Barry."

"We'll see," Mani rose up and stretched out her arms, bathed in blue moonlight.

"I'd better get my shit." Angel patted his vest pockets to find a flashlight. "I'm pretty sure it's just down this path in some bushes."

"Your mission must have a big budget. Where're you staying? Is there a five-star Jungle Hilton I don't know about?"

Angel shrugged his shoulders. "Wrapped up in my canopy wing on a branch, I guess… again."

"You can stay at my place, more comfy than a tree. It has a roof." Fifty yards down the path, Mani stopped and pointed into the darkness on the right. "I live up there. My Jungle Mosquitotel. Not five-star, but a billion stars right outside."

"Hmm. I walked by here today. I think my stuff's right around the next bend."

"What a coincidence." Her half-smile said it wasn't an accident.

"I don't believe in 'em," Angel disagreed. "No coincidence… guidance from Mai Bang."

After they retrieved his harness, backpack, and supply bags, Mani led him to a vine-covered rocky wall at the foot of the ridge. "I used to come here as a kid. My secret private place. No one knew about it." Tugging aside a labyrinth of vegetation, she motioned for him to step through. The flashlight beam flickered on the craggy sides of a tunnel expanding into a wider cavern. "It's not much, but right now it's home to me."

Her name means Gem, same as the kid's new girlfriend in my dreams. She lives in a cave in a ridge. I live in a high-tech cave in The Ridge. I dreamed I was in a cave. Angel stood spellbound, taking it all in, and then turned toward Mani. "You got Wi-Fi here?"

RED
Upside Down

DURING THE NIGHT, RED FELT A STRANGE SENSATION—fabric swinging on her neck as if blown by a breeze. Lying on her back, she pried open her eyes, squinted through the murky bedroom light, and was shocked to see four feet of her sari waving straight up in the air.

As her vision cleared, Red gazed beyond the sari to the ceiling, but instead saw her empty bed on the floor with a crumpled paisley blanket on top of the bedding. Panic attacked as her eyes moved from the grandfather clock at the front of the bed to the upholstered chairs and dressing table on her left to the armoire and full-length mirror on the right—they were all upside down.

She jerked upright to see the ceiling fan, custom-made from wooden airplane propellers, eye-level beyond her feet.

What the… I'm lying on the ceiling!

The drape of her sari hung down, not up, swinging in the breeze from the fan. Expecting to drop at any moment, she rolled onto her stomach, her hands scrabbling across the white plaster ceiling, searching for anything to grab hold of.

"Azeez!" she screamed, but the word stopped short as if spoken in a padded room.

Terrified, she crawled toward the armoire. The floor was nine feet below her; the top of the armoire only three. Red stretched an arm down to it, expecting comforting support, but none came. She was stuck on the ceiling.

Clutching the wardrobe's latticework at the top, she pulled herself to her knees, then to a squatting position, then to her feet, and tied the loose end of the sari around her waist to keep it from hanging in her eyes.

Is this someone's idea of a macabre joke? Bug. It has to be Bug's doing!

Hoping this prank is confined to the bedroom, Red stepped gingerly across the ceiling toward the door, avoiding the swirling fan. Panic launched another attack as she approached the open door and noticed its knob level with her chin and the doorway header waist-high up the wall.

No one could have done this while I was gone!

Desperately she scanned the inverted living room/office ahead and climbed over the doorframe. The desk, laden with pens and stacks of paper, was upside down. The shelf on the wall with the Samurai warrior standing at attention was upside down.

She raced to the picture window, tripping on sunken ceiling lights in her bare feet. The end of the sari unwound and rose, again swaying above her head. Her petticoat bunched up around her knees. Red pressed her forehead against the pane and peered out. The airplane, the hangar outside, and the ground were all upside down.

The whole world's upside down! Or I'm upside down! Gravity must have reversed! No, no, my God! It's only affecting me! Only me!

"Azeez! Azeez!" Red ran across the ceiling to the outside door, reached up, turned the latch, and flung it open. "Azeez! Help me! Azeez!"

She climbed over the frame, holding its sides in a death grip, then stepped out and down to the underside of the overhanging roof.

Azeez hobbled across the grounds as fast as he could manage while pulling on his pants over his underwear. He was naked from the waist up.

Tripped by a roof brace, Red slipped over the edge, her feet heading into the night sky toward the stars. She caught the arched tiles of the rooftop with her hands and hung on with all her might, legs dangling upward into infinity.

"Miss Red!" Azeez yelled. "What are you doing up there? Why are you standing on your hands on the roof?"

"I'm being sucked into the sky! Everything is upside down! Do something!" As Red screamed, she could feel herself separating—splitting away from herself—one experiencing, one observing. *This cannot be happening. It is impossible.*

"Yes, yes, Miss Red! Hold on! I am getting the ladder!"

Red's grip weakened and slipped from hands to fingers. Fear strangled the words in her throat. "I can't hang on anymore!" *Perhaps I don't want to.*

With an aluminum ladder balanced on his shoulders, Azeez shouted encouragement. "Hold tight! You can be doing it! You are strong!" He leaned the ladder next to Red on the roof and scampered up, stretching out his arm. "Take my hand, Miss Red!"

"I can't! I'm flying away!" *I'm flying...*

Azeez grabbed her right wrist and held it firmly. Momentarily steadied, she released her hold on the roof and caught his other hand, feeling the upward tug on his arms, nearly lifting his entire body off the ladder.

"Okay, Miss Red! Bring your feet down to the roof! I am holding you!"

"I can't do it! The force is too much!" *I don't need my feet anymore.*

The gravity from the heavens grew stronger, as if the stars had lined up behind her in a tug-of-war. Azeez' feet lifted from the ladder, and he hung in the air, rising upward slowly, faster, swiftly.

If I am to be an angel like Angel in my dreams, I can only save Azeez by letting go. I am going. I am almost gone.

Azeez stuck his toes under the roof tiles, but his ankle muscles couldn't keep his feet stiff, nor stop his ascent. "I am not letting go!"

The next moment, both of them were fifteen feet off the ground. Sweat lubricated their fingers and entwined hands, loosening their grips.

Red opened her fingers. *Goodbye, Azeez. Good luck to you.*

He dropped to the ground as she receded into a speck in the black sky, finally disappearing into the darkness.

The speck in the black sky lethargically watched the Earth dissolve into another speck in the black sky.

She wasn't cold. She wasn't hot. She wasn't afraid. She just was. And she was flying… in a place she'd never envisioned was possible… not a place… in space. She passed Mars in a moment, then gigantic Jupiter and ringed Saturn in another. Billions of stars shrank behind her as billions more grew in front.

She flew through the Orion Arm of the Milky Way, its halo of cloudy luminescence expanding as she soared toward its center. The neighboring Andromeda galaxy loomed large, still two million light-years away. Clusters of dust and gas coursed in spirals on their way to becoming new solar systems. Up close, stars a fraction of the sun's size or a hundred times larger revealed their true colors—red dwarfs, blue giants, two yellow stars orbiting so near to each other they appeared to be a glowing cosmic peanut.

Music faded in from the background of her being, from a dream just round the bend, or a million light-years behind.

This is my quest
To follow that star
No matter how hopeless
No matter how far

Red, the autopilot and the passenger, felt content. It seemed as though she were going home and exploring new dimensions at the same time, but there was no time, only space. Fear fell away—no fear of Baldev, Murakan or Bug, of finances, of failure, of cancer, of pain. Thoughts of the past and future ceased. Nothing to think or do except be. To be in awe? No, just be.

Approaching the center of the galaxy, a dense bright congregation of ancient stars in a spheroidal bar bulging in the middle, she could see its dark core—an area of spacetime where matter and light only passes inwards, where gravity prevents anything, even light, from escaping. The supermassive black hole looked like a whirling disc, twisting the radiance of other celestial bodies close to it.

Though the void swallowed stars, planets, and everything surrounding it, perhaps spitting out new galaxies into another dimension, she heard no sound and felt no vibration, only peace as she sailed into the obsidian emptiness.

THE FAINT SUNLIGHT OF DAWN ON HER LIDS COAXED RED'S EYES OPEN. Beneath her paisley blanket on the bed, she gazed up at the rotating ceiling fan, the familiar hum of its motor massaging her ears, and trembled from the terror of her nightmare. Right beneath the terror, serenity sat calmly, soothing the soul she'd never imagined she had. Red sat up and looked down at the floor.

Thank god.

It was the floor, and the long, draping end of her sari rested on it.

Where did that come from? The alcohol? I've been plastered on the floor before. Chemo drugs? God only knows.

In spite of the living horror she'd experienced at the beginning of her dream, Red felt a fresh outlook on dying and lay back to honor it.

If that's what death is all about, bring it on.

MONA
Gene Therapy

After a phone call to let Zarita know of their arrival plans, Mona strolled through the yard with Marco at her side. Into the driveway pulled a VW Beetle: bright scarlet with black spots on its body, hood and fenders, headlights painted like eyes, and a white grin on its front bumper. A four-wheeled ladybug. *Hmm. Who's this? No one just stops by.*

The driver got out and waved, smiling like a salesman, then walked through the wildflowers toward Mona. Marco, her mobile security system and character detector, padded up to him, sniffed, wagged, and received an ear scratch from this new human, now free to enter his inner sanctum.

"You must be Miss Mona Arcade, or is it Angela Mariposa?" he asked, removing his straw Panama hat and bowing. "Which do you prefer?"

"Mona's fine unless you're talking to my paintings. You?"

"Gene Etherton." He stuck out his white-gloved hand. "Pleased to make your acquaintance."

Fuller Brush man? Donations for a rest home? As Mona gazed into his friendly, wizened eyes and shook this elderly man's hand, something stirred inside her. "Who are you, Mr. Etherton?"

He smiled. "Oh, only a volunteer for Monarch Watch who's been salivating over your delicious paintings at the Butterfly Center."

"You're too kind," Mona blushed. "How'd you find me?"

"I'm sourcing potential sites for Monarch Waystations, which I see you've already created," Gene said, stretching out his arms to the sides. Marco interpreted this as 'bring me a stick,' which he did, and Gene tugged on it while he talked. "Milkweed heaven! I spoke with the manager at the Center, and she mentioned you and your work for our flying friends. I asked if she thought you'd mind if I dropped by, and she said, 'If you want to talk monarchs, she'll probably ask you to live there.' So… here I am."

Reminds me of my handsome psych professor in college. Tweed jacket, ascot, old-fashioned but timeless. "Well, do come inside then. I'm getting ready for a trip, so I don't have much time to spare. I must say, your car's adorable."

"It's definitely a conversation starter. Marvelous creatures, these little ladybugs, devouring garden pests." The wide grin and twinkle in his eyes matched his car. "Did you know they can play dead? If a predator gets too close, they might fall lifelessly into the bushes or the ground."

Sounds like what I do when I faint, but I'm certainly not telling him that! "When I was a kid, I used to play with them on the beach in Wisconsin. Mama said ladybugs bring good luck."

"I agree." Gene's smile was now a permanent fixture on his face. "One brought me here today! In Scandinavia, some say their name relates to Freyja, the 'Lady' in old Norse mythology, the goddess of love, sexuality, beauty, and fertility."

Mona wasn't sure what to say to that, but her steps seemed to have a bit more bounce as she and Marco led him to the deck.

Gene's eyes roved from the adobe Alamo wing on the left to the palm tree jutting out of the roof and onto the sloping east wing. "What a charming house… or palace you have here. Not architecture. More like 'artitecture.'"

"It's eccentric like me, but it's home," she replied, opening the front door. "Would you like a refreshment?"

"Cool water would be splendid, thanks. Where are you off to, if you don't mind my asking?"

"Mexico, to see a friend and millions of our mutual flying friends." Mona led him into the kitchen and pointed to Bea's framed monarch photo on the wall. "I'm going to stand in front of the tree in this photo."

"Oh, my!" he exclaimed. "I must go there."

"Exactly what I said when I saw it. Now I'm *doing* it."

Mona brought over two tall glasses of ice water, and they sat at the counter beneath the photo. Marco brought a tennis ball and demanded that Gene throw it.

"Why, thank you, Miss Mona. You are as cordial as you are comely."

She couldn't recall the last time anyone had said she was attractive or pretty, let alone comely. Marco retrieved the ball, and Gene threw it again.

"Where do you live?" Mona asked, intrigued by the way his moustache wiggled when he talked. "Your accent tells me you're not a native Texan."

"San Antonio now, originally Havre, Montana, way up north. As they say, 'It's not the end of the world, but you can see it from there.' I couldn't take the cold anymore." Gene hugged himself and shivered then tossed the ball again. "Frost would settle in my bone marrow until midsummer."

"Sounds like Wisconsin. My papa used to say he dialed 911, and they told him to call back in the spring."

"Good one." Gene laughed and stroked his gray goatee. "I'd guess they tell the same stories in both our hometowns." The photograph on the wall caught his attention again. "I wonder how many fourth-generation monarchs from Montana and Wisconsin are wintering in that tree?"

For a moment Mona had been lost in the tang of his aftershave lotion, a familiar odor like pine cones or juniper berries, but three words he said snapped her back. "Fourth generation monarchs? What are they?"

"Some folks call them winter or Methuselah monarchs, truly the old ones in their migration cycle."

"I've never heard of them. Marco! Chill! Lie down and listen to this. Sorry, go on."

"It's okay. I used to have a shepherd. They're the best."

"He isn't normally so… so affectionate."

"I like him. He feels it. He likes me. Isn't that how it works with dogs?"

"Almost always," Mona said almost impatiently. "Now please, about these winter monarchs."

"The first three summer generation adults only live for two to five weeks in the US. The fourth generation lives for seven to nine months—surviving the long journey south, several months in Mexico, and then a shorter trip back into the southern states in the spring."

"But I thought butterflies only lived for a few weeks. I knew monarchs migrated to Mexico, miraculously over several generations, but…" Mona felt her knowledge being put through a shredder and her mind trying to staple the strips together into a new order. Her nebulous family history was scattered somewhere in the pile. "I've been painting monarchs for years. It's my name, for heaven's sake, but I've missed something along the way."

"It's confusing I know. A miracle, as you say." Gene leaned closer, reveling in the discussion of these creatures he adored. "Think of it like a family on a multigenerational journey."

Gadzooks! Now he's reading my mind.

"Let's imagine your great-grandmother was born in Mexico, perhaps on that specific tree in the photo, then flew north and gave birth to your grandmother and died. Your grandma flew farther north and gave birth to your mother and died. Your mom gave birth to you—her daughter—and died. Your ancestors only lived for a short time, but you live many times longer and travel all the way back to Mexico to start over as the future great-grandmother of another cycle."

Mona was utterly and profoundly stunned. This intriguing man had clearly recounted the hazy events in her family lineage. The only thing stirring in her being was the words from her birth mother's letter. *I truly know there is an important reason for you to survive. I pray every day that you do not pass so quickly like your grandmother and me.*

"I need a glass of Merlot," she mumbled, shaking her head, blinking her eyes. "How about you?"

"If you're having one, I'll join you."

Mona brought two goblets, the Merlot, a bottle of sparkling soda, and a bowl of ice cubes. "I like my Merlot cold and bubbly. You want yours neat or spritzed?"

"A Merlot spritzer? Why not? Never had one."

Mona was not about to tell this complete stranger her life story, but she needed to know more. "I'm learning a lot here. What else can you tell me about these winter Methuselahs? At seventy-three, I feel like one myself."

"Me, too. You have three years on me, but I thought I had ten on you."

"Oh, stop it. Let's stand in front of the mirror and count crow's feet."

"We'd need a calculator," Gene said, raising his glass. "To the seventies!"

"To the seventies and beyond," Mona added and clinked his glass. "Seriously now, please tell me more. I don't know what to ask. Just talk."

"Well… they don't look any different. They go through the same life stages as other generations until they become adults. But then, instead of reproducing and laying eggs, they migrate to a warmer climate where they can survive until the spring. They focus on drinking nectar to give them strength for their journey south. They're not sexually mature yet, kind of like a child before puberty. When they arrive in the Mexican forests in November and December, the cool weather puts them into a deep sleep, similar to hibernation, to conserve their energy until the weather warms in February. Their bodies change, and the mating rituals begin. Once they become sexually active, they only live a few more weeks. Many fly north into America."

I never married. I lost interest in men. Maybe later. For a few weeks. "It's all quite magical. How do they know where to go? To head south on a route they've never flown before?"

"The jury's still out. Instinct passed through DNA from their ancestors like a cosmic relay game? An inner compass so they can navigate by the sun? We may never know."

Every time he spoke, Mona felt this stranger stepping closer to being a friend she enjoyed, a companion she could trust. Perhaps he could be even more than a friend.

"Monarchs weigh less than a gram and can fly 2,000 miles to a specific tree," Mona said. "I weigh 100 pounds and have trouble finding my way into town to the library."

During the house tour, Gene was like a kid at the county fair, enthralled with it all. For two hours that zipped by in moments, they chatted and laughed and shared—about her trip, his travel lust, her paintings, his former career as an environmental biologist, her amorphous plans for the future, his wife who had passed on some years earlier.

Antonio and Bea entered through the front door to find them lounging next to each other on the davenport with two empty goblets, one drained wine bottle, and Mona's sketches strewn across the coffee table in front of them. With matching curious smirks on their faces, Antonio and Bea spoke in unison. "Hi."

Mona felt like a teenager whose parents had suddenly appeared in the room unannounced. "You're home! Let me introduce you to my new friend." She pushed herself up as Gene steadied her. "Gene Etherton from Monarch Watch, meet my roommates: Antonio, writer extraordinaire, and Nurse Queen Bea, who I'm sure will eventually turn photographer."

Hands shook, how are you I am fine lines were delivered and received, chitchat dwindled.

Gene turned to Antonio. "Well, I'd better be heading home, to your namesake, San Antonio."

"What is it? Four hours at least."

"I meander. Might stop in Corpus for the night." Gene gave Antonio his Monarch Watch business card. "You have a card? Here's mine."

"Sure," Antonio said, searching in his wallet.

Mona broke in. "I'll take one, too. No, wait a minute. We'll trade." Mona padded delicately to her bedroom, returned with a packet of her greeting cards, and handed them to Gene. "Twelve monarch cards for one of your business cards. You owe me."

"I do," Gene said, his eyes reaching into hers. "You've been the perfect hostess and a scintillating conversationalist. Thank you so much." He turned to Bea and Antonio. "It was great to meet both of you and hope it can happen again when you get back. Have a grand journey!"

Mona led Gene to the door, opened it, and took his hand as he walked out. She felt a spark when they touched, like one that comes after scuffling across a carpet, but there was no carpet, only a wood floor.

"Thanks for dropping in. My phone number's on the back of the pack."

Gene smiled, nodded, and departed.

As Mona closed the door, Bea said, "I hope he didn't feel like he had to leave cuz of us."

"No…" Mona's voice had a dreamy feel, like the look in her eyes. "He'd been here for almost three hours. He's got things to do and knows we have to get ready for our trip. Gene's a good man. I hope to see him again somewhere."

Antonio and Bea glanced at each other behind her back and exchanged winks.

ANGEL
Gem in the Jungle

Mani knelt to light the candle on her permanent table, a broken stalagmite rising up like a flat-topped beige butte from the floor. She sat on a lower one next to it.

"Let me give you the palace tour." She didn't get up, just pointed around the circular cavern. "This is like, the living room, dining room, kitchen, rec room, den, and bedroom. The men's room's anywhere outside."

"Nice digs." Angel extracted himself from his harness backpack. "You live in a black hole."

"It's the perfect hiding place. Light can't escape."

"I love your decorating style. Late Stone Age, isn't it?"

"Uh-huh." She smirked, her eyes sparkling in the dark. "I need a Neanderthal man to carve petroglyphs on the wall. Maybe you qualify."

"I don't think so," he said, touching his brow. "Forehead doesn't slant enough." Angel bent down to open the dry bags stuffed with supplies he'd ordered from the Skipper. "So you were born here and live in California. How the heck did you get there and back?"

"You want the quick answer or the thirty-year story?"

Still enchanted by this woman, Angel imagined another thirty-year story he just might be able to handle with her. "Um… How 'bout somewhere in between, then you can fill in the gaps later?"

"Sure, but if I'm going to spill my beans, you'd better do some spilling along the way."

"Fair enough," Angel agreed. "Mind if I open my presents during the journey? There's gotta be food in here."

"Go for it. I'll have a hot croissant and a Greek salad."

"Doubt if they come in a can." Angel sifted through his bags as Mani sifted through her past.

"I was hatched in a village near here that doesn't exist anymore. Lived there until I was like, eight. Lao Dad and Hmong Mom died in a raid by bandits, probably relatives of this ghost maniac. My aunt and uncle raised me."

Angel spilled a bean of synchronicity. "I was hatched in a village outside of Luang Prabang that doesn't exist anymore."

"What? You're kidding, aren't you?"

"No, scout's honor," Angel pledged, raising three fingers with his thumb holding down his pinky.

"Gimme five, homeboy!" Mani's broad grin almost ripped off her jaw.

Angel's scout salute opened and met her hand halfway in a high five. "Go on, keep talking. I spilled one bean."

"Then we fled to a refugee camp in Thailand and lived there for two years. I don't remember much except filth, crowds of people, and wanting to get the hell out of there."

"Sounds horrible," Angel said, sitting in front of a pile of camo fatigues and boots for Barry, C-4 explosive packs, det cord, and a roll of 3,000 firecrackers.

"At least I got to play in the mud. Some charitable agency relocated me to Minnesota when I was ten. I thought it was the North Pole or another planet, but the natives were as nice as the winter was fucking cold. My uncle had been a traditional doctor in our village back home and started an herbal medical clinic in St. Paul."

"Commercial break. I have good news."

"What is it?"

"Snack time!" He held up a jar of Skippy peanut butter and a box of Ritz crackers. "The Skipper is the man."

"Mmm, this is my Skipper." Mani grabbed the jar and opened it. "Who's your Skipper?"

"Deputy at the Drug Enforcement Administration, my main man in DC. Got any knives besides the ones you dropped in the ravine?"

"Don't remind me. Anyway, I don't need 'em." Mani plunged a finger into the Skippy jar, then into her mouth. It came out clean.

"I cannot believe you just did that."

"We're in a fuckin' cave here. Loosen up."

"Don't get me wrong," Angel said, holding up his palms. "I've done that before, too. Alone. Never with a woman."

"So what? Are we like on a date here? I'm a cavewoman. Be a caveman." She shot him a mischievous smile. "You gonna spread the PB on the Ritz or do I have to?"

He snatched the jar from her. "You talk. I'll spread."

"Where was I?"

"Frozen."

"Oh, yeah. After high school, I got a scholarship at the U of M and majored in ethnobotany. Thousands of Hmong people lived in St. Paul—leftover communists, leftover CIA supporters from the Vietnam War, half of 'em turned Christian. Hmong bickered with Hmong over invisible clan borders leftover from Laos, many trying so hard to be American, they forgot who they were, and like, felt embarrassed being Hmong! I've always been proud of my heritage."

Angel pulled a log over by the stalagmite table and sat. As fast as he could spread PB with his finger and set up the crackers, they both knocked 'em down as Mani unfolded her life.

"I'm only half Hmong and got tired of all the bickering. Besides, I grew up with like, six months of warm rain, not six months of fucking precipitation in every form possible. I had to escape. So I threw a dart at a US map on my wall. It hit Los Angeles and screamed, 'Go west, young woman!' I quit working at my uncle's herbal clinic and hitched to California."

"What year are we talking now?" Angel asked.

"2005, I guess."

"So how old are you?"

"So how much do you weigh?" Mani snapped back.

"What?"

"Kind of a personal question, isn't it? Asking a woman her age?"

"Even a cavewoman?"

"Just kidding. 29, but feeling every speck of it. You?"

"33 years and 165 pounds, the last time I checked. Thought maybe we lived in California at the same time, but I was a Marine grunt by then. LA Mom took Lao Dad, Grandmother Dao, and me back to her hometown in '87. They could only handle it for a few years and moved to Phoenix."

"LA was a scary place for me at first," Mani said, shaking her shoulders. "I was like 22, a green sprout from another world. I rented a crummy room in the south LA Hood, then worked as a waitress and a bunch of other shit jobs. Took self-defense courses to survive on the street in front of my apartment! Later I scored a ranger gig with the National Park Service and lived happily ever after for five years in the forest near Mammoth Springs."

"Is that where you learned to fall out of trees and into ravines?"

"Shut up."

"I thought maybe you were falling for me."

"Dream on." She smiled, then became serious. "Maybe later. We got things to do."

"We?"

"There're people to save out there! My brother and some family I've never met. This Barry guy of yours."

Angel inhaled deeply. "Mani… I've got thirty-six hours to get him to a helicopter pickup in the valley, nice and quiet-like. *That* is my only mission."

"Oh, yeah? So who is he, anyway?"

"That's classified information."

"Classify my assify," Mani said, fed up. "You're almost *alone* in the middle of a damn jungle in my cave. Spill a few more beans… and pass me another PB Ritz."

Angel dropped his head and spread another cracker. "Okay, okay, okay… He's the nephew of the President of the USA and has a million-dollar ransom on his head."

"Ah… I see." The gleam in her eyes darkened. "A million bucks for one dude and the rest of the local captives aren't worth shit. USA business bullshit as usual."

A buzzing, rustling sound came from the exit passageway. Before Mani could take another breath, Angel had slipped out his ankle knife with one hand, his pistol with the other, and was crouching by the cave wall.

Mani laughed and shook her head. "At ease, soldier. It's only Horny, my roommate."

"Horny?"

A hefty, six-inch horned insect whizzed by Angel's head and landed near Mani and the candle.

"My pet rhinoceros beetle. He likes to hang out with me. C'mere, little buddy." Horny crawled onto her hand, and she stroked his shiny black-brown wings.

The dreams again. Tiger ordered one of these. Gem had one as a pet in the Congo. "Wicked. Can I hold it?"

"That depends on your combat decisions. And 'it' is a he. I might tell him to attack you."

"What decision do you want me to make, Mani?"

"Say you'll help me! Say we'll work together! Like, how're you gonna live with yourself after gun-packing GI Joe springs one guy and a helpless little woman saves thirty innocent prisoners? I'm sure *The Washington Post* would love that story."

"Blackmail now, is it?" What is happening here?

"No… it's a joke. I am not Mr. Ghost. I am Miss Real. So what's your plan? You gotta lotta firepower over there."

Angel sat silent for a few moments. *This is definitely not in the plan. I don't want to endanger Mani, nor anyone else. But… my plans already took one right turn today. I wasn't going to fly in until tomorrow morning.*

He began to understand why Leez had thanked him so heartily on the top of Phu Chi Fa and why the Kong brothers were so happy to carry his supplies. Word must have traveled among the locals about a "savior" coming to rescue their relatives. He watched Mani petting Horny in her lap, like Gem with the rhino beetle on her lap in his dream. Angel thought of the joy Tiger felt when Gem appeared in his life, a rare girl from the rainforest.

He spoke dubiously, listening to his own words, tallying up the hours of surveillance and preparation his plans would require. "Plan A is to get Barry out quietly and invisibly. Locate and prep two escape routes, one booby-trapped. If Plan A goes south, Plan B. Create chaos with pre-planted explosives. Make sure Barry gets to the chopper even if I have to crawl out on my own." *Or stay here.*

"Hmm. The best-laid plans. So American. Probably blow up my family along the way." She glared at him. "And Superman, how will you do all this in thirty-six hours?"

"I've got satellite photos and maps," Angel muttered, a feeble attempt to convince himself of any chance of success on his own. "I've done missions like this before."

"Sorry, soldier…" she barked, jumping up and pointing down at Angel, "but you don't know *shit*. Like… you don't know *where* Barry is, you don't know *which* building is what or where, you don't know the security routines, you don't know the jungle. You may be good, but you're not *that* fuckin' good." Mani pointed to herself as she paced around the cavern. "I'm no commando, but I do know shit. I've been here for two weeks. I was ready to spring my people, but this Barry fucked up my plans. Overnight they doubled their guards and now patrol the whole area like they're expecting a goddamn battalion to sweep in. I've built a rope ladder up the ridge in a place no one ever goes, nor would imagine could ever be an escape route. You'd have to take out the roving security guards first, with or without me. My people will sneak out the back and up the mountain while you hightail it down the valley on the other side of the Ghost Zone."

Paralyzed for a moment, similar to his dream on the jet, once again Angel saw the light at the end of the tunnel leading out of the cave into the jungle with Mani and the full moonlight shining behind her. *Perhaps I am her savior.* After a few moments of tension, their eyes locked together, he jumped up and saluted her—not Boy Scout style—Marine style. "Yes, ma'am… General Mani. My previous mission stands amended. Your wish is my command."

She squinted at Angel, lips pursed, scanning his body language with her bullshit meter. Angel continued saluting, a smile of surrender on his face.

"Really?" Mani asked, not quite convinced his decision had flipped.

"Really, Miss Real. Let's get on it."

She bounded over, threw her arms around him, and gave him a big wet kiss on the cheek.

Angel stood stiff, arms at his sides, shocked and shy. "So… um… what'd'we do next?"

She pressed both hands on his cheeks, kissed Angel full on the lips, then hopped away, beckoning him to follow. "C'mon, soldier. Let's go look at the moon. No one comes out here at night."

Angel stuck close to Mani through the thicket to the main path and sat on a huge limestone rock next to her. They could've read a book in the bright silver moonlight. After a quiet time-out, Mani shared her reverie.

"I had a friend in California. She looked like one more spaced-out blonde, but that vacuum in her head seemed to connect to the cosmos. We called her Guru Girl and listened when she spoke. She used to say there are three phases of the full moon.

"The first one tonight, is the fierce temptress, luring you in with her sensuous songs and seducing the lunatic out of your soul. The second, tomorrow night, is the omnipotent queen, neither good nor bad, a guiding-force, compelling you to choose your destiny and follow through with your decisions. The third sweetheart moon is a loving entity who engulfs you in her arms, sheltering you before sending you on your way into a new cycle." She turned to Angel, cocked her head, and spoke softly. "I'm all of those."

Angel had never encountered a Mani before. Half Hmong mountain girl and half LA ghetto girl. Having no idea what to say, he draped his arm over her shoulder, and they sat in silence, soaking up the full moon.

Soon Mani shattered the mood. "We should plant all your bombs around Mister Ghost's mansion and make a monster tunnel so he drops back down into hell."

"Must be the temptress in you speaking. Sorry, I'm not that kind of a guy. I save people. I don't kill them."

"But you're a Marine, aren't you?"

"Used to be. Now I'm freelance. I admit I may have caused death in the past, but now I do everything I can to prevent it. Can I still be in your battalion, General?"

Mani smiled and took his hand in hers. "You are my battalion, my only battle lion."

"I gotta get some rest. And get up in a few hours to check out Ghost Land. Tomorrow night I set up my fireworks display, and right before dawn, we do the deed."

"Sounds fun," she said. "Need a guide?"

"Generals guide from the safety of their plush offices. I know how to get back there."

"Wrong. I live in a cave, remember? I'm no general. I'm a captain who leads the battle charge. Besides, I've got to find my knives."

"I was going to surprise you with them," he whined.

"Oh, you're already a big surprise." She punched him in the biceps. "Let's go check out your maps and photos for a few minutes."

Angel spread them out on the cave floor. They knelt down together on hands and knees, a candle to one side.

Mani took over, her straight black hair dangling down to the maps. She was lit. "Barry's in this wood house on stilts, three guards outside and one inside. In the back where this ridge slopes down is the concrete bunkhouse for the workers, my people, twenty or thirty of 'em. One door, one guard with the key. My rope escape ladder goes up through this vertical gully, nothing in the way except trees and brush. The next building over here is where the Ghost Soldiers sleep. Two lookout guards stand on this water tower 24/7, right next to the drug factory. Propane tanks are outside towards the tower, gas tank faces the parking lot."

"What are these guards like?" Angel asked, knitting his brow. "Are they real soldiers or hired thugs?"

"Thugs. It's a job. They get paid. They have a place to live and eat. I'll bet they get drugs, too."

"So they're not fighting for a cause." He let that fact sink in for a second. "Just because."

"Right on. Some are too young and too green to be playing with guns. Khun P. must think the ridge and jungle are the walls to his fort or that the Ghost Zone is really invisible. I was surprised when there were so few perimeter guards in the jungle."

"What about the roving security you mentioned? What's their route? How often do the guards change?"

"Every four hours. Ten p.m., two a.m., and six a.m." She traced a path with her finger on the SAT photo. "Two guards patrol this route around the buildings 24/7, but each walks alone, so you only have about a seven-minute break before the next one comes along."

"Ever see Mr. Ghost?"

"Nope… Never met anyone who has."

Angel let out a sigh and leaned back. "This is all great info, but I gotta see it with my own eyes. The only surprises I want are mine." He smirked. "Sorry, Captain… ours."

"We'll do it. Full moon makes the trek back easy."

"What about you, Ninja Girl with knives? I don't want you to get hurt or be in the thick of this."

"Don't worry about me. I'm no ninja, except for the black outfit, but I know some moves. I'm more like a black cat woman than a ninja—lurk in the shadows, catch mice, run away."

"Well, if this mission goes as planned, you'll be in and out in a flash."

"I had a cool tool made for protection in the ghetto in LA," Mani said. "A portable black umbrella with a retractable knife concealed in the tip like a ninja hanbo. Had to use it a couple times. I called it my 'slumbrella.'"

"Slumbrella. I love that! I want one of those."

After an hour of hashing over the plan, they received a clear message that brainstorming and dinner were over—the PB jar and cracker box were empty. Angel took the canopy wing with its tangle of lines out of its pack and tried to form it into a mattress.

"Pretty bumpy and hard over there." Mani pointed to her bed of broad leaves and a blanket under a mosquito net fastened to stalactites on the cave ceiling. "Put it over here on the flatlands."

Once they'd spread it out, Angel stepped back, smiling. "It fits. My fake camo leaves on top of your real ones."

As he set his watch alarm for 3:30 a.m., Mani brought over the candle and set it by the bed. "Don't tell me what time it is. I'm pretending we'll get up in like, eight hours."

"Which side do you prefer?"

"The one next to you." Her words were a soothing Cupid's arrow through his heart. "Good night, my battle lion," she whispered. "Thanks for stopping by."

"My pleasure, Captain."

As she lay down next to him, Angel thought of the other questions he'd like to ask. *Captain, may I…* But this was already more than enough. *Only thirty-odd hours ago, I looked up at the ninja in my dream and asked myself, "Is that me up there?" Now I'm lying next to my gem. Who'd've thought…*

As usual, visions of the imminent mission flooded through him, anxiety churning out best and worst-case scenarios, playing each one out to success, pre-living each moment, and setting his resolve in stone. As Mani sank into sleep, safe and secure with her army at her side, Angel blew out the candle, and the cave turned pitch black, but for the ember at wick's end.

RED

Send in the Clowns

Red shivered in the cold shower, trying to revitalize her body after two nights of heavy necking with Scotch. The previous month had carved up her emotions and left them rotting for the dirty dogs, flies, and bugs, but today was D-Day, Demolition Day, when she'd send in the clowns with exploding props to set her world straight.

She wasn't in a sari mood and dressed in blue jeans, a long-sleeved white blouse, and a red scarf. Over three cups of tea and an English muffin, she watched nothing happening in the hangar at Aero Dynamic on her smartphone. *Gandhi's birthday. It's dead over there as I expected. Chocks away!*

At ten a.m. Red met her three hench-people in the limo at the Lodhi Park lot and Hari opened the side door for her.

"Ah, the perfect chauffeur. Natty as usual, Hari."

Before she could step in, Dietrich stepped out, blue-blazered in Atlanta style with a caramel poplin shirt, linen pants, and tassel loafers. A black-haired and goateed Colonel Sanders. "Pleased as punch y'all could make it, ma'am," Mason Butler drawled, his alter ego for the day. "Do join us inside, Miss Scarlett. It's hotter out here than hinges on the gates o' hell."

Red sat by Toma as Dietrich joined Hari across from them. "Well, you look rich and sound Georgian to me, but then, I've never been there. Should fool the natives."

"Miss Scarlett O'Hare," southern belle Toma crooned, "I am just tickled pink to see y'all!" She'd outdone herself with another low-cut outfit accentuating cleavage and alluring thighs. She ran a finger up the leg of Red's jeans. "So casual on Gandhi Jayanti."

"Toma," Red began, then corrected herself, "I mean Melanie... you are simply dazzling again. Dressed to kill."

Her last three words hung in the air while Dietrich and Toma glanced at each other, wordlessly saying, "Who's going to bring it up?"

Dietrich took the lead. "Speaking of dressed to kill, we want to make sure that doesn't happen. Bombs are... well, I don't know. Serious business.

Maybe overkill."

"Everyone was so kind and friendly at Aero," Toma chimed in, concern clouding her face. "We met Murakan for a minute. Seems like a nice fellow."

Red listened attentively but was churning inside. This cannot fall apart now. Except for the remark about Murakan being a nice fellow, she felt much the same, but her emotional stake in the situation pierced through reason and compassion. *I need to finish this final act.*

Though she hadn't pondered Devika's wisdom twenty-four hours earlier, it had dissolved in her blood like an Alka Selzer tablet in a glass, inconspicuously delivering its elements throughout her being. Red didn't want to harm anyone, especially the workers she'd seen on the remote camera, everyday people doing their jobs, some of them pilots like her. *What can I say to calm their fears? My fears?*

"I've grown fond of all of you, and I understand how you feel because I feel the same way. I do not want anyone to get hurt. I've murdered billions of insects and birds in this lifetime and might get out of dusting altogether. Flying is my passion, not killing. I've watched the remote camera at Aero today, and business is at a standstill. The devices are small. I'll detonate them in the dead of night, when you're long gone and have disappeared from Delhi. I believe I'm paying you well. Is the amount a problem?"

"No, no, it's not that," Dietrich said, shaking his head and sighing. "We are not saints, but we've never done anything like this."

"I'd deliver them myself, but lack your great skills of performance and masquerade." *A compliment, now levity.* "And I doubt that FedEx sticks bombs on walls." *Now distraction.* "Toma? Dietrich said you had fun during act one. Can you tell me more?"

"Well, it worked out just as we'd planned. We took the tour, the manager played his part, and I slipped away into the hangar. I hid in plain sight like you said."

Now a reality check. "What about security? Cameras? Guards?"

"Only your camera that I put in the corner," Toma said with a shrug. "A gate man in a uniform. That's all."

"How about you, Hari? Anything unusual?"

"I was standing and watching the whole time. Everything was most usual."

"Let me say one more thing, if I may." *Now tug the heart strings.* Scarlett Red snagged Melanie Toma's eyes. "My former husband told me about the possible double meaning of a southern smile. It might apply here."

"I'll bet you mean like what Hattie said in *Gone with the Wind*, one of our favorite movies," Toma said, shifting up her floppy-brimmed fedora. 'What gentlemen say and what they think are two different things.'"

"I suppose it is. Murakan may seem civil, but behind his smile is treachery. Even his name gives him away. Murakan means six-faced in Hindi. I haven't spoken of it, or even dared admit it to myself until now, but I feel in my bones that he was involved in my father's mysterious disappearance and my mother's death." *Now let it sit.*

"That's terrible," Toma said, touching Red's shoulder. "This isn't just about your business, is it?"

"No, it isn't." Red lowered her head.

Dietrich leaned over, resting his hands on Toma's knees. "I wasn't there. It's your decision to do this or not. 'Frankly, my dear, I don't give a damn,'" he quoted with a grin. "What's your woman's intuition say?"

Toma sat silent for a few seconds, then donned her Melanie smile and mimicked Scarlett O'Hara in the movie. "'If I think about that right now, I'll go crazy. After all, tomorrow is another day.' Let's do it."

Tally-ho! "All right then." Red removed the box of explosives from her purse and showed Toma how to arm them. She could see the apprehension in her eyes. "Don't worry, honey. There's no chance of detonation until I activate them with my phone and punch in a special code. What time are they expecting you at Aero?"

"Five p.m."

"Dietrich, call me when the deed is done." Red wanted to leave before their resolution waned. "Thank you so much for helping me. I hope to see you again sometime when this is behind us." Stepping out of the limo, she stuck her head back in. "Good luck to you all."

Back in the security of her Mercedes, Red's hands were shaking. The final act of her production had begun, and her directing was over. All she could do now was wait and watch her spy camera at home. More words from the movie came to mind. *"There was no going back, and she was going forward." Gone with the Wind. It sounds like flying.*

Red felt antsy for the rest of the day. She wasn't hungry and drank too much tea. She couldn't look Scotch in the face after last night. She watched the clock and stared through the spy camera on her phone screen. It was beyond boring. At least the clock changed. By 4:30 p.m. she was nervous as Cat Astrophe slinking behind her ankles. She kicked him out of the condo.

Miles across New Delhi, Red's cast pulled into Aero Dynamic Enterprises, intimidated by its opulence and the enormity of their undertaking. Unlike the India right outside the gate, all the structures were first-class, silver and black, sparkling as if they'd been constructed yesterday. Offices sat to the right of the roundabout, the arching duster hangar ahead, three more hangars to the left across from several other windowless buildings on the drive. Parking planes and dusting crops wouldn't even cover the maintenance costs, but perhaps covered up the lucrative activities hidden behind steel walls. Anxious and early, Red's players longed to send this task into the past. Hari parked and stood next to the limo.

Suman, the manager they'd met two days before, presented them to Murakan, dressed down for the holiday, but still elegantly shiny in his black silk kurta—a collarless shirt extending down to his knees. He was perhaps Dietrich's age, but looked older, harder, sharper.

"Howdy, Mr. Patil," Dietrich drawled, looking down four inches into Murakan's eyes. "Ah'm pleased to make your acquaintance."

"My pleasure as well," Murakan replied, smiling. "Your charming wife has told me a little about you." He turned to Toma and extended his hand, the corners of his eyes wrinkling deeper than crow's feet. Vulture's feet. "Melanie, isn't it?"

"Yes it is. It's so nice to see you again."

"You are a most frightening distance from Georgia, Miss Melanie." Murakan's smile broadened. "I presume you're an Atlanta Redskins fan?"

"Y'all must mean the Atlanta Braves," Dietrich cut in. "The Redskins are up in DC."

"Ah, yes. Atlanta Braves, Washington Redskins, and the Columbus Indians."

"Pardon, but that's the *Cleveland* Indians."

"Oh, of course. So confusing. Isn't it odd they are named after Indians, supposedly in India, the place where your Columbus assumed he had landed...? What was the year again?"

"1492."

"Oh, of course. Not long ago, compared with our 5,000-year history. Well, thank you for considering Aero as a home for your airplane. A Cessna Skyhawk, I believe?"

"Cessna Skyland, JT-A," Dietrich said, extracting a fact from his online research. "The bird stays up in the air longer'n a Skyhawk."

"We don't see many of them around here." Murakan's intense eyes floated above a thin grin. "Do you fly yourself, Mr. Butler?"

"Naw. I let my pilot handle the stick while I lounge in the back, takin' in the wild blue yonder out the window."

"I do the same, my mind outside, gone with the wind...but enough chat for now," Murakan said, turning to Suman before striding away. "Please persuade our guests into the fold with our state-of-the-art facilities, then bring them to my office so I know you've done your job successfully."

AT 4:55, THE INTERCOM BUZZED AT ADMIRAL AVIATION, startling Red at her desk. "Miss Red? A police detective is here to see you."

Bollocks. She glanced at her watch. *Five minutes until showtime.* "Please bring him to my office, but tell him I can only spare ten minutes."

Now was not the time Red wished to see anyone, but she didn't want to arouse suspicion. She changed from jeans into a skirt, secured a scarf around her head, and made it to the door as they arrived.

"Good day, Miss Admiral. My name is Detective Darshan and I am working with the Public Prosecutor's office. Azeez tells me you are busy, but this should only take a few minutes."

"Holiday, you know. Things to do, places to be." *He seems vaguely familiar.*

Darshan looked as if he'd been working twenty-four hours a day for sixty years and had never glanced at a mirror. Unruly eyebrow hairs strayed upward, and white, nose bristles fought their way into his grey moustache.

"Please make yourself comfortable on the couch," Red sat at her desk and slipped the smartphone into a drawer. "Have we met before, Detective?"

"Yes, some years ago. Your mother, Chandra, used to be my superior at the Prosecutor's office."

"She was always my superior wherever we were."

He laughed politely. "Chandra was a remarkable woman, and I am still sad she passed away. My belated condolences to you."

"Thank you so much. Now, how may I help you?"

"As you may know, we have reopened unsolved cases, including a few your mother had been involved with before her unfortunate accident on the bridge. One of the kingpins under investigation is Baldev Ishwar Gupta. Your father had some association with him, yes?" He might as well have poked into a raw nerve with a dentist's drill.

"Mr. Darshan, I've gone over this with your department before, to no avail whatsoever. None of your so-called professionals could come up with one clue regarding his disappearance."

"That is unfortunate. I hope our current investigation may give us insight into his case as well. A newspaper reporter has similarly vanished. Can you tell me of any relationship between Chandra and Baldev?"

"She couldn't stand him, considered him a complete con-man goonda, and nagged my father constantly about his dealings with him. She wanted to put Baldev away and made no bones about it." Red looked at her watch openly, hoping the hint would be heeded.

"What is your relationship with Baldev?" he asked.

"I have no relationship with him," she barked, then backed off. *Where is he going with this?* "I've met him a handful of times over the years," she amended. "I think he's a vile man."

"I agree whole-heartedly, Miss Admiral. We're trying our utmost to take him down. What about Murakan Patil?"

An internal electric shock bulged her eyes for a split second. She hid her face by checking her watch again. *Steady on. Give him a shred of the truth, then get him out of here.* "I met him once, for a moment at an auction. He purchased one of our used crop dusters. What's he got to do with Baldev?"

"We're not sure, but he is Baldev's nephew, you know."

Red's chest constricted into a knot, but she somehow managed to continue breathing. "Mur… M…" She covered her mouth and feigned coughing while choking on his words. "No… I didn't know. He must be vile as well," she mumbled, as flippantly as she could manage. "Now I must be off, Mr. Darshan. I have holiday plans."

"Yes, I understand," he said, handing her his card. "If you think of anything that may help us—"

"I'll give you a call." Red finished his sentence and led him to the door. "Good luck. The lot of them should be behind bars. Azeez will see you out. Cheers."

She rushed back to her desk and took out her smartphone. 5:10 p.m. Except for the dwindling light and lengthening shadows, the hangar looked the same—three dusters and a truck, no workers, no pilots, no Toma. By this time at Aero, the tour was over, a near repeat of the previous one, and Red had no way of knowing she'd missed Toma's performance.

After passing the hangar at Aero fifteen minutes earlier, Toma had excused herself. "I need to freshen up. You showed me where before, Suman. I'll catch up with y'all."

On the way into the toilet, she slipped one bomb under the horizontal stabilizer of a duster's rear wing, and on the way out, another among barrels of chemicals. Crossing diagonally to the front, she dropped a handkerchief from her purse, and while picking it up, stuck the last bomb under the fender of the yellow Caterpillar service truck used to fuel and lube planes in hangars or on the tarmac.

Suman led Toma and Dietrich into Murakan's office, where he sat behind his luxurious desk, flanked by wall-mounted big game heads bagged on African safaris.

"Come in, come in! Jack is waiting. A taste of your USA." Murakan spread his palms toward three Waterford crystal glasses next to a bottle of Jack Daniels Tennessee Honey Whiskey and a silver bucket of ice. "Please have a seat."

Reluctantly, they both sat in the chairs in front of his desk, aching to get the hell out of town. They hadn't signed on for act three.

"That's some sweet nectar y'all got there," Dietrich said, "but we need to hit the road and—"

"Nonsense!" Murakan waved away the plea with a flip of his hand. "It's Gandhi's birthday! A national holiday, in fact, a global day. The International Day of Non-Violence. You *must* have one glass with me to celebrate."

"Okay," Dietrich surrendered. "Just one."

"Neat or with ice?" Murakan asked Toma.

"Ice, thank you."

"Neat," Dietrich said.

Murakan filled one glass with ice, poured three hearty shots, and handed over two. He raised his glass and toasted. "To Mahatma Gandhi… Bapu… the Father of India." He downed Jack in one gulp.

Dietrich emptied his. Toma sipped hers.

Behind them, outside by the limo, two guards lifted Hari's limp body off the pavement. He'd chugged one sedative-packed Jack to settle his nerves and asked for another.

"Do you have any questions about our high-tech world at Aero Dynamic?" Murakan asked with the trace of a smirk on his face as he glanced out the window at his guards hauling Hari away.

"No, siree," Dietrich said. "Y'all have a mighty fine operation here. We'll be parkin' our plane at Aero."

"When might that be?"

"Not sure. We'll let y'all know."

"I must show you our security system."

"I was wonderin' about that," Dietrich said, Jack warming up his torso. "I didn't see no cameras anywhere."

"Well, isn't that the most delicious kind of security? No one knows they are being watched!" Murakan pressed a button on his desk. A second later, two beefy apes came through a sliding door concealed in the back wall and positioned themselves behind Toma and Dietrich. "Meet the Kakkar brothers, former Olympic weightlifters. My mobile security system."

Wobbling slightly, Dietrich turned in his chair and gazed upward. He didn't know Indians could be that big. Like Murakan, they both wore black kurdas, their bulging biceps and shoulders stretching the fabric to its limit, their mouths petrified into a line. "Looks like they'all jog on their arms," Dietrich said, blinking his eyes, his drawl thicker.

Toma finished her Jack and set it down with a clank as Murakan rose from his chair.

"Dietrich Sheppard, mein guter Freund, let me demonstrate the rest of our security system with a short movie featuring your wife Toma in Scarlett Red Admiral's fanciful burlesque."

Hearing each of their real names in one sentence sent chills from their toenails up to their dyed hair. Bug-eyed Toma trembled while Dietrich tried to stand. Cued by an imperceptible nod from Murakan, four heavy gorilla hands clamped onto their shoulders from behind, imprisoning them in their chairs.

Murakan clicked on a large LCD wall monitor behind his desk and stepped aside. "And now... please pardon my bastardization of that age-old fable... Little Red's Hiding Hoods."

Stunned and wavering in their seats, Toma and Dietrich watched themselves walking with Scarlett and Hari in Lodhi Park, viewed from somewhere above.

"Aren't these new surveillance drones simply splendid devices?" Murakan asked.

No one answered.

On the screen, Dietrich juggled scarves, then Toma climbed onto his shoulders.

"Ah..." Murakan sneered. "Such agile, acrobatic clowns."

The scene changed to the cast of four inside their white limo, and Red's voice seemed to boom out of the speakers. "You could delicately venture into the loo while checking out locations for three fist-size, adhesive-backed explosives."

Murakan leaned toward Dietrich with his palms flat on the desk and hissed, "Our security system extends far beyond your imagination."

The final scene showed movie star Melanie Toma, a half-hour earlier, slinking through Aero's hangar. Even without sedatives coursing through them, neither Toma nor Dietrich would've known what to say. They'd never been caught red-handed before, never dealt with an evil creature like the one glowering down at them.

Murakan sat, removed three bombs from the drawer, lay them in front of Toma, and grinned. "Miss Melanie, you must have misplaced these on your tour. Perhaps you should stick with exploding cigars."

She could hardly keep her head from lolling onto her chest. Dietrich's elbows barely supported him on the desk.

Murakan tipped up the whisky bottle and took a deep swig. "You see, our designer drugs coated your glasses, instead of dissolved in the liquor. While you are both still semi-coherent, you should know two more things." Murakan's grin was gone. "One, your friend Ganesh is also part of our security system. If he doesn't tell us what he hears, we'll remove his ears. These little firecrackers would never have popped until we set them off. And two, I heard your touching speech about avoiding death in the limo today. Understand that we have no qualms about killing here."

He stood abruptly, grabbing the bombs while growling commands to the Kakkars. "Strap them to the chairs in the cube along with their fake chauffeur. Put a bomb in each of their laps and set the countdown for five minutes past midnight. We don't want anyone dying on Bapu's birthday. Now take them away! I have a gala to attend."

MONA

The Day before Tomorrow

Mona's bucket list trip began tomorrow, before dawn. Airline tickets had been purchased, Bea's job terminated, Antonio's sabbatical granted, Zarita notified, and Marco's dog sitter confirmed.

Mona couldn't bear to cage him in a kennel during her absence. Luckily, her friend Laura, the librarian, was hopelessly in love with Marco and Mona's house and her collection of bizarre books, which would never, ever, in a million years, grace the Mission library shelves. She always agreed to come at a moment's notice, secretly praying Mona would not return. Laura's standard greeting at the library was, "Hey, Mona. Nice to see you. When are you leaving?"

Mona stopped at the bank to buy traveler's checks and at her lawyer's office to pick up a document. She then met Sasha for lunch at Manzanito's, the best Mexican food in Mission, Texas. Perhaps for the first time in a decade, Mona and Sasha were both on time *and* in the same place.

"I'm not sure if you look charged up or beat up," Sasha said as Mona sat at the table. "Your hair looks like your head's unraveling."

"And good afternoon to you, too," Mona shot back.

"Sorry, sweetheart." Sasha rested her hand on Mona's arm. "I'm a little stressed myself with the relatives descending on me tomorrow. I had to do my makeup three times before I could leave my condo."

"It's okay. I'd say I'm just very sad and very happy."

"Together they make sappy."

"That, too." Mona hesitated, running her fingers through her tousled black hair. "I met a man yesterday."

"Do tell." Sasha leaned as far in as her tiny old body in a tight, black dress would allow. "I've never heard you use those words in that order before."

"I felt things I haven't felt for years."

"Where?"

"My head, my heart, my loins."

"That's not what I asked," Sasha said, smirking, "but thanks for telling me. And I've never heard you use the word 'loins.' I meant, where did you meet him?"

"Oh." Mona blushed. "He just dropped in. A dapper, mature man from Monarch Watch."

"Mature, you say. How old?"

"Seventy."

"A young whippersnapper," Sasha scoffed. "You cradle robber."

"I'd given up hoping to find someone my age I could really connect with. It could happen to you, too, Sasha."

"Ha. I doubt it. I'm halfway to 90."

"No. You're 85. That's halfway to 170."

Sasha winced. "Ouch and touché. Now we're even for my head unraveling comment."

"Heck, I'm almost halfway to 150. As if we're going to make it that far."

"You never know. Brain in a bottle. Saw it on TV."

"I'll probably never see him again," Mona sighed, "but we were so comfortable together, like old friends. So much in common. He listened and shared his feelings and told me some things that still have me reeling."

"What things?"

"Oh, I'll tell you later. Too much to process right now."

"You'll forget. Tell me now. I may not be around much longer."

"Don't say that!" Mona was shocked at how loudly she'd spoken and lowered her voice and her head as she glanced at other diners in the room. "I'm sorry to shout, but that's exactly what I've been feeling… not about you, about me."

"Now, what are you talking about? It's me here. Sasha. Tell Sasha what's going on."

"I… I don't really know. I've told you about all these strange visions I've been having lately. Now they actually feel good, but I don't know where they're coming from or what they mean. And I'm finally going to Mexico, which feels so final, like maybe I should move there. And Zarita's going to die. I know it. She knows it…" Mona's head dropped into her folded arms on the table as her chest swelled and eyes overflowed.

"Let it out, sweetheart," Sasha whispered, pressing her head against Mona's and glaring at the nosy folks at the next table. "Maybe we should go somewhere else. I'm not hungry, anyway. Thirsty, yes. I was about ready to trip a waiter with my cane to get a drink."

"Okay," Mona agreed, stealing a few paper napkins to dry her tears. "How about the park down the block. I think it has a lemonade stand."

"Do they serve vodka?"

"We're in Mission, not New Orleans."

"I can dream, can't I?"

They hobbled out to the sidewalk, Sasha using her cane, Mona using Sasha. The day matched both of their moods, overcast and gray. Mona talked as they walked.

"You know, when an old friend passes who's the same age as you, you look at your own life with a magnifying glass. I have this feeling I'll be passing on soon, too."

"I understand," Sasha sighed, "whatever soon means. I've felt that for fifteen years now. Then I forget about it, then I feel it again, forget it, feel it, all in one day."

"I can't believe I'm finally going to meet Zarita," Mona said, suddenly happy. "To exchange words with arms and eyes and hearts. It's a dream come true."

"I'm sad I can't go with you."

"Me, too, but Antonio and Bea are coming with me."

Sasha stopped walking and turned to Mona. "That is wonderful. I couldn't bear imagining you going alone. I've felt green with guilt, but this news tickles me pink."

"We leave tomorrow... early. They've been like my kids, but now they're like my parents taking care of me. Sweet beings, they are."

Two lemonades and one park bench later, they sat in the shade, soaking up the smell of freshly cut grass and the dahlia blooms surrounding them.

"Our plans have expanded," Mona said. "This has become my bucket-list trip. After seeing Zarita, however long that takes, we're going to a Maya ruin and then to a monarch sanctuary near Bea's hometown. I can hardly wait for every step of the way."

"My guilt has now been replaced with envy. Maybe I can join you after my clan leaves."

"That'd be great if you could! We'll keep in touch."

For a few languid minutes they sat with the breeze, watching the life of Mission ramble by.

"Do you have a bucket list, Sasha?"

"Used to. Crossed them all off. Now I only have a 'fuck it' list. Can't golf. Fuck it. Can't dance. Fuck it. Can't go on your bucket list trip. Fuck it."

Mona's laughter swelled with every word. "Oh, Sasha. You always grab me and lift me up when I'm down. I'll miss you so much." Her tears of joy melded with tears of sorrow as she threw her arms around her dear friend.

"Good thing we left the restaurant," Sasha said, rubbing Mona's back.

Mona sat up, wiping her eyes then smoothing her hair back with damp palms. "Whew. Lately I'm in and out and back and forth, on the edge of a thin ridge. Happiness down one side, sadness down the other."

"You'll get through it," Sasha assured her. "What can I do to help?"

"There is one thing." Mona took out a document and gave it to Sasha. "The shock of the news about Zarita made me change my will. You just said it. 'You never know.' The proceeds from my artwork and card sales still go to the Butterfly Center, but I've willed the car, the land, the house, and everything in it to Bea and Antonio. Besides you and Zarita, they're the only family I have."

"You're a good woman, Mona Arcade," Sasha said. "Have you told them?"

"No, but I can see the look on their faces when they find out. My lawyer has a copy of my will, but I'd feel better if you had one."

"Now I'm going to have to live longer than you. I hope you have a lawyer younger than me."

"Thank you for doing this, Sasha."

"You're welcome, Mona. I guess I have a bucket list again… with only one thing on it."

"I have a present for you."

"Vodka for my lemonade?" Sasha asked.

"This work is a one-of-a-kind that I'll never have the patience to do again." Mona handed her a tiny canvas, the exact size of a business card. "I recreated that five-foot monarch I painted that's hanging on your wall, so you could carry me around in your wallet."

"I have to put on my eyes," Sasha said.

"Mine got worse by the time I finished it."

Sasha squinted at the painting through her thick lenses. "It's amazing! This is so sweet of you, but you know I already carry you around in my heart all the time."

"Likewise." Mona fidgeted for a moment. "Sasha, I don't want to go, but I've got some things to do. Can I give you a lift home?"

"If you have time."

"You wait here. The Ranchero's just up the street."

After a quiet ride, each of them lost in their own feelings about her imminent departure, Mona pulled into the condo parking lot as Sasha spoke.

"I had one of those weird experiences like you had. I was talking to a friend and telling them about one of our routine Friday rendezvous. When I finished the story, I didn't know if it really happened, or I imagined it, or it was just a funny story someone told me."

"Which time?" Mona asked, all ears.

"Some years ago, we were playing cards at that tavern on Mayberry street. I looked up at you and my mind went blank. I was completely embarrassed, but you know I never let that get in the way. So I said, 'I'm sorry, but I can't remember your name.' You stared at me for a minute and said, 'How soon do you need to know?'"

Mona snickered.

"Did that *really* happen?" Sasha asked.

"You're asking me? I don't remember. You don't remember. I could've said that. We'll never know for sure."

Neither of them wanted to part, but Sasha took the lead. "This isn't a goodbye, just a see you later."

Mona got out, came around the car, and opened the door for Sasha. "I'm gonna miss you, my guardian angel."

"Thanks for the ride, sweetheart. You call me. Anytime."

They hugged hard and long, then Mona got back into her Ranchero and pulled away, her eyes once again dripping with joy and sorrow.

When she walked through the front door at home, Antonio and Bea, her worker ant and bee, scurried about packing, sorting, cleaning, and calling clients while grabbing bites from the nachos, guacamole, and tacos on the counter.

"Hi!" Bea said, brimming over with glee. "The countdown has begun! Dinner's in the kitchen. Need any help getting ready?"

"No, I'm pretty much packed, thanks. Only a few last-minute things to finish."

The word 'last' echoed in her mind as she plodded into her bedroom. Searching through her chest of drawers, Mona found a small antique book—*Chinese Gems of Wisdom*—that she'd discovered while cleaning the storage room. She'd tucked it away to peruse later. *Later is now. Maybe Flank left this just for me. A present for the present.*

More than a century old, its leather cover still glistened with gilded letters, and its pages were still sturdy and white. Reading the copyright date of 1895, Mona surmised it had been printed on cotton rag paper that didn't yellow over time. She browsed through the woodcuts scattered throughout the book. Each page contained only a few words.

Mona started at the beginning and read the first entry, an anonymous Chinese proverb. "A book is like a garden carried in the pocket."

The next page held a morsel from Confucius, one she'd always loved and lived through her multifaceted spiritual practices. "There are many paths to the mountain, but the view is always the same."

With both thumbs on the edges of its thick pages, Mona opened the book to the middle, landing on the wisdom of Lao Tzu, her all-time favorite sage. "Life is a series of natural and spontaneous changes. Don't resist them - that only creates sorrow. Let reality be reality. Let things flow naturally forward in whatever way they like."

It made her feel better about the way her emotions had been bouncing between sadness and joy. She flipped the page to another Lao Tzu quote she'd never encountered. "What the caterpillar calls the end, the rest of the world calls a butterfly."

This one captured her, and she turned to the next page, expecting more Lao Tzu. The next words were like a cold slap in the face though she felt a fire begin to rise up her spine. Mona read them again and again, blown away by their message and shocked she'd never heard them before. Pieces of the jigsaw puzzle she'd been struggling with in her soul lifted off the floor and assembled themselves. A hazy revelation forming in her mind, she walked out to her studio on the bluff to clear them up on canvas.

Mona looked at the blank canvas on her easel.

It's too big, and oils won't dry in time. I'll take this one with me.

Her eyes wandered to the antique watercolors she'd saved from junior high school in Wisconsin. In the center of the tin cover, under the words World Paint Box, prop planes flew and passenger ships steamed around a green globe. Illustrations of children encircled the image—American kids with suitcases, a girl in a sari, a Latino boy dancing under a sombrero, an Eskimo, an Asian, a lad in a kilt.

Why not? These old colors will come to life again.

She took it down, and it took her back to her childhood. Some of the tiny rectangular paint blocks in the bottom tray were gone. Red, yellow, and black were thin and cracked, almost empty. Many were caked combinations of the other hues surrounding them. Splotches of all the twenty-seven colors stained the back of the cover. She dug out some small brushes and fetched a glass of water.

Pen and ink to begin, watercolor to finish.

With an old-fashioned, split-nib dip pen and India ink, Mona drew herself and a mirror framing her so she was merely a reflection. She completed the rest of the image with broader black strokes, then propped the sketchbook on her easel and let the watercolors "flow naturally" as Lao Tzu had advised, "in whatever way they like."

Returning to pen and ink, Mona wrote the quote that had inspired the piece at the bottom, signed it, and left it to dry until morning.

After discussing times and logistics with Antonio and Bea, her last and final activity for the day was the opposite of activity. Mona went into her meditation room, guided by the words of Buddha. "Don't just do something, sit there."

She lit the white candles to the side of her altar and twelve sticks of sandalwood incense in the middle, then sat on the round cushion that helped her into the cross-legged lotus position as much as her fossil hips would bend. Resting her hands in her lap, right over the left, she closed her eyes and breathed deeply, rhythmically, letting thoughts of the past, today, and tomorrow drift away. She focused on the low sound of the heart beating in her chest and the high-pitched whine of the nervous system in her head. She chanted the words gathered along her pathway to the mountain.

"I call upon and honor my guides, teachers, and angels. Please lead me to kindness and compassion, to awareness, understanding, and acceptance, to awakening, enlightenment, and union with the god/creator/spirit for the greatest good of all."

Into the black void of her meditation floated faces, strangers morphing into friends, elderly wise men into animals, cloudy colors into geometric patterns and symbols on stone walls, blue sky back into darkness. Then, as had happened recently during the day or night, anytime, Mona heard a familiar rustling sound, smelled a breeze spiced with pine, and felt a tickling sensation on her skin.

She opened her eyes, and as her five senses took over, the sound, smell, and feeling disappeared.

ANGEL
Endless Day and Night

Mani and Angel slept shoulder to shoulder, soldier to soldier, but once in a while during the night, a stray arm draped over the other's body and spontaneous unconscious spooning evolved.

Triggered by his internal clock, Angel woke at 3:20 a.m., ten minutes before his watch alarm. He crept out of the bed of canopy wing and leaves, lit the candle, and watched Mani resting in the golden flickering light.

I've never felt like this before. Could this be the infamous love at first sight? The one I thought could only happen to other people? I'm on my hundredth sight and it still seems like the first. Mmm. Such inner peace. No desires, no needs. Just watching her sleep is plenty.

At 3:29, he gently rocked Mani out of her world and into his. She rose like a zombie, splashed water onto her face from a bucket, and lit the tripod butane camp stove to brew some herb tea. "God, how many times have I done this lately? I'd rather go sightseeing at noon."

"It'll be over and done soon," Angel assured her.

They didn't talk much while preparing to hit the trails. Angel packed the tools and toys he'd need for the day plus a few Soldier Fuel energy bars and packs of FSRs: First Strike Rations from his DEA care package. Angel kept a safe distance from Mani. For twenty-four arduous hours, his sweat had been fermenting and the stench threatened to overwhelm the pleasing mossy odor in the cave.

Mani dressed in North Face and Patagonia forest green gear. A name-brand ranger. As she stepped outside through the vegetation covering the doorway, she tripped forward onto her hands and knees.

Flashlight in hand, Angel raced ahead to help. "You okay?"

"Yeah," she muttered. "Legs're still asleep."

He took her hand and pulled her up. "I've seen you fall out of a tree, into a ravine, and now over your own doorstep. Do all Hmong people have two left feet?"

"Shut up."

"Next time I'll have to carry you over the threshold." *Jeez, did I just propose to her?*

Crickets and tree frogs chirped in the trees by the stream, and an occasional cuckoo coo-cooed its predawn yawn. Full moonlight made the path easy to follow. The temperature was cool, the air pristine, the scene perfect for a stroll, but soon Mani's lower limbs awakened, transforming into strong, slender leopard legs, challenging her battle lion to keep up the pace.

They retrieved her knives from the ravine, then climbed up to where they'd first met. Once again they lay together, under leaves instead of on top of them, behind a slight rise, and scrutinised the Ghostscape below.

"What's the workers' schedule?" Angel asked, scoping out the scene through night-vision goggles. "It's dead down there."

"Seven to eleven, every day."

"Check these out." He swapped his goggles for her mini-binoculars.

"Woah! These kick ass," she whispered. "I need a pair to get around in the cave."

"You look like a deadly insect with those on."

"Thanks. I'll keep 'em."

"Not tonight, honey. I'll need 'em to spot Ghost Soldiers. You can glue two candles on your shoulders and one on your head."

Under an elemental blue sky with vagrant clouds lingering on the ridge tops and a vast umbrella of foliage, this banter went on all day as they avoided perimeter guards, traipsed along the trails, planning and prepping Angel's two escape routes. On the first path, a safe distance beyond the Ghost Zone, they fashioned booby-traps by cutting short bamboo staves and pounding them diagonally into the ground toward potential pursuers. They sharpened the protruding tips and covered them with leaves. One moment the air was thick with tension; the next moment, they relaxed into their own private galaxy.

"Back in The Ridge, they call me 'The Alien' cuz I'm so weird, and no one has any idea what I do." Angel marked the path five feet before the staves with a folded palm frond pierced with a twig to keep it upright and visible. "But I don't feel like an alien here. I feel at home."

"That's cuz you are home, like me. What's The Ridge?"

"Where I live… or lived. Pokeberry Ridge in the Appalachian Mountains in Georgia." He grinned as they walked beyond the trap. "Home of American hill tribes."

"Da, da, dang, dang, dang, dang, dang, dang, dang," Mani sang, plucking a stick of bamboo like a banjo. "I think y'all mean them hillbillies."

"Kissin' cousins, bills from the hills," he drawled.

"You know," she said, scratching her head, "someone once told me the toothbrush was invented in Georgia."

"No..." Angel fell into her trap.

"Yeah. If it had been invented anywhere else, they'd've called it the teethbrush."

"I'll hafta tell that one to the Ridge boys. They'll get out a noose 'n' string me up."

"Bring home one of your bombs and wear it as a necklace. Like, with a grenade ring in your nose."

"Um, maybe... if you'll wear the candles."

At other strategic locations they stretched dark canopy line eight inches above the trails to trip or tangle unsuspecting legs, or as trip wires for a bamboo whip—a green pole bent to the ground across the path and hidden under brush, possibly deadly as it flew back upright with spikes lashed to the end, but only a shocking deterrent without the barbs. Angel didn't want deadly, only disabling, a reminder for the Ghost's army to slow down. Spikeless but wrapped with thorny vines, his whips only left a bloody message written on skin. These areas he marked with one forked stick stuck into the ground, another leaning in its crotch.

"This trail's like my life," Mani mused. "Spikes, tripwires, too many sharp surprises. Been smooth sailing for a while, but the comfort zone gets a little ho hum."

"What's next for you, after you're a hero and all?" He paused and saluted. "Sorry, Captain. A she-ro."

"Pff, I dunno," she sighed. "Everything I own's packed away, ready to rot. Like, I think I need a new road, a new horizon, something new. But I tell you, it's bitchin' to be back in the tropics. The sweet smells and the talking jungle. This thick air feels like a warm wet puppy on my neck."

"I'll be itchin' for a comfort zone after this Ghost Zone. Been on too many trails around the globe leadin' to shitheads in shitholes."

Setting the last trap on a second trail where Angel might split off alone was more complex. If the Ghost Soldiers were still hot on their heels, he'd lead them away from Barry and the route to the extraction point. He wrapped several small trees on both sides of the trail with detonation cord, a high-speed fuse that doesn't burn, but explodes instantaneously along its entire length. Six loops of det cord around a utility pole would cut it neatly; fifteen could catapult the severed upper section twenty feet into the air. Angel planned to ignite the cord in real time during the chase, creating a logjam at the junction, and then draw any leftover soldiers toward him onto a divergent escape path. His preferred scenario was still a clandestine getaway—no hunters, no traps, just a walk in the woods.

At noon they picnicked at the edge of a clearing. The Soldier Fuel energy bars hit the spot. They'd passed on the mystery meat extracted from a First Strike packet after Mani's one-word description after one bite. "Blechhh!"

They strolled another mile down the valley and across the stream on a narrow wooden bridge leading to flatter land. Angel lashed one of the C-4 explosive packs under the bridge. 500 yards farther, he hid the GPS bug used to locate his supply bags in a tree on the edge of a dry rice field where the chopper could land safely.

He called in the coordinates with the special phone Agent Nat had given him and assured her, southern-style, that everything was hunky-dory. "Say hey to Cowboy Doug."

"Good luck out there," Nat said. "FYI. Ransom went from one to ten million bucks. Mister P must've found out Barry's the president's nephew."

"Huh, greed gone hog wild. Don't worry. I'll get the boy out. Catch up with y'all soon after dawn."

The call reminded Angel of the regular local phone Nat had provided as a backup, and he dug it out of his pack. Even though he felt a million miles from civilization under the towering teak tree, a cell tower might be right over the ridge.

"Hey, Mani. You have a cell phone on you?"

"Doh. Of course. Always."

"What do I have to do to get your number?"

"Simple. Give me yours and those night goggles."

"Number now, goggles later? Captain, may I?"

"Sure. Give me your number and I'll call it."

Angel looked at the phone and shook his head. "Jeez, Louise. My number? I have no clue."

"And you thought you could do this without me."

"Temporary insanity."

Mani told him her number. He walked behind the tree and phoned her.

"Hello?"

"Christopher Worthington Sengtavisouk here."

"Who?" she asked, surprised.

"That's my given name."

"Now I understand. Mind if I stick with Angel?"

"Most do. Now Miss… Miss who? I don't even know your last name."

"Zuah."

"Like you live in a zuah?"

"You mean like *you* should? No way. It's Hmong for sharp, like smart, witty, intelligent."

"That fits. Okay, Miss Zuah, I'm running for chairman of WHAT and hope you'll vote for me."

"What?" she asked.

"Yes. WHAT."

"What's what?"

"You don't even know what's what? You're one of its members! WHAT is the Worldwide Hmong Attack Team."

"I see. But you don't qualify. You're not Hmong."

"Close enough," he said, "I am among the Hmong."

Mani smiled and sat on a root of the teak tree. "Um… I dunno… Who else is running?"

"No one."

"How many members are there?"

"So far, only two."

"Well, I'm gonna have to think it over," she teased, leaning her head back on the trunk. "Like, a whole mob of people will want to join tomorrow."

"That's why the election's today," he said.

"Sounds shady to me. How long's your term in office?"

"One day. And I don't have an office. We'll hold a new election tomorrow."

"In that case, you have my vote."

"Great. It's unanimous then."

"Congratulations, Mr. Chairman."

He stepped around the tree, still talking on the phone. "Ua tsuag, Captain. I'd love to celebrate with a hot shower."

"Good luck." Mani smirked and stood up, speaking into the phone but looking into his eyes.

Angel raised his right arm and pointed across the paddy. "You think it's safe to jump into that stream over there?"

"I thought you'd never ask," she said, backing away. "I wasn't avoiding you today because I didn't like you."

"Good to know. I am a little ripe… almost rotten." He pressed both elbows against his sides, sealing his armpits. "I've been trying to avoid myself."

They hiked over to the stream and along its banks to a bend where it rushed over glossy rocks into a tranquil pool surrounded by a grove of

Ratchapruk—Golden Shower trees. As he stripped down to his Avengers boxer shorts and waded in, Mani gave him a botany lesson, her eyes roving between the trees and nearly naked Angel.

"Cute. Superhero shorts. You see this tree here? The national tree of Thailand. Blooms like yellow waterfalls in April. They call it the 'disease killer' in India. Potent Ayurvedic medicine for ulcers, fever, and fungus among us. Dry yourself off with the leaves. Might help your pits. Nice pecs, by the way."

"Thanks," he said, scrubbing himself with sand. "I think I see some wave foam over here."

Mani's dimples framed her smile like parentheses. She turned and wandered off toward the brush.

Angel watched her fade into the sublime scene. He was far enough from the Ghost Zone to feel safe. Water buffalo lolled in the rice paddy mud across the stream. Floppy-eared, humpback cows ruminated contentedly with white cattle egrets pecking flies and ticks off their backs. As Angel gazed down the valley, trying to determine the distance and route to the Mekong River, he heard Mani shout.

"Angel!"

He bounded out of the pool, slipped on his boots, and vaulted into the brush, laces flapping around his feet. "Mani! Where are you?"

"C'mere quick. Be quiet!"

She sounded okay, but that didn't lessen his panic. He found her crouched behind thick bushes.

"Slowly, slowly," Mani warned, pointing at two huge multicolored moths clinging to the bark of a tree.

It's the same moth that Tiger ordered. And the one mounted at the Smithsonian. Weird. "Wow. Atlas moths," Angel whispered, "the largest moths in the world."

"They hardly ever fly during the day. Maybe they coupled last night. They live less than a week."

"I heard they don't even eat. No mouths. Just mate, lay eggs, and die."

"How come you know so much about 'em, soldier?"

"I saw these in a dream. I'll tell you later."

"Watch this. She's female, larger than the male." Mani slipped her fingers under one moth's front legs and coaxed it onto her hand, which disappeared from sight under the Atlas' twelve-inch wingspan. "She's calm… ready to go home. She's almost completed her mission for this lifetime."

Angel bent down and examined it, his eyes inches from the moth's soft, furry head and legs. "She's beautiful. I'll bet the Butterfly Mother sent her."

Mani's voice took on a trance-like timbre, as if she were reading from a book or a page from her past, the same tone he'd heard when she told the tale of the Butterfly Mother and the phases of the full moon. "Like the butterfly, a moth signifies change; this one, a big change. Butterflies bask in the sunlight by day. Night is the realm of the moth, and they bask in the moonlight. They call upon you to listen to the inner voice in the darkness of your soul. They're totems of your ancestors come to visit, bringing messages from beyond life and death."

Her words and pastoral manner reminded him of his shaman grandmother. *Moth. It's right in the middle of her name. Grandmother Dao.* Angel felt as though she were speaking through Mani and thought of a letter Dao had once written to him, a message that had stuck in his soul, but one he might not have been able to hear then.

My grandson, you circle the world like a moth around a flame, flirting with death among artificial illusions made by man. I say, embrace the natural way. Follow the sun by day and fly straight to the moon at night. Do not be distracted by the funeral pyres of desire. Do what makes your heart soar. It will carry you higher than your mind can imagine.

The sun was about ready to set behind the ridge as its shadow crept across the valley, cooling the light breeze. Mani set one large insect down carefully while Angel swatted the tiny ones snacking on his legs.

"We'd better head home," she said. "I'll show you the way to the trail you came in on yesterday."

They hiked leisurely, their thoughts flipping between the peace of the moment and the chaos that would erupt tomorrow. The day had been an odd amalgam of love and war—tender moments while setting traps for young soldiers, perhaps trapped in a daunting life from which they might not have had the choice to escape. The air felt electric, charged with uncertain options and outcomes.

Mani stretched out her hand to help backpacking Angel up the steep incline and continued to hold it as they turned and walked on the path toward the cave.

Once they'd arrived, Angel said, "I gotta get my toys ready for the party."

"You do that. I'll fix dinner." Mani lit a lantern, heated a water pot on the camp stove, rummaged in plastic bags, and prepared wild food gathered in the jungle.

As he sat on a rock stuffing bombs and det cord into his pack, playing the plan in his brain, Angel realized he would not be sitting in the chopper tomorrow. He felt at home here. He'd wave goodbye as it lifted off, then return to this magnetic woman to let his intense emotions play out.

He spoke her name quietly. "Mani?"

She turned and looked into his eyes, searching for the meaning of the strange new tone in his voice. "Angel?"

"I've changed my plans."

"Now what?"

"I'm staying."

"Staying? Like, staying where? When?"

"Here. Tomorrow. Once it's done..." The next two words Angel only thought, because he couldn't quite get his tongue around them. *With you.* "I'd like to remove those traps so no innocent bystanders get hurt."

"Angel baby... the whole valley'll be swarming with angry army ants." She leaned over him with a ninja knife in her hand and concern in her heart. "That could be more dangerous than the mission ahead of us."

"Yeah... you're right. We'll see how many traps get sprung." He looked up like a little kid talking to a little girl on the playground. "What're you gonna do?"

"Well, there's no way in hell I'm stayin' here." She pointed her blade towards the valley. "I have three trucks lined up to take the workers to another village down the other side of the ridge. Maybe I'll hang with my bro for a while."

"Sit down and stop threatening me with your knife," he demanded, grinning.

She sat lotus-like in front of him. "Better?"

"Better." *No, you're the best.* "When I got back from Bolivia six days ago, I'd planned to put my dogs up and be a vegetable for a month. This gig came up after only eleven hours of vacation." Praise every god and goddess. "I'm due for one..." His voice trailed off, but his sigh said there was more. "And..."

"And..." Mani repeated.

Angel stared off for a moment, then back into her peaceful, inviting face. "You want the truth?"

"I like the truth. Shoot."

"Mani... I... I can't..." His palms were up. His foot bounced on its heel.

Mani eyes had fastened onto his."Yes, you can."

"No, I can't."

"Can't what?"

"Can't imagine... leaving you," he stammered. "Can't imagine not being near you. I just can't imagine it!"

"Me either. Now that wasn't so hard, was it?"

She was so calm it almost irritated him. He folded his hands, looked at his lap, and started bouncing his right foot. "I know it's all happened so fast. And it's confusing. And it's intense. And—"

"Angel."

Blinking, he raised his eyes to meet hers. "What?"

"It's been magical, mysteriously magical. And you, Angel Phoenix... you are a miracle, a miracle in my life."

Angel couldn't speak, only gaze into those two black portals of hers, dizzy, like swirling in space, falling into them. No escape and no desire to.

Mani stooped low and rested her hands on his knees. "How many messages do you need, sweetheart? They came to you in your dreams before we met and have kept coming like comets from the cosmos."

"I didn't dare believe they were all true."

"You're a daredevil. You dared to fly in here to save Barry. You're daring to help me save my people. Be a *dare angel* and dare to save yourself for me."

"I've never felt like this before about anyone." He choked up. "I've faced death and destruction, but this is even scarier."

"I know what you mean. But now we're facing life." She took a deep breath, ending in a mischievous smirk. "If I've had any worries, it's that we might spontaneously combust and explode like one of your bombs."

In place of the tears threatening to well up in Angel's eyes, a snort of laughter burst out. "There isn't another woman in the world like you."

"Sure there is, but like, I'm not gonna let you find her. If this straight talk isn't enough for you, lemme give you one more message, special delivery." She kneeled in front of Angel, pressed his palm gingerly over one of her eyes and fluttered her lashes on his skin, then on his bare arm, then on his nose and forehead.

Angel's whole body quivered inside like a blooming cherry tree filled with honeybees.

She put her hands on his cheeks. "Know what those were?"

"Um... no. What?"

"Butterfly kisses."

Angel's smile was audible. "Mm... felt like a butterfly."

She rose and stepped back, pointing with her knife from Angel to the bed. "Get over there."

"Now?" His eyebrows shot up. "What about dinner?"

"Dinner can wait. Heaven can't."

"You sure about this?"

Mani set down the knife, sat on his wing canopy draped over her leaves, and put a finger to her lips. "Shhh..."

Angel crawled across the cave floor. "Captain, may I?"

"Shut up." She grabbed him by the collar, pulling him on top of her.

They transformed into Morpho and his newfound mate in the rainforest in his dreams. Arms and legs fluttered like wings. Fingers touched and tapped like antennae. Leaves shook and bounced beneath them. Angel's world went away and his world became Mani.

An eternity later, as they lay still, entwined, Angel wrapped around her body on the outside, Mani wrapped around his inside, the words of a friend floated through his mind. *Once you touch Asian skin, no other will ever do.* He knew now it was true. *And what a spirit is living inside her skin.*

They both knew in their hearts and souls this wasn't a one-night stand. It was a one-life stand. But with the nebulous uncertainty tomorrow held, neither of them knew how long that life might last.

RED
Countdown

By seven p.m. at Admiral Aviation, Red's shoulders ached and her palms itched. She paced around the condo, checking the spy camera screen that never changed, drinking too much oolong tea and avoiding the Glenfiddich bottle on the shelf, testing her smartphone to make sure it worked, again and again.

They should be done and gone by now. Why haven't they called?

At Aero Dynamic, nothing moved in the cube. Dietrich, Toma, and Hari sat unconscious in the dark, duct-taped to three stationary concrete chairs.

By eight p.m. in Red's condo, the aches had marched up to her head and set up camp where the tumor had been removed. She stood, she sat, she went outside and looked at the main gate, the sky, her watch.

Something went wrong. The limo broke down… No, Dietrich would have called… They never went to Aero. They stole the limo and the bombs and my money and left town. Fucking wankers.

At Aero, Dietrich stirred and raised his chin off his chest, slowly lifting his eyelids, but nothing changed. The cube was as black as the inside of his closed eyes. He couldn't tell where he was and couldn't speak through the tape wrapped around his mouth and head. The tomb smelled of death, or what was left of it. Eventually he could make out two dim red lights glowing across from him, slightly illuminating two seated figures, and a red glow below his vision. He looked down at his lap. An LED screen attached to a bomb counted down second by second. 3:58:23… 3:58:22… 3:58:21…

By nine p.m., Red felt winded from heavy breathing attacks one minute and spontaneous hyperventilation the next. Her lungs ached from the pounding of her heart. She dumped Scotch in her teacup and sat twitching on the couch, playing out every scenario she could fathom.

They're criminals. They disappeared like my father. They're dead. They had an accident like my mother. They're spineless miscreants. They chickened out… No, they're smart. They knew my plans wouldn't work. They saved themselves. They saved me. Thank God, I didn't have to press the red button.

At Aero, all three actors had awakened in their prison cube—a twelve-foot square underground dungeon with three-foot-thick concrete walls and ceiling, an inverse bomb shelter that stifled sounds inside instead of shielding explosions outside. They grunted and squirmed, trying to liberate their lips from the duct tape. Dietrich's raw wrists stung from chafing against the back of the chair as he struggled to free himself. The saliva Toma had to keep swallowing didn't ease the irritation in her parched throat. Hari needed to piss and pressed his shaky legs together but finally let it flow into his trousers. The urine odor seemed more visible than the numbers counting down their lives in their laps. 2:47:13… 2:47:12…

By ten p.m., Red decided nothing would happen tonight. Her production was a flop, but maybe a godsend. She felt helpless and searched for hope in Devika's words. Some of them soothed her anxiety, some slapped her on the side of her soul.

You might have misinterpreted the messages in your dreams. *"If you seek revenge, dig two graves."*

Red ran her dreams through her head, focusing on her current dilemma.

Butterfly Morpho was pinned on the forest floor. One boy picked him up and crushed his body. The second boy held the envelope. The third dropped it into the killing jar. Three young boys.

Three teenagers attacked innocent Tiger and were arrested while shoplifting.

Three men demolished Angel's Fakehouse. He whipped two and taped them to a tree. One dove into a ravine. All three were apprehended.

Then she remembered a message closer to reality.

Three terrorists ran from a house after a bomb accidentally exploded and destroyed the roof. One accidentally blew off his own legs with a grenade. No accidents, instant karma. I sent in three actors to get my revenge. I didn't heed the messages. I was destined to fail.

Quivering but temporarily inspired, Red brewed some ginger tea as Devika had suggested, spiced it with spirits of Scotch, and flipped through the booklet of Sanskrit chants she'd given her.

At Aero, hope had vanished. Discomfort grew into stabbing neck and back pain. Each actor sat silently in the dark, staring at darker corners in their minds as an ghastly fate stared back. 1:50:47… 1:50:46…

Around eleven p.m., Red went to the bedroom, rested her forehead on the glass of the grandfather clock, and stared at the swinging pendulum slicing off the seconds of her life. Exhausted and inebriated for the third night in a row, she gave up trying to figure out what she would do or what might come next. She collapsed onto the bed in the fetal position, clutching a cushion and a cliché.

Tomorrow's another day.

Murakan returned from his holiday gala, ready to play with the pets who'd strayed into his trap. Each carrying a flashlight, he and the Kakkar brothers descended the stairs into the cube. One bodyguard strong-armed the steel and-concrete door open; the other led the way into the darkness. Three flashlights shone into the beleaguered faces of the prisoners, each blinded by one beam, terrified by what might lurk behind it. Murakan's voice had a lilt to it, like an annoying game show host.

"You three have two choices: life… or death. You can either work for me, or continue working for Red Admiral… and be vaporized in…" He leaned over to see the LED in Dietrich's lap. "In thirty-three minutes and forty-two seconds."

Three mouths came alive, mumbling unintelligible words that stuck to the duct tape.

"You'll all be able to speak soon enough," Murakan said, "but I only want to hear one word from each of you—life or death." He put his hand on Hari's shoulder. "We can always use a driver. You played your part well."

He turned and squatted down between Dietrich and Toma, eye-level with their puffy red faces. "Ganesh speaks highly of you two and your unique skills. Your acting was authentic, and we can certainly find work for you scaling walls and fleecing the public. Juggling scarves, I'm not so sure."

Murakan chuckled as he stood, then instructed one of his bodyguards to peel the tape off their mouths while he finished his proposal.

"You passed your test today, but tomorrow is the final exam... should you select the appropriate word. It's quite simple. A tit for tat! Just return these devices to their owner at Admiral Aviation. No killing required or desired. Merely misplace them in three buildings. One of my associates will accompany you to make certain everything goes smoothly."

As the Kakkar brothers unwound the tape and mumbles struggled into words, Murakan sliced the musty air with his flattened hand.

"Silence! One word is all I have the patience to hear!" He was a small man, but his voice resounded in the tight space. The captives went quiet, stretching their mouths and licking their bruised lips. "Leave one device on the floor between them so they can all see it," Murakan commanded the Kakkars. "No need to waste two." He walked over to the doorway. "You have twenty-seven minutes to select your word... your destiny. Feel free to scream. I guarantee no one will hear you... or care a whit."

The guards closed the door and left them in the cube, now a little darker. One LED flickered on the floor. 00:26:09... 00:26:08...

Hari was the first to speak. "Life." Then shout, "Life!" Then howl, "Liiife!!!"

"Get a grip," Dietrich grumbled. "He can't hear you."

"Murakan is the devil," Toma said, eyes glazed.

Hari became a ventriloquist's dummy, his mouth flapping as if some internal hand controlled it. "I am a most excellent driver. I can be working for the devil. I can be driving anything with wheels. I like to wear socks that are matching my uniforms. I will—"

"Hari!" Dietrich barked. "Zip it! Lemme think for fuck's sake. He needs us... well, he wants us... for one job, maybe more. Who knows? He might be listening to us right now."

They talked until there was nothing left to talk about without words they didn't want Murakan to hear—until the five-minute countdown began. 00:05:00. The red zeros on the LED seemed to darken the cube and inflame their fears.

Hari had convinced himself that Murakan would never return and wept. Toma and Dietrich ignored him and professed their love for each other, for the life they'd shared together, for their daughter Christina.

00:01:00... Hari flipped between bawling, mumbling about his driving abilities, and shrieking. Toma prayed fervently, even though she'd never prayed before. Dietrich's shoulders heaved, arms straining against the tape, his torso lurching an inch to either side.

00:00:03... 00:00:02... 00:00:01... At the zero jackpot, nothing happened except a long beep from the bomb. They all sat motionless for ten seconds, not even breathing, expecting a blast... The door swung open.

Hari scream-wept, "Liiife!!! Life! Life..." and dropped his head onto his chest.

Murakan waltzed in between his bodyguards with Baldev following behind. "Good choice, Hari," Murakan said flippantly, then turned to Toma and Dietrich. "What's yours?"

They both whispered in unison. "Life."

"Excellent! Free them!" Murakan turned to his uncle and gave him the floor with a sweeping arm gesture. "They're all yours, Baldev."

Dressed in his customary shiny suit and tie, Baldev unwound the string on a manila envelope. "Soon you can shower and rest before your final exam tomorrow, but first I must show you our life insurance policies... more like death assurance policies for you. If you're silly enough to think about escaping, or stupid enough to divert from our plans..." He dropped a photo into Hari's lap. "Take a look at your mother, Lila, at home in Cochin with her new cleaning lady, sent by you in honor of her birthday tomorrow."

Hari stared at the print, puzzled.

Murakan weaseled in. "Quite ironic, really... our little Anima posing as a cleaning lady. An efficient servant, but so messy during her executions."

Hari's eyes went wild as he jumped up and started flapping again, drooling like a beagle puppy. "I am a most obedient servant. I will be pressing my uniform and polishing my shoes everyday. I will be shining the car keys."

"Good boy, Hari." Murakan petted the top of his head. "Now sit!"

Hari sat panting.

"Now stay," Murakan demanded.

Baldev dropped a stack of photos into Dietrich's lap. "You might like to see your daughter Christine in Kerala during this past week—at her school, the dance studio, your sister's home. Your decision and your actions will determine if she will be able to do the same next week."

"No. No. No. No." With each word, Toma's head jerked sideways as if deflecting any thoughts except Christine's cheery face. She adjusted her rumpled skirt and tugged at her deranged hair, her eyes pleading with Dietrich. "We'll do just as he says, right Dietrich? Exactly! Right?"

Dietrich wrapped his arms around her shoulders, scowling at Baldev and blowing a mental bullet hole through this new devil's head. "Yes, yes. Don't worry, sweet one. Nothing will happen to our angel."

"Smart," Baldev jabbed, his squint fencing with Dietrich's scowl. "I thought you'd understand."

Murakan took over. "Now off to your sleeping quarters, a step up from your current lodging. I've taken the liberty of having your clothes and belongings delivered from your hotel, compliments of Aero Dynamic, your new employer."

Hari heeled behind one Kakkar while the other herded Toma and Dietrich with his nightstick flashlight.

As he passed Murakan, Dietrich shoved a promise through his clenched teeth. "We'll be your German Shephards and do your dirty work for you."

"Marvelous!" Murakan said, clapping his palms together. "Of course you will!" Then he turned deadly serious, speaking down to Dietrich as he looked six inches up at him. "You will fetch when I say fetch. You will roll over when I say roll over. You will shit when I say shit. And now…" He thrust his hand toward the door and pointed. "Go and lie down!"

MONA
No Hands on the Clock

MARCO THE SHEPHERD BOUNDED INTO THE BEDROOM AT DAWN with two tennis balls in his mouth and batted another with his paws while Mona packed her carry-on. He dropped the two wet ones at her feet and sat, proudly wagging his tail. He knew the routine. They were going on a trip, and Marco wanted to make sure his favorite toys came along.

"You sweet boy," Mona said, kneeling and wrapping her arms around his neck. "You have to guard this house and make sure Laura the librarian behaves. I'm going to miss you *every* minute of *every* day."

Marco whined, then followed her through the house like Shadow had done when she was a kid.

On the porch, Mona cuddled and Marco licked while Worker Ant and Queen Bea loaded the bags into the rental car. As they drove away to catch the plane in Monterrey, Marco let out a big dog sigh and slumped down by the front door, already waiting for her return.

Feeling like little Mona leaving home with her parents sitting up front, Mona pressed her forehead against the backseat window, tears streaming from her cheeks onto the glass. Once her Marco emotions subsided, she perked up.

"I remember riding home from church with Mama and Papa in Wisconsin when I was about six. Good lord, sixty-seven years ago!" She leaned forward and pointed through the windshield. "I told them I wanted to fly south to Mexico like the ducks in a V in the sky."

"Homeward bound!" Antonio said, one arm draped over the wheel.

"I don't know how I'd even heard about Mexico back then! It must be in my DNA, like a monarch who knows how to migrate back to where her great great grandmother lived."

After a quiet ten minutes, Mona shouted from the back seat in four different voices.

First, whining: "I'm thirsty!"

Second, lower: "I'm hungry!"

Third, frantic: “I have to go to the bathroom!”

Four, Mona, sixty-some years ago: “Mama, Billy’s looking at me!”

Bea turned to the rear. “What’s going on back here?”

“Oh, I’m just pretending to be me and my friends on a trip with my parents.” Voice two: “I’m bored.” Voice three: “Are we there yet?”

“Mona, you are the youngest old person I’ve ever met! What’s your secret?” Bea asked.

“It’s not Merlot.” She shook her head and sat back. “No. It’s all in your mind. People think they’re only one age—the latest one. As you get older, you have more options. I can be three, thirteen, thirty-three, fifty-three, depending on the situation or my mood. I have seventy-three choices!”

Everyone played somber and subservient through the U.S. border check, but lightened up on the Mexican side. An elderly officer peered through the open window at Mona, looked down at her passport in his hand, then back at her and smiled. “It says you’re seventy-three, señorita. You don’t look a day over fifty to me.”

“Mentiroso,” Mona grunted in Spanish. *Liar.* That caught the guard off-guard.

“No, no. I am being serious, Miss…” He looked at the passport again. “Miss Mona Arcade.”

“I’m only thirty-nine,” she smirked in English.

“Ho, ho, ho,” he chuckled, his dimples deepening. “Then you must have drunk too many Corona beers!”

“Merlot, gracias.”

“Well, Miss Mona, my name is Julio Alvarez. Stop here on your way back and we’ll drink a bottle together.” He winked and handed over her passport.

As Antonio pulled away, he grinned like Mona’s Papa in the rearview mirror. “He was hitting on you, Mona!”

“*She* was hitting on *him*!” Bea said. “Mona’s been a man magnet lately.”

“The clock’s ticking.” Mona fluffed up her shoulder pads. “Maybe it’s finally time to mate.”

She wanted to grab the clock and spin its hands into the future. She’d waited six decades to meet her penpal, and that moment was only six hours away. The car couldn’t get to the airport soon enough, nor could the plane fly fast enough.

They rented another car in Villahermosa, the capital of the state of Tabasco. Although the clouds bouncing on the flat horizon and the thick tropical climate and vegetation enchanted Mona, the fifty-mile drive to

Zarita's home outside of Teapa seemed to last an hour short of forever.

Petite and tidy with bright yellow walls and baby-blue trim, Zarita's adobe cottage nestled in a grove of fruit trees next to a brook babbling in Spanish and crooning corridos.

"You go in alone, Mona," Bea said, helping her out of the car. "It's beautiful here. We'll stroll around and soak it in, right outside if you need us."

Mona took a deep breath and walked toward the cottage.

The nurse waving in the doorway shouted, "¡Buenas tardes, señora Mona! ¿Cómo está?"

Mona knew enough Spanish small talk to get on with most anyone. "Muy bien, gracias. ¿Y usted?"

"Bien, gracias." The nurse held Mona's shoulders and kissed her on both cheeks. "I am Landa. Zarita is so happy to see you. ¡Por favor, entre!"

"How is she, Landa? I was a nurse for many years. Tell me the truth."

"Zarita is a strong woman, but her heart is weak. She will not eat. She is ready to go home, but waiting for you."

"Thank you for your honesty. I've known her most of my life, though we've never met. I'm so sorry she is going, but we'll honor her journey and send her off with joy."

Landa led Mona into Zarita's blue bedroom, a cozy space adorned with Maya temple rubbings, photographs of archeological digs at Palenque, and a floor-to-ceiling mural of the Galactic Butterfly painted on the wall at the foot of the bed. Zarita lay peacefully, her eyes closed. Mona's heart soared and sighed and soared again as she sat on the bed and gently rested her hand on Zarita's.

"Am I dreaming, or have I died and gone to heaven?" Zarita's eyes opened slowly, lifting her lips into a smile. "My dearest friend… you are here."

"Yes, I am here."

For a few moments, they let their hearts speak through their eyes.

Then Mona murmured, her voice wavering, her other hand on her chest. "The pounding of my heart probably woke you up."

"I wasn't sleeping, only waiting." Zarita's smile widened. "Thank you so much for coming. You are busy I know."

"I'm seventy-three, like you. Not busy, just a busybody."

"My body is busy packing up to go."

"I know, dear." Mona squeezed her hand. "I'm so happy to see you, but so sad at the same time. I'm sure I'll follow you soon enough. Landa says you're not eating."

"No, I ate plenty in this life. I feel good being empty. I drink. I breathe.

Now I get energy from you."

"For sixty years I've wished for this moment. For sixty years I've sat on my little homemade stool Papa made me, facing south, reading your letters, imagining you in front of me." Mona shook her head and looked down. "Oh, why didn't I come before?"

"Because what we shared was so special, so simple. Beyond words, beyond the world."

"You're being a poet again."

Zarita let out a frail laugh. "No, no, just being. Did you bring paintings to show me?"

"One, and my sketchbook. But first... two friends are with me, wonderful young people who've been helping me. They're outside wandering through your lovely yard and haven't been to see their relatives yet. Do you mind if they come in to meet you for a moment?"

"Your friends are my friends." Her eyes turned concerned. "But Mona..."

"What is it, Zarita?"

"I do not want you to leave for even a minute. You can stay here. You and I can have a... What did you call it? You invited me to your house to sleep when we were fourteen for a... a what?"

"I remember... a slumber party."

"Yes, that was it! A slumber party. Partying while slumbering. That sounded fun."

"I'd like that," Mona sighed. "I was sorry you couldn't come, but I told my friends all about you and showed them your letters. Your English was pretty funny back then."

"So was your Spanish. You only knew the words taco, Zarita, and Mexico, and I think you pronounced Mexico wrong."

Mona went to get Bea, Antonio, and her bags. She told them she was staying; they understood. Once inside the bedroom Mona moved aside and nudged them ahead. "Zarita. Beatrice and Antonio Vega. Bea's the little one, Ant's the big one."

"I am so happy you are here! Please sit close to me. Mona tells me you are wonderful, so I think you are wonderful."

Antonio walked to the bed and pulled up a chair. Bea sat in his lap and spoke to Zarita in Spanish. It had been a few years, but it was like riding a bike. "I'm so glad to finally meet you. We're two members of the Mona Arcade Fan Club."

"Hmm," Mona hummed. "They must be the only two members."

"No, three members," Zarita said. "Me, too."

Antonio took Zarita's hand and rested his other hand on top of hers. "I feel like I already know you a little. Mona told me I should write a book about you two from your letters. I'm trying to do it… if you don't mind."

"Who wants to read about my silly life? Digging holes, getting dirty, collecting broken pots?"

"If I can write it well, many, I think. Mona named the book. It's called *Two Lives.*"

"Good luck then. Most of it should be about Mona. Maybe Landa will buy one… if you write it in Spanish."

"That's a good idea!" He bounced Bea on his knee. "Maybe my sweetheart will translate it."

"How much is it worth to you?" Bea asked.

"A thousand," Antonio said, eyes hinting at a different agenda.

"Dollars or pesos?"

"Massages."

"It's a deal."

"I'd like to read it," Zarita said with a faraway gaze, "but I do not think I can bring a book with me where I'm going. Nor will I have hands to turn the pages."

Antonio and Bea and Mona could have felt nervous and fidgeted and said things like, "Nonsense, you'll get better!" or "Don't even say that! Look on the bright side!" Instead, they let the compassionate silence speak.

Zarita already looked on the bright side, or perhaps at that fabled, white light at the end of the tunnel. Most likely she gazed at the bright stars surrounding the black hole in her own inner galaxy, or at the Galactic Butterfly on the wall symbolizing humanity's home galaxy, the Milky Way. To Zarita, death merely meant being born from one womb into another. In another form? She was ready to find out.

Mona finally found a few words. "Zarita, soon you will live in my heart and can read the words through my eyes."

"Sweet Mona. You always know the right thing to say."

"Dumb luck. Or maybe… 'Listen more. Speak less.'"

"I have books for you, but I cannot reach them," Zarita said, pointing. "Bea, will you please bring three of those blue books on that shelf?"

"Of course." She hopped up and got them.

"One for each of you. Mona said you will go to Palenque next. It is my favorite place in this world, and I wrote about it. Some parts are technical and boring, but the book might help you understand where you are."

"Thank you!" Bea exclaimed. "I'll treasure this forever."

"Forever," Zarita sighed. "We'll see what that means."

Antonio rose and put his hand on Zarita's shoulder. "You are a kind and remarkable woman. An inspiration to me, for sure. We'll let you two catch up on life."

"Thank you for coming to meet me," Zarita said, holding onto his fingers. "Please take care of my dearest friend."

"We will. I hope to see you again tomorrow."

After they left, Mona sat on Zarita's wide double bed. They talked about dreams realized and unfinished tasks, about life so far and what might come next.

"I did a lot in life, but I'm tired of doing," Zarita said. "And I'm just plain tired."

"I know how you feel."

"It's comfortable here, on my soft sheets and under my old blanket, and I don't want to get up anymore."

"I still get around okay," Mona sighed, "but getting up is a struggle for these old bones. They stick together if I sit too long and then snap, crackle, and pop like Rice Krispies when I try to get up."

"Most people are so afraid of death, but you know… I don't remember life being so bad before I was born."

"Me, either," Mona said, gazing at the Galactic Butterfly. "I suppose that's what some religions are for, to convince us we don't really die. I talked to one young lady who thought we all come back and live on Earth forever." Mona looked back at Zarita. "Can you imagine? Coming back to a mailbox full of unpaid bills? Having to do laundry forever?"

Zarita snickered, then closed her eyes, still smiling. "Please give me a few minutes to rest. My heart's either going wild or slowing down."

"Relax, dear. I'm here. Moment by moment."

Mona took hold of Zarita's hand and wrist, stealthily feeling her pulse with one finger. She'd been here so many times before, but never with a loved one like Zarita. Time slipped by as if she were watching a sunset, unable to see the movement of the sun, but knowing it's going down.

In a few minutes, Zarita's eyes fluttered open. "You said you have drawings. Please show me."

Mona retrieved her sketchbook from her suitcase and sat again.

"Lie down next to me so we can both see them," Zarita said. "There's plenty of room."

She helped her slide over and creaked into the bed. "Now you'll hear my bones break when I get up." Mona looked over at her sketchbook, just out of reach. "Mierda," she grunted in Spanish. *Shit.* "I forgot my sketchbook on the table. My memory's going fast." Mona got out of bed. "What was your name again?"

"Zarita. Sara in English. It means princess."

"See? I forgot that, too." Mona climbed back into bed with her drawings. "Okay, princess. Show and tell."

As they pored over the pages, the admirer showered the artist with compliments, as the artist brushed them off. Mona turned to the sketch of the woman in the hospital, drawn before getting Zarita's letter about her heart attack.

"That was my hospital room," Zarita marveled. "Exactly. Somehow you were there with me."

"Look. The clock has no hands. Spooky."

"No… real. Now my clock has no hands. Real spooky."

Mona flipped through other drawings of two teenagers in a pink VW Bug, the building exploding, the huge cocoon hanging from a branch in a dead tree. "I don't know where these sketches are coming from. Weird visions appear at any time, during the day, during meditation."

Zarita looked and listened intently, filled with love, weariness at bay. Mona told her about the photo Bea had taken of the monarch swarm on the tree and how she felt compelled to go there.

"The butterflies are calling you home," Zarita said quietly, her voice like an echo from beyond. "They are messengers from your infinite ancestors in the Galactic Butterfly."

"I feel you are right. Let me show you one more I created last night before we left, one that seems to tie everything together."

On her legs, bent up into an easel, Mona set the drawing of her reflection in the mirror, washed over and beyond the ink boundaries with vibrant water paints, like a child filling in the blank areas in a coloring book.

"Which one is you?" Zarita asked.

"I don't know. I feel like both of them."

They lay side by side, these friends forever, reading the quote that had inspired Mona's drawing, soaking in the wisdom between the lines and brush strokes, savoring the joy of sharing their wonder, their love.

Mona felt a shiver rise up her spine… no, a warm breeze from below, passing through her solar plexus, through her heart, through her neck, between her brain and her eyes, and out the top of her head. The room was still. The air, the leaves, and the dusk outside the open window were silent.

She turned her head. Zarita's eyes were closed, her lips curved into a serene smile, her chest at rest. Mona lifted her hand and gently checked Zarita's pulse. With a deep breath, she lay her head back on the pillow as the bubbling spring from her soul created pools of tears in her eyes that flowed down her temples like waterfalls.

ANGEL
Springing Time

By one-thirty a.m. they lay on the rise gazing down into the Ghost Zone—Mani in ninja black, Angel in green Ghost Soldier camo. He wanted to watch the routine and the changing of the guards at two a.m. and have plenty of time to secure the explosives before springing the prisoners right before dawn. Like spreading peanut butter into each corner of his toast, this task required patience and precision—as much time as it took. Uncommon for the season, the clear sky was a blessing. Rain would do Angel no good whatsoever.

"No gates, fences, or dogs, you say?" he whispered.

"Only around Khun P's mansion up the hill. Gated walls, at least four guards. I've heard barking up there."

"Only cares for Number One. Workers are his dogs."

At two-fifteen, Angel began to crawl backward. "I don't know how long it'll take to set my surprises. After you tell your bro to get the folks ready, ve-ry qui-et-ly, meet me back here. Call if you need me. Cellphones on vibrate only."

"I'm gonna vibrate your cells later, Angel baby."

Shooting Mani an A-OK sign, he slipped away with nine C-4s and a roll of det cord in his pack, pockets loaded with other tools of his trade, night goggles strapped to his head. His first target: the water tower in the east corner of the Ghost Zone, roughly a square—Khun P's mansion was to the north, worker and soldier's dorms to the west, guard huts and Barry to the south below the rise.

He had to time his trek precisely, ducking from bush to building, behind one roving guard, well ahead of the second walking the same circuitous route while constantly aware of the two guards' sight lines on the water tower. A concrete tripod supported the water tank and the guard lookout post beneath it. He secured and activated one C-4 pack on the leg facing the guard huts so the tower would fall in that direction. Another went on the bridge over the ravine which split the compound in half, two more under the petrol and propane tanks on two outside walls of the drug factory. *So far, child's play.*

Angel felt light on his feet, leftover buoyancy from their heavenly encounter earlier that night. He knew in his heart this was his last mission, that his life was at a turning point, but had to keep reining his mind back into the present. *Maybe I'll start a little paraglider flying school…*

Lurking behind a pickup in the parking lot, Angel let the second guard pass, then put a bomb under the truck, stuck four lengths of det cord into its plastic explosive core, and wrapped them around the wheels and up into the gas tanks of nearby vehicles. Angel checked his watch. *One hour gone. Four C-4s to go.*

Slinking over to the drug warehouse diagonally across from the factory, he placed two C-4s—one through an open window and one on the lean-to generator shed at the other end. He decided to save one for the escape trail, but couldn't resist the urge to leave another as a kick in Mister Ghost's groin, though it meant approaching the most heavily guarded area up a winding drive. It took another hour. *Fair karma trade. Bad guys crush my Honda; good guy blows up bad guy's Mercedes.*

At 4:29 Angel made it back to Mani and lay beside her on the rise. The Zone was still black, but the morning mist lurked like ghosts below.

"How're you doin'?" Angel asked.

"Butterflies in my stomach, but okay."

He glanced at his watch. "Thirty-minute countdown. You have a good hiding spot near the back of the worker dorm?"

"Yeah. The door leads to the toilets. Jungle on one side and behind. My escape route goes from there up to the rope ladder in a crevice in the ridge."

"Wait there until you see me take out the guard at the door, and then we'll spring your people. It'll be awhile."

"How can I help you?" Mani pleaded.

"Hey! You're saving thirty. I'm saving one. I can handle it. It's my job… my last official mission."

"Well, I hope so. Where'll we meet? Not the cave."

"I dunno," he said, shaking his head. "Down the valley by the Mekong, I guess. I'll call you when I get there."

"I *will* find you. I am *not* going to lose you."

"I'm counting on it." He took out a crumpled First Strike Ration label with scribbling on the back. "I wrote somethin' for you." His red face looked purple under the blue moonlight.

"When?"

"When I was invisible. Read it later."

"Is it a love note?"

"Maybe." He rolled onto his back and pulled her on top of him. "Can you see your reflection in my eyes?"

Mani looked hard, then gave up and gave him a kiss instead. "No, but like, I know it's there."

"You are the angel in this Angel's eyes."

"That is so sweet!" she whispered, kissing him again. "What a softie! Are you sure you can handle this mission?"

"For sure. It led me here and now leads me back to you."

They lay in each other's arms, soaking in the silence before the impending jungle storm as Angel demonstrated his newly acquired skill at butterfly kissing. Reluctantly pulling away, he removed the remote C-4 detonators from Mani's pack. He velcroed them to a wide strap, attached it around his stomach, snapped on his goggles, and crawled over the ridge. "See you at the dorm."

He retraced his steps to the water tower. A wooden stairway spiraled up the water outlet pipe between its three legs. For a minute, Angel watched the two guards above. *One's almost asleep, looking in; the other's dreaming, looking out.*

He slipped the Sig Sauer from his holster and screwed on the silencer, then crept up the stairs and onto the platform between them. The guard facing into the compound sat with his forehead on his folded arms on the railing, perfectly positioned for a dual chop in the brachial plexus nerve center on both sides of the neck. Angel tucked the pistol into his belt. *Too easy. Gently now. Don't kill him.*

The guard slumped to the floor as Angel darted around to the other side of the lookout and jammed the Sig's muzzle into the second guard's preoccupied temple. "Don't move and you live. Speak and you die."

Angel's command of the Lao language was minimal, but short succinct sentences worked best, anyway.He moved in front of the guard, who stared, mesmerized, into the silencer tube. Angel saw he was only a kid, twenty maybe, knees shaking, eyes aghast, likely horrified being confronted—in his mind—by a real, live, goggle-eyed alien. *Poor boy. Looks like he might shit himself.* "I only want the prisoner. Do as I say and you'll be okay."

The kid nodded like a perpetual motion rocking chair.

Angel tranquilized the first guard with his syringe gun to keep him comatose. He ripped off a length of duct tape stuck to his pant legs. "Wrap this around your mouth and head."

The kid did it, still nodding.

"Now carry him down the stairs, slowly, quietly." *Fuckin' A. This'd be so much simpler if I could just kill someone. Safe on the ground behind a bush, rifle, scope, silencer...*

With Angel's pistol on his neck and the unconscious guard draped over his back, the kid stepped down the stairway, then walked twenty-five yards into the brush.

"Put him down and lie next to him." Angel stuck the syringe into his neck. "Sorry, kid. Time for beddy-bye," he sighed in English, then waited for him to drift away.

No one here seems to expect anything but mosquitoes. Eliminating the roving guards was textbook work. Tranquilizer dart from his blowgun while hidden in bushes, Marine rear take-down tactics, duct tape mouth, tie arms and legs tight with Kevlar fiber canopy line that eats through skin if given half a chafing chance.

Angel tucked away his goggles, donned a guard's hat and jacket, and then slung the AK-47 over his shoulder. *Four down, five to go. Dorm guard on deck.*

Angel took the four-inch combo flashlight/stun gun from its sleeve on his hip—4.5 million volts of power with 160 lumen LED beam capable of temporarily blinding eyes. Its baton-shaped, black aluminum alloy body was a weapon in itself. Sticking to the standard roving security route, he sauntered around the corner of the dorm, hiding in plain sight. He veered casually toward the guard seated by the door, greeted him, and blazed his eyes with the beam. As the man's hands flew up to his face, Angel slammed the flashlight down onto the guard's knee, and then up into his chin. *Goodbye. Hope I don't see you later.*

Mani ran up as Angel syringed the guard to sleep, grabbed the keys, and opened the dorm door. Her brother emerged first and hugged her right off the ground.

"Meet my bro, Somjai," Mani said.

Angel stumbled through "Nice to meet you" in Lao or Thai. He wasn't sure which.

Somjai gave Angel a respectful wai, bowed, and said, "Thank you, thank you, thank you."

"Gotta go. Daylight's on its way." He turned to Mani and wrapped her in his arms, whispering in her ear. "Get 'em outta here. Barry's next, and all hell might break loose. By the way, I think I love you."

"Don't think. Feel."

"Okay, fine. I feel I love you. See you soon."

He smiled, pecked her on the lips, and was off. Angel now faced his most challenging task and hadn't quite figured out how to handle it. His theme song wafted through his mind.

To fight for the right
Without question or pause
To be willing to march into Hell
For a heavenly cause

As Angel strolled on the security route, he saw Barry's twenty-by-fifteen-foot wooden prison house on stilts, facing away from him toward the bend in the road. One sentinel at each rear corner, one in front, and he hoped, only one inside. *Don't fancy hand-to-hand combat with nine remote detonators strapped to my stomach.*

A brainstorm struck as he thought of the first time he'd met Mani. *Snake.* He took a pack of Marlboros out of his pocket, reserved for close encounters of the friendly kind, and unsnapped the mace-gun holster on his belt. Amazon's website said one cartridge delivered seven 25-foot blasts.

Pausing three feet from the nearest corner guard, he asked in Lao, "Cigarette for a light?" Angel held up the pack. "Marlboro?"

The guard grinned.

Angel handed one over and stuck another between his lips. The man shielded the breeze with one hand, lit his Bic with the other, and brought it up to the cig. Angel jerked to the side, staring behind the guard, visibly alarmed. "Cobra. Don't move."

The guard froze and slowly turned his head. Angel whipped out the mace gun and shot him in the eyes. He grunted, fingers flailing over his face, then took a swift kick in the gonads. Angel dropped to the ground with him as the second corner guard started toward them. "Stay back. Spitting cobra."

King cobras were terrifying enough, but a spitting cobra could nail its victims from six feet away, potentially blinding them permanently. The other corner guard stopped short, ten feet from Angel, well within the range of his mace gun. One long burst and he was eyeless as well. Two baton blows to the sightless sentinels' temples and both men were out cold. Angel looked at his newest toy with approval. *Not bad, Amazon. Eighty-four bucks online.*

Slipping underneath the house between its stilts, Angel lay in wait for the front guard who must have heard the grunting and groaning. *Which way'll our third little piggie come? Left? Nope. Right.*

He watched two feet tip-toe along the house and step around the corner to the rear. Halfway along the back wall, the creeping guard kneeled beside his fallen comrades.

Angel grabbed the guard's ankles and yanked him under the building, dragging him facedown in the gravel. He sprang onto the guard, pinning him to the ground, and pressed the stun baton into the back of his neck. It crackled like a spark on steroids as the man's arms and legs spasmed. *Enough. Don't want cardiac arrest. Just guard at rest.*

He'd hoped that Barry's chaperone inside the house would join the backyard party as well, but no luck. He stole up the front porch steps and to the door. *Locked. Now what? Hmm. Snake scene, take two.* Angel lay on his stomach and knocked, moaning in Lao. "Help. Help me. Snake bite."

Nothing.

He moaned louder, scratching the door with his fingers. "Help, please, help."

The lock clicked, the door cracked open, and the muzzle of an AK-47 stuck out.

Angel lifted his head and let it smack back down. "Help me. Snake bite."

As the guard took one tentative step out the door, Angel rolled over, spraying the man's entire head and neck with mace. He took the groaning man down with a leg kick, delivered a temple blow with the butt of the mace gun, and hauled him through the door.

Barry sat in a six-foot square bamboo cage, dazed as if he'd just emerged from a coma, naked except for stained shorts. Red bruises and blistered cigarette burns spotted the baby-white skin on his fullback body.

That's the exact cage I saw in my dream, only I was in it. "Barry," Angel whispered, kneeling to search for the keys in the guard's pockets. "Barry!"

"Wha… What's happening?"

"I'm Angel. DEA Jonathan sent me. I'm gonna get you outta here."

"It's about time," he mumbled.

About time? Fuck you and the horse's ass you rode in on! Stuffing his ire, Angel unlocked the cage door and graciously offered candy to the stranger. "Chew on a couple of these Soldier Bars, buddy. They'll perk you up, and they taste good, too." Angel pointed to a gallon jug. "Is this drinking water over here?"

"Yeah." Barry crawled out and creaked up, favoring one leg. He couldn't stand or lie straight in the cage.

Angel guessed Barry's body specs while mixing him an electrolyte drink in a plastic cup. *Six-foot-three, 240 pounds. IQ: minus 11. Personality: brick.*

"Barry, my man. This Gatorade'll get you goin'. I've got some clean fatigues stashed in the brush outside. Eat and drink up, and I'll be back in two shakes."

"Thanks."

He is a hippo. A limping hippo. Angel sprinted to the bushes and back, uneasy about Barry's leg, the mist lifting and dawn slipping in. *God help me! If I have to carry him, we're both dead meat.*

Once back in the prison house, he set a canvas bag in Barry's lap. "Pants, shirt, boots and socks, thanks to Mr. DEA Doug in Thailand who has a chauffeur and a chopper waiting to escort you out of this shithole."

"Thanks."

Impressive. So far he's said eight words. Might of reached the end of his vocabulary. "Okay, Barry. I only have time to brief you on the plan once, so listen up. One—a GPS bug is pinned in your pants pocket so Doug knows where you are. Two—here's a GPS locator for the chopper extraction point in case we get separated. That bug's in a tree next to a dry rice paddy where it should land. Three—once we leave the perimeter of the compound, stick close and follow in my footsteps, literally. I've booby-trapped the trails to slow down the soldiers. Four—I'd like to sneak out nice and quiet, like church mice wearing slippers. Five—we're outta here in five minutes, period. Now, I've gotta check on something, but I'll be back in three minutes. Stay inside and get your shit together. Both our lives are on the line." *And the lives of thirty others.* "Okay?"

"Roger that," Barry grunted.

"Any questions?"

"No."

Angel sprinted up to the worker dorm with the AK-47 on his shoulder. The guard was still a lump and Mani's people had slipped away. *Good. All quiet on the northern and western fronts.*

He took out his phone to send Nat an SMS and punched in, "Ass…" He wanted to end the first word there, but finished it. "Asset recovered. ETA to extraction point: one hour."

As he walked back, assuming his masquerade as the roving guard, compassion seeped in. *Give Barry a break. Think about what he's been through. Put yourself in his shoes, even though they'd fit like canoes.*

He'd hoped to escape undetected, but seeing the brutality inflicted on Barry's body made him shudder and reconsider his plan. He thought of Mani's imprisoned people and the other innocent pawns under the spell of Mister Ghost, and the sorrow of all their families. *If I leave the bombs intact, I've only delivered more powers of destruction into the hands of a maniac. No, we're gonna have a fireworks display and knock him down nine notches.*

Approaching the end of the dorm, Angel heard shouting ahead. He looked across the road past the prison house to see three half-dressed Ghost Soldiers brandishing weapons at the last guardhouse. *Fuck, fuck, fucking fuck!*

Backed into the far corner of the porch, Barry clutched a guard to his chest with one arm and a machete to the man's throat with the other.

RED
Squashed

Red awoke exhausted at eight A.M. after a fitful night's sleep plagued with dreams of drowning, trying to fly a duster underwater, and whirlpools dragging her down. As she mulled them over in bed, their meaning became clear. *I'm in way over my head and the tide keeps rising. Get out. Baldev wanted to buy this place. If I meet him face-to-face, maybe he'll make me a better offer.*

The phone rang, and Red plodded out of the bedroom to answer it. "Admiral Aviation. How may I help you?"

"I'm Lata Dhawan, manager at Cotton Crops, Ltd. We are needing aerial application, today if possible."

"I'm sure we can assist you," Red said, surprised to hear from them. "What's your immediate problem?"

"Many hectares are infested with bollworms."

"I believe we have the required pesticides in stock and two dusters for delivery. I'll have to check with my warehouse, but I must ask… aren't you currently a client of Aero Dynamic Enterprises?"

"We are, but they're too busy to respond to our needs."

Self-satisfaction glimmered in Red's eyes. "I see… We can take care of you. May I have my scheduling manager ring you back in a few minutes?"

"Yes, please. I'll be waiting for the call."

Red hung up and pressed the intercom button. "Good morning, Azeez. How are you?"

"I am doing fine, Miss Red. And you?"

"Chipper. Do we have bollworm insecticide and two dusters free today?"

"Yes, I am thinking we do, Miss Red."

"Then call Lata Dhawan at Cotton Crops and schedule an application. Now." Red smiled, drumming her fingers on the desk. *Well, well. Perhaps Murakan's karma has caught up with him.*

Azeez had the dusters fueled, filled with chemicals, and ready on the tarmac by ten. Two pilots taxied away as Red walked up behind Azeez.

"Hello, what's this? Who's flying that first duster? That's not Jay, is it?"

Startled, Azeez whirled around to face her. "No, it is a pilot named Ravi, Miss Red. Jay is sick but sent over a friend to replace him."

"He may be a pilot, but is he a crop duster?"

"Yes, yes. He has even been flying for Cotton Crops before and will show Amit the way." Azeez' cell phone rang in his pocket, but he didn't answer.

"Bollocks!" Red griped. "This could be a big client for us. He'd better be good."

"It is the best we can do on short notice." His phone continued to ring.

"If you say so, I suppose I'll have to trust you. Azeez, answer your phone."

"Whoever it is, I will call them back."

"By the way, did you figure out what you wanted to tell me after our little skirmish yesterday?"

"No. Yes. I… I mean no, Miss Red."

"No, yes, no? What do you mean, anyway?"

"Yes, but no, not right now, Miss Red." His phone rang again. Azeez looked at the screen and rejected the call.

"What's wrong with you? Take it. Maybe it's important… another client."

"No, no, no. It is only a friend," Azeez said, agitated.

"Have you been wearing your mask while handling the chemicals?"

"Yes, Miss Red, always."

"I think I'll make an appointment with Dr. B for you."

Azeez wiped his forehead with his sleeve. "No, no, I am feeling fine."

"Well, stay out of the sun. I'll be in the bedroom. I'm knackered today."

His phone rang again as Red walked away.

The recent days and nights had taken their toll, wiping out her energy bank account. Scotch seemed to have eaten a hole in her digestive system. She napped on and off, awakened by the rumbling in her stomach or to the sound of distant thunder.

In the gatehouse, Azeez' cellphone harassed him like a swarm of malaria mosquitoes. He sat and stared out the gatehouse window, sweating by the air conditioner, waiting for the dusters to return and the backlash of not answering the phone calls.

Late that afternoon, while brewing a cup of tea, Red picked up her smartphone to check the spy camera at Aero, now an automatic reflex. All day it had only shown workers and pilots doing their normal routine. This time the screen displayed the image of a woman in a sari. Confused, Red pressed buttons to make certain she'd connected to the camera. The same image reappeared. Scrutinizing the screen, Red realized it was her, in her red-and-black patterned sari and scarf, standing in Lodhi Park. She froze as still as the photo of Scarlett O'Hare looking back at her.

Inside the gatehouse, Kamal started barking and pacing in circles. Azeez leaped up and pressed his head and hands against the window. A white limo had turned onto the road leading to the main gate of Admiral Aviation. By the time it stopped in front of the gate, Azeez was slinking around the perimeter of the grounds with the bulldog at his heels.

Dietrich and Toma got out of the limo and tried to roll the mesh gate to the side, but it was electronically locked. Dietrich leaped onto the hood, then Toma climbed onto his shoulders and made her way over the barbed wire at the top. She jumped to the ground, picked up a rock, smashed the window in the gatehouse door, unlocked it from the inside, and searched for the gate opener.

Red heard the sound of breaking glass, threw on jeans, slipover, and a scarf, then ran to the office/living room as Azeez flung open the front door.

He stood shaking in the entryway, gripping the door frame with both hands. "Miss Red! They are here! Hurry! We must run!"

"Who's here?" She had never seen such horror on his face.

"They kidnapped my sister they threatened to hurt her they made me follow you and tell them where you were going." Azeez couldn't talk fast enough. He slapped his hands to the sides of his head and pushed his fingers up through his hair. "I have been lying to you Miss Red I'm sorry. I was not knowing what to do I was so scared."

"Who?" she demanded. "Who threatened you?"

Cowering behind her ankles, Cat Astrophe arched his back, hissed, and fled into the bedroom.

"Bug Murakan Baldev. They drugged me and took me to Aero. Bug made me let him into your condo that night. He made me follow you to Lodhi Park—"

A soft, fleshy thunk dismembered the rest of the sentence. Azeez' eyes blinked as his body jerked and wavered, arms dropping to his sides. Red lurched forward to catch him, but he fell into her outstretched hands and slipped facedown onto the floor.

She dropped to her knees, shouting desperately. "Azeez! What's wrong? Azeez!" Spotting the thin dagger stuck in his upper back, she raised her gaze to the black stick figure standing four feet outside the doorway.

Bug. Red's eyes tightened into slits. "You. You..." she whispered, the syllables sliding out like two fangs from her gums.

"We meet again, Miss Red Admiral." He lifted his arm as if to shake hands and greeted her with a gun. "Get up."

She didn't budge, a red fox protecting her cub.

"Leave him... now!" he shouted, punctuating his command with the subcompact Beretta.

She glared beyond the barrel into his inert eyes and backed away.

Bug stepped over Azeez's body, hissing, "Sit on the couch behind you."

"A knife in the back of an innocent boy?"

"No, a spy like you."

"Why?" she pleaded. "Why!?!" she wailed.

"He served his purpose."

Red's voice descended into a low growl. "And what's your purpose, you fucking monster?"

"To return your misplaced devices. To bounce your karma back at you. To deliver you into your future."

A cell phone buzzed in Bug's pocket. He stared at Red as he took the call. "Hari! The plan has changed. You need to put the bomb in another location. Call me when you're in the warehouse and have it in your hands."

"Are Dietrich and Toma here, too?"

"You mean Melanie and Mason? Friends of Scarlett in her saris, Miss-cast Red Admiral? Welcome to act three of your child's play, though your actors have new scripts written by Murakan and Baldev. They're *our* actors now. Murakan's spy camera in your limo has been an amusing sitcom. Your exploding props from Ganesh would never have popped. He only sells them. Murakan makes them."

Abashed and seething inside, Red wrenched her emotions into survival mode. *Danny's three rifles in the case behind the desk. Revolver in the drawer.*

Bug sat in the chair at the front of her desk, his Beretta trained on Red, and took a three-by-five-inch metal box from his bag. "Detonation switches. You'll soon see how they work."

"What do you want?"

"You know what we *want*, and will *get*, whether you're alive or..." Bug slapped his palm on the desk. "...dead, like crushing your little namesake, a Red Admiral butterfly, Miss Dead Admiral. That choice is yours."

"Dirt. Fucking men and their fucking dirt."

"Yes, your microscopic piece of dirt in the middle of Baldev's massive project. It will be ours, today by your hand or tomorrow after your death. Your only heir, this street urchin on the floor, is gone. Your two dusters are already at Aero Dynamic. These buildings must come down eventually, so we're just removing them ahead of schedule."

Bug's phone buzzed, and he flipped up the first safety catch on the detonator box. "Are you in the warehouse with the device, Hari?" Bug smirked at Red. "Excellent work. Cheers." He pushed the red button as casually as turning on a hall light at home. The floor vibrated as the blast set off a chain of chemical explosions.

Through the windows, Red watched the warehouse mutate into a billowing thunderhead of smoke with lightning flames flashing upward. She covered her face with her hands. Hari hadn't been just a hired hand. She'd grown fond of him and his cheery smile. Peeling her palms off her cheeks, she spoke like the devil herself. "I will see you die."

Bug laughed at her words and fierce delivery. "Oh, Miss-erable Red Admiral! So much like your Daddy Danny and Mommy Chandra. They could've so easily saved themselves and sold Baldev the business… but nooo… sooo stubborn."

Red knew the answers to questions she'd sought for so long but never dared uncover were a few heartbeats away. She just had to suck them out of this beast. He was so full of himself, some of them had to leak.

"So Danny wouldn't sell, and you killed him?"

"Oh, no, no. Danny disappeared in the cube at Aero."

"The cube?" Red asked like a little girl in class.

"Murakan's bomb shelter. It keeps the sounds of deadbeats underground… and vaporizes them."

"Chandra wouldn't sell and you disposed of her, too?"

"I never touched her." Bug threw up his hands halfway, as if he'd just been half-arrested. "I might've hired a cement truck that day to disrepair the bridge…"

Red sat stone still, the answers to her questions fusing into one sentence. *Baldev gave the order, and these assassins killed both of my parents.* She felt like a volcano on a lonely island under attack by pirates. Magma boiling so far down, for so long, searched for a way to the surface. Devika's words didn't work anymore and needed a twist. *"If you seek revenge, dig two graves." Two so far… three more to go.*

She groped for some clue about what Danny would do, and it came to her in a flash from the past.

"Lemme show you the new addition to my desk," Danny had announced in his workshop. "Someday it might save my life… or yours. You know in movies where the good guy has to sign something at his desk while the bad guy sits in front of it, watching to make sure he doesn't take a gun out of the drawer…?"

He'd replaced the wide drawer with two narrow ones. In a compartment he'd built between them, Danny rigged a twenty-gauge, short-barrel shotgun with a series of levers so both barrels could be fired simultaneously by shoving a pen through a small hole in the right side of the desktop. Its muzzle hid behind filigree on the front of the heavy rosewood desk. *He planned for this moment! Act four, new script.*

Red looked at Bug in the hot seat, centered in front of her desk cannon. Channeling her inner inferno into tears, she began to weep.

Bug's phone buzzed again. "Have you placed your device? Good girl. Join Dietrich in the condo hangar."

"No, not Toma! Nooo!" she cried. "No more killing! It has to stop! I can't take it anymore!"

Red pounded her fists on the cushions and then paused. She pulled off the scarf to reveal her bald scalp and spoke in low tones, head down. "You win. You can have the land. It's only a bloody graveyard now. Give me something to sign."

Bug smiled like a cat batting a crippled mouse crouching in the corner. "Finally Miss-guided Red Admiral has come to her senses!" He dug out a document and gestured behind him with the gun. "Of course, the price has dropped with the imminent destruction of your buildings."

"Let's get this over with," Red whimpered. She struggled to her feet, bracing herself on the couch and the wall, then staggered behind the desk.

As she plopped onto the seat, Bug placed the document in front of her and leaned back in the chair. "Keep your hands up where I can see them."

Still sobbing, Red lifted the gold Montblanc from its holder, slipping the weighted base forward to expose the trigger hole. With her left elbow on the desk, her hand holding her forehead and covering her brow, she pretended to scan the document as the pen in her right hand hovered above the opening. With eyes fixed on the hole, she spoke the first two words softly, the rest rising into a scream.

"You have misread Miss Red Admiral, you fuck!!!"

And plunged the pen down.

The deafening discharge reverberated in the room. Bug flew backward in the chair, his knees, groin, and stomach torn apart by the shot. Thrashing on the ground like a giant centipede ripped almost in half, he dropped the Beretta to clutch his mangled flesh.

Red's pent-up rage erupted. Leaping to her feet with fiery adrenaline surging through her body, she shoved the desk forward, tilted it up onto its front legs, and let it fall onto the squirming Bug. The crunch of his rib cage silenced his howling. Red dashed around the desk, grabbed the gun off the floor, and pointed it between his eyes. An image flashed into her head. *He's pinned like Morpho on the forest floor.*

"I told you before that bugs can be squashed."

A gasp squeezed out the grimace of agony and disbelief on Bug's face.

"For Mommy Chandra." Red shot a third eye in the middle of his forehead. Aiming the Beretta at his heart, now with real tears overflowing down her cheeks, she fired five shots into his chest. "For Danny Boy."

MONA
Picnic at the Palace

Part of Mona died with Zarita. For hours she lay beside her friend with one foot mentally in her own tomb. Both of their lives passed through Mona; their words and the different worlds they'd created sharing the spotlight in the darkness.

She remembered her parents' swan song and understood how Papa must have felt after Lily's heart gave up. He wasn't the same—incomplete—just counting sheep, chores, and seconds until the end, or the beginning. Marco put his affairs in order, sent Christmas cards, and delivered gifts to friends and relatives. Then one evening, resting in his oak rocking chair, he went to sleep, peacefully joining his other half for the holidays.

The morning after Zarita's passing, Mona felt half hollow, as if only two valves of her heart were pumping. Antonio and Bea drove past the ambulance in the driveway and heard the news from nurse Landa at the front door. They found Mona in the living room, a mere shell on the sofa.

Bea hugged first and spoke next. "We're so sorry to learn about Zarita."

"I felt her leave her body with joy… in the midst of a quiet moment together." Mona gazed through them as if they were holograms. "I'll take her with us in my heart."

"Me, too," Antonio said. "I'm glad we met her."

"I'm going to stay here until tomorrow morning with Landa. And soak up Zarita's spirit."

"You want company?" Bea asked.

"No, no, you two go exploring. She said that the Grutas del Coconá is an enchanting cavern with stalagmites, stalactites and an underground river."

"Okay, will do. We'll check in on you later."

Mona helped Landa turn the hospice back into a home and fasten the traditional black wreath on the front door. Relatives were on their way for the *velorio*, a ritual wake that might last for days. She pressed her face into the clothes hanging in the closet to refresh her senses with Zarita's denim work shirts, lingering cologne, and the ancient dirt she'd dug for decades.

Later, at the plank picnic table under the bougainvillea arbor, she sketched Zarita's cottage and life to etch the memories in black and white. Flashes of iridescent blue and camouflage brown dancing through the air caught her eye. A blue morpho fluttered around Mona's head, as if trying to glimpse the drawings over her shoulder. After landing and lifting off and tapping the tabletop and lightly fluttering up again, the morpho butterfly finally landed like a baby bird with fledgling feathers. She climbed onto the sketchbook, fanning her wings calmly, showing off the sapphire above and owl eyes on the underside.

"You forgot to say goodbye last night, eh?"

Mona's murmurs soothed her delicate visitor, who seemed to rock backward and look up.

"That's okay… you just drifted away. I felt you go… I'm a little jealous." Mona leaned down, resting her elbows on the table, head in her palms. "You look good in blue, as usual… your favorite color."

The butterfly's antennae swayed, seeking smells and sensing the position of the sun. She rose up, flapping her new wings leisurely as if waving goodbye, then flitted away through the trees alongside the brook.

That evening Mona toured the bedroom shelves and discovered her original sixty years of letters, all written by her hand on yellowed note book paper, flowered stationery, butterfly cards, magazine articles, or on anything she'd deemed fit for script. She read deep into the night, resting on the bed under the old blue blanket, laundered over the years into a thin cotton sheet, with Zarita lying inside her.

When Antonio and Bea arrived early the next morning, Mona was poring over her sketches under the arbor.

"No moping, no mourning," Mona sighed, dragging her cheeks into a smile. "Zarita told me she wanted cheers, not tears."

They stood in front of her in their twin bright-blue tropical shirts and jeans—Antonio's arm around Bea's shoulder, hers around his waist.

"You look like two blue morpho lovers." Mona shook her head and reconsidered. "No, the females are always bigger than the males."

"Sometimes I feel like Beatrice is bigger." Antonio helped Mona rise from the bench. "You don't wanna mess with her."

"That's exactly what Papa Marco said about Mama. But then, she had a rifle in her hands."

As they prepared to leave, Landa hugged Mona and handed her an envelope. "I forgot to give you this letter Zarita wrote in case you didn't get here in time. You were the flame of her candle in the window."

"And you have been wonderful, full of wonder, exactly what we both needed. Gracias and good luck to you."

"¡Buena suerte, también! Hasta luego."

Mona climbed into the backseat of the rental car. "Okay, Azeez. Take us to bucket list number two."

"Azeez?" Antonio asked, turning toward her.

"Azeez? What do you mean?"

"I mean Azeez. You just called me Azeez."

"Did I?" Mona turned red. "Huh. Well, it's a nice name. It means friend in Hindi."

"I didn't know you spoke Hindi," Bea said.

"I don't. I just know."

Bea and Antonio glanced at each other, raising their eyebrows as they started down the drive.

On their way to the neighboring state of Chiapas, the trio lingered at overlooks through the Tumbalá mountain foothills and in village street markets to watch everyday people doing everyday things.

Zarita's book never left Bea's hand, and she routinely instructed her two students during the ride. "Okay, class. Listen up! Zarita is our guide today. 'The magnificent yet middle-sized Maya city of Palenque flourished in the seventh century. After its decline, Mother Nature reclaimed the land, absorbing its towers, temples, roads, and aqueducts into a dense jungle of cedar, sapodilla, and mahogany trees. The lost city wasn't rediscovered for another 1,000 years.'"

"Outstanding," Antonio said. "A lost, deserted city like Atlantis… or Gary, Indiana."

"We could spend a week at Palenque." Bea's excitement escalated the more she learned. "The excavated ruins are within one square mile, but that's less than ten percent of the city. The jungle still covers hundreds of buildings!"

During the whole trip, Mona didn't say much, only stared. She seemed a little off. Off in another world.

Around noon, they wandered across the parking lot through cool air so humid it seemed half a percent shy of a drizzle. Inside the cleared area, the trio felt tiny, standing in the grandeur of the ruins, spellbound by the ancient city—a sleeping beauty that had thrived for 1,000 years, then slumbered for 1,000 more. The Palace of Pakal commanded their view with its four-story Observation Tower jutting above its grounds, with a water pressure system and saunas for royalty hidden below. The landscaped plazas and towering jungle surrounding the site were as emotionally powerful as the ruins themselves. At the clearing's edges, thick vines twisted like boa constrictors crushing tree trunks, then intertwining up the branches into spidery webs.

Mona checked her site map. "I want to go up there," she said, pointing at the steep stairway leading up a taller structure to the right. "The Temple of the Inscriptions. Zarita's favorite spot. The funerary monument of Hanab-Pakal."

"Think you can make it?" Antonio asked.

"We'll see."

They started up the stairway together, but soon Mona lagged fifteen feet behind and below with an umbrella for a cane.

"Angel!" she shouted. "Mani!"

Antonio and Bea glanced to the sides, then behind to see who Mona was calling. "Who's Angel?" he asked, climbing down toward her.

"You're Angel," Mona said, then looked at Bea. "He's your angel, right, Mani?"

"Sure, Mona, always." Bea followed Antonio down to Mona. "But who's Mani? Not me."

Mona was puzzled. "Mani means gem or jewel."

"Not in Spanish," Bea said. "Gem is gema or joya."

"No." Mona paused and sat on the step. "In Sanskrit."

"Sanskrit? Like in India? You speak Sanskrit?"

"No, but I know it's a name in Laos, too. And the spirit of the moon in Old Norse mythology.

Bea felt her forehead. "Are you okay, Mona?"

"Having visions... like I told you before. They just seem more real now."

Antonio frowned and suggested heading for their hotel.

Mona objected. "No, I... I feel fine. If you were really Angel, you'd have a chopper waiting to take us to the top of the mountain."

"A chopper?" he asked. "Like a motorcycle?"

"No... a helicopter."

By now, they were all deeply puzzled.

Mona spoke through the wordless discomfort. "Just help me climb. We'll make it. I'm not dizzy. I'm not going to faint. I truly like my visions. They seem more real than reality, whatever that is."

It took forty-five minutes to get to the pillared monument on top, a mini-Parthenon, but the view and the climb took their breath away and didn't give it back for several minutes. The clouds were so close Antonio and

Bea tried to hang on them. Regal tombs and temples atop step pyramids seemed to stare up at them with disapproval. The Temple of the Jaguar… the Count… the Cross… the Skull… Structure XII with a bas-relief carving of the god of Death.

Mona seemed herself again and pulled out an envelope. "Zarita left me a letter with Landa before we arrived. I haven't read it yet, and if you want, I'll share it with you."

"I'd be honored," Antonio said.

"I'd like that a lot," Bea echoed. "I'll prepare the picnic."

Mona unfolded the crisp paper carrying Zarita's shaky handwriting and read aloud, her legs dangling down to the first step.

My dearest friend, Mona,

You are on your way. You may not make it before I am gone, but you are already here. I love you like a dog. (That looks funny when I read it again, but you are a dog person, and I know you feel the same way about Shadow, Chipper, Merlot, and Marco.) I loved all my dog friends from the moment they came into my life until the day they left, and every moment afterwards.

Mona paused to wipe her eyes. "Zarita said no tears. Right. Fat chance."

"You had a dog named Merlot?" Bea asked.

"My graceful girl. An Irish setter, auburn with the hue of Merlot, vintage 1984." Mona read on.

I have neglected to send these words about you and the day you were born. If some of my associates or the Maya elders read them, they would shake their heads, but I listen to ancient words passed down, and to modern scientific writings, and to all their interpretations along the way.

The inspiration for these words comes from those who resonated with José Argüelles, born in Minnesota near your hometown in Wisconsin. His approach was syncretism, combining different, often contradictory beliefs, and melding them with various schools of thought and his own spiritual journeys.

His Dreamspell calendar, with the Galactic Butterfly at its center, drew from such diverse ideas as Maya time cycles, the I Ching from China, a magic square devised by Benjamin Franklin, numerology, and fringe archaeology.

Mona took a breather.

"Chow time." Bea announced. "We're going to need fuel to understand this. Can you chew and talk?"

"Sure, but my mother always said that was rude."

"She's not here, and it's not rude to us."

"Okay," Mona said. "Talk to us through the meaning of me, Zarita."

You can learn more about it if you choose. It may sound a little complicated at first, but let it sink in and brew for a while. I feel these words will resonate with you, perhaps giving you insight into where you have come from, what you are, and where you are going.

"Should I go on?" Mona asked, picking up a corn chip. "It's already complicated, and we haven't even gotten to the good stuff.

"Go for it," Bea said. "I could sit here forever."

No one was in a hurry to get anywhere. She began after a crunch or two.

"Mona Arcade, born on September 13, 1941."

She stopped. "Land sakes. I always feel like a fossil when I see my birthday written out." And began again.

Your Galactic Signature is the Red Spectral Skywalker, composed of your Tone and five Seals arranged like a cross, glyphs that also represent the days of the year: your conscious self or who you are in the center; your higher self or guide above; your subconscious or hidden helper below; your challenge or gift to the left; and your complement to the right, something that comes naturally for you.

Red Skywalker is your conscious self, and also your higher self and guide, a time/space traveler, jumping between dimensions and experiencing heaven on Earth. Unlimited in form, it often chooses to be an angelic messenger. (Sounds like butterfly Mona Arcade and her mother Angela Mariposa, doesn't it?)

"Cut." Bea sliced across her neck with a burrito. "Antonio's a writer. He might grok all this, but I need visuals. Let's see now…" Bea looked down at her props. "The Galactic Signature is our whole meal and the Seals are the five dishes. One red bean burrito at the center and one on top. You and your mom." She set two burritos on the waxed paper. "Which side's the challenge or gift?"

"To the left," Mona said.

"Salsa on the left. A gift for your tongue or a challenge if it's made from habanero peppers. What's on the right?"

"Your complement," Mona replied, "something that comes naturally."

"Cheese dip. It goes with anything." Bea set down plastic cup to the right. "And our subconscious hidden helper on the bottom?"

Mona checked Zarita's drawing in the letter. "Good memory. Better than mine."

"Corn chips! They help you pick up the other goodies."

"What do you call a nacho that isn't yours?" Antonio asked Bea, scraping a glob of dip with a chip.

"I don't know. What?"

"Nacho cheese." Antonio smirked. They chuckled.

"Funny, but out of line. Detention after school."

"Great. I get to spend more time with the teacher."

"So where's the tone?" Bea demanded from her class.

"It doesn't say." Mona shook her head, then surveyed the green scene stretching out to every horizon. "I think it's all around us."

"Good answer. A-plus. You may continue reading."

The energy of Red Skywalker kindles a yearning for reunion with the soul and represents balance in your being, not static, more like the flow of a dance. You can use a state of imbalance to relax and steady your waltz through life.

The glyph of Red Skywalker seems to have a boundary, but instead symbolizes the illusion of duality and separation from the spirit. Step through the illusion anytime. You have the ability to do so. Red Skywalker is the bridge between two realities."

"It all makes sense now," Bea said. "Two burritos, balance, the illusion of duality…"

Your hidden helper is Yellow Star propelling you toward wholeness, to an expanding image of your self, to new perceptions.

"Nacho. See? It's yellow." Bea propelled one into her self. "Go on."

Mona read on obediently.

Yellow Star is like fireworks exploding into a cosmic milkweed bloom, scattering seeds from its pod to fly throughout the universe.

Bea threw a handful of chips into the air toward the nearby birds rubbernecking for stray crumbs.

Blue Night is your challenge and may signal an unconscious fear of change.

"Salsa!" Bea chirped, holding up its cup.

Mona coughed, cleared her throat, and continued.

You have created a home where you live, a box where you view the outside world. Go within yourself and cut the bonds of old structures and judgements. Opportunity knocks, and transformation awaits. The truth hidden in darkness holds the greatest potential for light.

"I'm getting a little hoarse," Mona said, turning to Antonio. "Would you mind taking over? You're a good writer. You must be a good reader."

"Sure. Take a break and listen. This is for you."

"Must be the cheese next," Bea mumbled.

Antonio read the rest of Zarita's letter aloud.

Your complement is White World-bridger, asking you to surrender, the opposite of giving up. Let go of control and how you think things should be. It requests that you die a symbolic death to release your limiting beliefs, to unveil your higher self by severing parts of the ego that no longer serve you.

And finally, your Tone is Spectral. Number Eleven. Change and disintegration, the ray of dissonance and its resolution. Once again, it says, "Let go!" Whatever has defined you is being stripped away. As the walls crack and your facade dissolves, The illumination of your true self shines through.

I'm tired. My hand is weak. I'm glad I had written most of this earlier! I imagine you reading this at Palenque at the Temple of Inscriptions. Look around for me. I hope my spirit lingers there on its journey to the Milky Way.

Your friend forever, Zarita

They were still for a spell, chewing the remains of the picnic and ruminating on her words.

"She is our tone for today." Mona folded the letter, her last letter, and slipped it out of sight. "Zarita let go. Disintegrated into her true self."

Bea had become merely another student in the class. "Maybe these messages explain your visions, Mona. You seem to be at some sort of turning point in life."

She only nodded and looked around for Zarita. Mona couldn't see her, but she felt her.

A guard on the ground shouted, demanding in fractured English and precise Spanish curses that they get off the temple. They'd missed, or ignored, the no climbing signs.

Bea gathered the cups and bags. Antonio helped Mona up and guided her down every step. They strolled toward the parking lot and groveled past the guard, who, at noon when they'd arrived, had been entranced by an enchilada under his sombrero. As Mona walked by, the guard grinned, gave her a thumbs up, and clutched his thigh with his other hand in tribute to her strong legs.

"Man magnet," Bea muttered.

An hour later, Antonio stopped the car in front of the Hotel Chablis Palenque.

"Don't they have a Hotel Merlot Palenque?" Mona asked.

"No worries." Bea said. "If they don't serve Merlot, we'll find you some red food coloring."

Mona was about to grab the handle when the door opened and a hand reached in to help her. Her eyes followed the arm up to another vision. *From the past? Another life? Where?*

"Mona Arcade, my dear. Welcome to Hotel Chablis. A Merlot spritzer is waiting for you."

The face was familiar, but the setting was all wrong. Then it hit her. "Gene Etherton! What in heaven's name are you doing here?"

"I couldn't miss the opportunity to experience that photograph on your wall in person. And…" he said, blushing through his white mustache, "I missed you and our talks."

"Well, criminently! It's great to see you again."

Matchmaker Bea and her clandestine communicator Antonio stood behind her, grinning impishly.

Mona put out her hand toward them. "Of course you remember Tiger and Gem?"

"Tiger and Gem?" Gene asked, confused.

"Sure," Bea agreed, elbowing Antonio in the side. "Antonio's always been my tiger!"

Antonio took the cue. "And Bea is my precious gem."

ANGEL
Ghost Zone Chaos

Seeing Barry cornered on the porch, Angel flipped off the safety catches on eight of the nine detonators under his jacket. Slipping out his Sig, he ran toward the guardhouse, shouting in Lao, "Don't kill the foreigner! We need him alive!"

Angel stepped onto the porch between two of the guards and saw soldiers down the road to his left. Stealthily, he pressed one detonation button. Pause. Two more. Pause. Number four. The first blast buckled one leg of the water tower. As it leaned toward the guardhouse, the petrol and propane tanks exploded, ripping through the drug factory and propelling the tower sideways like a water balloon. The last blast took out the bridge.

When all heads jerked toward the roar of fire and flying debris, Angel put a bullet into the guard's thigh to his left, then into the other guard's thigh on his right. Suddenly Angel's internal radar blared as he saw Barry slice his captive's throat, fling him aside, and raise the AK-47 slung on his shoulder.

Barry doesn't know it's me. He thinks I'm one of them! Angel leaped to the ground and ducked under the porch as Barry sprayed the other three guards with the AK-47 and kept spraying, practically cutting them to shreds. Angel pressed three more det buttons—five fiery gas tanks blew five vehicles into glowing spare parts in the parking lot as geysers of flames consumed the warehouse next to it.

"Barry!" Angel poked his head up and saw the lunatic look of revenge in his eyes, the sly smile on his face. "Barry! It's me! Angel! I'm on your side!"

Barry seemed to snap out of it and stepped over the bodies, still threatening him with the automatic. "What?"

Angel took a chance and leapt to his feet, throwing his hat and his AK-47 to the ground, a mud bath created by the water from the tower. "What?" Angel yelled. "What the fuck happened here?"

"That bastard tortured me." Barry pointed his muzzle toward the dead guard with the nearly severed neck. "Payback time."

Five-feet-eight inches of fury leaped onto the porch and slapped six-feet-three inches of psychosis across the face. "Goddamn it, you fucking idiot! I said stay inside! You wanna die here?"

"Sorry, I had to do it."

"Sorry, my ass! If you don't follow my orders, I'll fucking shoot you myself!" Angel pressed another det button, tore the other eight off their Velcro chest strap, and threw them aside. Khun P's Mercedes up the hill became the fireworks finale for everyone in the Ghost Zone to ogle. "Now let's get outta here."

MILES AWAY ON THE OTHER SIDE OF THE MOUNTAIN, Mani heard the explosions and squinted toward the east, her lips tight. The sun was up but hidden behind the ridge, its rays only coloring the clouds behind her to the west. Cheers rose from the free men and women boarding the trucks she'd arranged to pick them up, but Mani had a bad feeling in her gut. She put her arm around Somjai's neck. "You can handle it from here, bro. I gotta find Angel."

"Where? Not back there." Alarmed, he turned to face her. "Don't tell me you're going to the cave?"

"No… somewhere by the Mekong. I can wind around this side of the ridge to the river. Angel changed his plans at the last minute. He's not leaving on the chopper." She put her hands on both of his shoulders. "I can feel he needs my help. I only met him thirty-six hours ago, and it's crazy I know, but…" Mani sighed, "I love that man."

"You just saved us all." Somjai shook his head and rested his finger on her chest. "I'm sure your heart will find a way to save him, too."

Mani gave him an iron hug, then, with a "see ya later," she disappeared into the jungle.

DAWN HAD SURRENDERED TO DAYLIGHT on the other side of the ridge. Angel led Barry over the rise, down and up the ravine, and onto the booby-trapped escape trail. No one followed at first, though they could hear shouting and barking in the distance. The energy bars and electrolytes seemed to have revived Barry. The exercise had loosened his limbs, but he still favored his right leg. They skipped over or around the traps and heard snaps and shrieks of pain somewhere behind them.

"How's the leg?" Angel asked, glancing over his shoulder at Barry.

"Old football injury. Only hurts every other step."

"Terrain eases up soon. Hang in there."

Fifteen minutes later, they arrived at the junction where they'd part ways.

"Hold up," Angel said, dropping to his knees and opening his pack. "They're still hot on our ass, so I'm gonna draw 'em away from you on this trail to the right."

"How're you gonna get out?" It was the first time Barry had considered anyone besides himself.

"That's my challenge. Yours is gettin' to the chopper. This trail leads to the extraction point, 100 yards or so after the only wooden bridge you'll cross. I strapped a C-4 pack on it." Angel gave him a small detonator. "Blow it with this. Flip this safety catch, then press this button. Got it?"

"Got it."

"*After* you cross the bridge." Angel smiled. "Got it?"

"Got it. After."

Angel's raised palm requested a high five and got one. "You'd *better* do it like I tell you. I won't be there to shoot you if you don't."

He punched in an SMS to Agent Nat—Extraction ETA twenty-five minutes—then handed the phone to Barry. "This button's direct dial to DEA mission control. Chopper'll be there in twenty-five."

"Sorry I was such a dickhead back there," Barry said, looking down. "I wasn't myself yet."

"I don't think I am, either… yet. Things happen in strange ways. If you hadn't been a dickhead and gotten yourself caught in the first place, I wouldn't have been here to help a friend spring her family and other prisoners. Tell Mr. Doug the villagers are free, too, maybe thirty of 'em."

Both heads shot up as they heard noises down the trail.

"Now get outta here," Angel ordered. "You're gonna ruin my reputation if you don't make it."

"Thanks a ton, Angel. You're a star." Barry loped away with two stolen AK-47s flopping on either shoulder.

Twenty yards up the divergent trail, Angel located the friction fuse lighter at the end of the det cord he'd wrapped around the trees at the junction of the two paths. Hidden in a thicket, he put on his pack and draped two strings of 1,000 firecrackers over his neck. The day before, he'd set another 1,000 in the trees to be lit by the det cord.

With an AK-47 in his lap, Angel waited until he spied the first soldier thirty yards behind the junction. He pulled the wire handle to ignite the safety fuse that burned to the det cord and then fired several bursts over their heads. Ten seconds later, the entire length of the det cord exploded with a thousand crackles and pops. The grove at the junction became a logjam and a mass of tangled branches.

Angel jogged a zigzag route across the trail and into the jungle on each side, firing randomly, then flinging a string of firecrackers to his right. He hadn't been far on this trail and only knew it headed around a middle ridge and down the valley to the Mekong, maybe three miles away. Angel paused to listen and heard faint thrashing. *Hope they're all following this party.* He dropped the empty AK-47, lit his last 1,000 crackers, and broke into a run.

MANI WAS SPRINTING IN THE SAME DIRECTION, two ridges to his right. She stopped to catch her breath, drink, and rest. Sitting on a log, she remembered the note Angel had given her and took it out of her pocket. She smiled at the child-like scrawl of this fastidious superman.

Did I come here for several reasons? Yes.
To rescue Barry? No, to bury the past.
To find my future? No, to receive my present.
To stay the same? No, to embrace the change.
To defeat a ghost? No, a spirit called me home.
To watch the sun set? No, to feel the moon rise.
To see my mom? No, to meet my children's mother.
To save many souls? No, to savor one.
I am now here for one reason. Yes. You.

As she read, Mani's tears began like a few drops falling from clouds but became a rushing stream. Another explosion jerked Mani to her feet. She forced her stiff legs to move forward, then let her heart carry her toward the Mekong River, and beyond to the sea if need be.

TO ANGEL, THAT LAST EXPLOSION meant Barry had triggered the C-4 at the bridge and was on his way, almost home. *Hip, hippo hurray! Hope he blew it up after he crossed.*

The trail had started to incline a half-mile behind him, but now became an official climb. *This had better head down soon. The Mekong ain't up.*

He plunged on, confident in the directions Mani had given him. The trail soon funneled into a path hugging a rock wall on his right and blue sky on his left. One wrong step meant a sixty-foot plummet into the jungle below. Ahead he could see that the path veered 120 degrees to the left in the V of the canyon, wound around the next sharp bend, and then out of sight. *There is my final bomb site.*

When Angel reached the V, he wedged his last C-4 pack into a fissure in the wall. If he could carve a large enough chunk out of the side of the ridge wall and destroy the path, any pursuers would be forced to turn back.

As Angel sprinted away from the bomb, a gang of Ghost Soldiers appeared behind and level with him, now straight across the narrow valley, forty yards of air away. He pressed the remote det button. The blast demolished the path, showering the valley with boulders and transforming the V into a wide U. Passage became impossible for the soldiers.

Angel pivoted from the scene, but as he vaulted around the bend, a bullet ripped through the lower side of his abdomen, knocking him off the trail and into the breeze. One hand grabbed an overhanging branch. He swung out and back, caught a foothold, and collapsed onto the path.

MANI HEARD THE EXPLOSION IN THE DISTANCE, and seconds later a sudden pain stitched her side, not uncommon for runners, but this was different. She stopped, put her hand next to her stomach, and bent over until the cramp eased away. She turned onto another path leading down to the river. Unbeknownst to Mani, Angel lay on the path she'd just left, a mile around the edge of the ridge, clutching his abdomen.

BREATHING AND BLEEDING HEAVILY, Angel cut off one trouser leg with his knife, wrapped it around the detonator chest strap, and tightened the strap over the wound. He could see the rice paddies down in the valley. *Good news. Chopper's landing. Bad news? I'm on the wrong fuckin' trail.*

He struggled to his feet and headed down the steep slope through the jungle to the Mekong below. Angel hopped and fell from one tree trunk to another; barbed brush and vines tore apart bare skin and clothing. He reached a ledge with nowhere to go except straight down. *Wish I had wings. Guide me, Butterfly Mother.*

Replacing the pain in his side with the image of Mani in his heart, he jumped fifteen feet down to a slanted grassy area, bounced off and rolled over shrubs, sticks, and stones bruising his bones until finally coming to a halt, flat on his back. He'd heard the snap of his ankle, but that pain melded with the agony coursing through his entire body. He took the cellphone from his thigh pocket, called Mani, and put the phone to his ear. Silence. It was dead. *Shit.*

Mani thought she heard her phone ring as she approached the banks of the Mekong. She grabbed it and listened. Nothing. She called Angel. Nothing. Signal strong, but number unavailable.

Rolling onto his knees, Angel crawled to a stand of small trees. He sawed one off at the base with his blade, carved it into a staff, and hobbled toward the river. The "I'm Possible Dream" sang itself inside him.

And the world will be better for this

That one man, scorned and covered with scars

Blood still trickled from his wound and caked on the skin of his leg. He'd run out of water and the sun baked his salty sweat into a crust. His vision wobbled.

Still strove with his last ounce of courage

To reach the unreachable star

Staggering to the shore, he knelt by the river and splashed water on his face before crawling to a rock overhang on his right. Fighting stupor, he lay on his side and spotted three figures heading his way. The figures grew larger. Angel could see they were soldiers. *Can't run anymore. It's over.*

From the edge of unconsciousness, his brain hatched a final plan. Angel rolled onto his stomach and positioned his body as distorted as he could handle, arms bent under his body, one hand holding the pistol, the other, his mace gun loaded with a full cartridge.

Peeking out from under the brim of his hat, he glimpsed their faces. *Three teenagers, barely soldiers, only boys. One AK-47.* They approached Angel cautiously, as hope took another step away. *I am Morpho, pinned to the ground, with three kids ready to put me away.*

One prodded Angel's back with his automatic. Another kicked him in the leg. Angel didn't move, which was easy since he was numb and ready to pass out. The soldiers mumbled to each other, then two kneeled down to turn him over. As they flipped him, Angel buried the trigger, covering their faces, heads, and bodies with a continuous stream of mace. He fired one Sig shot at the blur of the boy holding the AK-47, then Angel's world went black.

MANI JOGGED ALONG THE MEKONG, her feet pounding the sand, heading east where she knew Angel had to be. Hearing a gunshot ahead, Mani dashed toward the sound until she saw one lifeless body and three others writhing next to it. She darted into the fray, grabbed the AK-47, and trained it on the soldiers. She'd never even held an automatic rifle before, but was ready to fire it. Keeping an eye on the soldiers, she dropped to Angel's side.

"Angel baby!" The sight of his blood and lacerated skin tore her up inside. "Angel, talk to me!"

She shook him. No response, but her fingers on his neck felt a pulse. Mani rose and stepped toward the blinded soldiers. She put a foot on one kid's neck and the rifle barrel into another's chest. She spoke in Lao, her words slashing through their moaning like a steel sabre. "Unless you want to die right now, take off your boots and pants."

They hesitated.

She screamed. "Now!" She kicked one in the head and pressed her foot and barrel harder into the other two.

They did it.

"Now take off your shirts!" When they were naked except for briefs, Mani growled, "Crawl to the river and wash your heads or I'll slice off your banana glands and feed them to the catfish."

While they bathed, Mani became the stern mother. "Khun P is finished. His world is destroyed. Go home. Get a real job. There's more to life than living in hell with a drug lord."

They bowed, scampered down the shore, and vanished into the jungle.

Angel was still out cold, his breathing shallow. He needed medical attention as soon as possible. Mani remembered passing a scorpion-tailed fishing boat and sprinted back along the riverbank until she found it, then waded into the water with the AK-47 pointed at the two fishermen.

RED

The Glorious Quest

A MUFFLED WHEEZE FROM AZEEZ snapped Red out of herself. She raced over and dropped to the floor next to him, relieved to see the minimal bloodstain on the back of his white shirt. *Oh, thank you, God.* With a hand resting on his head, Red spoke as calmly as she could, with anger and joy fighting inside for attention. "Lie still, Azeez. You're going to be all right."

"Wha..." His gasp struggled into feeble words. "What is happening?

"Bug threw a knife in your back, but you're hardly bleeding at all. He's dead. You'll live. I'll get you to a hospital as fast as I can. You can tough it out, Azeez. Don't move. Just breathe."

"Yes, Miss..." Azeez went out again.

Dietrich and Toma must be right outside. Red opened the back door into the hangar and stepped out, the Beretta eye-level at the end of her straight arm. She crept along the wall, crouching low to spot legs under the Tiger Moth. No one. She stole up to the duster and peered through its propeller blades. Her betrayers huddled in the far corner, fifteen yards away, waiting for cellphone orders from Bug. Swerving round the prop, Red strode toward them. "Do *not* move a muscle. I don't want to shoot you, but trust me, I will if I have to."

"Scarlett!" Dietrich shouted, his hands in the air, one holding the explosive. "Where's Bug? We heard gunfire!"

"Dead. I crushed him. So is Hari. Bug was going to blow you both to pieces, too."

"You can put the gun down," Dietrich said, his upraised palms echoing his words. "None of us wanted to do this in the first place. They had Hari's mother. They threatened our daughter. They would've killed us."

Still ten feet away, Red spoke from behind the Beretta. "They're all fucking monsters. They killed my parents. You have to get out of here."

"I'm sorry, Scarlett," Toma cried. "They said they'd hurt our daughter!"

"It's Red." She lowered her arm. "This is the real me... bald, cancer, my life in flames. I had no idea what I was getting into. Sorry to drag you in."

"What do we do now?" Toma pleaded.

"My man Azeez is dying inside with Bug's dagger in his back. You must take him to the emergency room now. It's right down the road, right on your way." She gestured toward the hospital with the Beretta, then stuck it under the waistband of her jeans. "Drop him off with the limo, then get home and save your daughter."

"But what about Murakan?" Dietrich asked. "They had photos of Christina and knew where she went every day."

"You keep saying 'they.' Who are you talking about?"

"Murakan and Baldev and their bodyguards."

"Baldev?" Red jerked back in surprise. "When did you meet the goddamn mastermind behind this?"

"Last night in Aero's dungeon, the cube. He was there when we left today."

"Baldev's at Aero." Red's brain churned as she listened.

"They knew about your little play all along," Toma sighed. "We were just three stooges in their grand plan."

A message missed from her dreams rushed through her. *Three shoplifting stooges. The teens who attacked Tiger—Tom, Dick, and Harry. Toma, Dietrich, and Hari were sent to blow up my Tiger Moth. If I'd been more aware, Hari might be alive.* "You're lucky to make it out of the cube. That's where they murdered my father. Let me think about this while we take care of Azeez. Toma, bring the bomb from the other hangar." *So Baldev's at Aero. Brilliant.*

"Murakan put a spy camera in the limo," Dietrich said. "I'll get rid of it." He drove the limousine to the condo door. They filled the back with cushions, carried Azeez out, and carefully laid him on his stomach.

Leaning on the hood for support, Red sketched out a plan. "This is our only chance. They're dying to get this piece of land. I'll ring Baldev and tell him I'm driving over to sign his fucking document. They won't know I'll be flying in from the opposite direction. I'll phone a detective who's ready to put them away. If the police fail again, I will personally exterminate them like I did with Bug. Now, *please* take Azeez to the emergency room."

"We'll do it," Dietrich assured her. "You can't imagine how terrible we both felt betraying you."

"Forget about it. Get Christina and leave the country while you can."

"I'm so sorry, Red," Toma said again.

"Me, too." Red hugged her. "You both may be bad'uns, but you're good ones."

The limo sped away as Red paused to summon her weepy voice, then rang Baldev to deliver her bogus plea for mercy.

"Miss Admiral," he said suspiciously.

"Oh, Baldev, thank heaven you're there," Red cried. "I'm ruined! My buildings are gone! Everyone's dead! I'm sorry. My chemo drugs made me insane. I didn't know Murakan was your nephew. You can have the land. Just please… please… stop the killing!"

"Let me speak with Bug."

"He was burned badly and went to the hospital. The warehouse exploded and flaming chemicals flew everywhere! He said you were at Aero and have a contract for me. Please Baldev, please, I beg you, let me drive over and sign it, for God's sake!"

He was silent.

Red's sobs spoke for a moment, then she whimpered, "Baldev, you were Danny's friend. We used to be friends. We played poker together. I paid my debts. I don't care about Admiral Aviation anymore. I just want to be able to fly. Maybe I can work for Murakan."

"All right. I'll wait for you."

"Oh, thank you, Baldev, thank you, thank you! I'm on my way." She hung up and rang Detective Darshan's direct line.

"Darshan speaking."

"Red Admiral. You came to see me yesterday."

"Yes, yes, Miss Admiral," he said, perking up. "What can I do for you?"

"Can you record this call right now? I have incriminating evidence about Baldev and Murakan."

"Yes, I can if you choose."

"I choose."

Two minutes later, Darshan was back on the line. "We're recording."

"Baldev wanted this place for his land development scheme and issued orders to extort me into selling it for next to nothing. He tried the same trick on my parents. His assassin Bug has harassed me several times and just stuck a dagger into my employee Azeez' back, then blew up my warehouse that's still blazing. Bug admitted he caused my mother's accident and that Murakan Patil murdered my father, and then Bug threatened me with a gun. I killed him in self-defence. I'm taking two of his unexploded bombs back to Aero Dynamic, where the two dusters they stole from me this morning are now parked, and where I believe both Murakan and Baldev are waiting for Bug's return. I'll either subdue them or send them to hell straightaway since you professionals can't seem to manage it. Got it?"

"Yes, Miss Admiral, but please—"

She hung up. Red knew his team would spring into action, but she'd arrive first. She donned her flight jacket, zipped the detonator box inside it, and stuck the bombs into her pockets, wondering what Angel would do. *He wouldn't even be in this fix in the first place.* Inside the hangar, Red strapped on her father's leather cap and goggles, and whether the odor was real or not, she smelled his British Sterling aftershave. *Fly with me, Danny Boy.*

Full of petrol and fertilizer, the Tiger Moth was a missile ready for a mission. Red swung the prop back and forth, flipped the magneto switches, twirled the prop, and the Tiger thundered. Red kicked aside its wheel chocks, climbed into the cockpit, and taxied onto the runway, well aware she hadn't flown for months.

Red felt a familiar rush as the duster lifted off Earth. She knew her plan was sketchy, beyond her experience, but not beyond her abilities. *Land secretly, threaten Baldev and Murakan like a suicide bomber, hold them until the police arrive.*

Consumed by the clouds above and the fresh wind coursing over the open cockpit, Red felt invigorated, and her revenge gave way to rapture. Unable to resist the urge to execute her favorite aerobatic maneuver, she pushed the 145-hp engine hard, dragging the old biplane higher and higher. At 4,000 feet, Red leveled off, and its pistons took a welcome breather. From this vantage point, she recognized Aero's location ten miles ahead in the sprawling Delhi cityscape. Flying in an S pattern, Red checked the sky above and below for other aircraft. *Empty. Excellent.*

She shoved the stick forward, and the duster dove. The hands of the altimeter unwound like a hyperactive clock running in reverse while the airspeed indicator ratcheted up. When she reached 150 mph, Red eased back the stick, then harder until it could go no further. The Tiger Moth roared into a steep climb, crushing Red into the seat, her body weight tripling. As it arched back on itself, Red craned her neck, anticipating the moment she'd cease seeing only sky, when terra firma would reappear.

At the top of her loop, the g-force decreased until, for an instant, Red achieved weightlessness, hanging upside down in the harness.

"Mmmm." *Joy of joys!*

She hadn't felt such ecstasy since her dream of drifting through the Milky Way. Red pressed the stick forward, and the duster soared gracefully out of the loop, resuming a level flight path. She idled the engine, took out her phone, and rang Baldev.

"Are you here already?" he asked.

"Close. I'm wondering where to find you."

"We're in the gazebo in front of the duster hangar. The guard will bring you around." Baldev paused. "What's that rushing sound?"

"The top's down on my Mercedes. I'll be there in a few minutes." She threw the phone down and throttled up.

Suddenly Red collided with her karma. A bar-headed goose—the only bird known to migrate over the Himalayas, the cosmic ambassador of all the airborne or earthbound creatures she'd killed, maimed, and gassed—smashed through the windscreen, scattering glass into the cockpit. The goose ricocheted off Red, snapping her head to the side, and disappeared behind the duster. Dazed, Red pulled the stick back to regain the altitude she'd lost. *Bloody hell! What next?*

Trying to rub the stabbing pain in her neck, she sliced her hand on glass shards sticking out of her skin. Blood dribbled under her collar, down her chest, from wrist to elbow. A whirlwind of exhaustion cut a swath through her, and Red felt herself splitting in two as she'd done in her recent dream—half was surrendering, the other half forging full speed ahead. Angel's words flew between them. *I need to be invisible and a big fuckin' surprise.*

With Baldev and Murakan on the tarmac, she couldn't land unseen. A big fuckin' surprise was the only option. *Plan B. Suicide bomber on the ground to one in the air. Kill two birds with one Tiger.*

Time and Red's stamina were running out as the duster ticked off the miles. Her fingers fumbled with the bloody zipper on the jacket, took out the detonator box, set it on her lap, and flipped the safety catches.

Setting her sights on Aero, she nudged the stick forward. The plummeting plane ate up altitude as it sped down like a falling star from heaven. Red held the duster in its dive until the indicator read 140 knots, the maximum its frame could withstand.

The Tiger Moth shook and complained, its rivets rattling, but somehow held together. She eased back on the stick, leveling the plane 500 feet above the city, one mile from Aero Dynamic, Baldev, and Murakan.

Red wasn't invisible but could run cloaked by the blinding sun behind her, silently. Entering full stealth mode, she shut down the engine, transforming the biplane into a third-rate glider with the aeronautical properties of a log with wings. Thirty years of flying Danny's ol' Tiger Moth had built the computer in her brain to calculate the precise combination of time, speed, and trajectory to hit her target.

Under the bamboo gazebo in front of the hangar, Baldev and Murakan sat smug, engrossed in toasting their triumph as the Tiger closed in on its victims. Red felt her energy ebbing. Forcing every blood corpuscle not flowing out of her neck into her head, she kept on course as moments slowed to nanoseconds. Thoughts and images swirled in from all directions—

Her father Danny's irresistible smile.

Her mother Chandra's irrepressible frown.

Azeez' perky face. "Yes, yes, Miss Red, always."

The wisdom of sweet Devika. "I can neither stop the wheel of karma, nor reverse it."

The lady at Lodhi park shouting as they fled the bird and insect attack. "Heading back home, I hope."

The doctor counting down the seconds of a cancer patient's life. "Ten... nine... eight..."

The contentment she felt drifting into the black hole. "Nothing to think or do except be."

Then the music from her dream Angel began to play and blew them all away.

And I know if I'll only be true...

Snapping back into reality, she focused on the gazebo looming ahead to the right of Baldev's silver BMW and the fuel truck inside the hangar.

To this glorious quest...

As the scene expanded in Red's vision, Baldev and Murakan spotted the Tiger charging out of the sunset, leaped up from their champagne, and stumbled toward the BMW.

That my heart will lie peaceful and calm...

Mustering her last iota of strength, Red guided her cruise missile into the devils madly trying to open the car doors. As she stared into the frozen whites of their eyes, her hand fell onto the two red buttons in her lap.

When I'm laid to my rest...

Dual blasts inside her jacket pockets metamorphosed the Tiger Moth into a flying fireball, hurling the car and fuel truck into the airplanes behind them in the hangar. In an instant, Red was no more. She became the red giant star, exploding into a multicolored supernova from her dream.

The domino of explosions from the Tiger to the car to the petrol truck merged into an inferno engulfing the entire building, uniting enemies, separating beings into individual atoms—*at om*—at home in the void, knowing neither whence they came, nor whither they go.

MONA
Out of the Picture

In the courtyard of the amber and cream adobe hotel, the quartet communed with breadsticks, Merlot wine, fizzy water, and a bucket of ice. Mona was bushed. "Tomorrow my muscles will be stiff as my old bones."

"Stick your dogs in that hot tub," Antonio said.

"I might melt. I'm feeling wicked."

Bea gave Mona a gentle poke in the ribs. "Wicked good or wicked bad?"

"I'll let you know later."

Gene's elfin eyes peered up from his bowed head. "I hope you don't think we were too wicked by planning this sneaky rendezvous."

"No, no." Mona rested her hand on his knee. "This is perfect. Everything's perfect the way it is."

They ate too much food that was too good, discussed tomorrow's travel, and then the quartet split into duets.

Mona and Gene meandered through town on the placid Palenque sidewalks. Her skin felt thin, a faint line between here and there, matter and spirit, life and death. Mona couldn't keep her feelings inside even if she tried. They spilled out and Gene soaked them in. He listened a lot, talked little, and they often walked in silence. She could confide in Bea and Antonio, youths with limitless horizons, but sharing mundane aches and pains, wonder, and whimsy with a kindred soul in the twilight of life warmed her to the core.

Soon Mona was strolled out. "Gene, this has been delightful, but my body's begging for bed."

"I completely understand. I came to see you, and the monarchs, and to help however I may."

Gene walked Mona to her hotel room, and she took hold of his hand as he opened the door. "You are a gem… or a tiger… maybe both. I'll see you before the sun does."

"Mona dear, let me leave you with something I recently learned. Scientists have discovered that one gene in a monarch's DNA might be responsible for making its muscles stronger and more efficient for its epic journey. Think of me as that one Gene." He kissed one of her fingers and ambled away.

At daybreak, no light broke through the clouds hugging the streets and buildings. Mona sat at a stone table to sketch the city awake while waiting for her companions to arise. After they'd fueled up on huevos rancheros, the expedition to Bea's hometown began.

The drive back to Villahermosa, the flight to Mexico City, and the three-hour rental car ride to Ocampo seemed to take less time than locating the key to Bea's uncle's house, their inn for the evening. Her absent-minded and currently absent Uncle Sanchez had said he'd hidden it on top of a window frame. It wasn't there.

Several calls later, Bea finally reached him to learn he'd forgotten exactly which window. A search of each one produced no key, so they presumed it had dropped off the frame and burrowed into the powdery dirt. After unearthing two keys that didn't fit, rusty hinges, and crusty cat shit, they found the proper one as dusk—and the rising dust from their digging around the house—fell.

Their accommodations had three attributes. One, they were authentic in a bachelor, traveling salesman, Mexican uncle sort of way; two, Uncle Sanchez was not home to pound down Coronas until dawn; and three, they cost nothing. The house was tidy, except for his dirty socks on the coffee table and two plates in the sink with fried egg remains fused to the pottery glaze. Once Bea had wiped the wooden chairs in the living room with rubbing alcohol, her mind turned to bucket list number three, and she gave everyone the rundown. "The Monarch Butterfly Preserve is an hour away, and the monarch colony is a trek from there—an hour downhill and another hour uphill on foot." She eyeballed Mona. "Think you can handle it?"

"If I'm going to make it, we'd better start now."

"They used to rent horses. Have you ever ridden, Mona?"

"It's been a few years. Fifty or so. We had a chestnut paint when I was a kid. I'm game."

"How 'bout you, Gene?"

"I'm from Montana. It's illegal not to be able to ride."

"Great. We should get there early to catch the monarchs in the trees."

After an indoor picnic of greasy but great market tacos, they hit their hard sacks early. Mona's elation seemed to levitate her above the bed.

The next morning she dressed in an orange cotton shirt above her black slacks to match the colors of the monarchs. The quartet headed out as the sun behind the mountain created a corona around its peak.

On the drive through the Snowy Mountains Range to the Preserve's visitor center, the temperature was a stand-off between the air cooling as they gained altitude and the rising sun warming it. Bea resumed her role as a tour guide. "It's not peak season, so it shouldn't be packed."

"I hope the trees *will be*…" Mona said, "with monarchs."

"I'm sure there'll be millions, but their numbers keep dwindling. A fraction of what they were." Gene's sour face stared out the side window. "Deforestation. Pollution. Destruction of milkweed habitats where they lay their eggs, where the caterpillars feed. So sad, really."

Tour guide Bea put on her happy face. "All right, perk up! We're here to enjoy what's here. It's just round the bend."

After viewing the info film at the visitor center and learning things they already knew, they saddled up and followed their trail guide into the trees—Gene and Mona sharing a black appaloosa, Bea and Antonio each riding a sorrel pinto. The four of them were live wires behind a dead plug. To the guide, it was another boring day, plodding up to a bunch of bugs and back. He said nothing, but no one wanted chatter anyway, unless it came from birds. They'd come to hear the forest.

Mona whispered into Gene's ear. "I can hardly believe I'm finally here."

"A once in a lifetime experience," he sighed.

"I am so excited that I feel like I might come apart at the seams or explode or something."

"Maybe you should sit in front of me so I can hold you inside yourself."

"Oh, no," she insisted, almost frightened. "You hold onto the reins and I'll hold on to you so I don't float away."

Gene started humming a tune that titillated Mona's ears.

"What song is that?"

His rich baritone voice caressed the notes as he sang. "To dream the impossible dream. To fight the unbeatable foe."

Mona was entranced.

"To bear with unbearable sorrow. To run where the brave dare not go."

Mona breathed deeply and hugged his waist harder. "I love that song."

"It is beautiful," Gene said. "I don't know the rest of the words, but I can whistle them."

Amplifying her anticipation of what was to come, these present moments intoxicated Mona's senses. The soothing vibrato of Gene's whistling. The sweat of the horse heating her thighs. The straight, stately trees like sentinels guarding the trail. The brown patchwork of fields, bordered in green extending down the valley, glimpsed through gaps in the forest. The tangy smell of fir trees with a eucalyptus edge. It all seemed familiar to her.

After half an hour of quiet riding, the rocking of the horse took Mona back home as a teen on their chestnut paint, and back further into her mama Lily's arms. At times she felt as though she wasn't even touching the saddle. When they reached the footpath and dismounted, Mona was dizzy and had to brace herself against the hitching post, but not because she might faint and fall down. She felt she might fly upward.

Bea saw that Mona was smiling, but seemed disoriented, or at least unsteady. "Mona, you look seasick. Or horse sick or something. How're you feeling?"

"Light."

"Lightheaded?"

"No..." Mona said, looking up and shaking her head. "Light... light-bodied."

"You want to sit for a minute?" Bea asked.

"I've been sitting. Walking would be good."

The junction of the trail and the footpath was the end of the line for the horses and the beginning of a half-mile hike up to the monarch hibernation colony. They hadn't seen another human on the horse trail, but now joined the smattering of tourists who'd trekked from the center. Gene found a smooth branch for a walking stick for Mona. A group of teenagers on a tour with a teacher passed them.

"There they are," Mona said.

"Who?" Gene asked.

"Tiger and Gem."

Bea heard her and turned. "Where?"

Mona pointed ahead with her walking stick. "That young couple holding hands in the back."

"You know them?"

She spoke matter-of-factly. "No."

"Then how do you know their names?"

"I just know."

Gene, Antonio, and Bea stood motionless in front of her. Other hikers had to step around the four of them.

Mona's face was serene as she looked from Gene's inquisitive eyes to Antonio's to Bea's. "I think we'd better stop and chat at that bench ahead."

Gene and Mona sat on the wooden slats with Bea and Antonio on the cast iron armrests at each end. A tall, slender woman with tawny skin and long auburn hair strolled by alone.

"That's Red Admiral. She lived in India."

"You've met her?" Bea asked.

"No, but I told you about her before. She was the snippy woman in the park who told me to go away, but I feel sorry for her now."

"She lived in India?"

"Yes, but I've never been there."

They all had that look in their eyes again.

"I know you don't believe me. Go ask her what her name is." Mona gestured with her chin. "You'll see."

Antonio didn't know what to say. Gene watched and listened intently. Bea's voice went medical as if Mona were a shock victim.

"We believe you."

"I doubt it. I'm not sure if I do. Bea, you and I have had several conversations about these visions of mine, these images I've been drawing that come from somewhere and I don't know where." Mona spoke as if some invisible strength was growing inside her. "I'm sure you've shared this with Antonio, and I told Gene a bit last night. They've been happening more often, and now they're getting clearer the closer I get to the colony."

"You said you felt light. What else?" Bea asked.

"I'm not an RN anymore, but I'm still plain old nurse Mona. I feel fine… just light, almost like I could jump thirty feet like they do on the moon. This isn't Alzheimer's. This isn't psychosis. This isn't my mind. It's beyond the brain."

Gene rested his palm on her shoulder. "What can we do for you, Mona?"

"Trust me. I know you're all worried. These visions—or whatever they are—feel good. They're beyond feelings. Let me say what I have to say and do what I have to do, whatever that may be." Mona rose effortlessly from the bench and dropped her walking stick next to the path. "It's a splendid day! Now let's hike."

She led the way toward the home of the fir tree from Bea's photo. A few hardy monarchs followed through the forest in the same direction. As they approached the colony, an Asian couple jogged ahead of them on the path.

"Angel and Mani," Mona said. "He's a good man. A star. And Mani… well, indomitable. His moon."

Mona strolled into the clearing at the edge of the colony and entered one of her own visions. Like her personal little scouts, several monarchs fluttered in front of Mona. Millions more covered the oyamel tree trunks like bark. In place of fir needles, the branches seemed to have shimmering orange leaves. The sun's rays had warmed many, seducing them out of the swarms where they'd huddled together as a living buffer from the weather. Many were Methuselah monarchs, the fourth-generation who lived for months instead of days, and had flown thousands of miles from their birthplaces in North America to return to the homeland of their departed great-great grandparents.

Mona walked to the middle of the clearing and turned slowly in a circle. She saw other familiar faces in the crowd of tourists, but only knew their names. Victoria, Jonathan, Donny, Azeez, Dr. B, Devika, Toma, Dietrich.

Words from Zarita's letter flew into her mind.

Let go! Whatever has defined you is being stripped away.

Mona could see the illusion of duality, a translucent swath of undulating air crisscrossing the scene in front of her eyes.

Step through the illusion anytime. You are the bridge between two realities.

She took off her jacket and let it fall to the ground. Now wearing only orange and black that mirrored the monarchs, Mona walked toward the exact oyamel fir tree she recognized from Bea's photo.

Her three companions trailed behind, dazed by the play surrounding them. Monarchs lifted from the trees and landed on Mona's head and shoulders and clung to her shirt.

She laughed gleefully and stretched out her arms like branches toward the tree as an orange-and-black cloud descended, clothing her from head to foot. She giggled, tickled by butterfly kisses on every inch of exposed skin. She became the tree and the monarchs, a tiny part of the image she'd seen so many times in her meditations. Words in the letter from Angela Mariposa, the birth mother she'd never met, fluttered through her heart.

We will be together again, someday, somewhere, in some form, maybe a butterfly. That is my name. Maybe that's what I will be.

Antonio and Bea tried to step forward and help Mona, but Gene held them back. "Don't worry. They won't hurt her. They're gentle monarchs. Her namesake."

Mona felt joyfully invisible beneath the thick mantle of wings, the sensations surging through her body almost orgasmic.

As the walls crack and your facade dissolves, the illumination of your true self shines through.

Suddenly, in a whispering explosion, the monarchs burst away in all directions like seeds blown out of a cracked milkweed pod in the fall, and soared toward their mates in the sky.

The space where Mona had been standing was empty. She was gone. The paper she'd been holding in her hand drifted to the ground.

In a stupor, Gene, Bea, and Antonio moved toward the spot, each looking around for Mona. They peered down, as if the piece of paper were a hidden trapdoor on a magician's stage. Bea picked it up—a page from Mona's sketchbook, the painting she'd done the night before leaving Mission and had only shared with Zarita two days earlier.

In the mirror on the wall to the left, a reflection of Mona. On the right, creating the reflection, a monarch butterfly. She'd written the words below the painting that had inspired the image, a quote from the Chinese sage, Zhuang Zhou, slightly altered from male to female. Mona's three companions each read it in their own time without saying a word.

I dreamed I was a butterfly, fluttering hither and thither, and then I awakened. Now I wonder: Am I a woman who dreamt of being a butterfly, or am I a butterfly dreaming I'm a woman?

ANGEL
Saving the Savior

When the two old men in the fishing boat spotted the fierce woman in the water pointing an AK-47 at them, they dropped their net and reached for the clouds.

"I'm not going to shoot you," Mani said in Laotian. "I need your help. My friend is hurt."

Motionless, they stared at her.

Mani took a chance that they weren't Ghost Zone cohorts. "He rescued thirty villagers from Khun P."

Both fishermen grinned widely with savvy sparkles in their eyes. "Angel Butterfly?" one shouted. "Where is he? What can we do?"

Mani grinned back and responded in Hmong, the language he'd spoken. "Are you from the village of Kong?"

They both nodded. One man gave her a thumbs-up, and said, "You must be that little Zuah girl I remember from the refugee camp. A feisty one back then, too."

"We heard about a strange girl slinking around the jungle," Hallo Kong said, "You should have let us help."

"Sorry. I haven't been here for twenty-one years. How could I know who to trust?"

She climbed in the scorpion-tail boat and directed them round the river bend. The Kong brothers retrieved Angel's unconscious body, laid him on the pile of fishing nets, and headed downriver.

Mani noticed a double-deck wooden vessel ahead of them, at least forty feet long with sun decks on top and curtained windows along the sides. "What kind of boat is that?"

"Cruise boat from Chiang Saen to Vientiane," one of the Kongs said. "Rich tourists."

"Does it stop in Luang Prabang?"

"Yes."

"Take us to it."

He shot her another thumbs-up and veered toward the boat.

As they drew near, both Kong brothers waved their arms. Mani was ready to fire the AK-47 in the air, just to see what it felt like. The cruise boat slowed as if it were expecting them, and the scorpion-tail pulled alongside. A uniformed sailor leaned over the railing and looked down.

"We've got an injured man who needs help!" Mani yelled.

"Angel?" the sailor asked.

"Yeah. Angel Butterfly." Mani shook her head in amazement, wondering how this secret commando could be so famous.

"Some American agent called and said to look out for him. We'll bring him aboard up front."

A crowd of crew helped Mani and the Kongs hoist Angel onto the deck. An elderly bearded guest shouted to her. "I'm a surgeon! I'll look him over."

"Careful," Mani warned. He's in bad shape."

The next half-hour was a whirlwind of activity. The boat captain notified DEA Doug who said they'd chopper in a doctor with medical equipment. Maids prepared a vacant luxury suite for the patient. A crew member brought in the boat's cache of first-aid supplies. Mani helped the surgeon clean and bandage Angel's wounds, skills acquired during her years with the National Park Service. A couple of times he grunted and almost regained consciousness.

After the surgeon had fully examined Angel, he spoke with Mani and the boat captain outside the suite. "He's going to be fine. His vitals are strong. The bullet went clean through his side, missing any major organs. His makeshift pant-leg-belt contraption kept the bleeding to a minimum, probably saving his life. Sprained ankle, bruised ribs, bump on the head, but I don't think he broke any bones. We'll see what the medic says when he gets here. The boy needs stitches, so I think it's best he isn't moved."

"Where in the hell am I?" Angel's voice barked from inside the suite. "Or am I in heaven?"

Mani smiled. "He sounds okay." The three of them went into the room.

"My captain!" He saluted Manu with a bandaged hand. "Are your people safe?"

"Happy and dandy," Mani said through her smile and kissed his other hand.

"Barry?"

"Home free."

"How 'bout you, sweetheart? You look beautiful." No mention of himself, only about others.

"I'm fine, baby, but I need a shower."

"How do you feel, son?" the surgeon asked.

"Like I've been run over by a hippo. Am I gonna live?"

"You only need a few stitches and rest. A real medic's on the way. I'm only the guest doctor."

"So where am I anyway?" Angel asked, surveying the suite and trying to sit up. "The Ritz in New York? Doc, help me here, the room's swayin'."

Mani put her hands on both his shoulders, eased him down, and rested her forehead on his, filling Angel's vision with her angelic face. "Will you please calm down, soldier? You're safe and unsound as usual… on a Mekong cruise boat on its way to Luang Prabang. You're a hero… You're *my* hero."

"I'll go and watch for the chopper," the captain said, raising one eyebrow.

"I'll get back to my vacation," the surgeon echoed.

Mani turned toward them as they left. "Thank you so much."

Angel slowly raised his hand and stroked her hair with his swollen fingers. "You did it, Ninja Girl."

"We did it, Superman."

"We did, didn't we? We make a damn good team."

Mani laid her head on his chest. "You had me scared for a while there."

"I'm sorry, darlin'. Me, too. Thought I was a goner. The last thing I remember is squirtin' the kid soldiers."

"I heard your gunshot and came running. I was right around the bend."

"I shot the Sig?" he asked. "Did I hit anyone?"

"No, I took care of 'em."

"How?"

Mani rose up wearing her coy face and looked him in the eyes. "I made the blind boys strip down to their briefs."

"Hmm… I'm jealous."

"Want me to lick your wounds? Doctor's orders."

"You're my kind of doctor." He nodded his head and winced. "Ow. It hurts right here."

"Later, baby. You get some rest now. I'll be right here."

As Angel drifted off, he mumbled, "Cool… Sailing to Luang Prabang… We'll visit my mom… so you can meet her and…"

An hour later, the chopper delivered the medic to the ship via rope ladder, then landed on the shore, waiting to transport any passengers back to base. The medic gave his lively patient a blood transfusion, stitched his wounds, and conferred with the skipper and the surgeon. Angel had made it clear to him that there was no way he would "desert his post in this fancy floating motel except in a body bag." The medic left some sedatives, pain-killers, and IV electrolyte drips for the surgeon to administer.

Angel slept soundly for hours. Late that night, he stirred, and Mani was bedside in a moment.

"How you feelin', baby? You looked like one sleeping."

"Better, thanks," Angel whispered. "I went far away."

"I don't want you far away."

"Just dreamin'."

"Wha'd'ya dream?" she asked.

"About you. You were my dream. Now you're my dream come true."

"Sweet mouth," she purred. "Lemme kiss it."

"I have two favors to ask."

"Anything. Ask away."

"One, there's a GPS bug in my pants pocket. Throw it into the river. I want no one to know where I am."

"My pleasure," she said.

"Two, can I use your phone to make one quick long-distance call? Captain, may I?"

"Like, how quick?"

"Very, very, very quick. I wanna thank the Skipper for a sec, and then I'm all yours."

"For how long?"

Angel gently pinched her cheek. "As long as you want."

"Deal. Why are you thanking him? He should be thanking you."

"I want to thank him for sending me to you."

"You got a way with words, baby." She handed over her phone and hugged him. "I loved your love note."

Angel phoned as Mani perched on the other bed, watching him.

"Jonathan Skipper here."

"Hey, Skipper. Strangel here."

"Angel Phoenix… You did it."

"We did it." Angel talked to him and looked at her.

"We?"

"I met my match."

"Mister Ghost?" Jonathan asked.

"No, my gem, my teammate." Angel traded smiles with Mani. "She's the one I've been lookin' for, and I wouldna found her if you hadn't called. Thanks, man."

"You're welcome. Who is she?"

"I'll tell ya later, but then you're gonna want to hire her. We'll be off the radar screen for a while."

"Your Angel radar?"

"No, yours. My GPS bug is drowning at the bottom of the Mekong. Don't try to find us there."

"Okay, then, you take care now, Angel. Thanks for everything. Wish I could tell the world what you did."

"A few know. That's enough. See y'all before y'all see me."

Angel put the phone down and looked at his angel on the next bed. "I'm done. Finished. Game over."

Mani smiled, slipped over, and sat on his bed. "Strangel, eh? The name fits. Time to lick Strangel's wounds?"

"Yeah," he said, pointing at his mouth. "I tell you, do my lips ever hurt."

She bent down and licked his lips, then gave him a passionate kiss while lifting her legs to lie beside him. She fell off the bed and onto the floor.

Angel smirked, unable to rise and help her up. "I'm rememberin' you fallin' out of a forked tree, into a ravine, over your own damn doorstep, and now outta my bed. You lied to me. Mani doesn't mean gem or moon. It means clumsy."

From somewhere out of sight, about three feet below, Angel heard that voice he adored.

"Shut up."

MONA
Finally Flying Again

In the oyamel fir tree, two months later—The sun warmed the wind whispering through the branches of the tree where she rested, protected from harsh weather and frigid nights. Perceived by her antennae's twenty-four-hour clocks and solar compass that had guided her southern migration, the longer days and rising temperatures triggered two primal alarms.

Mona awoke.

Dreams of Morpho, Tiger, Angel, Red, and an elderly woman with a walking stick floated away like snapshots dropped into a stream. The clicks and grunts and babble of language inside merged with the soothing rustle of monarch wings surrounding her. The strange sensations along the course of her five-month, 2,000-mile journey from birth in Wisconsin to the Snowy Mountains of Mexico faded into the perfume of the oyamel sap and springtime blossoms.

During the months of semi-sleep in the hibernation colony, Mona's reproductive system had finally matured. Her two front brush-footed legs and antennae detected the scent of flowers and male pheromones in the air.

On her four hind legs, she walked across the wings of other sluggish monarchs to a twig on the fringe of the tree, preening her coiled proboscis and stretching the muscles in her thorax and abdomen. She fanned her wings to dry traces of the morning dew.

Poised like a paraglider on a cliff, she surveyed her domain, then flew toward the blooms and grooms below as the two primal signals grew stronger.

Drink. Mate.

www.ingramcontent.com/pod-product-compliance
Lightning Source LLC
LaVergne TN
LVHW041057080826
845145LV00007B/1603